The Death Pictures

Simon Hall

Published by Accent Press Ltd – 2008

ISBN 9781906125981

Printed and bound in the UK

Cover Design by The Design House

For both our fathers,
laid low but no less loved

Acknowledgements

Paul Hill for his indispensable critiques, Darin Jewell, my agent, for continual help and encouragement, Dr Susan Taheri for medical advice, Dr Abi Burridge for psychological insights, Hazel and Bob Cushion for their faith and guidance, Carol Ackroyd and Maureen Twose for their wonderful support, Simon Read, my editor, for his feedback, Devon and Cornwall CID for advice and assistance, Al Stewart for his excellent photography and of course Jess, my writing widow, for all your love, help and patience.

Prologue

HE WAS AMAZED AT his calm. After so many long weeks of painstaking research and careful planning, it was finally his moment. He'd come to think of himself as the star of a show he was about to launch. He'd expected to shake with nerves, find his mouth dry, his body rigid and breathless, like an actor on the opening night of a spectacular. But no nerves had bitten. There was just control, a vacant calm. The cool detachment of the professional he had become.

They would label him a rapist, psychopath, monster. Avenger was the word he preferred.

She had the honour of being the first. The winner of his glorious league. He allowed himself a smile at the memory of why, the beautiful day they had met, two months and four days ago.

She was alone of the six chosen ones to score full marks in every category he'd decided to assess. He'd mentally checked them through as he sat in the café, next to her, pretending to be engrossed in the racing section of the paper. She was stirring brown sugar into a cappuccino and moaning about her ex-husband to her vacuous, over made-up nodding friend. He could hardly believe it when he heard her words, had to force himself not to react, to stare intently at the paper.

The 3.20 at Exeter racecourse, he still remembered even that. Remembered too the bitter, stewed tannin tea, the sticky chessboard lino floor and the tubby, bumbling waitress who smelt of turning sweat. The blackboard with the changing chalk, the ghosted outlines of the week's tasteless offerings. Shepherd's Pie was the special that day. Three pounds ninety-five, with two veg. It was a squalid hunting ground, but necessary.

'He still bothers me every week you know. Every week he wants to take James out,' she'd bleated. 'The court gave him fortnightly visits, but he's always on about seeing James more. Doesn't he understand we've got a new life to live?'

1

She had branded herself. He wrote 'bitching about spurned victim' carefully in the margin of the paper and lovingly shaped a slow tick next to it. The highest scoring offence of the five rankings, and her the only one on his list to achieve it. Five points. She was already setting herself apart as his champion.

He checked his watch. She must have the allocated ten minutes of all his potential contenders. It was important to be fair. He wasn't picking his targets. They were choosing themselves.

He took a last drag at his cigarette and stubbed it out in the dirty plastic ashtray. The final seconds ran down. Time now to test the four other categories. He stood quietly, left the tea half drunk, folded his paper and walked out into the street. No one had noticed him. An ordinary man in an unremarkable place on an average day. Six different cafes he'd chosen for his interviews, in six different areas of the city. The police would look for links between the women. They'd find none. His plan was perfect.

Opposite, he noticed a newsagent. Buying some chewing gum and studying the notice board of cards in the window would give him the required time to see what she did next.

Seventeen minutes she took, the slow bitch. He'd read about the new ironing service three times before her reflection emerged from the café. She hugged her friend, took her son's hand, then set off along the pavement and up the hill.

He followed on the opposite side of the road, just as they did in those military magazines he'd studied. He'd done his research. She passed a bus stop, didn't hesitate. She was walking home. Good. He had the leisure of time to measure her against all the categories and give her a fair ranking. But he already suspected she was going to be the new leader. He liked her. She was becoming his favourite. He was looking forward to getting to know her better.

He stopped to admire the sleek power of the new touring bikes gleaming proudly outside the motorcycle shop. An admiring finger ran over the handlebars of a red Yamaha, but he walked on before the hovering young assistant could trap him in sales talk. He had a greater purpose.

He increased his pace a little to close the gap, needed to study her as she walked. He couldn't mark the four point category until she got to her house. Did she merit the three points for dressing provocatively? He knew he wanted to award them, but restrained himself. He had to be fair, impartial.

It was neither a warm nor cool day, classic English springtime. Her top was cropped and tight under that fitted denim jacket. It rode with her walk, waving flashes of the taut, pale skin of her waist. He screwed up his eyes to focus and hissed softly. A small spider's web of grey-green stretched from the base of her back. He didn't allow himself to wonder again why tattoos so angered him, forced his thoughts back to the assessment. Her jeans were figure-hugging and she wore high-heeled, open-toed sandals. It was a simple judgement. It had to be three points.

Did she have the contrived wiggle? That too always goaded him. Waving their bloody arses around in the hope men would stare, then those pathetic protestations of outrage if a guy had the cheek to do exactly as they wanted. He calmed himself and glanced over as she bent down to talk to her son, then walked on. He turned away, caught his breath. Yes, definitely, the bitch. Another two points.

They all got one mark in the final category. It was what distinguished them for his attention. It was their starter question, the warm-up, just like on the old quiz shows he used to watch with his Dad so many years ago. All had a child, but no partner. An abandoned father, discarded somewhere in their past. Just like him.

He often imagined the men as he went about his beautiful work. They were the audience he played to. He'd like to meet them, put a brotherly hand on their shoulders. 'Don't worry, mate,' he'd tell them. 'I'm on your side. I know what it's like. I understand. I'll make them pay for what they've done.'

He lit another cigarette, cupping his hand around it against the awakening breeze. Only one more issue to resolve now.

The second most important. Her house. The grander the home, the more money she'd leeched from her ex. Four points for this.

A sudden surging urge hit him, to sprint across the road, catch her, slap her, do it now, but he forced himself to wait, breathe, relax. He stopped at a Pelican crossing, pressed the button, counted the seconds until the lights turned. She wasn't moving fast, couldn't get away. The traffic growled to a reluctant halt and he crossed. Ahead, she turned off the main road. He lengthened his stride.

He reached the corner of the street, stopped, checked carefully around it. Fifty yards down, on the opposite side of the road, she was fumbling a key into a front door. Her son stood on the wall, balancing his way along it, arms outstretched, calling for her to watch. He ducked back, waited a moment. There was no one around, but he pretended to tie his shoelace, just to be safe. He counted to 13, his lucky number, turned down the street and strolled past her house.

He allowed himself three sideways glances, no more. Each blink of his practised eye captured it like a photograph. Semi-detached, at least three bedrooms, possibly four if the loft was converted. Late Victorian, he estimated. Double-glazing. Satellite TV. A new slate roof, whitewashed stone and duck-egg blue paint on the windowsills. Mannamead, a very good area this. A well tended front garden. Probably a nice little enclosed lawn at the back too. A valuable house. That gorgeous iron gate at the side, his warm invitation into the back garden and, when the time was right, the house itself. He walked on contentedly, filled with the warming satisfaction of awarding her the final four points.

His smile crept wider at the delight of the memory. It was two months and four days ago now, but still so fresh, so vivid in his mind. She'd scored a full house. She'd won his league. She'd hit the jackpot. And now it was time for her reward.

The strength was within him, he was sure, but he took a moment to be certain of his purpose and to reinforce his will. He knew just how.

He thought back to a summer's night, so similar to that

4

which caressed him this evening, the time when he had first met the one whose name was now never mentioned, whose face was just a black, scarred silhouette, when they had first held hands and kissed in the hiding place between the stretching plates of sentinel rock on the deserted beach. He wound the memories on to the first night they had made love, semi-drunken after that awful Italian meal, laughing about it as they walked home, the first time she had accepted his invitation to come in for coffee. On further, to the night the baby was born and the wonder so heady in his addled brain as to make him doubt it had really happened, only the screams from that tiny, wrinkled ball of fresh humanity insisting on existence in its newly found world. He let the memories drift, fill him, and then summoned the one he needed, the day she had announced she was leaving.

He reached out and stroked his knuckles over the rough red brick of the patio's low wall. He felt its edges scratch and scrape at his skin. It was a delightful pain. He pressed a cheek against the cold glass of the window, closed his eyes and enjoyed a second's anticipation.

He felt as he imagined a great predator must, relaxed in the certainty of his power. The oblivious prey was chosen, never suspecting its fate. Now it was just up to him to decide the moment of his victory. It was a just and God-like emotion and it was delicious.

She was there, stretching out, he could see her through the tapering slit of the draped curtains. The chair hid her body, but there was a ruffling of damp, dark hair about its back. The flickering light of the television shone from the smooth white legs that stretched out under her burgundy dressing gown. Her toenails were red, newly varnished. He knew her son would be in bed now, she would have had her bath, be relaxing in front of the TV with a glass of red wine. She'd be warmed from the soaking waters, clean, a faint smell of scented soap drifting around her from the gentle night air slipping through the welcoming window. The thought stirred him. He could taste her flesh now.

He reached out carefully, felt the latch. This was further

than he'd gone before, no turning back now. No turning back. It was time. The long controlled rage bit at him, eager to be released. And at last, at last, it could finally run loose.

He reached into his jacket, pulled the stocking over his head and snapped the surgical gloves onto his fingers. A momentary shot of panic as he fumbled for the sacred object, searched the inside pocket, checked the other side, relaxed in a wash of relief. It was there, bending, creaking slightly under his loving touch.

He ran his fingers up the plastic to its pinnacle, allowed himself another smile. His calling card. The summary of his triumph, how he would become known, first by the police who would hunt him, then the journalists who would write about him, then, most of all, by the thousands of people who would gather on street corners, in pubs and outside shops to talk, hushed words, looks cast quickly over shoulders, shocked. His fingers rubbed again around the sharp plastic peak. The first of his set of calling cards.

He slid it back inside his jacket, reached for the other object, held it out and tipped it up. The slow oil oozed softly onto the hinges. His calm fingers found the catch. It shifted silently. A soundless shoe found the certainty of the window ledge and he levered himself up. The boom of an advert break startled him into stillness, but the figure in front of the TV didn't move, the legs still stretched out, languid on the servile leather pouf. The first thrill of the surging excitement hit him as he rode the expectation of those legs buckling under his pounding weight, her eyes wide with silent horror.

A second's darkness, silence, then another advert illuminated into life, rang out and he was inside the room, striding, quick and careful over the carpet, breathless with the anticipation, his heart banging now, so hard he thought she would hear. And finally the figure moved, turning, the damp hair swinging slow as the head faced him, the fine cheekbones rising, the mouth slowly opening, readying for the scream, but his shaking hands were on her, stifling, the only sound her strangled gasp, his rushing breath of exulted release, the cheerful theme tune of the flickering television and the bumping tumble of the glass, gushing its bloody liquid across the cream carpet.

Sometimes it was difficult not to cry, but he couldn't say exactly why the tears were gathering now. Before him was a masterpiece that he had created and which would live on for hundreds of years, perhaps even thousands. And he was dying. Which was the reason for the tears? A little of both perhaps, he thought. Whatever, it didn't matter. All that was important now was the completion of his grand vision, the wondrous legacy he would leave.

He swallowed and felt the tumour, hard and alien within him. It was always there, deep inside, always growing, hungrily eating away at his life. It was a cowardly enemy, but an insurmountable one. It would never show itself and it could not be defeated. And its victory was near now as the momentum of its lethality grew. His only consolation was that the cancer would die with him.

The familiar watering stung at his eyes and he wiped them with a sleeve. She would not see it. She was suffering enough, readying herself for life alone. No more breathless walks on the dizzying, jewelled coast, shared bottles of heady wine in the warm snug of a stone-walled pub, even the mundane yet strangely precious nights just watching the television together. And she was prepared for what he had asked her to do. It was a daunting sacrifice for one as good as her. Her role was vital and he knew she was heavy with doubt, but she had promised. He trusted her to carry it through. It was his last wish, the way he wanted to be remembered. His lesson.

He reached out with the fine brush and mixed a little white into the fluid gold crescent of paint on his pallet. Above the head of the younger of the two images of himself, he added a point to a star. It was complete. The final picture was finished, the last clue to the riddle, the closing detail in the spectacular epitaph he was writing for himself.

He laid the pallet down, reached for the light switch and turned to walk back into the house. Another persistent tear tickled his eye. He hesitated. He couldn't face her yet. Not yet, she couldn't see him suffering. It hurt her too much.

He gazed back at the picture and relived the anticipation of the sensation he would never see. It was a fantasy he couldn't tire of. No one would solve the riddle, he was sure of that. It was too clever, too perfect. In a lifetime of wonder, this was the zenith.

He would achieve immortality, joining the exalted ranks of the finest artists, with the timeless works they left behind. He still wasn't quite sure which was the most powerful motivation. That, or the opportunity to enforce some justice in an immoral world. He licked a finger and smoothed a spraying eyebrow into order. It didn't matter. The historians could argue about his reasons, and they would, for many long years. All that was important was that it happened.

The thought cheered him, as it always did. He would die within days now. His hand rose to his chest. The tumour had almost finished gorging itself, but time enough remained for all that was required. He reached for the light switch again and this time flicked it off. He could face her now. The knowledge of the amazement, fascination and scandal that he would leave behind had given him strength. It always did.

He glanced back at the silhouette of the canvas and the dark outlines of the two images of himself. Whatever they claimed about him, it could never be said that Joseph McCluskey's death had no meaning.

Chapter One

THE SCREECH CUT THROUGH the air, bounced off the walls and sliced into Dan's skull. Lizzie slammed the phone down and sprung to her feet. She looked tall today, her icicle stilettos four inches high, a bad sign. The newsroom fell quiet as she glared around. Journalists began to sink below the safety line of their computer screens, like soldiers in their trenches, fearful of the coming barrage.

'We've lost one of the top stories,' she barked, a sharpened fingernail jabbing accusingly at the air. 'The bloody lawyers have vetoed the exclusive on the shagging councillor. So there's a three-minute hole in the programme. Who's got something that can fill it, and fast? Come on, quick, quick, quick!'

Silence, apart from the merciless tick of the radio controlled clock on the wall. Dan stood, frozen, as her roving eyes settled on him.

He just had time to reminisce about what a pleasant day it had been. For once, there was no breaking news of murders, mutilations, explosions, fires, crashes, rapes or robberies that would force him to scramble to yet another miniature war zone. He felt much better off after getting through almost half of his paper mountain backlog of expense claims and he'd even researched a couple of stories too. The one about hoax calls to the police was his favourite for tomorrow. The Superintendent in charge of the 999 call centre had a tape of so called emergencies that included a request for a pizza, a report of a racing pigeon making its home in someone's back garden and a broken washing machine. It would certainly amuse the viewers.

He'd even had time to wonder about whether he should call Kerry. They hadn't got together for days and he wasn't so sure he wanted to see her at all, but he wasn't doing anything else tonight, it was spring, the weather was pleasant and a grapple in the sheets would be a fine way to end the day. But then, she'd see it as some form of commitment – again - and he didn't know if he could face the hassle.

He'd checked his watch. Coming up to five o'clock it said, so probably about ten past. Dan mouthed the routine curse for the backstreet jeweller who had sold him the cheap Rolex. It hadn't taken long to find out why the price was so reasonable. He'd started packing up his satchel. Time to quietly sneak off. He could get home, take Rutherford out for an evening run, then decide whether to call Kerry. There was no rush. It was an unusual feeling, but he seemed to be reasonably relaxed.

The contentment vaporised as Lizzie launched.

'You!' she barked, striding over, her heels stabbing hard into the carpet tiles of the floor, the black bob of her hair flying. 'You've been doing so-called 'research' today. So… what've you come up with?'

Dan put down his satchel. 'Hoax calls to the police…' he began. 'But I don't have the tape of them yet…'

'Useless then,' she snapped. 'What else? Come on!'

'Err… big rise in the number of people being killed on our rural roads…'

'Got enough to talk for a couple of mins about it?'

'Err…'

'Done then. Get out there. I'll send the outside broadcast truck. I want you on a rural road. I want emotion. I want you yapping movingly for two mins. I want one of those places with a pile of flowers next to a spot where someone's copped it. And I want it good. Go on then, what are you waiting for? Go!'

Dan jogged and swore his way down to the studios' car park to meet Nigel. He was leaning on the bonnet of his estate, polishing the lens of his camera. 'Quick,' Dan gasped. 'Scramble call! Head north, towards Dartmoor. We've got to cobble together something for the programme… somehow. Bloody Lizzie.'

Nigel battled their way through the traffic while Dan worked on his script. Every second saved could be vital in beating a deadline. 5.20, a tortuous time to leave the city, the sluggish roads clogged with weary commuters. And still the location to find and the live broadcast to sort out. It was going to be tight. The precious minutes ticked mercilessly by. Dan noticed his heart had begun racing.

They headed for the A386, leading out of Plymouth towards north Devon. A racing track mix of single and dual carriageway, long, inviting straights and sudden, deadly bends. It'd seen a series of fatal crashes, particularly motorcyclists.

He'd spoken to the mother of one young lad, Jason Rayner, a year ago when they'd covered a story about the rising number of bikers being killed in the region. Jason had died on this road when a lorry pulled out in front of him. His family made sure there were always flowers left to mark the spot.

Dan remembered the interview well. Jason had been just 22 years old. He was a keen motorcyclist, had passed his advanced test and used to ride out into the South-west's countryside to enjoy his other hobby, landscape photography. He'd been entirely blameless in the crash, as was so often the case with the deaths of bikers. The lorry driver simply hadn't seen him.

The man was charged with causing death by dangerous driving, but it was notoriously hard to prove and the case had collapsed. He'd eventually been convicted of careless driving and given a fine of two hundred pounds, with six points on his licence. Jason's family had described that as an insult.

The interview with Emma Rayner had been powerful and poignant. She hadn't cried, instead maintained a calm but intense dignity, which somehow had been more moving. She was only a young woman herself, in her early 40s, and had gone on to join the charity Roadpeace to help campaign to reduce the number of deaths on the roads. Dan had spoken to her a couple of times since about various motoring safety issues. They'd always got on well. He'd even been invited to Jason's funeral, a gathering of hundreds of friends and family and filled with touching eulogies.

An idea started to form. He could easily talk for a couple of minutes to take up the required airtime. Painful experience of hearing the dreaded words, 'Fill, fill, we don't have the next report,' in his earpiece on many an outside broadcast had quickly taught him the art of padding. But better, so very much better, to hear what losing a young life in a crash meant from someone who really knew.

Dan delved into his satchel, found his contacts book. Early in his career he'd got into the habit of writing down the phone number of every person he spoke to, and had been glad of it so often. It distinguished a good hack. You never knew when you'd need to talk to someone at short notice.

'Emma,' he said gently into the phone. 'It's Dan, from *Wessex Tonight*. How are you?'

She sounded genuinely pleased to hear from him and they chatted for a couple of minutes before he explained what they needed to do. He called, he said, because it was only fair to warn the relatives of people who had died that their cases were about to be featured on the television. Even many years on, some still struggled to come to terms with their loss and could be shocked at the images suddenly appearing before them, often as the family sat down for dinner.

'That's fine Dan, absolutely fine. You've always been very sensitive about what happened. You know my views. The bigger the publicity the better. If featuring Jason's case might make people drive more carefully, you've got my full blessing.'

Dan thanked her, paused, then explained his idea.

She didn't sound surprised, just amused. 'What, right now? You don't ask much, do you? I'm about to cook tea.'

'Anything good?'

'A bit of pasta. Nothing that can't wait, I suppose…'

'So…'

'But I don't have any make-up on.'

'I wouldn't say you needed it. Me yes, certainly, but not you.'

'Charmer. You think I'm cheap enough for a bit of flattery to persuade me?'

Dan kept quiet. A series of good-natured tuts echoed down the phone, then, 'I'll be there in half an hour. As it's you.'

The car's glowing clock read half past five. Less than an hour until they were on air. Behind, in the morass of traffic,

12

Dan could see the outside broadcast van. He worked through a quick mental calculation. Twenty minutes to get the satellite link working. Another ten to talk Emma through the interview. Fifteen more for him and Nigel to sort out how to present the broadcast. They could do it. Just.

'Got to get some fuel,' Nigel said, turning the car off the road and into a petrol station. 'We're running on fumes.'

Dan groaned. 'Not that time's against us or anything.'

'Sorry, it's been so busy lately I haven't had a chance to fill up. But if I don't get some petrol we're going nowhere. Just two minutes. I'll only get a few quid's worth.'

Dan ground his teeth, went back to working on his script, then looked up, noticed something on the forecourt. Another idea kindled. It was remarkable how the jabbing pressure of a looming deadline could spur your brain into action. He got out of the car, walked fast over to the kiosk, jogged back.

Nigel gave him a look. 'What're you up to?'

'Shhh. No time. You'll see later.'

The cameraman accelerated around a roundabout and the road broke free from the concrete of the city, onto the open moor. The horizon stretched with a ragged line of the famous tumbledown piles of granite of Dartmoor's tors. Golden gorse flecked the hedgerows as they sped past. Weatherbeaten ponies chewed hard at lush pockets of grass. Dan kept watch. He scanned each junction eagerly. No flowers... no flowers.

The miles clicked by. 5.45 now. No flowers... no flowers... no flowers.

Dan shifted uncomfortably in his seat. His back was sweating. If they didn't find somewhere to do the O.B. in the next few minutes they'd be out of time. He'd never before missed a deadline and didn't want to make this an unhappy first.

He breathed out a hiss, tried to remember exactly where the crash had happened. It must have been farther out of the city than he thought. Still no flowers. More time slipped past. 5.50.

A flash of colour caught his eye. 'Stop!' Dan yelled. Nigel slowed hard, bumped the car off the road. A blare of angry horns from other drivers buffeted them. They ignored it, clambered out of the car.

A tapestry of flowers lined the fence, interlaced reds, blues, yellows and pinks, ruffling gently in the breeze of the passing traffic. One card read, "Jason, always in our thoughts..." Another, "Forever missed, your smile lit up our lives." Jason's mischievous face grinned out from a photograph, handsome, dark haired and swarthy.

Dan's mobile rang. 'Hi Lizzie,' he said, making a face at Nigel. 'Yes, I know the programme's in real trouble unless we get this sorted. Thanks for pointing that out. Yes, I know you're relying on us. If we could just get on with it...'

A babble of words burst from the phone. 'Yes, I think you're right Lizzie,' Dan replied nonchalantly. 'We should have thought of asking someone who's lost a relative in an accident to join us for an interview.'

The phone buzzed as the attack intensified. 'Oh, sorry, yes, what I meant was *I* should have. Yes, I entirely agree, it would have made much better television... far more emotional.' He paused, waited, gave Nigel a knowing wink, then finally added, 'Oh, hang on... that was what I meant to tell you... it's just what I've already done.'

The Outside Broadcast truck skidded to a halt beside them. Nigel held out a microphone and Dan took it, started rehearsing his lines.

'There are few roads you can drive down in the countryside without seeing a poignant memorial to a fatal crash,' he intoned in his best sombre voice, kneeling by the bouquets. Nigel nodded, focused the camera.

Emma arrived at quarter past six and gave Dan a hug. He wasn't surprised to see she didn't look in the least flustered by the prospect of broadcasting live to half a million people. They were ready with three minutes to spare. Close, but he'd known tighter.

The director barked a cue into his earpiece, Dan showed the camera the flowers, crouched down to quote one of the tributes, explained what had happened to Jason and Nigel panned the shot to find Emma.

She talked movingly about losing her son, the pain it still

caused every day, her anger at the senselessness of his death and appealed for people to take more care on the roads. Her words were as powerful as ever, couldn't have been better scripted or delivered by Hollywood professionals, Dan thought. After the broadcast he thanked her, then reached into the back of the car and gave her one of the bunches of flowers he'd bought at the petrol station.

He waited until Emma had driven away, then carefully placed another of the bouquets at the end of the line of tributes. It just didn't do for anyone to suspect that such a hardened hack as him had a soft centre.

Nigel gave him a look, then peered into the back of the car. 'There's one bunch left. So who's that for?'

Dan adopted an enigmatic smile. If he did decide to go and see Kerry tonight, the flowers should soothe his passage into her sheets beautifully.

Dan took Nigel for a quick beer at the Moorland Inn after the broadcast. It was his way of saying thanks for rushing around and making sure the story got on air.

Lizzie called. Not to thank him Dan noted, but to burble about a story for tomorrow.

He sipped contentedly at his pint and held the phone away from his ear, but still managed to catch most of the words.

'It's an extraordinary story, one of the best we've ever had. It'll send the ratings soaring. I want top coverage and lots of it. I want reports and live broadcasts. I want emotion. I want poignancy. I want... are you listening to me?'

'Yes, yes of course. Every single word.'

'Right, well, you know the story of that dying artist McCluskey and the Death Pictures riddle? It's that. I want you to mug up on it. I want you to be our expert. I want you all over it. I want you to know it inside out. Are you back home yet?'

'No, I, err... I'm... checking out another story first.'

'Right, well, one of the researchers will drop off a briefing at your flat. You'd better read it until you know every detail. Tomorrow's a big, big day. I want top coverage.'

They finished their pints and Nigel drove them back to Plymouth. Just as Dan climbed out of the car, his mobile rang again. He sighed wearily and was going to ignore it, but Adam's name flashed up on the display.

'Hi mate, how you doing?' he said.

'Bad. I've got a really nasty case and I need your help.'

'Fire away Adam. I owe you after all the help you gave me on the Bray story.'

'We've got a rape, Dan, and it's a weird one, very weird. A guy forced his way into a woman's home and attacked her. It was savage, one of the worst I've seen. She's a right mess.'

Memories of the case they'd worked on together filled Dan's mind. The shotgun killing of Edward Bray, the notorious businessman, how he'd been allowed to shadow the police investigation, the uncovering of the conspiracy of Bray's enemies that had led to the murder. How he, a journalist, had seen the vital detail that solved the case. How they'd become unlikely friends and the Chief Inspector had confided in him about the rape of his sister, Sarah, its shattering of a promising life.

It was that which had pushed Adam to become a detective, a sort of legitimised vigilantism, he'd said. No wonder he sounded dangerous.

'You hear this all the time, Dan and it's become a classic police cliché, but I'm worried the guy could strike again,' Adam continued. 'He did something very odd in the house, which makes me think this is just the start. I need a broadcast to warn women and to get out the description we've got to see if anyone recognises him. Can you get something on air for me?'

Dan paused, could imagine Lizzie interrogating him about the story. Who can we interview? What pictures can we show? He knew what she'd want, but didn't know how to tell Adam.

'Dan? You there?' The phone buzzed with the detective's anger. 'We've got to get this bastard.'

'Yes, I'm here, mate,' Dan replied. 'We can probably help you, but there's one problem. We have a policy of not doing too much crime. There's so much of it about we could easily fill the programme every day and leave the viewers scared witless. We just tend to do the major stuff, and only then if we can talk to the people who are really affected. And in this case, that'd mean talking to the victim.'

He heard a hiss of breath over the humming of the phone line.

'Is she up to talking, do you think?' Dan continued. 'We could make her anonymous. I know it sounds daft, but we'd need to hear from her what effect it's had.'

Silence, a couple of clicks on the line. Dan could imagine Adam squeezing the phone in his grip.

'She's in a dreadful way,' the detective said finally. 'But she's trying to be strong. She's already talking about not letting him beat her and saying she'll help us all she can. I think she might be up for it. I'll have a chat when I go back in to see her. I'll call you later.'

She seemed swollen with her suffering. Her face red, blotched, streaked and stained from the tears. Her head hung loose, lifeless, as though she couldn't find the strength to support it. Her eyes were narrow lines from the endless tears and flinching as she revisited her torment, again and again. One of her hands hung over the stark, sterile white of the hospital sheets, a fiery diamond lightly gracing the wedding finger, a glittering contrast to her hunched darkness. Her fiancé had been traced, was on his way down from Birmingham and he dreaded the man's reaction when he arrived, dreaded her seeing it too. He'd find a different woman to the one he'd loved.

Adam could sense the freeze spreading inside her, the shrinking of feeling before it, the blossoming of fear and mistrust in its wake. He'd seen it before, with Sarah, seen what it did to her. A life tainted in one sickening, uncontrolled, attack. She could act a smile now, years on, but she could never feel it.

Rachel would be the same. She would survive, physically recover, allowing friends and family to enthuse about how much better she was looking. They'd all try to instil life back into her. But it was what it did to you inside, the severing of the fragile bond with humanity. No one would ever know that but Rachel. She and the small band of fellow sufferers who'd been violated by a man's sexual rage.

Adam turned away again, looked out of the window, west, to the sun settling on the springtime fields of the Tamar Valley. Shadows stretched ever longer over the amber glow of the patchwork land. He hardly registered its beauty.

He clenched a fist, breathed out slowly through tightened lips, allowed himself to enjoy a fantasy he knew would stay with him until the case was over. It was how it had been with the other rape investigations. Tracing, chasing, tracking and cornering this man, not the metallic clunk of the handcuffs, but instead his fist planted in the rapist's face, his knotted knuckles, beating, pounding, time and again, then the hard leather heels of his shoes stamping, pummelling, feeling the dull crack of a skull and smelling a spurt of blood, grinding him into oblivion.

He would get him. Adam almost whispered it to himself. He would. Twice before he'd faced these cases, renowned as some of the most difficult to investigate, let alone get a conviction. What was the current statistic? About six per cent of complaints of rape led to a successful prosecution? Not for him. Two out of two.

But he'd have to be careful. He couldn't risk another warning, or a closer look at how he'd solved the other cases.

In the first, it'd just been raised eyebrows from the other detectives and a friendly word in the ear from the Assistant Chief Constable. He could still hear the shouting and screaming in the bar and feel the fist flying into his face, his skin splitting under its clubbing impact.

'We won't go too deeply into why he assaulted you, eh?' Hawes had said, an arm on his shoulder in the quiet of a corner of the police station car park. 'We won't ask why you happened to fancy a drink in that very same pub he was in. We won't go into his claims that you'd been following him all day and he lashed out at you in frustration. No one would believe the word of a rapist, would they, eh? We'll just think it was good luck that you happened to be in the same pub as our prime suspect and he was drunk enough to have a go at you. We'll overlook our frustration at not being able to take a DNA sample from him because he'd committed no crime. Up until he attacked you that is, eh? We'll forget how fortunate it was that we could finally take a swab after we'd charged him with the assault. It was just down to luck that it matched the sample taken from the woman he'd raped. No one in the force would ever dream of suggesting you pushed him into attacking you so we'd have grounds to get some DNA from him, eh?'

Adam rubbed at his right eyebrow and the tiny scar Mick Barwick's fist had left. He was a squat, powerful man and it had meant four stitches. But it was a price worth paying. He'd gladly exchange it for Barwick's twelve years in prison.

The other case had brought a formal warning. WPC Radcliffe was young and keen and had been up for the operation, but Adam had stupidly forgotten to get the required approval from the Assistant Chief. An oversight, he'd assured the raging Hawes as he stood to attention in his office. It was a detail lost in the intensity of the hunt for their man. Just an oversight, nothing more.

Hawes wasn't mollified, nowhere close. Jo Radcliffe had been badly shaken by Hill's attack on her in the park, he ranted. It didn't matter that there were cops in the bushes, waiting for him and that he'd been arrested before he could do anything more than grab her. It was unacceptable to compromise the safety of an officer without approval from the highest level. DCI Breen would consider himself formally reprimanded and nothing like it would ever happen again.

That was the only stain on his service record, Adam thought, and he'd gladly take it. Neil Hill had got 14 years. They could prove he'd committed two rapes and suspected him of another couple of attacks. That was enough for the judge. A reedy man in his mid 20s with an odd smell of damp, Hill was a classic inadequate who'd never had a girlfriend. He picked only on very thin young women and used masking tape to strap his victims' hands together as he raped them. He'd developed a way of working and had got a taste for it.

He'd have attacked again unless they'd caught him, again and again. Adam allowed himself to relive the memory of how he'd twisted and jammed Hill's arm behind his back, dislocating his shoulder. How he'd enjoyed the cracking sound and the man's agonised scream, how it'd tempted him to push the arm just a little harder. He'd expected to feel some guilt, even a little shock at himself, but jubilation was all that came.

The door swung open, banging into the white wall, juddering on its hinges. Rachel flinched, her eyes widening, looked helplessly across at Adam as though pleading for protection. A young, white-coated doctor stood in the doorway.

'Who's in charge here?' he said sharply, jabbing a pen around the room.

'I am,' snapped Adam. He strode from the side of Rachel's bed to within a foot of the doctor. The man took a step back. 'Detective Chief Inspector Adam Breen,' he went on. 'And you are?'

The doctor held his stare, then looked away to Rachel, lying on the bed. She held one hand over her heart as though trying to calm it.

'This woman is far too frail to be questioned at the moment,' he said. 'I wouldn't hear of it...'

Adam reached out an insistent arm and guided the doctor out of the small private room. His words faded and he followed meekly.

'Look, doc, it's this simple,' whispered Adam into his ear. 'I need a description of this guy and the details of what happened, then we'll leave her alone.'

The doctor had a callow complexion and a darkly lined face. He hadn't introduced himself, but a well-worn blue badge said Andrew Lovell. His eyes were framed with blood red circles and his black hair stuck up in spraying patches. Hell, I wouldn't want him treating me, thought Adam.

'I wouldn't hear of it. She's only just come in. We need...'

'It's like this, doc,' Adam cut in. 'This woman has been raped. That's raped. She hasn't sprained an ankle, or cut her finger. She's been raped. The man broke into her home – her

20

own home – and attacked her while her kid was upstairs in bed. That's upstairs… in bed.'

He checked the doctor's hand for a ring and saw the silver wedding band. 'Now I don't want to scare you,' Adam continued, 'but at best that means there's a guy out there who doesn't think twice about busting into women's homes to attack them. I said at best, because I'm hoping he's gone home, gone to ground somewhere to feel bad about what he's done. At worst, he's wandering around the streets now feeling very good indeed and looking for his next victim. And that could be anyone. My wife, my family...' He paused. 'Even yours. So we need a description, and we need it now.'

He let the words linger. Doctor Lovell met his stare, seemed to have turned paler. He picked at a piece of paper on his clipboard.

'Ok then,' he said. 'Ten minutes, no longer. She needs sedation and rest.'

She'll need a lot more than that in the days to come, thought Adam. He walked back to Rachel's bedside, making a point of closing the door softly behind him.

Back in his flat that night, Dan read through the briefing notes on the Death Pictures. He hardly needed them, knew the story well enough, as did most of the country now. He had one of Joseph McCluskey's prints on his wall, a silkscreen of a cracked rainbow with a silhouetted female angel above it and a faceless man kneeling below. It was number 377 of 450, signed in pencil by the artist. He'd bought it years ago after an unexpected tax rebate, in the days when they were just about affordable.

An original was out of the question on a journalist's salary, particularly now McCluskey was close to death and had become so very famous. Eighty-five thousand pounds, the most recent of the Death Pictures had sold for, according to his notes. He patted Rutherford's back as the Alsatian lay by the side of his great blue sofa, scratching hard at a floppy ear. 'That's plenty more than double our pay, mate. No more doggy treats for you if we wanted a picture like that. And stop scratching, or your ear'll drop off.'

The briefing went back to McCluskey's early life, more detail than he needed but it was interesting to read. Born in Plymouth, undistinguished years at school, went on into the sixth form for a year, didn't like the idea of more education, left and began painting. No formal training, he just decided to have a go. His work was quickly recognised as having what the cuttings of the time called 'great potential', and for once that wasn't the usual journalists' hype. He started off in portraits – the briefing implied that was a sure way to fund your living expenses, flattering the pompous who desired immortality on canvas – then moved into more abstract work.

One cutting detailed his first London exhibition, a minor gallery but it was a start. More followed, the venues growing progressively bigger and better known and his paintings began to sell around Britain. His lifestyle was as colourful as his works, making lurid stories for the tabloids.

'The Dishonourable Lady' read one photocopied headline. A minor titled member of the local aristocracy had posed naked and highly suggestively on the steps of a National Trust home for one work, causing a predictable outcry. She was barely 20, he 40. An affair had duly followed, outraging her family. It was all good publicity and the painting had sold for a record sum for a McCluskey. There was a string of women, his technique apparently a simple one. Paint them, then bed them.

Dan couldn't suppress a chuckle. He put down the notes and got up to fetch himself a beer from the kitchen, thinking what a creative way of working McCluskey's was.

He pondered what ale to have from the multicoloured collection of cans in his cupboard and thought of Kerry, whether she would be interested in a call or text message from him. Stour, he decided, pulling the red tin from the plastic netting of its pack of four, good Kentish ale. It reminded him of his college days. A thought of Thomasin in her tight yellow summer dress lingered teasingly too, like the beautiful ghost she was. Dan pulled open the tin and poured it quickly, watched bubbles fizz through the amber liquid. He forced his thoughts back to Kerry. It wasn't a night for sinking in memories of a lost past.

'Either commit to giving it a chance, or leave me alone,' she'd said, and he hadn't heard from her for ten days now. There'd been no sex since, and he wouldn't mind a quick bout, but after that, then what? He knew he'd lie there, feeling guilty about the implicit promise he'd made and not sleep, then spend the next few days trying to avoid her. It was a well-worn path. Maybe the flowers could stay in the vase in the hall. They brightened the place up.

His mobile rang and he jogged back into the lounge, shifting a sniffing and curious Rutherford away from the phone with his knee.

'Hi, Adam, how you doing?'

'OK, Dan, just about OK.' He sounded tired, his voice thin and hoarse. 'I'm off home, but I just wanted to call you first. She'll do it. She wants a couple of days to compose herself and recover a bit and she wants me and Suzanne there too, but she'll do it. Oh, and she wants to be anonymous as well. Is that all OK for you?'

'Sure, Adam, that's fine. I'll be sensitive with her, don't worry. You going to call me when you're ready to do it?'

'Yes, I will.'

Dan waited for Adam to say goodnight and hang up, but nothing came, just the hum of the phone.

Finally he asked, 'Are you OK?'

'Just about.'

'Sarah?'

'Yes.' The phone rattled with a sigh. 'And Annie and Tom.'

He'd fancied a night in on his own, a couple of beers, reading up on the interview with McCluskey and a decent sleep, but Adam was a good friend... Well, at least it would stop him trapping himself with Kerry again.

'There's beer here if you need one.'

'I'll be there in 20 mins.'

Dan sat back down and scanned through the rest of the briefing. McCluskey's paintings begin to receive national acclaim. A series of major exhibitions. The odd tabloid story

23

about broken relationships and spirited feuds with other artists. Becomes a Royal Academician, to the horror of some of the older art establishment, some very spicy quotes there. 'This is the Royal Academy, not a sordid Soho Drink and Porn Club you know…'

Dan chuckled again and patted Rutherford's head. He was beginning to like the man more and more.

Married to Abigail Duggleby, ten years younger, met when she modelled for him. Much cynicism about the chances for the relationship in the press, all confounded. Twenty-two years on they were still together and apparently happy and devoted, even as he prepared to die.

Ten months ago diagnosed with cancer of the oesophagus, a secondary tumour in his liver making it inoperable, given nine months to a year to live. Decides to spend his remaining months finding reconciliation with all his enemies – quite a number according to the notes – and raising money for charity. And here's how, the idea that captivated the country.

'Ten pictures I will paint,' a newspaper article quoted him as saying, 'roughly one for each month I expect to remain on this planet. Each will be auctioned off for a charity of my choosing. Each will have a very limited number of prints made, also to be sold for good causes. I will keep one of each of the sets of prints which will be exhibited on my studio wall. Hidden within the sequence of ten pictures there is a coded message of great importance to me. The answer to the riddle has been left in a safety deposit box in my bank in Plymouth, to which only my wife Abigail has the key. From the moment of my death, you have six months to solve the riddle. The person who does will be given the original of the last of my pictures. If it's not solved, it's up to Abigail what happens to the painting.' There was a photograph of the artist standing by an easel, moodily glaring at the camera.

They'd become known as the Death Pictures, and the rest of the folder contained images of each of the nine so far revealed, along with notes on what had happened to them. The first original had sold for just under thirty thousand pounds, the money going to a grateful St John's Hospice in Plymouth.

From there, the values had risen fast. The final picture was expected to be worth more than a hundred thousand and there had already been countless attempts to solve the riddle. None had been successful.

Tomorrow, Joseph McCluskey would unveil the last of the Death Pictures at his studio on Plymouth's Barbican and Dan, along with scores of other journalists, would be there to interview him. Not just a quick chat though, as Lizzie had made clear.

'I could send anyone for that,' she'd said. 'I've no idea why, but people seem to open up to you. He must be nearing his time now. I want you to do a proper interview with him, a good long and detailed one that we can use as an obituary when he does die. His wife Abi is a friend of a friend of mine. She asked if we could do something like this. She even asked for you. She said Joseph liked some of the other reports you've done, particularly on the Bray case. It's a huge story, so don't balls it up. I want it long, I want it good and I want it poignant.'

One final note in the file, from another reporter who'd interviewed McCluskey after the unveiling of the first Death Picture. 'Man's an arsehole. Full of himself. Horribly arrogant. Answers questions with questions. Thinks he's cleverer than everyone else. If interviewing, be prepared for a rough ride, and don't bank on getting anything useful.'

Dan rolled his neck and stared out of the bay window. Interesting. Was that why Lizzie wanted him to go? Because they hadn't got a good interview from McCluskey in the past? He felt himself starting to look forward to the meeting.

The doorbell buzzed. Rutherford jumped up sleepily, managed a half-hearted bark and gave Dan a questioning look. 'Ok fella, no worries, it's just a friend in need, lie back down,' he reassured the dog.

He opened the door to find Adam leaning against the wall outside. The top of his shirt was unbuttoned and his tie drooped forlornly down his neck. Dan handed him a can of Bass and he walked heavily in, taking off his suit jacket, which he flung at the coat stand. It missed.

'Shall I stick a duvet on the spare bed, mate?' asked Dan, picking the jacket up and dusting off some fluff. He must get round to doing the hoovering sometime, he thought. That, or get a cleaner in, more likely.

Adam flopped down on the sofa and nodded.

'Yeah. Duvet, bed, and some whisky beside it.' He took a deep draw on the beer, then another, while Rutherford sniffed at his impeccably polished shoes. 'What a bastard of a day,' he groaned. 'And I know there's worse to come if we don't get this guy soon. Much worse.'

He couldn't sleep. He'd expected that, but wondered why it would be. Guilt or excitement? Now, at last, he knew.

His naked body cuddled up around the second of his calling cards, like a child with a precious Teddy Bear. He stroked it, his fingers toying with the plastic point of its peak, rubbed it through the tingling hairs on his chest. Those ecstatic minutes earlier wouldn't leave his mind. They played again and again, the memory never losing its sharpness or thrill. He wouldn't sleep at all tonight, he knew that now. He was too awake, too alive. Too eager for the next time.

Chapter Two

HEAVY SNORING WAS GRUMBLING through the door of the spare room, so Dan whispered 'shhh' to Rutherford, slipped the lead around the dog's neck and they edged quietly out of the front door. He could do with a good run to clear the thickness in his head after the beer and Adam's outpourings of last night. He had a big interview to do today and wanted to feel fresh for it. He suspected he'd need to be sharp to handle Joseph McCluskey.

April had brought with her a fine morning, the awakening topaz sky bisected by the single white vapour trail of a lonely jet. A pair of magpies hopped and chattered to each other on the roof of the garage next door, oily rainbows shining in their blue-black feathers. Wasn't it two for joy? That'd be good, he could do with some. Spring was warming the world but there was still a nudge of chill in the air, so he broke into a jog. Rutherford matched the pace effortlessly beside him, the pads of his feet beating a soft rhythm on the tarmac.

They headed down the hill from Hartley Avenue into Thorn Park and Dan freed Rutherford from the lead. The dog shot off through the watchful chestnut trees, skidded across the dewy crystal grass to stop to sniff a scent, ambled back, then sprinted off again, just missing his master's legs. Dan nodded to another dog owner who smiled understandingly at Rutherford's antics, then began running laps of the park. A couple of miles would do, to wake him up and give him time to go through the competing thoughts jostling in his mind.

So Adam's on-off marriage was off again. It was like a soap opera.

When they'd first met, in the weeks leading up to Christmas, Adam had been living in a one-bedroom flat away from Annie, his wife and young son Tom. Dan had initially thought it had been the usual story of a man putting his work before his family. Sad but familiar, mundane even. Then Adam had told him about Sarah, how what happened to her had driven him to become a detective and how he couldn't betray her by giving it up, not even by easing back.

He'd agreed with Annie to ask his Chief Superintendent for a better 'work-life balance', as the police had called it, and for a while it had made a difference. But that was over Christmas when the festive spirit meant there was a lull in the violent and deadly crimes that demanded a Detective Chief Inspector's attention. He'd spent more time with Annie and Tom and they were edging towards reconciliation. But then there was a murder to deal with, a drugs killing, then a kidnapping, and now this rape.

Annie knew what a rape case meant. She'd been through it before, knew that she would scarcely see her husband until it was solved. And even when he was there beside her, his mind would be away, exploring the alibis and angles of the investigation. Her patience had stretched and finally snapped. Adam was back in the hated flat again.

They'd been through it all last night. What should he do? He wanted his family and his job, but couldn't bear the thought of betraying Sarah. As always, Dan had no answers; he was there to listen and keep Adam plied with beer until he fell into a dark sleep. It had become a familiar supporting role.

An excited yelp signalled that Rutherford had found a stick. Good timing, Dan was glad of the respite it offered from the run. The beer was still a heavy weight in his stomach and head. But first they had to go through their familiar routine. He wrestled the dog for it, and faced with growling, jaw-locked determination he pretended to give up, looked around and found a better stick under a lime tree. Rutherford immediately dropped his and galloped towards the new prize, giving Dan a chance to grab the original and hurl it off through the trees. The dog sprinted happily after it.

So what about Kerry? Should he give it a try with her? He liked her, but that was about it. Was liked enough to justify continuing a relationship? He couldn't see himself ever falling in love with her and wanting to spend years together, probably not even months if he was honest. He knew she felt very differently. Those hints about two flats being far more expensive to keep than one were hard to ignore, but he'd set his face and managed it.

Talking to Adam last night had put him off any real desire to get involved with her anyway. Better to be alone than live like he did. But life could get lonely, it was only human to need someone to cuddle after a dark day, and the sex was good too. Perhaps he'd call, or text her later? Another runner passed him, moving fast, purposefully, a young man carrying a backpack, probably training for the navy. Leave it for now, there were other things to think about besides Kerry. The Death Pictures. A fascinating story, he had to admit.

He began another lap of the park, picking up the pace to stretch his legs. That other runner had shamed him. A pigeon flapped fussily from a hedge as he passed. So what do I say to a famous and apparently cantankerous artist who's probably got a month to live? The classic cliché of the journalist's question – 'so how do you feel?' – wouldn't be a good idea for someone as spiky as Joseph McCluskey, would it? How do you think a dying man feels?

He'd been given this job like a presidential order, because Lizzie expected McCluskey to open up to him. Well, that might be a problem. He couldn't think of anything to ask the man at the moment. Maybe some hint about the solution to his riddle? That'd certainly get the viewers interested, and Lizzie would love it. But he couldn't see McCluskey going for it. He'd kept silent on any clues so far.

Something would come to him, it always did. Sometimes he just needed the adrenaline rush and panic of a deadline to focus his mind. And then there was the interview with Rachel, the rape victim, later in the week too. He didn't even want to start thinking about what to ask her. He'd certainly have to prepare that well, didn't want to hurt her more.

Dan wiped his forehead with a sleeve and checked his ever-unreliable watch. Five to eight it said, so it was probably about five past. The Rolex had never kept accurate time, but at least it looked good.

'Come on dog,' he shouted to Rutherford, whose head was buried in a hedge, tail a wagging blur of grey and black fur.

'That pigeon's long gone. They can fly off, you know, just like I wish I sometimes could. It's time to get back. I've got lots on.'

Dan grabbed a quick coffee from the canteen, scanned the newspapers, avoided the prowling Lizzie and logged in to a computer in the safety of the library to check his emails.

None were particularly interesting, although one was irritating. It quibbled about his pronunciation of schedule in a recent report, that making the ch sound like a k was the American way. He found his standard response and pasted it in.

'We apologise, but the mail server is experiencing technical difficulties. It could be several days before your communication gets through, if at all.'

It was a ten-minute drive down to the Barbican. Dan had planned to use the time to think of some poignant and penetrating questions for Joseph McCluskey, but still nothing came to mind. Instead he kept wondering about Kerry, if Adam could be trusted to lock up the flat properly, and whether he should get a cleaner.

Nigel turned off the main road, steered the car around a corner, then braked sharply. 'Bloody hell,' he gasped.

'Wow,' agreed Dan, loosening the seat belt, which had locked around him.

They'd stopped just in front of a crowd of people milling across the street, indifferent to the impatient horns of the cars that were trying to pick their way past. They were clustered around McCluskey's studio, the building almost obscured by the multiple layers of onlookers. Dan did a quick count. Several hundred he estimated. And it was only just before 10 o'clock, still an hour to the unveiling. There were a couple of satellite news vans too, their dishes stretching skywards.

Nigel turned the Renault up a back street and found a space. They got the kit out of the back, Nigel took the camera and rucksack containing spare batteries, tapes and the long furry gun-shaped microphone. Dan balanced the tripod over a shoulder, his notebook under the other arm.

'Some shots of the crowd first, I think,' said Dan, staring at the pack and thinking his way through the story. 'Let's get them now, before we have to push our way through. They're important in showing the incredible interest the Death Pictures have generated.' Nigel nodded. They stood back from the crowd and he set up the tripod and started filming.

From street level you didn't get a real sense of the mass of people surrounding the studio, thought Dan. Some perspective, we need a high shot. There was a surf shop on the other side of the street with what looked like a stock room above, its windows dark with brown boxes. That would be ideal. He walked over and introduced himself.

'Sorry, mate, can't help you,' the manager said. He had a pen behind his ear and looked flushed. 'I'm on my own, see. I haven't got time to go upstairs and shift the stock around.'

Dan smiled understandingly and pretended to open the door to leave. 'That's a shame,' he said over his shoulder. 'It would have fitted in nicely with the shot we were going to do from the opposite side, looking back at the crowd with your shop's logo above them. I reckon half a million people will be watching tonight too with a big story like this. Oh well, if we can't do it…'

From the shop's first floor window it made a great scene. Like a medieval siege, Dan thought. The crowd had swollen to perhaps five or six hundred, pressed against the double glass doors of the studio. He admired it as Nigel filmed.

The gallery doors opened and a wave of people washed forwards. There were shouts and cheers from the crowd. A chain-of black suited security men linked arms and struggled to hold them back. A good-natured chorus of 'Why are we waiting?' began.

Dan checked his watch. It said ten past ten, so probably only ten twenty, nowhere near time for the unveiling. What was going on? The bouncers forced clear a space and a chubby, dark haired shape wearing a body warmer and with a camera slung around his neck was shoved quickly out. The doors slammed shut behind him. Dan laughed aloud, making Nigel look up from his viewfinder. He should have guessed.

Dirty El.

The figure pushed his way through the crowd and shambled quickly off towards the city centre, the camera bobbing up and down in front of him. Dan couldn't stop chuckling. He grabbed his mobile from his back pocket.

'Hi, Dan mate, how you doing? Bit busy at the mo…'

'OK, El, let me guess.'

'Guess what?' He was out of breath, moving fast, a sure sign a lucrative deadline was looming. Nothing else made El break sweat.

'This is what. It's almost ten twenty-five *The Wessex Standard* goes to print in 20 minutes and hits the streets about eleven. I'm guessing they were desperate to get the last Death Picture into the paper. It's a huge story for them. They couldn't wait until tomorrow and the official unveiling would have been too late for today's deadline. So they send the dirtiest, most conniving photographer they know in early to try to get a snap for them.'

No answer, more panting. 'Might have been.'

'Did you get it?'

More panting. 'Enough for a cover. Gotta go, at the offices now.'

They finished the high shots, shook hands with the manager and went downstairs to get a few interviews with the crowd.

'He's a great artist and we've got one of the last chances to see him,' a young woman with a shock of black and purple hair shouted at him as Nigel filmed. 'In years to come he'll be world famous, him and the Death Pictures. I'm just hoping to get a glimpse of him and, if he'll sign my print, that'll make my life.'

'I have to admit I'm being mercenary,' said a balding, middle-aged man in a suit. 'I've taken a couple of hours off work. I do crosswords and I've got a few ideas what the answer to the riddle might be. I want to get one of the first shots at it. I'd love that picture. I could pay off my mortgage with what it'll be worth. I could even afford to divorce the wife.'

'I just love him!!!' screamed an older woman at the camera. 'He's a great painter and so sexy!' She waved some photos of McCluskey at the camera, pouting with her vibrant red lips. 'I want him to sign one for me, with lots of kisses.'

'That'll do for interviews,' Dan said, as he and Nigel pushed their way through the crowd to the doors. 'All good ones. That's a first. I wish it was always that easy.' He showed the bouncer his press pass and invitation.

The man peered at it with tiny eyes and scowled. 'Ok mate, but behave in there please,' he said. 'We've already had to throw one of your kind out. He let off a firecracker at the back of the gallery and while we were all looking to see what it was, the sod pulled the curtain away to get a shot of the picture.'

'That's disgraceful,' said Dan, trying to swallow a laugh.

She'd never quite understood why, but she'd applied to go on the course about dealing with victims of sexual violence and had become the specialist liaison officer for Plymouth. It had been distressing but strangely rewarding too. There was something about these crimes that marked them out from the standard assaults and muggings, even many of the killings they had to deal with.

It was the domination and humiliation, the violation, the most degrading and debasing of attacks. With the assaults the body usually healed in a few days or weeks. With the killings, that was it for the victim, sad, but nothing more to worry about with them, just catching the attacker. With these rapes, the victim was left alive, always conscious of what had happened, the knowledge stalking her like a cold shadow for the rest of her life.

'How are you feeling, Rachel?' Detective Sergeant Suzanne Stewart whispered the words. Hospitals made you do that, she thought.

Outside a young blonde nurse hovered, peering occasionally through the slit of smoked glass. Fifteen minutes she'd been given, strictly no more. The boyfriend – fiancé – Martin had been sent to get a coffee, Suzanne needed to be alone with Rachel. They'd managed to get a brief description of the man, for what it was worth. A rough height and build, a stocking over the face, a smell of tobacco. No words though, he'd stayed silent, no clues about accent or upbringing. It wasn't enough. There had to be more.

'A bit better, Suzanne, thanks. Just a bit.'

Rachel's voice was thin and hollow, speaking an effort of will. She managed a faint smile, but it was almost imperceptible. Her head lay back on the pillows, her raven hair played out around it. Her once full lips seemed to have shrivelled after the attack, the bleaching making them blend into her pallid face. Her eyelid twitched as she spoke. Suzanne felt a familiar growing anger for the man who had caused this, had transformed a woman friends had spoken of as bright and vivacious into a wraith.

'I don't want to bother you any more than I have to, Rachel,' she said, taking the limp hand that lay on the sheets. It was safe, her fingernails had been checked for any fibres or skin she might have clawed from the attacker.

Anyway, they had all the DNA they needed, the man hadn't bothered with a condom. So now another lingering torment. The wait for the result of the Aids test. And why hadn't he used a condom, when he had worn gloves and there were no fingerprints? Was he so excited he couldn't control himself? Didn't he care about leaving evidence? Did he have a criminal record, but one which dated back to before the DNA register? Did he want to be caught? Did he have Aids, and want to infect his victims? Was this about revenge?

If it was revenge, it didn't seem to be specifically against Rachel. All the men she knew – particularly the exes – had been checked and had good alibis. Nothing in her past showed any reason why a man might have a grudge against her. Even the men living along her street had been checked to see if there was any chance one might have been harbouring a pervert's fantasy. They'd found nothing.

So could the motive be a more general revenge? Against dark haired women? Single mums? Thin women? Women who happened to be wearing a white coat or a dark hat on a particular day? Suzanne knew that for a psychopath or sociopath with a festering motive in his past, any such reason could be a full justification for his attack. Or was he just hunting women? Any women? Because of something that had happened to him, were all women legitimate targets? Or was this simply about power, domination and lust?

She knew where the answer would come from and closed her eyes for a second at the thought. They'd only be sure when he attacked again. And they thought he would, were sure of it in fact. Because of that strange object they'd found and the question she had to find a way of asking Rachel.

Suzanne checked her watch. Her fifteen minutes were almost up. She had to ask it now, but despite all her experience, didn't quite know how.

The fragile eyes stared at her, questioningly. Following her thoughts? She hoped not.

'Sorry, Rachel, I was just thinking for a moment,' Suzanne began, as soothingly as she could. 'What I wanted to know was; have you remembered anything else about the attack that could help us? Anything at all?'

The head shook slowly, the eyes slipping closed with infinite tiredness. There was a whispered 'no'. Suzanne wasn't surprised, knew now to expect a suppression of memory, a reluctance, even an inability to relive the horror of the attack. She knew they wouldn't get anything more from Rachel Bloom for days, perhaps even weeks.

That TV appeal DCI Breen was so keen on would have to wait. Now there was just one thing she had to know before she left. The object they'd found in Rachel's living room, in front of the pictures of her and Martin, hand in hand at the beach, dressed up at a wedding with both their parents, all smiling at the camera at a birthday party. Just the one question, but how to ask it without inflicting more pain, stirring more fear, more vivid, haunting nightmares?

'Rachel, there's something else I must ask. It's the last thing for now.' Suzanne smiled as best she could, but it was lost. The woman's eyes were still closed, her head resting back on her pillow. A couple of cards stood on the cabinet beside her. "Sorry you're not well" they said in friendly typefaces, pictures of sunny countryside and a playing kitten. Shopper-friendly euphemisms, but then Suzanne couldn't imagine a rack of 'With sympathy for your rape ordeal' cards.

'Rachel, can you hear me?' she whispered.

A slight nod, the eyes still shut. Suzanne knew it was time to leave, but she had to ask first.

'Do you remember the man leaving anything in your house? Did he say anything... anything about...' Suzanne hesitated. How to phrase it? What words? 'Anything about... the occult... or... witchcraft?'

Now the woman's eyes opened wide, and Suzanne could see the flash of fear in them. Her face looked ready to crumble, her chin trembling, her fingers finding some security in twining repeatedly together. 'No,' she said in a trembling whisper, her voice shaky and breathless. 'No, he didn't say anything.'

She looked about to ask a question when the door swung open and the nurse bustled back in. Suzanne struggled to hide her relief. 'Time for a nice wash now, isn't it, Rachel?' the woman trilled in a Scottish accent. 'You'll have to excuse us please.'

Suzanne quickly said goodbye, mumbled that she'd be back later and closed the door behind her.

Outside in the corridor, she toyed with her necklace and breathed out, leant back heavily against the white wall. Would Rachel have to know about the witch's hat they'd found in the living room, the small black cone of cheap plastic with the white stars and yellow crescent moons, the type children wear at Halloween parties? And that it had been placed proudly, perhaps triumphantly, on the mantelpiece, alongside her family photos? And would she have to know the packaging was screwed up and left inside it, the wrapping which said it came from a party pack of six?

Dan had once had what he called a mini relationship – lasting for one night – with a Plymouth historian he met in a bar, and from a memory of her conversation guessed the building they were in probably dated from Tudor times. He seemed to recall the city lost much of its historic soul in the Blitz, but the Barbican survived. Funny he could remember that, but not her name.

The studio wasn't large and the walls were thick, exposed stone. It was hardly designed for a modern press pack with their TV lights, cameras and radio recorders. The ceiling was low and the stone was an efficient insulator. The room was getting uncomfortably hot with the crowd of journalists, cameramen, photographers and security staff all jammed together.

On a low dais at the front of the room were two black curtains, tightly drawn and held up by a gleaming gold rail. They were slightly parted with a dagger-shaped slit in the centre near the ceiling, the spotlights in the roof revealing nothing but a hint of colour and shape. An ornate golden cord dangled at the right hand end of the curtains.

Fanned out around the platform was one of the biggest press packs Dan had seen. Cameramen and photographers stood in the middle, the journalists behind and to their sides, some seventy in all. Outside, the crush against the glass doors had grown, layers of people now stretching back across the road and the cobbled square behind.

Dan checked Nigel's plastic digital watch. Ten pounds it had cost him, but it was always accurate. Nigel had the sense to be practical, not flash, Dan reflected ruefully, and wondered if he would ever learn the lesson. It was two minutes to eleven. He still hadn't thought of what to ask McCluskey yet.

A man barged into his side, and Dan shoved back.

'Come on, mate, let me in there,' he said. He was chubby, in his late forties Dan thought, his face shining with sweat, a fat-lensed camera hanging around his neck. He smelt strongly of cigarettes. The pass pinned to the lapel of his leather jacket said *Daily News*.

'Come on mate,' he went on, leaning into Dan again. 'You're just a reporter. You don't need to be so close. That's for us snappers.'

Dan held his ground. Positioning was all in a press pack.

You never knew what could happen. If McCluskey said something extraordinary, he wanted to be at the front to hear it. Besides, a good TV reporter always watched his cameraman's back. With Nigel focused on looking down his viewfinder, he had no idea what was going on around him. And more to the point, he hated the *Daily News.* It was a scandal sheet, the kind of paper that gave journalists a bad name.

'Forget it, mate,' Dan hissed. 'You should have got here sooner. Didn't your mother ever teach you about early birds and worms?'

The photographer leaned into him again, tried to get his shoulder in front, but Dan was too quick, turned his back and pushed the rucksack with the spare batteries and tape into the man's face. It was a familiar trick.

'Arsehole,' he muttered and moved away, trying to squeeze through the crowd to a better position.

'You winning friends and influencing people again?' asked Nigel, looking up from his viewfinder.

'Just holding my ground,' said Dan with a grin. 'He was from the *News*, and you know what I think of them. And...'

A door to the side of the curtains swung open, interrupting him. A man hobbled slowly out onto the dais. The room instantly quietened and all the camera lenses turned to follow him. Dan had been expecting a big introduction from some master of ceremonies, but none was needed. Everyone here recognised Joseph McCluskey.

He had been a tall man, perhaps six feet two, but the cancer had bowed him. He walked carefully, almost a shuffle, but he watched the crowd throughout, his eyes dancing over them, a sparkle of savoured amusement in them. He stood by the side of the curtains, took the cord and went to pull it, but then stopped. He looked down at his watch and slowly smiled. He lifted his hand to the cord again, then stopped, lifted it again, then stopped. A rumble of nervous laughter filled the room.

'It's not quite time,' he said, and his voice was still clear, although throatier than Dan had heard it in other interviews. He was much thinner now, almost gaunt, but still a handsome

38

man in a haunting way, his hair rich and dark, the flecks of grey adding fine fissures of detail. His trademark eyebrows sprayed shaggy and unkempt. White teeth shone in his smile as he surveyed the press pack.

'All this just for me and my little doodles?' he chuckled. 'Or do you think you can solve my riddle? Would anyone like to have a guess?'

There was another ripple of hesitant laughter. This was like no other press conference he'd known, Dan thought. Always they, the media had the power. They leered down over their prey like a pack of voracious predators. Always the victim needed the media and the journalists knew that. They relaxed in it. The control was theirs. McCluskey had turned that around. They needed him, his final Death Picture and any words he deigned to give them about what it could mean, or how to solve his riddle.

McCluskey spoke again, his voice harder. 'OK, here's how it goes. I'll unveil the picture. You can get some pictures of me in front of it. Then I'll say a few words. After that, I'm off.'

He looked around, challenging the hacks, but no one said anything.

'Unlike you lot, I've only got a little more time here, so I want to go and spend it with my wife, not messing around with the likes of you.'

He smiled again and there was another wave of laughter.

McCluskey checked his watch. 'It's time,' he said softly. 'It's time.' The room was silent.

'OK then, are you ready?' he asked. A few hesitant calls of 'yes' bounced from the crowd. 'Then here we go. Welcome to history.' He stepped to the side of the curtain and pulled the cord.

A blaze of white camera flashes flared out, making the artist blink as he watched the reaction. The quiet remained, the journalists scribbling notes on the atmosphere of the moment, the details of the canvas before them. Nigel was moving his shot in to the artist, a close up of his exhilarated face, his eyes shining and dancing wildly. They flicked from the painting to the press pack, savouring their entrancement. Outside faces pressed against the glass doors, like children at a sweet shop.

Dan found his eyes drawn to the painting. All the Death Pictures had been the same size, about five feet high by four wide. All were oils, all framed in black wood, all with different subjects, some places, some people, some abstract and surreal. But this was different. This was a self-portrait, two in fact.

On the left of the canvas stood a younger Joseph McCluskey, when he was in his 40s, Dan guessed. He was proud and erect, arms folded in front of him, staring out, expressionless. At his feet was the earth, a perfect sphere of blue and green. On the right he looked as he did now, thinner, shorter, older, the 66 years he'd lived for. Now he looked down, not straight out and his arms hung by his sides. And, in this image, there was the earth above him, smaller, as though in orbit around the man. The background to the painting was all black, punctuated by a speckling of stars.

Between the two men was a clock, the classic alarm type, silver rimmed, two bells on its top, a grey face, the hands set at five to twelve. Below the clock ran a cascade of numbers, like a river flowing down to the bottom of the canvas, numbers Dan didn't think had been painted at random. There was a 9, an 11, a 5 then a 3. In the next line a 91, an 85, a 77, a 53 and a 42. In the third line a 29, 31, 32 and 37, then at the bottom a 109 and a 133.

Dan had no idea what they meant and wondered if anyone else would, but he knew that was the point. Somewhere in there was the answer to the riddle without a question, and people would be buying his prints, newspapers, books and magazines in their hundreds of thousands as they tried to solve it. Around him he could see his fellow hacks staring at the picture, all silently going through the same thoughts.

'So that's it, ladies and gentlemen, the last of the paintings you kind folk of the media have been so good as to name the Death Pictures,' rasped McCluskey from the dais. 'Of this image, I've decided there will be three prints made and signed. Two will be auctioned for a couple of charities I have in mind.

The remaining print will be placed here on the wall of my studio, along with prints of the nine other pictures, in strict order of their creation. In those pictures, here, you will find the answer to the mystery. That is…'

He let the words hang, scanned the crowd, smiled mischievously again, '…if anyone is clever enough to do so. And as you know, the original painting of the last Death Picture will go to whoever solves the riddle. To who that may be, I say this.' He paused again, nodded to emphasise the words. 'Remember the moral of the story well.'

With that, McCluskey turned and walked out of the door to the side of the picture, ignoring the burst of shouted questions from the pack.

The cameramen and photographers rushed towards the picture to take their close up shots of its detail. Nigel was right at the front and in the middle, as ever. Dan watched, his mind full of what McCluskey had just said. What did he mean, remember the moral of the story well? Did it mean the answer to the riddle was some kind of lesson McCluskey wanted to teach? But what? What was so important to him that he would hide it in a riddle the whole world seemed to be trying to solve?

A barge in the back knocked him off balance and he lurched forwards. Dan looked round to see the *Daily News* man disappearing out of the door. What a pathetic revenge, he thought. But the irritation brought him back to the room and he felt a sudden stab of concern. What happened to his interview with the artist? Lizzie said it had all been set up, was relying on him to bring in a compelling obituary for one of the biggest stories she'd handled. Returning to the office to tell her McCluskey had disappeared and he hadn't got it would be an invitation to demote him to reporting on church fetes, if he was lucky.

He felt a panic stirring. As he stood at the back of the room, looking around him, wondering what to do, there was a gentle tug at his sleeve.

'Dan Groves?' It was a thin, dark haired woman in her mid 50s, pale blue eyes and sharp cheekbones, despite the years.

He knew her from somewhere but couldn't place the face.

'Please don't say anything,' she said, 'but I'm Joseph's wife Abi. He hasn't forgotten the interview, but he wanted to do it quietly, away from all this fuss. In a minute I'll take you to another part of the studio where you can have a chat. He's looking forward to it.'

She smiled, but it was rueful, no warmth in it. 'He says he never thought he'd have a chance to write his own obituary. And he's got something he wants to show you, something no one else has yet seen. He's very proud of it. It's wonderful.'

Chapter Three

DAN MADE A POINT of trying never to be surprised, and if he was, certainly not to let it show. It wasn't cool or professional for a hardened hack, but he didn't know what to say about the room she led them into. He stood and stared, despite himself.

'It's the memorial he wanted to leave,' said Abi quietly, standing with them as they gaped at the walls. 'It'll be opened to the public so they can come and see them. The answer to the riddle is here. Have a look and do some filming while you wait for him. It's important to see them in order.'

They were the Death Pictures, for the first time complete and all together in one show. The room was windowless, the only light coming from the rows of spot lamps suspended from the ceiling. The walls and floor were stone and almost unnoticeable, seemed to fade away next to the paintings. The pictures were the room, thought Dan. They commanded attention, didn't allow the eye to wander. It was like a Pharaoh's tomb. Joseph McCluskey's memorial to himself.

One picture hung by the door, three each on the other walls. Dan had seen them individually, on the television and in the press, but never as a group. Beside him Nigel drew in a long whistling breath.

The first picture showed a woman, young, thin, perhaps 30 or so, flame haired against the lush green background of a forest. She was beautiful, pouting at the camera with succulent lips. But what drew Dan's gaze was the huge mobile phone straddled between her legs, as though she was riding it through the trees. The display had a phone number on it, the Plymouth code, 01752, followed by 225. The last three numbers were missing, looked as though they had yet to be typed in. All the pictures were very limited prints, the originals sold off for the various good causes chosen by the artist. This was number 3/4.

The second picture was unmistakeably Dartmoor. The gnarled grey tor in the background was familiar, but he couldn't quite place it. Somewhere around Merrivale he thought. Perhaps Vixen, Kings, or Great Mis Tor? White birds wheeled in a blue sky above it. In the foreground was a vicar, in cassock and dog collar, staring up at the rocks, a hand outstretched pointing to a small plane in the sky. Behind it trailed a banner bearing the legend 'Goodbye number one.' A dog dug up the earth at the vicar's feet. It was print 3/3.

Dan stood, hands on hips and gently shook his head. There were no doubt clues in the pictures, but more clearly a lot of mischief. He'd understood that from the few words McCluskey had said earlier and the last of the pictures. He couldn't help but think the man was having a great joke at the expense of the rest of the world. Nigel adjusted his tripod and started filming the first picture. He looked across at Dan who shrugged. He knew his friend wanted guidance about what details to pick out in his shots, what was important and what wasn't, but what could he say? He had no idea.

Picture three was a street, unremarkable, terraced houses, probably late Victorian, cars parked along the road. A red legged and beaked bird perched on a streetlamp in the foreground. From his past days as Environment Correspondent, Dan recognised it as a chough. The first few car number plates were clear, the rest blurred. A blue mini had 'OK 9', an old blue Ford '115 J', a yellow three-wheeler 'Yes 04', a red Peugeot 'Here 911'. The street sign was a blurred grey, but 'Road' was legible. A manhole cover lay open halfway along, a child wearing shorts but no T-shirt looking down into it. Print number 3/7.

Picture four was an abstract, what seemed to be a blazing, malformed sun in the sky above a desert. It was the simplest so far, just a few rocks, a couple of cacti and what looked like a pool of water. A mirage? By the water stood a clock, similar to the one he'd seen unveiled in the last picture. The hands showed a quarter past nine, but they were drooping. A snake wriggled by in the foreground, seeming to make an S shape. It was print 1/2.

Why just two prints of this picture, he wondered? Because the artist thought it less powerful than the others? Less of a work? Less important? Or just because he only had a couple of

44

beneficiaries in mind?

Number five showed the inside of a pub, clearly identifiable by the wooden sign above the bar, the Waterside Arms. Dan knew it well, just out of the city, over the River Plym in the old village of Turnchapel. It was one of his favourites. There were beer festivals every couple of months, a fine range of pies on the menu and an old-fashioned landlord who liked to know everyone's name. He treated them as treasured guests, not an inconvenience, unlike so many modern publicans. It was print 1/6.

The oddity was that the pub was deserted, despite there being half drunk pints and glasses on the bar and tables and a couple of plates full of food. Four darts stuck from a board, a double two, a nine, a 13 and a bull's eye. Why four darts, Dan wondered? A fruit machine showed three bunches of cherries on the win line. There was a broken bottle of whisky on the floor, a black and white cat sniffing hesitantly at it.

A woman dominated number six. Blonde, with a shoulder length bob, she smiled out of the canvas. She wore small rectangular glasses, dangling silver earrings and was holding a newspaper folded out in front of her. It was the *Western Daily News*. In the top left corner was printed 'Today's jackpot bingo numbers; 2, 22, 27, 39'. The paper's headline was 'It's a Fiddle!' There was a picture of a yellow fishing boat next to it, the number 98 on its prow. It was print 2/3.

Dan couldn't stop the run of thoughts in his mind. Fiddle, did that mean the answer wasn't in here? Or was it a double bluff? Was it some hint that if you went fishing for something to do with 98, you could come up with something? He checked himself. Damn! He was getting drawn into the riddle in exactly the way the artist wanted, and so just how he shouldn't.

Painting seven looked the simplest, but that made Dan suspect it wasn't. It was a portrait of Abi, looking much the same as she did now, except in the picture she had a perfectly formed tear rolling from her left eye. He looked across the room at her and she nodded. In the picture she stood against a coastline, just a simple line of green before the blue of the sea and sky. She wore a white T-shirt with a picture of a key on it, the number 09 alongside. The only other feature was a small red balloon drifting by in the sky on the right of the picture. On it was an exclamation mark. It was print 1/3.

Dan turned to the final wall. A print of the last of the Death Pictures was already in place, also number 1/3. The other two were the most striking of the set.

Number eight showed a child reaching into a goldfish tank, the watchful and wary creatures clustered at the sides of the aquarium. It was brightly colourful, the fish, the emerald green of the boy's jumper, the opaque blue of the water, the primrose yellow of the walls of the room in the background. Three fish faced the dangling hand on the left of the tank, four on the right. In the gravel at the bottom stood a miniature castle, grey but with a white portcullis. Outside it, also embedded in the gravel were five toy soldiers, all pointing rifles, and an armoured car. On its side was '17th light infantry.' It was print 2/5.

The ninth print was of a chessboard, with just the white king remaining, surrounded by a black knight, queen and pawn. A hand hovered in the painting but it wasn't clear to whom it belonged. A gold wedding ring shone on the index finger. In the background was a grandfather clock, the time showing five to ten, but the odd thing about it was there were no numbers 11 or 12 on the face. This time the clock's hands weren't limp but straight and sharply pointed. It was print 3/4.

'What do you think?' asked Abi. 'You're the first person from outside to witness it as he wants it to be seen.'

Good question, what did he think? Part of him wanted to say how impressive, stunning in fact, the pictures were. But Dan sensed he was feeling annoyed, as if he was being played with, used, and he hated that. Plus the pictures were full of intellectual arrogance and teasing, and that was even more irritating. On the other hand, he couldn't help but admire the idea, it was clever and intriguing…

Dan was saved from having to answer by Joseph McCluskey sticking his head around the door. 'They're still in there, lapping it up, photographing, filming and writing. Just like a flock of sheep,' he rasped. His face lit with a grin. 'Anyone fancy a cup of tea?' he asked. 'The shepherd doesn't mind making them.'

Adam was washing his hair in Dan's shower when his mobile rang. The shampoo was annoyingly sticky, that hair thickening stuff. He hadn't realised Dan was worried about his hair receding. You didn't have to be a detective to learn a lot about a person from their bathroom. He wiped the soap from his eyes, fumbled out around the sink and picked the phone up. Good job he'd left it to hand. You just knew a call would come when you least wanted it.

'Sir, Suzanne here,' came the rushed words. He had to listen hard to hear what she was saying. 'I think we've got another one. She's just called in. It took ages to calm her down before we could work out what happened. A team's on the way around now.'

Adam hoisted a greying bath sheet around his shoulders and tried not to think of the last time it was washed. He spat some soap from his mouth.

'Any details, Suzanne?'

'Sounds similar to the last one sir. Raped in her own home. She'd just got back from taking her little girl to school. It looks like he got in through an open window at the back of the house.'

The side of his fist hit the white tiles on the bathroom wall and a couple of bottles of after-shave rattled. 'Any more info?'

Suzanne knew exactly what he meant. 'I did ask, sir. She was in too much of a state to talk properly, but she said he did leave something behind. She hasn't touched it, but says it looked like some kind of kid's hat.'

He'd hardly needed to ask, knew it was the same man. Mission number two of six completed successfully he'd be thinking, congratulating himself, savouring another victory, lifting a pint and smoking a cigarette to celebrate. The bastard. No more, please no more. What did he mean *please*? It was his job to make sure there were no more.

'Her age?' Adam asked.

47

'About 30.'

'I'll meet you at the scene.' He dried himself quickly and strode into the spare bedroom.

They had a serial rapist on their hands, one whose way of working was already clear. Young women, living with their children, no man in the house. The attacks were well planned. And the motive, yes, sex, of course, but that was the easy answer. Wasn't he thinking it sounded like revenge too? The actions of an angry and embittered man? Someone who hated women, for whatever reason.

He wouldn't have time to go back to his flat for a change of clothes. Yesterday's suit would have to do, thankfully he'd hung it up carefully. The shirt was grubby though. But Dan was roughly the same size, wasn't he? He scanned the rack of shirts, chose a light blue one to match his navy suit. Dan's ties were a bit bright for a rape case, but he managed to find a darker blue and subtle diagonally striped one. It would do. He'd need to look decent, he had to get this on the TV. It was time to put out a warning.

The door opened again and McCluskey stood in its frame, his figure silhouetted in the daylight streaming from behind. He paused, silent and still, then projected his voice theatrically into the room.

'So you come not to praise McCluskey but to bury him?'

The artist began handing around tea and coffee from the tray he carried. Nigel took his but carried on filming. He was only on picture five, the detail in the works took time to capture. As they didn't know what was important he was trying to cover it all. If the answer was revealed, they'd need to show the parts of the pictures which pointed to it.

'I wouldn't be so Shakespearean,' replied Dan, prompting a slow nod from McCluskey. 'Anyway, the people we interviewed outside were full of praise.'

McCluskey made prolonged eye contact when he talked, as if he was looking into you. Those eyebrows were like the eager shoots of spring above the shining, mocking eyes. Dan held the stare on principle, but it was unsettling.

'Diplomatic,' McCluskey said slowly. 'But not your opinion. What does the man from the media really think of my little scrawls?'

Dan turned to the last of the pictures, then back again, giving himself time to think. 'I'd say they're fascinating,' he replied.

The artist studied him, but said nothing. He clearly expected more.

'There's so much thought in them,' Dan added. He swallowed a spike of annoyance, a buried memory of a feeling similar to being pushed for an answer by a disliked teacher in front of a classroom. 'Or is that just a bluff?'

McCluskey's spraying eyebrows rose. 'The answer is in there, I promise you that,' he said, turning to the first of the pictures. 'But so are many iron pyrites.'

Another test. The words were familiar, but how? Something from many years ago. Dan searched his memory, right back to school days. He thought he'd got it, took a gamble. 'Fool's gold?' he asked, trying not to sound hopeful.

McCluskey turned back, nodded. 'Very good. You wouldn't expect me to make it too easy, would you? And surely it's a better story for you if it goes on and on, with more of these hopeless wrong guesses we're inundated with? It keeps the suspense and drama going, doesn't it?'

'And the amusement for you, the shepherd? And the growth of the legend?'

He shouldn't have said it, Dan thought. It was hardly professional to be drawn into an argument with your interviewee, especially when he knew very well how much you needed his words. If he backed out now, refused to talk… But McCluskey didn't look ruffled at all.

'Yes,' he said simply. 'And what would you say is wrong with that? Trying to make some kind of a mark on the world? Provide a little enjoyment and entertainment for a few people? Perhaps even teach a lesson, achieve a little justice and right some wrongs in the process?'

The two men stared at each other, Dan determined not to break the look. What did he mean by righting wrongs? And what was this lesson he kept talking about?

'As you're going to be asking me some questions, I think it only fair if I get to ask you one first,' said McCluskey, still staring at Dan. 'If that's alright with you?'

Dan shrugged. 'Sure.' What else could he say?.

'We all have our little interests and weaknesses,' the artist continued. 'Mine happens to be crime. Not the mundane stuff, but the deeper plots, and what drives people to them. Your reporting of crime is always thoughtful. You're one of the rare few who tries to get behind the facts and into the underlying motives. You look for the insight and you seem to be able to understand people and see it.' He paused, the burning stare again. 'I like that. It's exactly what we artists do when we paint. Well, the decent ones anyway.'

Dan stayed still, facing the man, aware now that he wasn't the only one who'd prepared for this meeting. He could feel the room around him had gone quiet as Nigel and Abi listened in.

'Plenty was written about the Bray case,' said McCluskey, nodding slowly. 'It was an extraordinary one. And the word was that you saw the solution. But it was never made clear in the reporting what led you to it. How did you solve it?'

Dan let out a deep breath as his eyes filled with the past. He'd been over that so many times in his mind. It was too ridiculous to talk about, but still so vivid and strong. 15 years ago now. Thomasin, aged 21, the last two weeks of their final term at University. They'd been in the same year, but had only met in the last fortnight, and she was so beautiful, so clever, so funny, so warm, so loving… so perfect.

They'd tried to make it work, but the simple college days were fading and the merciless currents of life had begun pushing them apart. They hadn't had enough time together to establish the foundations to make the relationship last. Every other woman since had been compared to her, and none had ever come close. Nowhere near. How could fate play that spiteful trick on him so young?

Dan blinked the memories away and said finally, 'The best I can say is that I think I understood how deeply you can be affected by one single event in your life. I knew how some people can never truly be freed of that weight, and how it can stay with them until it drives them to one day find some resolution.'

McCluskey held the stare, nodded slowly. 'And in the Bray case, it was revenge?'

'Yes. He'd broken people's lives and that had to be avenged.'

'And in your case?'

Dan could feel the room's silence, the eyes on him, but why was he was still tempted to tell McCluskey about Thomasin? A feeling like being in a confessional? To this man he didn't know? No, not now, not ever. No one knew and no one would. No one would know about the catalogue of sticking-plaster relationships that had followed, the attempts to cover the cracks in a fractured heart. Continued to follow he thought, as Kerry walked across the stage of his mind, head held high, not looking at him.

'Mr McCluskey, I'd love to stay and talk, but we have to get the unveiling of the last picture on the lunchtime news.'

Another silence as they stared at each other, then a faint nod from the artist and a swell of relief in Dan. He thought he managed to disguise it, but he wasn't sure.

'You're very privileged you know,' McCluskey said, turning back to the last of the pictures. 'No one from outside has seen the series properly yet.' He looked up and reached out a hand to touch the alarm clock, as though wanting to adjust its time. 'Abi's acquaintance with your editor and her kind offer to let me write my own obituary swung it. It was something I couldn't refuse, and that doesn't happen very often, not to a man in my time of life.'

McCluskey flinched and let out a deep wracking cough, his body shaking. He took a couple of deep breaths and composed himself. Abi was at his side instantly, an arm on his shoulder, fear in the tightness of her face.

'OK, OK...' he said to her breathlessly, gathering himself. 'Now, time is something I don't have the luxury of, so shall we get on with the interview? In here, using the pictures as a backdrop?'

'Yes please,' Dan replied.

'Almost ready,' said Nigel, 'just give me a minute to get a couple of details of number nine and I'll be with you.'

'So what do you want to ask me?' said McCluskey, putting an arm around Abi who looked up to him in the most adoring way Dan had ever seen.

'I suppose I want to know how you'd like to be remembered,' Dan replied, surprising himself. So his brain had finally come up with an idea. 'And also about the last months of your life, the Death Pictures and your reconciliation with your enemies. All that sort of thing.'

'Fine,' McCluskey said, drawing himself up slowly. 'That's exactly what I wanted to talk about. Abi my love, please don't stay with us for this, it'll be too upsetting for you. I'll come and find you when we're done.' She turned without a word and walked out through the door.

Nigel positioned McCluskey so they had a backdrop of the last three pictures. He clipped a microphone onto his shirt and Dan took his position by the side of the camera.

'The first question, I'm bound to ask,' said Dan, bringing a wan smile to the artist's face. 'Can you offer any help to the thousands of people who are trying to solve your puzzle?'

'No,' came back the instant reply. 'Except to assure them the solution is in the pictures here and may come as a surprise. I certainly hope it will.'

A word in the answer surprised Dan.

'You said 'here'. Do you mean here in the gallery, with all the pictures in their position in the series is the place to solve the riddle?'

McCluskey nodded. 'You're listening. Very good. Or shall we say… I'd consider the studio by far the best place to solve the riddle. All the information you need is here in front of you. If you were to buy some prints of the pictures elsewhere, it may not be. It may, but then again, it may not.'

What did that mean, wondered Dan? That the answer may not be just in the pictures, but there was something here in the studio as well? He was tempted to look around, to see what it could be, but stopped himself. I'm thinking like I'm trying to solve the puzzle, not an interviewer.

'Could you explain what you mean by that?' Dan asked.

'No.' A shake of the head, the smile still there. 'It's all part of the mystery.'

Dan nodded. He'd been expecting that, knew he wouldn't get any further, had his next question ready. Time to move the interview on, he had lots to cover. But what did McCluskey mean? Was it part of this lesson he had to teach?

'You were given up to a year to live when you started the pictures. That time is almost up now.' Dan heard the whirr of the camera's motor next to his ear as Nigel zoomed the picture in for the powerful close up of the artist's face. 'What's it like feeling your time is running out?'

He'd expected some defensive reaction to that, probably even wanted it, but McCluskey remained inscrutable.

'It's like feeling the driest, most powdery sand slip through the fingers of your hand. It feels strangely beautiful. It looks beautiful. You'd like to stop it but you know you can't. You'd like it to go on for ever, but you know it won't. You know each passing second brings you closer to your hand being empty. And with that is the certainty that soon it will be empty.'

Dan tried to disguise the shudder he felt run across his shoulders. He looked down at his notebook to check his next question.

'You've made a point of reconciliation with all your enemies in these last few months. Why?'

McCluskey spread his arms, as though appealing to the sky.

'I want to go to the grave content. I want my soul to fly unburdened.' His words came softer now, and Dan wondered if he could see the cover of his preparation for the interview thinning, the real feeling starting to show. 'I don't want the nagging weight of unfinished business to bind me. I don't want the drag of regret to inhibit me. I want to leave this beautiful planet calm and at peace with it.'

McCluskey looked expectantly at him and Dan was

tempted to ask his next question, but decided to take a risk. He'd learnt early that the greatest art of the interviewer is knowing when to stay silent. It could leave you looking foolish, unsure where to take the discussion, or it could prompt real passion. Dan held the artist's look, said nothing.

'When I was told I had under a year to live,' continued McCluskey, his voice hoarse now, 'I was angry. In fact, I was livid. I raged and shouted and screamed at how unfair, how unjust it was. But then I realised it was an opportunity. How many of us get notice of our departure date? I realised I had a chance to do all the things I wanted to do and leave this earth without regret. Who among us can say that?'

Dan let the words settle, then asked. 'And why the raising money for charity with the pictures?'

'The easiest question so far. I have a little talent for doodling. There are many deserving causes. I don't need the money where I'm going. Why not help them out in their good works? I'm not a believer, but I have been a gambler. If I'm right and there is no God, I won't lose out. But if there is, I might as well insure myself and do some good works before I get to the Pearly Gates of Heaven. They might just squeak me a ticket in.'

Dan heard a quiet huff from Nigel. A gentle Christian, he was bringing up his sons in the same way and didn't like to see religion mocked. But that was a hell of a good answer, and he couldn't fault the logic.

'Finally, as you know, this interview is for broadcasting after your death.' Dan paused, let the words echo from the stone walls. Nigel zoomed the shot in again. This was the killer question, the most important of the interview. 'How would you like to be remembered?'

McCluskey looked down at the ground for a moment, then gestured to the paintings behind him. 'Remember me with this. Remember me as a man who had a small talent and did his best with it.'

Dan stared at him and thought he could see a moistening in the edges of his eyes, just a slight shine but it was there. At last, a question gets through his defences, thought Dan. At last.

'Remember me as a man who didn't always lead a good life, but tried to do his best in the end. Remember me as someone who liked a little game with his pictures, but only for the best of motives. Remember me as someone who tried to right the wrongs he saw around him before he left the sweet wonder of this beautiful and precious earth.'

Dan didn't often feel pressure when he was editing a report, but now the base of his back ached. McCluskey's teasing, vanity, games and riddles may have been annoying, but he'd been touched by that interview. They weren't using it in this item, instead saving it for his obituary. This was a story about the unveiling of the last of the Death Pictures, but he still wanted to do his best for the man. So many stories they covered were mundane, fillers, forgotten within minutes, meant nothing. This was one of the rare few that felt different.

To open the report, Jenny, the picture editor, put down the shot of McCluskey standing by the curtained picture, ready to unveil it. Dan added just a few words of commentary, less is more, the golden rule in television; 'So this is it, the last of the Death Pictures.'

The cord was pulled and the picture revealed. Dan said nothing over the shot, just let it run, the noise of the photographer's flashes and the viewers fascination with the painting meant no commentary was needed. Then they edited in a close up of the artist's exultant face and some of his words about the answer being in there.

After that it was shots of the crowd, one with the surf shop in the background. Then came the interviews with the people talking about why they'd come to see the unveiling. The shots in the gallery of all the pictures together were next, using lots of Nigel's close ups of the detail, the people, the places, the numbers. Dan added a few words about them going on display from tomorrow at the studio, with the riddle still to be solved. And as he sat in the edit suite, he found himself staring into the images, wondering what the message and lesson in there was, and why it was so very important to Joseph McCluskey.

* * *

The report led the lunchtime news, as befitted it, in Dan's view at least. He did a similar version for *Wessex Tonight*, just a little longer with some extra shots of The Death Pictures all together.

It was almost six o'clock. Lizzie had seen the report and approved it in her less than wholehearted way and Dan was packing up his satchel, ready to leave. He didn't take offence. He'd never seen her fulsome in her praise of a story in her life, merely satisfied or, if you were lucky, pleased. He sometimes wondered if exclusive footage of an alien landing would see her very pleased.

Dan sat at his computer and filled in a couple of expenses before he forgot. He was sure the company owed him hundreds of pounds in forgotten claims. Then he debated whether he could be bothered to stop in at the supermarket to get some food. But it would be busy and some beans on toast would hide the staleness of the bread, wouldn't it? That way he could take Rutherford for a run, then eat and have a quiet and early night.

He felt tired and lethargic, the hangover from last night with Adam. But might there be some time for a look through the Death Pictures, just to see if he could spot anything that could be a clue to the riddle? He hoped not, but suspected he wouldn't be able to resist.

He was about to log out of the computer and set off home when his mobile rang. Adam.

'Hi, mate, how you doing?' Dan asked, the phone balanced between his chin and shoulder.

'Bad. No, make that bloody terrible. We've had another rape, the same bloke as the first and I think there are more to follow.'

Dan fished his notebook out of his satchel and began writing. 'I've got to get a warning out and I've got to do it as soon as possible,' Adam continued. 'We've got to get this guy, or at least stop him striking again. The woman from the first rape will talk to you. She's still weak and nervous, but we've told her what's happened with the other attack and she wants to do it. Can you get something together now?'

Chapter Four

DAN RAN DOWNSTAIRS, TAKING them two at a time and jumping the final flight. He spun around the corner and into the studio's bar, a small but comfortable room full of soft, burgundy furniture and bowing plants. Faces turned in familiar anticipation, each expecting to be called away. One by one they relaxed as they followed his look to Nigel. He sat in a corner, chatting with a couple of engineers and sipping happily at a bottle of beer.

'How many have you had?' Dan asked.

'This is the first,' said the cameraman ruefully, putting it down and getting up from his stool. 'Unfortunately,' he added.

Dan took the bottle and finished it. 'Let's go then. Urgent one.'

They drove fast to the Tamarside Hospital, on the northern edge of Plymouth. A queue of cars waited on the entrance road, looking for places to park. Dan swore and looked quickly around, but there was no other way in. He swore again, making Nigel shake his head.

The queue edged slowly forwards. Behind them, an emergency siren wailed, flashing blue lights strobing inside the car. Ahead, drivers shifted onto the grass verge to get out of the way. Dan had an idea. He nudged Nigel, and pointed back towards the ambulance. As it manoeuvred clumsily past, they pulled out and followed hard behind it into the car park, ignoring the angry horns blaring out from the other cars.

Adam led them along a sterile, echoing, white tiled corridor. The hospital was vast and it was quite a walk to the ward where Rachel was recovering. He briefed them as they went, posters on walls, nurses, visitors and patients flying by in a blur.

'The High Honchos are so concerned we've scrambled extra patrols around Plymouth tonight. There are going to be more cops on the beat than you've seen in years. It'll be like a modern Dixon of Dock Green.'

Dan shot a sideways glance at Nigel, who nodded. That's what they'd be filming later, little chance of much rest tonight. Rutherford had been fed and exercised by Dan's obliging downstairs neighbour – minimal cost, a case of decent red wine a year – Nigel's sons were with Dot, his mother in law. They both had contingency plans for breaking stories, had to have.

'Part of this is a big media strategy,' continued Adam, walking fast and talking intensely. Dan and Nigel struggled to keep pace, laden down with the tripod, camera, lights and microphone they carried.

'You're in first because we trust you after the help you gave us on the Bray murder. In fact the Assistant Chief Constable says if you want to join me on some of the investigation again, that's fine. We need all the publicity we can get. It'll be the same deal as last time. You wouldn't be able to broadcast anything without my say so, but you'd get exclusive access.'

Adam gave Dan a look. His eyes were wide and his face was shining with a layer of sweat. He was walking unnaturally, almost mechanically. 'If you can, I'd like your help mate,' the detective added. 'I think we'll need it.'

'OK,' said Dan, who didn't have much breath for a longer reply. Adam was moving like he was possessed, his polished black shoes flying over the white tiles in a drumbeat of pace. 'I'll have to check with Lizzie, but I can't see her turning the chance down. It worked well last time.' Dan didn't add how much he'd enjoyed the excitement of riding with the police on a major inquiry.

They turned a corner and Adam leapt out of the way of an oncoming trolley. A drip was suspended above a prone woman, her breathing quick and shallow, anxious nurses bending alongside. Dan shivered. He thought he could feel the Reaper's gloating presence.

'Here's what you can put in your report,' went on Adam. 'Two women have been attacked and raped in their own homes. One was in Mannamead the night before last. The other was in Hartley. They're just half a mile apart. We're keeping the exact addresses secret to protect their identities. Both lived with their young children, one a boy, the other a girl. Thankfully neither witnessed the attacks. The girl was out at school, the boy was asleep in his bedroom. There was no man in either house. The attacker broke in through open windows. We don't have much of a description of him, but I'll give you the details of it later. We've got a press release ready.'

'OK,' panted Dan again. 'We won't be able to get anything out now until breakfast tomorrow, so we've got a bit of time.'

'As you'd expect, both women were severely traumatised by the attacks,' said Adam, spitting out the words. 'We have some good forensic evidence which has allowed us to put together a DNA profile. But it doesn't match anyone on the database, so we're looking for a new offender. We've got no meaningful description and no leads. I want to appeal for witnesses, or for anyone who's noticed a friend or member of their family behaving oddly. And I need to put out a warning to women in Plymouth to make sure their doors and windows are locked and that they take care when going out. The big point is we fear he may strike again.'

'OK,' repeated Dan. The tiredness had left him, the adrenaline of a big story always burned it away. He could see it had the same effect on Nigel. 'So what's the bit you're not putting out?'

'Strictly not for broadcast,' said Adam, stopping suddenly and turning to look at Dan. 'And I mean strictly. We need this kept back to filter out the cranks.' He paused, drummed a finger on the wall. 'And so as not to panic everyone. He's a weird one. He's left a kid's witch's hat at each house. And at the first place, he left the wrapping too. I think he did that deliberately. It was from a pack of six. I see it as a challenge, a taunt and a statement of intent. This man hates women and plans to strike again. Four more times, unless we get him first.'

Joseph and Abi McCluskey sat in their living room that evening, rewound the video tape and watched the recording of

59

Wessex Tonight. They hadn't had time to get home to see it, had too many calls, emails and guesses to deal with. All were wrong, some wonderfully creative and outlandish, but all nowhere close. They hadn't expected anyone to solve the riddle, were almost sure they wouldn't. But it was reassuring nonetheless and it meant they could continue as they'd planned.

Abi fast-forwarded through the programme – her husband was hopeless with technology – until they found the report. She cuddled into him on the sofa, the flames popping and flaring in the log fire. It wasn't cold, they didn't need it on really, but she was always worried that Joseph could chill easily and it made the room cosy. They shared a bottle of fine red wine. The doctors had advised against it, wouldn't react well with the painkilling morphine he was on, but what was the point of worrying about that now? They both knew his time was running ever shorter.

'Mmm… not a bad report,' he said begrudgingly when the story had finished. Their aged boxer dog Darwin waddled in and settled lengthways along the ember glow of the fire.

'Lizzie reckons he's their top reporter,' said Abi as she got up from the sofa to turn the TV off. 'And as you said, he's the one who saw the solution to the Bray case. So it was a good test. If he didn't spot the answer after the clues you gave him today, it's a decent chance no one else will.' She pressed play on the answer phone and a tinny voice crackled out. One message, from Kid, replying to the message she'd left him earlier and confirming he'd be round tomorrow evening.

'But he didn't see it, did he?' said Joseph McCluskey, stretching his legs out on the sofa. 'And it was there, right in front of him. I got the feeling from talking to him he is going to have a go at the riddle though. I hope he does. And I guess he was the right person to do the obituary with then. I just wish I could be around to see it, how it all goes, and whether he, or anyone else, cracks the code.' He took a sip of wine and breathed out heavily. 'God, I'll miss that, the taste of something so sweet and the feeling of you next to me.'

He stopped himself. They'd said their goodbyes, told each

other all they wanted to say. They'd agreed they wouldn't go over it again. It was too painful. 'You promise me you'll do exactly what we agreed when I'm gone?'

She snuggled back into him so he couldn't see the gathering tears. 'Yes. I promise,' she whispered. 'I know what all this means to you. I'd never betray that. Dead or alive, I'll always be loyal to you.'

Dan had prepared himself to meet a barely recognisable woman. He expected bruises and dried blood, swollen and closed eyes, scars and stitches. She looked utterly normal and had even put on some make-up, a little blue eye-shadow and a line of lipstick. What was it Adam had said? Most rape cases don't involve a beating. The man doesn't like to spoil his prize before the attack and afterwards usually just wants to get away. The damage is done in the mind, not the body.

Dan noticed his hand was trembling and he gripped the notebook tighter. 'Rachel, I'm Dan Groves, the reporter. This is Nigel, the cameraman.' He went into the familiar words he'd used many times when talking to distressed or bereaved people. 'I would say pleased to meet you, but given the circumstances that have brought us together I'll just say I'm sorry, and we'll make this as easy as possible for you.'

She nodded, managed a tight smile. 'Thanks. I wasn't sure whether to do this, but when Mr Breen told me what had happened to the other woman…'

She didn't need to finish the sentence. Adam and Suzanne Stewart stood at the back of the room, both with their arms folded, staring at Dan.

'I don't want to be identified,' Rachel said breathlessly, sitting up in bed as Nigel focused the camera.

'Don't worry, he's just checking it's working,' replied Dan in his best soothing voice. 'The law gives you absolute protection from being identified and I promise there won't be a hint of who you are. We won't even film a silhouette of you. We'll use a light to cast a shadow of your head on the wall and film that. I can show you what it looks like afterwards if that'll make you feel better.'

She slid back down in her bed, pulling the sheets up to her neck as though to defend herself. Nigel began setting up a light. 'What are you going to ask me?' she whispered.

Dan sat down on the corner of her bed. 'Rachel, this won't be easy for you, but I'm going to have to ask what happened.' She flinched, closed her eyes, trying to escape the eternal memory. 'I know it's difficult, but remember, this is for the TV and radio, so you can spare the dreadful detail. Just give it to me in broad terms that an audience can cope with.'

She drew in a deep breath, nodded again. She was fiddling hard with her engagement ring, its twists flashing darts of diamond light around the room. Dan watched, then said, 'These questions may sound daft to you, but remember, almost no one out there will have been through what you have. I'll want to know what effect the attack has had on you, and so how important you think it is this man is caught. Is that ok?'

She nodded, still fiddling with her ring. Nigel clipped a tiny microphone to her pyjama top.

'For what it's worth,' said Dan, 'I think you're being extraordinarily brave speaking to us, and certainly doing the right thing. People will empathise strongly with you, and it'll make anyone who could help catch the man much more likely to come forward.'

'I understand,' she said, and her voice was clearer and stronger.

'Rolling,' said Nigel from behind the camera.

'We won't use any names here,' began Dan, 'and I appreciate this is a very difficult question. But in simple terms, can you take me through what happened?'

She gulped, then again, took a deep breath, faltered.

'I… I...' she managed, twisting hard at her ring. Dan let her go, didn't want to interrupt.

She took another breath and rallied. 'I was sitting in my lounge watching the television. *Eastenders*, I think it was. I thought I heard a noise behind me, but I ignored it. I thought it was… Well, my little boy coming downstairs, and I try to ignore him.' She managed a tight smile at the thought. 'He's not supposed to you see, and if you take no notice he usually goes back to bed. The next thing I knew, these hands came from behind and grabbed me as I sat on the sofa, then he was on top of me…' Her voice failed again and her chest heaved. Her hand went to it. 'He pinned me down and… well… he raped me…'

Rachel's voice tailed off. Dan let the silence run, a chance for her to compose herself and for him to frame his question as sensitively as he could.

'Ok, that's enough of what happened, we don't want to take you back there any more.' She'd closed her eyes again and her lower lip trembled. 'Well, you're in hospital now, being looked after,' Dan continued. 'This may sound like a stupid question, but it's important for the viewers to understand. What effect has the attack had on you?'

She looked down at the engagement ring, stared into its rainbows. Then the words came in a rush of release.

'I feel violated. I feel I've had my inner self invaded. I feel cheap and sick. I can't sleep for thinking about it. Even when I'm awake, doing something else, it haunts me. I'm scared for my son. I don't know how much love I still have left inside me for him now. I can't go back to that house. I can never go back there. And I'm scared for my fiancé. He's done nothing, but I don't feel close to him now. I don't know if I feel like I trust him. I don't feel like I'll trust anyone again.'

Her words came in short, rushing gasps. It would make compelling television, but Dan felt a tightening in his stomach for putting her through it again. He knew he'd be ambushed by the memory of this interview in the months to come. Just one more question then, just one more.

'Finally, it's quite likely someone out there knows or suspects who might be responsible for these attacks. What would you say to them?'

'Turn him in,' she said instantly, the certainty of what she had to say giving her strength. 'Tell the police. Turn him in before he wrecks any more lives. I'm determined he won't have destroyed mine, but in the dark moments when I lie here and think, I'm not so sure about that. No one else should have to suffer like me, and my fiancé, and my son. Please, if you

63

can, please help the police and turn him in. Turn him in.'

Outside the hospital they found the police car that the officer guarding Rachel had driven in. Night had crept up on the city, but there was enough light from the streetlamps in the car park to interview Adam in front of it. The shot would look dark and sinister, matching the story perfectly. A standard soundbite please, Dan asked, about 15 seconds worth, that gives you roughly 45 words.

Adam had been through the media training which had become indispensable for modern day politicians, senior managers and just about anyone who might have to be the spokesperson for an image-conscious organisation when a story broke. Dan watched as he composed his three points into a crisp, punchy answer. He emphasised what shocking, vicious attacks these were, how the police feared the man would strike again, and how the public's help was vital in catching him. Dan nodded his approval. Adam's message was strong and clear. We need to find this man. Please help us. Otherwise…

Dan and Nigel loaded the kit into the boot of the car and drove back towards Mannamead to find some officers on patrol. They didn't talk and unusually didn't even turn on the radio. More drizzle was gusting in over the city and the car's windscreen wipers squeaked through their dutiful arcs.

As Nigel drove, Dan found his mind drifting back to the Death Pictures. There could be lots of symbolism in there, there were certainly plenty of places, but he kept thinking it was in the numbers. Weren't there numbers in all the paintings? He was sure most were iron pyrites, as McCluskey had put it, but he also thought the answer was in there somewhere. But how could numbers form a message or a lesson?

Should he do some work on it? Give it a try? Perhaps he'd buy a set of the pictures when he had a chance and just look through them, see if he could spot anything. It wasn't the hope of winning the painting. If he was honest, it was the challenge and the opportunity to prove McCluskey wrong, that the code could be cracked. It would be interesting to have a go, wouldn't it? No harm in it.

They stopped at a red light. Dan watched as a cyclist hopped his bike up onto the pavement and carried on, head down against the drizzle. Hang on he thought, didn't he say he wouldn't get involved in the riddle? Could rise above it? Wouldn't follow the madding crowd? Wasn't going to do the shepherd's bidding? He could, but he knew he was going to have a go anyway. There was a lovely space on the wall of his bedroom where the picture would look great.

'Bingo!' exclaimed Nigel, bringing Dan back to the car. In the road outside, a couple of uniformed policemen were talking to a man walking his dog. They parked up, pulled on their coats and he explained what they were doing while Nigel got the camera out of the boot. The pair didn't want to be filmed and began to walk off. Some cops were like that, hadn't told friends about their job or were just unhelpful. Find some others to film they said.

He saw Nigel's look, tired, wet and cold and longing to go home. He felt the same way himself. He needed a cuddle with Rutherford, the safety of his great blue sofa and a large whisky, after that interview with Rachel. It could take another hour or more to catch up with a different patrol.

Should he call Detective Chief Inspector Breen, Dan asked the men? Drag him out of the hospital where he was talking to one of the rape victims, tell him about the problem with finding officers to film? Surely the police would want to be seen patrolling on the TV, in front of half a million people, a strong reassurance for the public? Suddenly the officers didn't mind being filmed at all.

It was after midnight when Dan got back to the studios. He groaned at the thought that he still had a couple of hours work to do. The rain had grown relentless and drummed a staccato beat on the windows, the trees outside bowing and rustling in the westerly wind blowing in from the Atlantic. But the newsroom was quiet, deserted. For a place always full of shouts, TV monitors bringing in picture feeds and the electronic burble of computers, it felt soulless.

His tiredness was back, a cocoon of dull, fogging cloud, so Dan did something unusual and had an extra caffeinated coffee from the machine. Within a few minutes his head was buzzing from its attack.

The radio work would take the longest, so he tackled that first. He loaded the interviews into the computer and found himself writing 'the numbers, the numbers, the numbers,' while he waited. Damn McCluskey and his riddle.

He picked all three chunks of Rachel talking, about what happened, what effect it had on her, and how the rapist needed to be caught. Green peaks and troughs of waveforms danced on the screen as he manoeuvred the mouse to edit them. He also took the clip of Adam, then wrote some script to link it all together. It was an easy job, Rachel's words were so powerful he only needed to add a few lines of explanation. He also loaded up some of the sound of the officers on the beat, trudging along and talking to people about what they were doing, asking if anyone had any information.

He stopped for a moment and stared at the screen. A sudden yearning to go home teased him, a need to climb into bed, Rutherford on guard at his feet, sleep quickly and hope not to dream, instead find a wonderful, numbing void to end this day. He thought about Kerry, her long, golden hair and welcoming smile.

It was half past midnight. Rutherford was being looked after. A cuddle would be wonderful when he finally got out of here. Was it too late to text her? It had been a long time. What the hell, her phone could be off, or she could just ignore him. What was there to lose? 'Having a late night working with these rapes,' he typed. 'Terrible story. Make sure you take care out there. Hope all's ok. x'

He liked the bit about taking care. Good improvisation. It looked concerned and loving and was almost a justification for sending the message. Better than simple loneliness. He stood up, stretched his arms and rolled his neck and was about to get back to work when his phone warbled, surprising him.

'Heard about it, sounds horrid. Poor boy, being mixed up in that. Am home and happy to supply cuddles if loving needed. K. x'

How well she knew him. A flush of energy that had

nothing to do with journalism, radio or television ran through his body. Dan replied that he'd be an hour or so and got back to the editing.

He mixed in some sound effects of the officers' footsteps, then them talking to a couple on their way home from the pub. 'Good evening. Nothing to worry about, we're just checking you haven't seen anything odd, like a prowler tonight, or a couple of nights ago...' Then came his commentary, writing to complement the sounds.

'Extra police patrols have been on duty for much of the night in Plymouth, looking out for the rapist. He's now struck twice in three days, forcing his way into homes in Mannamead and Hartley to carry out his attacks. This woman – who doesn't want to be identified – was one of his victims...'

In came the first clip of Rachel, talking about the attack. He let her words run, so chilling were they, then his question about the effect it had. Time then for a change of voice, radio worked best with plenty of variety.

'The police are concerned the man could strike again,' Dan intoned. 'Detective Chief Inspector Adam Breen is leading the investigation. He advises all women to keep their doors and windows locked and to take care when going out...'

Then it was the clip of Adam. Dan joined on the last part of Rachel's interview, when she too talked about the need to catch the attacker. It didn't need introducing, the listeners would remember her voice. And that was the end of the report, nothing more needed to be said.

He wrote up a shorter version for the television breakfast bulletins and left a note for the early news team and Lizzie, pointedly marking the time in the corner. His watch said 1.15, so he guessed it was about half past. Rain was still beating down, so Dan pulled his jacket over his head and ran to the car. He didn't want to look dishevelled.

The roads were deserted and he drove too fast, north, out to the edge of the city, to Crownhill and Kerry's neat terraced house. A thought that he shouldn't be doing this nagged at his mind, but he ignored it. He knew very well he shouldn't, that come the morning he would regret it, but he knew too he was going to do it anyway. Sometimes life left you little choice.

At least he'd learnt one lesson. To make sure he didn't get involved in a protracted and awkward saying goodbye, followed by the inevitable 'discussing their future together' session in the morning, Dan set the alarm on his pager for half past six. That way he could plead an urgent news story, run for it and get home in time to take Rutherford for a jog before going to work. He got out of the car, checked his reflection in the window, shaped up his hair and gave himself a knowing wink.

Chapter Five

DAN GROVES WOULD LATER come to look on it as a day that changed his life. There was the beginning of the path towards the flurry of international fame which grew from his involvement in McCluskey's riddle and the extraordinary end to the story, and there was the meeting with the woman who would finally beat away the spectre of Thomasin and tame the swamp of the depression that had always stalked him. But it didn't feel like a seminal day at the start. Far from it. He felt under pressure – attack even – from two different aggressors.

What was usually known as the Murder Room had become the MIR, the Major Incident Room. Given the police force's lack of imagination, it was the best they could manage for an inquiry into a serial rapist, thought Adam, as he surveyed the gathering crowd of detectives. Four floors up in Charles Cross Police Station in central Plymouth, it looked out over the city and the bombed out Charles Church, the memorial of the Blitz from which came its name.

Dan stood in the place he'd adopted by the windows at the back of the room. Despite the number of times he'd been here during the Edward Bray investigation, he couldn't shake off the nagging feeling he was an interloper. He wondered if that would ever change. He caught a glance and a brief nod from Adam and relaxed a little. The boss may want him involved and some of the other detectives had come to accept him, but he was conscious many still thought he had no place here. There had been more than a couple of hostile looks already. He tried to stare straight ahead and ignore the nudges, sly glares and whispers.

It was just before half past eight. Last night's rain had blown through, its legacy another fine spring morning, the sky blue above the trails of traffic heading into the city. Dan hadn't managed much sleep last night and felt groggy, but just about OK. It wasn't the tiredness that was bothering him. It was the guilt. That and the trap he'd laid for himself.

He'd done it again. He'd let his lust lead him back to a place he shouldn't have gone. In the passion and afterglow of the night he'd said yes, we'll give the relationship another try. Yes, I do mean it. Yes, I'd love to take you out for dinner at the weekend to show my commitment. Dan sighed. When would he ever learn?

Another busy day stretched ahead when he longed for a quiet one. He'd called Lizzie and she'd been keen he should join the investigation. He knew she would, but he also expected the caveat that had quickly arrived. 'So long as you keep producing stories. There's huge interest in the case. I don't want you disappearing to play detectives like last time. We pay you to report the news. So I want stories, stories, stories. Got that?'

So it was Charles Cross for the briefing at 8.30, then back to the newsroom to cut the lunchtime and evening TV reports on the rapist, while continuing to keep an eye on the state of the investigation. Tonight would have to be a quiet one. He wanted a good walk with his dog – it was funny how he missed Rutherford when he was away, or busy – and an even better sleep. The chances of that had to be good surely? The news of the rapes and the extra police patrols was everywhere. No woman would leave any lock unsecured, or venture out alone.

'City in Fear' *The Wessex Standard* had put it, splashed across a thousand screaming billboards. A bit over the top, but the point was clear. The man must have seen the coverage, in the papers, on the radio and TV, and wouldn't think of attacking again. Not until the publicity had died down and people had gone back to their routines.

'OK, quiet please team,' called Adam from the front of the room. 'Let's get on with it. We've got a lot to do.'

Adam stood beside a series of four green felt boards, each the size of a typical classroom blackboard. Dan almost smiled. The detective loved those boards. So much of modern policing relies on computers Adam had said, but sometimes you need to see a web of connections to feel the links between people and events. That's the key to catching your man, spotting the

70

threads between the crimes that would lead you to him. The 30 or so detectives and handful of uniformed officers quietened. The young, keen and promotion-seeking took notes, the older, more confident or jaded just listened.

'Victim one,' said Adam, pointing to the centre of the left-hand board and a photo of a familiar face. 'Rachel Bloom, 31 years old. Attacked about half past seven in the evening at her home in Atlantic Road, Mannamead. Her son was in bed asleep, thankfully. The man got in through an open window. She's recovering in Tamarside Hospital.' He pointed at another photo. 'A kid's witch's hat found at the scene, along with the wrapping. It's from a pack of six, and you know what that means.' He surveyed the silent crowd, eye contact for all. 'But we're not going to let it get that far, are we?' Nods and murmurs of agreement bounced back at him.

Suzanne Stewart stood to Adam's side and took over, her style similar. Conscious or unconscious, that, wondered Dan? He suspected she was trying to impress, but *that* could just be his prejudice. They'd never got on and she'd hardly spoken to him since he helped to solve the Bray case. He wondered if she'd taken it personally.

'Victim number two,' began Suzanne. 'Eleanor Anderson, known as Ellie. 30 years old.' A photo was pinned to the middle of the second board, a blonde woman, long hair, blue eyes, cute little nose, a crinkling smile. Taken before the rape then, Dan thought. He couldn't imagine her looking so content now.

'Attacked in her home in Oaks Lane in Hartley, just after nine in the morning,' Suzanne continued. 'The man got in through a partly open window, which he then forced. She got up to see what the noise was and was raped in her kitchen. Her daughter was at school. A witch's hat was left on the draining board of the sink. She's also recovering in Tamarside Hospital.'

'So what do we make of all this?' asked Adam. 'All the usual suspects have been seen. That's thrown up nothing. All the background checks on the two women haven't given us anyone who might want to attack them. All their male

71

associates have been checked. Again nothing. We've got no real leads. So what do we look at now? Where do we go?'

A young uniformed lad at the front spoke quickly. 'House to house sir?' Dan looked over and for once appreciated the old cliché. He really did look as if he'd hardly started shaving.

'Spot on, Andy,' said Adam, ignoring the shaking heads and smiles from a couple of the older detectives. 'We're doing it. In fact, we've more or less done it now. Just a few more to go back to. Nothing so far.'

'The two houses are very close sir, just five or so minutes walk.' A smartly suited officer, also young, short hair, almost a crew-cut. 'Could it be someone who lives in the area?'

More hidden smiles from the club of experienced CID. 'Good thought Mike,' replied Adam. 'We've got a DNA profile but it doesn't match anyone in the database. No one in that area has a record of anything that might make them turn into a rapist. But if we don't get a result quickly, or if there's another attack, I will consider asking all men there to have a DNA test.' His eyes roamed the room again. 'Come on team, more ideas please. This is urgent, he could strike again at any time.'

A woman who Dan recognised from the Bray case spoke. 'The women are similar ages and profiles, sir. Do you think that's important?'

'Yes, Claire, I do. I'm wondering if these attacks were well researched. There was no man in either house. Both women had a child. Let's have a look at what connects them. Kids' playgroups, gym, social club, work, friends, anything like that, any connection you can find. You can work with Suzanne on that. And congratulations on the promotion too.'

She blushed as laughter rumbled around the room. Dan noticed Suzanne Stewart didn't look happy though, she was keeping her eyes firmly fixed on Adam, expressionless.

He took another sly look at Claire, studied her in what he hoped was a subtle way. She was pretty, wasn't she? A dark bob, his favourite hairstyle. Lovely brown eyes to match. A good figure too, cute and petite in that fitted black trouser suit. Dan glanced over again as she wrote a note on her pad. No wedding ring either... He stopped himself. Didn't he have enough to think about after last night?

Adam raised his voice. 'Come on then team, more ideas please. What kind of a man are we looking for?'

'A woman hater, sir,' said a chubby, middle-aged, dishevelled looking man towards the back of the room.

'Yes, Jack, I think you're right,' replied Adam. 'And why do men hate women?'

Some of the older men exchanged looks. Dan could see it in their faces. Divorce, expensive divorce.

'Relationship break up, mainly,' said Jack, who was running a finger over his wedding ring.

'Quite right.' Adam pointed back to the boards and tightened his tie. 'So let's see if these women have been through divorces. Or if they've taken their kids against the wishes of their ex-partners. Jack, can you get on to the Family Courts, the Child Support Agency and Fathers for Families to see if they've got anyone newly divorced, or who's been making threats, anything like that. Anyone who's spare can give you a hand with it. There's plenty to work through. We're also checking whether his sperm shows traces of HIV. It's possible he may be a carrier and blames women for his infection. Any other ideas anyone?'

There was a rumble of 'no' and some shaking of heads. 'A couple of you can see if we can trace where the witch's hats came from, but I don't imagine we'll have much luck with that. I'm going to see if any new leads have come in from the media appeals.'

Adam raised his voice again. 'So go for it team, and remember. We're up against the clock on this one. We've got an embittered man out there who plans his crimes and fully intends to continue with his game. It's a game which wrecks lives. He won't stop, so we've got to stop him. He's taking the mickey out of us and I know you're not going to stand for that. So let's go get him. I don't want to be standing here again telling you about victim number three. If I am, we've failed.'

To freshen his report for the lunchtime news and *Wessex*

73

Tonight, Dan and Nigel went filming some of the remaining house-to-house inquiries. 'Do some chats with local people too,' Lizzie had said, a four inch stiletto grinding into the long-suffering newsroom carpet. She was never satisfied. They were the only ones who had the interview with Rachel, yet still she wanted more. Dan sometimes thought of her as like a nest of baby birds. No matter how many juicy worms you brought, the beaks were still open and squawking, always wanting more.

The thought cheered him and eased his tiredness. One man wanted to know what was in it for him if he was interviewed. Dan wrote 'Present this for 10% off your next TV set' on the back of one of his business cards and signed it. The man laughed and talked about his fears for his 15-year-old daughter and how he insisted on giving her a lift everywhere now. The poor teenager must be chewing glass with embarrassment, Dan thought, being delivered to meet her cool friends in Dad's rusting Ford Estate. But it was a good interview. It made the point.

Another man gave them the familiar earful of abuse about being parasites. It was an occupational hazard of being a reporter. Dan couldn't be bothered to argue, just told him he quite understood and that when he got back to the studios he would tell the engineers to lock out the TV signal to his house if it was such an evil. He left the man at his gate, glancing up at the aerial on his roof and looking an entertaining mix of angry and worried. Suddenly he was feeling better.

He did a little address to camera himself with the police inquiries going on in the background. To stamp his authority on the story was the official reason, to grab his slice of the glory was the truth. Many a beer he'd been bought on a night out just for being on the TV. He told the viewers how to contact the police if they had information, through the Crimestoppers number or direct to the MIR at Charles Cross. The graphics unit could generate the number to appear across the bottom of the screen as he talked.

Nigel drove them back to base, and Dan found his mind again drifting to the Death Pictures. Could the riddle be something to do with the Waterside pub? It featured heavily, after all. It was almost the weekend and perhaps Saturday would be well spent with a research visit?

He could pick up copies of all the pictures in town, get a paper too, take the water taxi across the River Plym to Turnchapel, then sit, read and think. If he timed it right, he could spend a few quiet hours in the afternoon getting nicely lubricated, see what he came up with, then be in the mood for the live music they had on a Saturday evening.

The last time there'd been an Elvis impersonator, and didn't he get up on stage to help perform that version of 'I Just Can't Help Believing'? It was a memory he'd buried, and no wonder. All he could remember was a mass of laughing faces. It was always a bad sign when you got a text message from your friends in the morning saying 'Do you remember what you did last night?'

Yes, the Waterside sounded like a fine idea for Saturday. But then he remembered, he'd promised to take Kerry out. A surge of annoyance needled him. But it was his own fault, wasn't it?

The edit was simple. The new pictures they'd just shot first, the house-to-house inquiries going on and commentary from Dan about investigations continuing. Then a long stretch of the interview with Rachel. After that, some pictures of the night time patrols, then a clip of Adam, finally his piece to camera.

Lizzie bustled in to the edit suite to watch the report and professed herself 'pleased', quite an accolade. She'd changed her shoes and her heels were lower, perhaps only a couple of inches. She kept around half a dozen pairs in a cupboard in her office and had been known to change them several times a day. Dan wondered what had happened to improve her mood. Good viewing figures for last night's programme was the most likely explanation. She always spent fifteen minutes at lunchtime studying the overnight figures. If she was feeling mellow, perhaps he could he push his luck?

'Lizzie, I was up most of last night covering the story and I'm feeling whacked. I was wondering if…'

'Yes, you can,' she cut in. 'I wouldn't want to burn you

75

out. You never know, we might need you. We'll call you if anything comes up. Don't turn your mobile off.'

He made for his car before she changed her mind, drove back to the flat and was greeted by the ecstatic ball of flying fur and yelping that was Rutherford. He was planning to have a sleep but didn't feel too bad, so he decided to take the dog for a run and pick up a copy of the Death Pictures. He could always go to bed early tonight. Rutherford deserved some fuss and he wanted to start thinking seriously about McCluskey's riddle. The postman had been and Rutherford had chewed a couple of the letters. Dan was amused to see it was only the bills he'd attacked.

He changed into his trainers, shorts and old polo shirt, trying to ignore the smell of stale sweat. He'd have to do some washing soon. Maybe if he charmed a cleaner, she could help with that. They jogged down the hill to the shops on Mutley Plain.

'Rape Victim Speaks out,' was the banner headline on one of the *Standard* billboards. Dan stopped and scanned the paper. They'd lifted all the quotes from his interview with Rachel. He wasn't annoyed. Imitation was flattery, and cannibalism was one of the most common ways journalists found stories. He'd been tipped off by enough of their reports. The newsagents also had a folder of the Death Pictures as they'd been set out in McCluskey's studio, so he bought one. The quality of the colours was poor, but the detail and the numbers were clear enough. He couldn't stop himself from thinking the numbers were the key. Why would they be there otherwise?

They ran back up the hill and into Hartley Park, found a stick and played the fetch game for ten minutes while Dan got his breath back. A Dalmatian came sniffing over to Rutherford, who treated her with lofty disdain. At least one of us has some discipline with women, he thought.

'Go on boy, don't upset her, she's keen,' he shouted at his dog, who came trotting back over with a total lack of interest. Shame, he thought, an Alsatian-Dalmatian crossbreed would be quite a sight.

Back at the flat, Dan took Rutherford down into the garden to brush him. His guilt at neglecting his friend waned as the dog's eyelids drooped in ecstasy and he began that funny low whine of delight. A gang of sparrows squabbled noisily in the pine tree at the end of the lawn.

Tea was a cheese and ham frozen pizza, which tasted of nothing. He must get to the supermarket sometime soon, he thought. But where was the time? A chore like that would always be at the bottom of the list of things to do. The evening passed easily, *Wessex Tonight* and his report, lead story again. No matter how many times it happened, he always enjoyed watching himself on the television. Then it was Cream on the stereo, a contented dog at his feet and some looking through the Death Pictures. It scarcely mattered that he had no meaningful thoughts of any kind about the solution to the riddle.

At about half past eight, Dan decided to have a relaxing bath and then an early night. He ironed a china blue shirt for tomorrow while it ran. Most of his shirts were varying shades of blue. They went best with his eyes, so a past girlfriend had said. Her words had always stuck with him. It was odd how little things like that sometimes did.

Just as the tub was full and topped with foaming bubbles his mobile rang. Adam. He knew it was trouble before he answered, could sense it. The evening had been too simple and pleasant.

'Dan, can't speak for long but you'd better get moving.'

'Another rape?'

A brief pause. 'No, thank God, it's not a rape. It's McCluskey. He's dead. In his bath. Wrists cut.'

Dan felt his body tense. He pulled the plug out of the untouched bath and made for his bedroom and the clothes he'd laid out for the morning.

'In the bath you say? Suicide?'

Another pause. 'It looks like it. But I'm not sure. His wife says definitely not. She's distraught. And there's evidence of a break-in. A window's been forced.'

77

Chapter Six

DAN SECRETLY THOUGHT OF it as his equivalent of those dashing young World War II pilots, hearing the wailing of the siren and sprinting from their mess room, across the airfield grass and into the waiting Spitfires. He knew it was ridiculous, that his little rush to a breaking news story didn't come anywhere near comparison with the bravery and sacrifice of those who'd died for his freedom, however he couldn't help but like the image and it was an analogy that always drifted into his mind whenever a scramble call came through. Dan pulled on the newly ironed shirt and some trousers and wedged his mobile under his chin.

He had a well-planned procedure, all about priorities. First, the call to Nigel. He could do nothing without his cameraman.

'Urgent story, central Plymouth. Get going, will call you en route with details and directions,' was all Dan needed to say.

'On my way,' came the reply.

Then Rutherford into the garden for a wee. You never knew when you'd be coming back. The dog could hold out for up to twelve hours, plenty of time to call his downstairs neighbour if Dan was going to be away for longer. Grab his satchel and into the car. He always kept a coat, maps, some snacks and water in the boot, along with a basic overnight bag. There was a black tie and jacket too, in case the scramble was a Royal death. He could call the newsroom on the way to let them know what was happening, but the priority was to get to the scene.

It was only a few minutes to Royal Gardens. Dan remembered nothing of the drive, his mind full of Joseph McCluskey and what could have happened to him. Was it something to do with the riddle of the Death Pictures? Whatever, it was going to be a hell of a story. He'd heard the panic at the end of the line when he'd called the newsroom to tell them.

A line of three police cars and a van were parked untidily

in the road, a cordon of blue tape already set up around the house, a couple of constables on sentry duty. Dan pulled up opposite and clambered out of the car.

A gang of neighbours had gathered at the end of the street, some pointing, some shaking their heads. The number of police here said the death of Joseph McCluskey certainly wasn't being treated as suicide. Dan checked his watch. 8.45 it read, so it was probably just before nine. The outside broadcast van was on the way, a report and live broadcast demanded for the 10.25 bulletin. They'd have to shift.

A familiar face bobbed up from behind a car, a camera slung around his neck. Dirty El, grinning as ever at the scent of a big story. Dan had expected him to be first on the scene. He was a keen scanner of police radio frequencies.

'Evening, El. So what's the low-down? Doesn't look like a suicide to me.'

The smile broadened.

'Suicide my arse,' said the photographer gleefully. 'They've scrambled a load of detectives and all the Scenes of Crimes lot, along with forensics. Kerching! El can hear the cash register calling.'

As if on cue, a couple of white-overalled figures emerged from the door of the house, knelt down and started checking over the porch. Their fingers brushed across the steps and probed the cracks in the paving. They were frozen in jerky strobes of flashlight as El instinctively raised his camera and loosed off a series of snaps.

Two cars pulled up fast, a journalist from the *Standard* and another from the *Western Daily News*. The pack was gathering. Word got around fast on a big story like this. Dan heard a familiar voice and turned, saw Nigel jump out of his car, run around to the boot, fish his camera out, hoist it onto his shoulder and come running over in time to get some shots of the forensics men. Dan stood behind him, watching his back. They could work up a plan in a minute. For now, they'd see what pictures they could get.

The white-suited figures rose and walked carefully back inside. Nigel put down his camera and turned to Dan, who

79

couldn't help but burst out laughing. He was wearing a blue, paisley swirled pyjama top.

'You said scramble, so I scrambled,' Nigel said huffily. 'I've got a T shirt in the car.'

Dan patted his friend's shoulder and just about managed to control his laughter. 'Thanks for moving so fast,' he said soothingly. They walked back to the Renault to get the tripod and microphone and give Nigel a chance to change. Dan tried Adam's number as he stood by the car, but it was engaged.

'We don't know much, apart from that McCluskey is dead and although it looks like a classic suicide, there are some suspicious circumstances,' he said, as they walked back to the edge of the cordon. 'So whatever it is, we've got a story. If he's killed himself, it's just a big one. If it looks like he's been murdered, it's very big indeed.'

'Understood,' replied Nigel, slotting his camera onto the tripod and pointing it at McCluskey's house. 'What's the plan then?'

'The outside broadcast truck will be here in a minute. We've got to cut a report and do a live bit.'

They'd got enough pictures of the scene, Dan thought. A few bits of interview would be useful, even if it was just neighbours voicing shock. They walked over to the gang of onlookers and got a couple of clips of exactly what he'd expected, 'Oh, it's terrible something like that could have happened here. Who'd have thought it? Such a lovely man.'

As he finished the interviews, Dan noticed a flash of colour lingering at his side. Loud Jim Stone, the outside broadcast engineer had, arrived. 'I was about to go off shift,' he grumbled through the thicket of his twitching beard. 'Bloody inconvenient time for a death.'

Dan hid a smile. Loud's nickname came from his love of wearing Hawaiian shirts and his unrelenting grumpiness. In full, it was 'Loud and Furrow-Browed', but it was usually shortened for simplicity.

'Yeah, I was just about to get in a bath,' Dan replied. 'But we're stuck with it, Jim, so we'd better get on with it. Park the truck as close as you can to the cordon and set up the satellite link. We've got to edit a report and do a live.'

He checked Nigel's watch. Nine twenty. Allow 20 minutes for the edit, another 10 to get ready to go on air. That gave them about another half hour's filming. 'I'll be in the truck by ten at the latest.' Loud huffed again and lumbered sulkily back to the van. Dan thought he looked like a caveman with a toothache.

They rejoined the pack. All the journalists were comparing speculation and rumours. It always happened on a big story. What they didn't know, they invented, and usually with wishful thinking. The *Standard* reporter told them he'd heard McCluskey had been knifed by someone who'd knocked at the door and went mad when the artist refused to give him another clue to the riddle. Dan replied he thought it was a harpoon.

What they really needed now was some reliable information and a brief interview with Adam. Dan could call him, but knew the detective would be busy setting up the initial investigation and would come out when he could. Give it a few minutes.

El was back, beaming this time. He beckoned to Dan who stepped away from the pack to share the secret. The paparazzo loved mystery.

'What have you got then?' asked Dan.

'A double whammy I think you'd call it mate. I'm in clover.'

Dan had long given up trying to interpret El speak. 'Meaning?'

'Got a lovely snap round the back. All the lights are on and I got some silhouettes of what looks like forensics people through the frosted glass of the bathroom. That'll be worth hundreds to the nationals.'

'How'd you get round the back? Haven't the cops got it all sealed off?'

El bounced from foot to foot as if he was about to lift off.

'Yeah. But I knocked on a neighbour's door and asked if I could use their garden. And they wanted to know what was in it for them?'

'I dread to ask,' said Dan, 'but what did you tell them?'

'I saw a wedding list in the hall. Their daughter's getting married. So I asked if they'd got a photographer and the bloke said no, not yet, they're so bloody expensive, hundreds of quid a go. I offered El's services for nothing more than a few beers at the do and the use of their premises now. They couldn't get me into the garden fast enough.'

El cradled his camera like a Crusader with a holy relic. He began warbling a tune to himself, grinning all the while. Dan sensed one of the photographer's bizarre and usually dreadful limericks was about to be born. After a few seconds thought, El spread his arms in the manner of a thespian and burbled,

'There once was a snapper named El,

Who was devious and scurrilous as hell,

He spotted a tree,

Thought – that's for me,

And clicked off some piccies darned swell!'

Dan just shook his head.

'Got to be off now, going to file the snaps, and collect the cash,' El chirped. 'Wanna meet for a beer at the weekend?'

'Oh yes,' replied Dan. El was generous with his money when he'd had a good week and a blow out sounded great. Then he remembered Kerry and the date he'd promised. Well, he could work something out. Probably. But he knew what would give if he couldn't.

'Hang on El, you said a double whammy. What was the other bit?' Dan asked.

'I've got a commission, a lovely, luscious, lucrative one from a broadsheet. It could be worth thousands. I've got to find out who the mystery women were in the Death Pictures and snap them. I might need your help on that one. Seeya, mate, call you Friday.'

Dan rejoined the pack. He checked his watch. Half past nine it said, so probably nine forty now, and still no reliable information. What would he write? He jotted down a couple of notes. He could say it was McCluskey's house, that someone inside was believed dead in suspicious circumstances. That would give the viewers the idea of what was going on. Could he say it was the artist? He turned to talk it over with Nigel when the pack surged forward. There were a couple of shouts, 'Mr Breen, Mr Breen...'

Adam had emerged from the house and was walking towards them, straightening his tie. It was already impeccable. He held up his hands for quiet. Nigel pushed his way to the front of the crowd, camera on shoulder. Dan followed, attached by the cable of the microphone he was carrying. He shouldered a radio reporter aside and stuck the microphone under the detective's nose. The word hypocrite lingered in his mind as he remembered the row with the *Daily News* man at McCluskey's studio. But this was a big story and he couldn't risk not catching Adam's words.

'Ladies and gentlemen, good evening. You want to know what's going on here, but I'm afraid there's only a limited amount I can tell you. We received a call from a man which brought us to the house just before eight o'clock this evening. We found a 66-year-old male dead. The circumstances of his death are unclear, so we've begun a full investigation. That's all I can tell you for now, apart from to ask anyone who may have any information, or might have witnessed what happened here to get in touch with the police. Thank you.'

There was the usual barrage of questions from the pack. 'Is it McCluskey? Is it suicide? Was he murdered?' but Adam turned away and walked back into the house.

Good timing, my friend Dan thought, and wondered if Adam was trying to help him. He knew exactly when their news bulletins were, had featured on them often enough. It was 9.50, time to get into the van and edit the story. Nigel would stay out here, just in case anything else happened and to set up the cabling and their position for the live report. There was just one thing he had to do first, the key to the story. He picked up his phone.

'Dan mate, I'm busy.' Adam sounded stressed. Not surprising, this would be a big case, the High Honchos watching carefully, and he had the rapist to think about too.

'I know. Just a quick one, I need to be sure for my report. Is it McCluskey?'

'Yes.'

'Suspicious?'

'Yes.'

'Despite initially looking like a suicide?'

'Yes.'

'Thanks mate. Call me when you can.'

Loud shifted his bulk as Dan stepped up into the van. 'Start with a couple of shots of the house, the police cars and the officers on guard, please,' he said. 'I'll write something to go with them.'

Loud huffed, and began spooling through the tape, picking the shots. Dan scribbled some words on his notepad, keeping an eye on the monitors, trying to blend his script with the pictures. Most journalists would have started with the obvious, 'The police were called here at eight o'clock tonight...' He prided himself on not doing it like most journalists.

'The initial reports were of a suicide,' he read in his best deep and authoritative voice. 'But detectives now believe there may be suspicious circumstances involved in the death of Joseph McCluskey at his house here in the Hartley area of Plymouth.'

Loud finished laying the pictures and they put in a couple of clips of interview of the onlookers. 'Mr McCluskey has become a famous artist, particularly with his works which became known as the Death Pictures. He painted them – and donated the hundreds of thousands of pounds proceeds to good causes – after being diagnosed with terminal cancer.' Dan paused.

'Don't put any pictures in there Jim. I'll ask them to drop in some shots of the paintings they've got back at base,' Dan said. He picked up the microphone again. 'Mr McCluskey had been given perhaps another couple of months to live. But this evening it looks as though his life might have ended in an unnatural way.'

Loud edited a shot of the press pack and Adam talking to them over that part, then a bit of Adam's interview. Dan continued, 'Tonight forensics officers are checking Joseph McCluskey's house for clues as to how he died, and detectives are beginning their investigation. This is Dan Groves, for

Wessex Tonight, in Plymouth.'

He called the newsroom while Loud edited the last shots in, dictated a cue for the newsreader to introduce the report and instructions on dropping in the sequence of the Death Pictures. 10.15 now. Time to get ready for the live broadcast.

Dan stepped down from the van, knotting the black tie which he'd grabbed from the back of his car. Nigel had set up in a position looking back on the house and the cordon. Dan squeezed the tiny swirl of moulded plastic into his left ear and heard the studio rehearsing. Good. Now a couple of minutes of calm to reflect on what to say. Live broadcasting was always the riskiest part of the job. One little slip could land you in a whole lot of trouble.

One thing Adam said had been bothering him. A man called the police. Who could that have been? McCluskey didn't have any family apart from Abi. Surely it would have been her who found him? And what was that stuff about signs of a break-in, a window being forced? Could it tie in with the rapist inquiry? His attacks were very near here and he forced his way into homes.

No, that was speculation too far for this broadcast. He could ask Adam about it when they next spoke. So what would he say? They only wanted a 10 second live introduction from him to go into his report, then 25 seconds of summing up at the end. He should be able to manage that.

'Dan, can you hear us OK?' It was Emma, the director, in his ear. He gave a thumbs up to the camera. 'Excellent,' she said. 'We have your report. The extra sequence you asked for has been edited in. We'll do a studio link, then hand to you to set the scene there, then play your report, then it's you again off the back. You're top story. With you in just under two mins.'

He gave another thumbs up. 'Move to your left a bit please,' said Nigel. 'I want to widen out the shot and get some more of the house and cops in the background.' Some onlookers had gathered to watch, a couple taking photos with their mobile phones, the flashes illuminating him as he stood waiting. Presenting a live broadcast often attracted a crowd, sometimes making him feel like an animal in a zoo.

'Good evening. The police have begun an investigation tonight after the famous Devon artist Joseph McCluskey was found dead in his Plymouth home,' began Craig, the newsreader. 'They describe the circumstances surrounding his death as suspicious. Our Crime Correspondent Dan Groves is at the scene...'

'Cue Dan,' came Emma's voice in his ear.

'Yes, there's considerable police activity here tonight,' he said, gesturing round to the officers and house behind him. 'Detectives have cordoned off Mr McCluskey's home and forensics teams are inside there as I speak, trying to work out how he died.'

'We're on the report,' said Emma. 'Nice and smooth, good stuff. Back to you in less than a minute and a half.'

'Behind you,' called Nigel, pointing. Adam had appeared at his shoulder. 'I'm a bit busy mate,' said Dan. 'We're on air.'

'I know,' Adam replied. 'I was watching you on a TV in there. Very good. I'm off, got to go back to Charles Cross to coordinate things. I just wanted you to know we're treating it as a major inquiry. Thought that might be useful.'

'30 seconds to you,' came Emma's voice again. 'Get that idiot out of there please.' Dan gave a thumbs up to the camera and shoved Adam out of the shot.

'I can now tell you I've just heard the police are treating this as a major inquiry,' he said, as the story finished. 'The officer in charge, Detective Chief Inspector Breen, who you saw in my report, has left to go to Charles Cross police station to set up an incident room. That's the second major investigation undertaken by the police here in just a few days, coming on top of the hunt for the man who's raped two women in Plymouth.'

He popped the earpiece out and helped Nigel coil up the cable. 'Who was that plonker who almost got himself on air?' grumbled Loud as he lowered the satellite dish.

'That,' said Dan, 'was the Chief Inspector in charge of the case.'

'You'd think he'd know better,' growled Loud.

Dan said goodnight to Loud and Nigel and got into his car. He turned on the radio. McCluskey's death was the lead story, an excited presenter interviewing an art historian about the legacy he would leave. As yet unclear, seemed to be the summary of what the man was saying. It depended on what happened now with the Death Pictures riddle, and what the solution was.

Dan waited a moment to listen, then started the car. The adrenaline flush of the breaking story and the outside broadcast was ebbing and he felt the fatigue closing in again. He'd have loved to have sneaked off to bed, but knew he didn't stand a chance. That interview he'd done with McCluskey for the obituary would be needed for the radio in the morning. He'd have to write something up about the investigation for the TV breakfast bulletins too.

He could hand the job on to one of the overnight journalists, he thought. He looked at himself in the car's mirror and shook his head. There were plenty of up and coming, ambitious reporters who'd love him to be out of the way so they could have their chance at covering a big story. It would come. That was life's way, but not yet. This was a corker and he wasn't ready to give it up. Might as well retire the day he was.

He called Adam as he drove back to the office.

'Thanks for that little titbit mate, it made my live summing up at the end sound much more dramatic.'

'I thought you'd like it. Well, you've helped me enough.'

'I know you're busy, so I just wanted to check on a couple of things. Firstly, is there any update on the rapes?'

'No. The teams have been out all day on inquiries, but nothing significant yet. I'll have another look at it tomorrow when I've got the McCluskey case properly underway.'

'And is there anything fresh I can run on McCluskey for tomorrow morning?' Dan pulled in to the studio's car park and turned off the engine. 'I need a new line for the breakfast news.'

A pause and the hum of the line while Adam thought.

'We'll be going round interviewing the neighbours tomorrow to see if anything odd went on in the close this evening. Will that do?'

'Fine mate, thanks. Goodnight.'

'Just one more thing Dan. Give me a call in the morning. I think there may be a lot more to this case than meets the eye. We might need some publicity to see if we can get any witnesses coming forward. Goodnight.'

He'd cut the call before Dan could ask anything else. A mischievous one, our DCI Breen he thought, as he climbed the stairs to the newsroom.

He found the tape with the obituary interview in the picture library and sat watching it as the audio fed into the radio computer. He was surprised to feel a creeping sadness. Up until now, Joseph McCluskey had been a story that had to be got on air. There'd been little time for reflection and thought. Now, as he studied Nigel's shots of the Death Pictures and saw the man in front of him, talking, he found himself starting to believe all that had been written about him.

But he'd left behind something to live after him, hadn't he? For six months at least. His death would trigger another flood of interest in the Pictures and thousands more attempts to solve his riddle. Dan reached out and froze the tape on the first of the paintings, the woman on the mobile phone. What did the incomplete telephone number signify? And who was the woman anyway and why was she riding it? There had been plenty of reports in the press about McCluskey's range of lovers, even in his later years when he was apparently happily married to Abi. Was she one?

El would be working on that. He couldn't think of anyone better for the job. And as for himself, he knew he was growing ever more fascinated with the riddle. He was still sure the answer was in the cascade of numbers somewhere. He knew that try as he might, he wouldn't be able to resist attempting to solve it.

Chapter Seven

HE WAS RUNNING FAST through a forest, branches bouncing off his body as he twisted and turned, trying to force his way through the ranks and rows of sentinel trees. He was panting hard, his heart pounding, legs sinking into the sucking moss and mud. In his hand was the small envelope containing the answer to the riddle of the Death Pictures. He desperately wanted to stop, open it, look at it, but didn't have time, had to keep running. Behind him chased the raging mob, the men and women who'd spent months trying to solve the puzzle.

He'd burst through the trees into a clearing, the crowd shouting and baying, only seconds behind him. He was exhausted, his legs shaking, ready to crumble. He could hear their screaming triumph as they ran down their prey. There were three paths out of the forest. A woman stood beckoning by each. To his left was Kerry, ahead Thomasin, to his right Claire, the Detective Sergeant.

He stood, just for a second, deciding who to run to when Joseph McCluskey appeared before him, laughing manically. In his hand was a mobile phone. He spoke into it, his words booming around the trees as if amplified through a loud hailer. 'I've made fools of you all,' he shouted. 'Learn my lesson well.'

Dan glanced at the mobile in his hand. He was used to having bizarre dreams, but that had to be one of the oddest. A strong coffee, some toast and the anticipation of a day on a big story still couldn't shake it loose from his mind. He didn't want to think about what it could have meant.

The phone rattled at his ear as Adam emphasised the words. 'Not for broadcast, ok? That's strictly not... for... broadcast.'

Dan had called his friend as soon as he got in to the newsroom that morning, wanted to know what he'd been hinting at the night before. It was just before nine and he'd walked in to a deluge of questions from radio and TV producers. What would happen today on McCluskey's death? What would the police say? Had the riddle been solved? What did his death mean? Would the answer now be revealed?

'Fine,' he said to Adam, waving away the lunchtime TV bulletin producer. He'd rarely seen such interest in a story. A hectic day beckoned. Thank God it was Friday. The weekend would be a sweet respite.

'This is what happened,' said Adam. 'A guy called 999 about 7.55 yesterday evening to say he was round at Joseph McCluskey's house and he was dead in the bath. The guy's name is Lewis Kiddey, generally known as Kid. He's another famous painter. You're not taking notes on this are you?'

'No,' said Dan, who was. He wouldn't use it, but you never knew when the information might come in useful. 'Carry on.'

'We got round there to find this Kid downstairs in the lounge shaking. Upstairs in the bathroom was McCluskey. He was lying in a warm bath, dead. His wrists had been slit. There was a kitchen knife on the carpet next to the bath and lots of blood. It was a right mess.'

Dan's imagination presented him with a picture, and he shuddered.

'Sounds fairly straightforward,' he thought out loud. 'The guy was dying. He had cancer. He must have been in pain. He knew he only had a few days or weeks left, if he was lucky. So he decided to end it all.'

He put his pen down. What was Adam talking about, more to it than met the eye?

'That's exactly what I thought,' said Adam. 'But then things began bothering me and I started to wonder if that's what we were meant to think.'

Dan picked his pen up again. 'Meaning?'

'Meaning there was evidence of a break-in. A window in the kitchen at the back had been forced. There are no fingerprints and we don't think anyone got in, but it's hard to tell for sure and it's certainly suspicious. And then there's his wife.'

Abi. She'd seemed very gentle, kind, utterly devoted to her husband. Dan couldn't imagine her having a role in any kind of violence or death. 'What about her?' he asked.

'First of all, it wasn't her who found the body. It was this guy Kid. She was out walking their dog and popping in to see some friends for a chat. Now you might think that would be understandable if McCluskey didn't want her involved in his suicide, but I just can't believe it. She says he gave her no hint whatsoever that he was going to kill himself and she's sure he would have. We've only had a brief chat with her – she's distraught – but from all accounts they were very close. I can't see him topping himself, not without her knowledge at the very least. And from what I've heard, it's more likely they'd actually want to be together when he died.'

Dan pondered this for a few seconds, then said, 'I think you might be right. I interviewed him a few days ago and met her at the same time. They seemed incredibly close. What does Kid say happened? Any reason to suspect him?'

'Not really, not at the moment. Apart from him finding the body that is. He says he popped round for a chat, as they'd arranged a couple of days before, to discuss McCluskey's new picture. It was just a friendly thing. He says he found the front door open, which wasn't uncommon apparently. He went in, looked around and couldn't find anyone so he went upstairs. Then he found McCluskey dead in the bath. He called us straight away.'

Dan thought back on the research notes of McCluskey's life. Kid was frequently mentioned. Another famous artist and a pupil of the dead painter, they'd been close, then had some kind of falling out and feud, something it seemed McCluskey specialised in. Didn't he remember it was about a woman? He'd check that later. But Kid had been most prominently noted for some artwork which had won a national competition and annoyed the American president. There were reams of stories on it.

He was also the first person McCluskey had been reconciled with when the artist was diagnosed with terminal cancer. There was a photo of the two of them together, arms around each other, some quote from McCluskey about thinking of Kid as the nearest to being the son he never had.

He didn't sound much like a killer.

'There's no chance of a connection with the rapist is there?' Dan said slowly. 'He breaks in to houses, and in that area of the city.'

Adam breathed out heavily, making the phone rustle.

'Now you're asking. On the face of it I'd have to say I don't think so, but I can't rule it out obviously. It's something we'll have to look at.'

If there were a connection, it would make a very big story into a huge one, Dan thought. He couldn't see it, the rapist attacked women alone in their homes, not men. But as Adam said, it couldn't be ruled out.

'So what are you doing now?' asked Dan.

'I'm getting a post mortem sorted, fingerprinting and forensics on the house and the knife. Results expected Monday. In the meantime, we'll do the sweep of the crescent I told you about last night, talk to all the neighbours and see what we find out. We'll also have a look at McCluskey's past to see if there's anyone who might want him dead. But if he has been murdered, it'd be the most bizarre bloody case I've ever handled. Who'd want to kill a man who was going to die in a few days anyway?'

Rachel Bloom had signed herself out of hospital and was back at home. She insisted she'd had enough sympathy and wanted to get on with her life. Suzanne Stewart sat in the armchair in the lounge of her house and watched as she stalked from table to window, to kitchen, to fireplace, never quite settling wherever she stopped.

She straightened a photo, flicked some dust off the television, shifted a vase by a couple of inches. Her movements were tentative, nervy, like a bird fearful of a cat. She wasn't at home in her house any more, Suzanne thought. No wonder, how could she be after what had happened here? It was already on the market, no new home chosen, no possibilities even viewed. Escape was the only motive.

Suzanne couldn't tell her so, but her behaviour was absolutely normal for someone who'd been through such an attack. She couldn't tell her too that it would last for weeks and months and probably years. And some never recovered.

'Rachel, I'm sorry to bother you again, but I know you understand why,' Suzanne began. 'Are you sure you don't know Eleanor Anderson, the other victim? Is there nowhere you could think of that you might have met? Nothing you could have in common?'

Rachel shook her head, at the window now, smoothing the drape of a blue curtain. They'd been through all the obvious possible connections, where they shopped, went out, friends, who they socialised with, work, families, kids. Nothing had shown up. The two victims – so far, Suzanne thought, with a grimace, so far – didn't even look alike. All they had in common was they were roughly the same age, estranged from their partners, lived in a similar part of the city and lived alone, apart from their young children. But that could be reason enough.

If the rapist had been planning his attacks for a while, how long would it take him to follow a woman home, come back a few times, check for a man, then strike? Daytime saw thousands of women out in the city, trailing kids behind them, no wedding or engagement ring, their shopping a sure sign there was no man at home. Just stand behind them for a few seconds in a supermarket to see the food they bought, walk the same way home, catch the same bus...

A few days perhaps to build up a little list of targets, maybe longer, depending on how many victims he stalked. And for a man like they were hunting, it wouldn't be a chore. It would be delicious, a savoured mission. He'd enjoy every minute.

'How are you feeling Rachel?' Suzanne knew there was no point pushing her questions, she'd told them all she could. Done more really, that TV interview took some guts.

'OK. A bit better.' She was by the sofa now, chewing at a nail. The engagement ring flashed in the sunlight beaming through the window.

'Where's Martin?' Suzanne asked.

'He had to go back to work.' There was an edge to her words. 'He's got a big deal on at the moment.' She paused, stared out of the window, rubbed at an imagined mark on the glass with a sleeve. 'They're never there when you need them, are they?'

So it had begun. The crumbling of the relationship. How long could it survive? Suzanne looked down at the carpet, said nothing, sensed Rachel wanted her to leave. She had nothing left to ask anyway, hadn't expected to hear anything new, was just checking to see how she was doing. She struggled up from the enveloping chair.

'If you need us, you've got my number.' They'd left a mobile, programmed to call them, an emergency line. 'We can have a squad round here in minutes.'

Rachel was at the fireplace now, toying with her hair, folding a lock in and out of her fingers. She nodded and mumbled a low 'thanks'.

Back in the MIR, Suzanne went through the information they'd gathered yesterday. She stared at the racks of papers. It was quite a pile. She wasn't afraid to admit she felt nervous, a little scared even. It was DCI Breen's inquiry, but the High Honchos' priorities had changed.

They wanted him on the McCluskey case, the show attracting the big media interest. He was still nominally in charge of the rape investigation, but had made it clear he'd have little time for it, not unless there was a quick result on McCluskey. She'd sensed an anger in him about that, but she didn't think it had anything to do with her.

'It's your inquiry now, Suzanne,' he'd said, a hand on her shoulder. 'And I know you'll do great. Go get him.'

She'd felt proud and stirred at the time, as if he'd put his personal trust in her. But now... Now she could feel the weight of the two shattered lives, the need for them to have the small compensation of justice being done, the possibility of some closure for their suffering. Look at the man who did this, try to understand why. Hate him or pity him, it didn't matter. Either was some certainty, a help in the healing.

And what of the thousands of anonymous, faceless, fearful women out there who could become victims if she didn't find this man? Had they already been chosen, walking around invisibly marked, not knowing how one man planned to smash his way through their lives? The nerves jangled again. She wasn't exactly awash with resources either. Most of the detectives had been moved over to the McCluskey case. It was down to her, the newly promoted Claire Reynolds and a few constables. At least they'd left her this room.

So, where to start? Where would Adam Breen begin? She had a sheaf of papers detailing what the team had covered yesterday. Prioritise, she had to prioritise.

The obvious connection between the two women was their estrangement from the fathers of their children. Eleanor had been married, the relationship lasting for six years, exactly the age of her daughter. Rachel had lived with her partner for three years before the split. Both women had been asked the necessary question. Could it have been...? A definite no in both cases, but the exes had been traced and DNA tested anyway. Both negative.

She leafed through the papers. They said both men were bitter about the break-up of the relationships. Both had fought for custody of the kids. No chance. Unless the mother was insane or a drug addict or criminal the family courts always sided with them. Both men seemed to have accepted that and kept in regular contact, visiting their children weekly. Model parents, albeit from a distance. It was the modern way.

Her mind wandered to the comfort of her own little relationship. Small, but growing by the day. She kept that one secret from all at work. DCI Breen had once said that if you let anyone into your private life one day you'd find it written on the toilet wall the next. Spot on, as ever. Work was work and life was life and the two had a habit of exploding when they mixed, like incompatible chemicals.

She knew what some of the male detectives thought of her. 'Lezzer' was the word she'd overheard. She smiled grimly. Let them have their snide little jibes and gossips. Because she didn't wear tight tops, loads of make up, flirt with them and join in their pathetic banter, she was a lezzer. No, she was a professional, and proud of it.

* * *

Anyway, wasn't it better that was how they thought? At least then they left her alone. And what did they know? They wouldn't know was the answer, certainly not how she'd met Adrian. It wasn't easy, meeting people in her job. The hours were long and unpredictable and some men ran a mile when they found out you were a detective. But he hadn't. A warm and caring man, handsome too in an odd way. Six months now it'd been, and going strong. She allowed herself a small, warming smile. Buying that computer had been such a good move.

The case, back to the case. So the ex-partners were out. Where next then?

They were looking for a trigger. Release from prison, the usual one, had shown up nothing. Anyway, they knew their man wasn't a registered offender. His DNA profile didn't match anyone on the database. They knew too now that he wasn't HIV positive, one small mercy at least for his victims. Known criminals moving into the area had shown up nothing either. All the local sex offenders had been checked and ruled out.

So they'd gone back over the local divorces and settlements, Family Court custody cases and Child Support Agency claims for the whole of the past year. It was a depressingly long list. The teams had worked through most of it yesterday, but there were still some outstanding names. They would have to be checked. That would be the priority.

He could be in there, but then again, it was just the list of the broken relationships they knew about. If the rapist was motivated by hate for women, and it grew from a bust up with someone he was living with but had no children, it wouldn't show up on any paperwork, would it? True, true, but that didn't help. They'd have to start on the leads they'd got, not worry about those they didn't have. Not yet, at least.

Then there was Fathers for Families to be seen. The teams hadn't got round to them yesterday, but they would have to be a priority too. Today if possible. That was enough thinking for now. Too much could overcome you. It was time for action. She picked up the phone to call Claire.

Lizzie was fizzing.

'I knew it was going to be a good day,' she buzzed. 'Listening to that interview you did on the radio this morning was touching.' Dan wasn't taking much notice, but did she say touching? The only thing she usually found moving was a surge in the programme's ratings.

'He was quite a guy. I'm glad I decided to put you on it. I'm looking forward to seeing it,' she went on, her thin lips almost forming a smile. 'And the kids got off to school this morning without a single hitch. No lost lunchboxes, or coats or anything. That never happens.'

Dan sat at his desk in the newsroom, wishing she'd leave him alone to get on with it. He wanted to start thinking about how he was going to put today's story together. There were two separate strands. The police investigation into McCluskey's death and the obituary. Two distinct reports probably? It seemed the best way. He noticed the doodle he was sketching on his notebook looked like the mobile in the first of the Death Pictures.

'And wow, what if he has been murdered?' He realised Lizzie hadn't stopped. 'What a story. The ratings will soar. Let's hope the investigation goes on for ages, and then there's a court case. That'd be great. I want wall-to-wall coverage. I want daily updates. I want us to be the McCluskey station. I want… Where are you going?'

Dan hit the log out button on his computer, got up from his chair and reached for his satchel.

'I've got to go out. We need some more filming.' She eyed him suspiciously, a three-inch heel twisting into the long suffering carpet. He'd have to do better than that. 'As you said, it's a great story and I want to get on with it. I want to make sure we do the best we possibly can. I've got a feeling that McCluskey's fans will have started gathering at his studio.'

An eyebrow arched. 'Go on then. What are you waiting for? We'll talk again later.'

It had become the fashion in grieving and as Nigel drove

them onto the Barbican, Dan saw his guess was right. It wasn't yet half past nine, but there was already a crowd of thirty or forty onlookers outside McCluskey's studio. A couple hugged each other. Several people were staring up at the building in silent reflection. Others laid flowers or copies of the Death Pictures with messages attached to them. Most of the flowers were bluebells, creating a necklace of living colour around the grey stone of the studio walls.

Dan wandered over to the surf shop while Nigel took some shots from the ground. 'Same deal as last time?' he asked the manager. 'Done,' came the instant reply. They were given a coffee each too as they looked down on the crowd which had now swollen to about a hundred. 'Come back anytime,' the man said as they left. 'We had quite a few people popping in after the last report.'

Nigel got down on his knees to film some low shots of the bluebells and prints. Dan overheard someone saying that the flowers featured in one of McCluskey's best-known paintings. He jotted it down to check and put in his report. He read a couple of the messages while Nigel filmed, and had an idea. It was a big story. Tonight's programme would get a great audience, so… It was only right he should appear in person.

Dan clipped the small radio microphone onto his jacket and tucked the cigarette packet sized transmitter into an inner pocket. Nigel manipulated the receiver into place on the back of his camera. Radio microphones were great for the flexibility of being able to talk while walking around unrestricted by cables.

'Hearing you loud and clear,' called Nigel, adjusting his headphones. 'Go ahead.'

Dan knelt by the flowers. 'It's a spontaneous tribute to a much-loved artist,' he ad-libbed. 'Some of the messages are touching. One says simply 'You brought colour to my life.' It's signed Louise. Another, 'Your riddle has stumped me, but I've enjoyed many happy hours trying to crack it. Thank you. Andy.' And here, this one, from Sue says, 'Go paint the heavens in peace great artist.''

Nigel shot a couple more close-ups of the flowers and

cards, then they did a quick interview with some of the people. It took three, all talking rest in peace and what a great man before Dan got what he expected. As if on cue, a young woman broke down into sobs. The image, and her words, summed up the shock and loss of the story.

As Nigel drove them back to the studios, Dan debated what to do about Kerry. He couldn't put it off any longer. He'd have to call her. She was expecting commitment, romance, wining and dining, and he didn't want to. It was as simple as that.

He looked down accusingly at his nether regions. Another fine mess you've got me into, he thought, shifting uncomfortably in the car's seat. Some 'research' at the Waterside, with the Death Pictures and a session with El was what he fancied. But if he didn't take Kerry out, it wouldn't exactly look good, would it? 'I've had my fun, thanks. Now goodbye,' would be what she'd think. And would she be so wrong?

He called her number and the phone rang. How about a compromise? Take her out tonight, get it out of the way, do the beer thing tomorrow? He'd rather have a quiet night in, but he had promised. Damn what remained of his conscience.

'Hi, Kerry, it's me.'

'Hi! Great to hear from you.'

Oh balls, he thought, she sounds delighted. But he noticed he still didn't feel any guilt.

'So, you fancy some dinner then?' Dan thought he managed to make his voice sound passably keen.

'Lovely! When?'

'Tonight?'

A slight hesitation. She'd been expecting tomorrow when she had more time to get ready, perhaps even wanted to spend some of the day with him. It was what they'd done when they were newly together, enjoying the excitement of discovering each other. But that hadn't lasted long.

'I was hoping to do tomorrow so we could have more time,' Dan added hurriedly. 'But I've got to work on the McCluskey case. It's a big story for us.'

A familiar excuse he thought, but at least this time it

contained a slice of truth.

'Sure,' she said quickly. 'I'll get a taxi and pick you up on the way. About eight?'

'Great. Look forward to seeing you.' He was relieved to hang up.

Dan heard a giggle building beside him. He tried to ignore it, but it wouldn't stop.

'Yes, Nigel?' he said warily.

'She doesn't know you very well, does she?'

'Meaning?'

'You sounded like you were arranging your own execution, not a date.'

'Just drive us back to base,' replied Dan.

Matt Rees had been the South-west's biggest news story for half of January. A low pressure system hung over the country and the wind and weather were being sucked in from Siberia. The temperature lurked just above freezing in the daytime, a few degrees below at night. It was the middle of the month, the time psychologists say is the most depressing of the year. The long, sweet holiday and celebrations of Christmas lingered only in extra weight on thousands of waistlines. The bills for the fortnight of excess were ominous in the post. The days were short and rejuvenating sunlight scarce. Summer was a distant and unconvincing prospect.

Rees had added to the gloom of motorists by bringing them a New Year's present of long and frustrating traffic jams. He'd spent 10 days on top of one of the concrete towers of the Tamar Bridge, the main road link between Devon and Cornwall, dressed as Batman. One of the three lanes had been closed in case he fell or dropped some of the tins of food he carried. The tailbacks, particularly in the rush hours, had lasted for hours. At a time of year when other stories were scarce, journalists had been secretly delighted by his protest. He'd filled hundreds of newspaper pages and hours of radio and TV airtime.

'It really made an impact that did. I won't apologise you know. I happily admit it, but I won't apologise. It was just what we needed to get some attention to the corruption and prejudice against fathers in our system. I'm going to stand for parliament in the next election and I bet I get some good support. At the very least it'll force the other candidates to think about children and access issues. And another thing...'

'Mr Rees!' Suzanne cut in. 'I've told you. I'm not here to talk to you about that.'

'Oh,' he said. 'I thought when you said you were from the police...'

'It's your work as co-ordinator for Fathers for Families I'd like to talk to you about.'

'Oh.' He looked at her again, his expression relaxing. 'In that case, would you like a cup of tea?'

Suzanne accepted. It would give her a break to think. He got up from the chair in the kitchen of the advertising agency in Plymouth city centre and put the kettle on. He had receding blond hair, nearly gone at the temple, and was a tall man, six feet plus. He was thin with it, almost gaunt. No superhero this, she couldn't imagine him filling a Batman costume convincingly. No rapist either, the description didn't match.

'Mr Rees, I appreciate your help,' she said, taking the mug, but refusing the offer of sugar. She usually liked a spoonful but had cut it out from her diet. She was trying to lose weight, keep trim for Adrian. 'And I'd appreciate your confidence,' she went on. 'As I told you, we're hunting this rapist and we believe he may have a dislike of women.'

Suzanne leaned forwards towards him and lowered her voice like a fellow conspirator, a trick she'd learnt from Adam Breen. 'Could you tell me if anyone has recently joined your group and seems particularly angry? Or if anyone who has been a member for a while has suddenly changed, become more embittered perhaps? Said something odd? Particularly against women?'

Matt Rees had copied her lean forward, but now shifted back on his chair. 'You're asking me to talk about some of my friends here,' he said slowly. 'That's difficult. I have a duty of loyalty to them, but I'd also do anything I could to help you catch this man.'

101

He looked down at the ground, interlaced his fingers and stretched his hands. 'Difficult,' he repeated.

Suzanne said nothing. She could see the man had something to tell her, but wasn't sure whether he needed pushing, persuading or just being given time. An unexpected nudge of nerves hit her.

'Look,' he said, raising his head. 'All of the people I know in Fathers for Families are non-violent. We only break the law because we feel we have no choice, and we only do so peacefully.' She nodded, sensed this wasn't the time to begin a debate. 'So I think it's OK to tell you. There is just one man I worry about. Do you need a name?'

Suzanne nodded again, trying to disguise her excitement. She scribbled quickly on her notepad.

'He's called Will, Will Godley. He works at the dockyard. He's always the one we have to keep an eye on. He's been in a bitter dispute with his ex-wife over access to his sons. He's full of rage and just lately it seems to have got worse, quite a lot worse. He's been saying we should step up our campaign and do something that really gets noticed.'

Matt Rees hesitated as though wondering whether to let the words go. Finally he blurted out, 'He said it was time we showed women we can fight back against them.'

He'd had to argue hard to hold on to both reports, but Dan didn't want anyone else writing them. It was his story. Plus he didn't have a great regard for the other reporters. Most of his colleagues were competent in putting facts together in a pattern, but couldn't make the elusive jump between information and understanding. They could tell you what happened, but struggle with why it was important. He hushed the sarcastic voice in his mind that said it was because he wanted all the glory too.

'Are you sure you can do both stories?' Lizzie had asked sharply, a heel wearing away at the carpet by her desk. 'The ratings are going to be massive tonight. I want top quality coverage. I could easily put someone else on McCluskey's obit, or the investigation into his death.'

Dan noticed a couple of other journalists hovering hopefully nearby. Everyone wanted a slice of the action on a big story. He edged to his left to block them from Lizzie's view.

'Absolutely. You know how fast I work. I've done all the interviews and filming. I know all the material. I know the story inside out. It'd be a waste of time someone else trying to get up to speed with it. I might as well go and get on with it now. I want the reports to be as good as possible, too, you know.'

She'd studied him for a few seconds, the stiletto still scraping another hole in the patchy carpet. He could see she was wavering on a decision.

'And don't forget I've got the contacts with the police,' Dan added quickly. 'It's me they want to shadow the investigation. It's me they trust. If they see someone else working on the story, it might scare them off and stop us from getting any more exclusive insights into the case.'

She'd looked at him for another second, then an eyebrow arched and he relaxed. 'Go on then,' Lizzie said. 'What are you waiting for? Get on with it. But you'd better make sure they're good.'

The first report was on the investigation into Joseph McCluskey's death. It began with the bluebells and messages, then had some of the people who'd come to pay their respects. Dan had discovered the bluebells were inspired by one of McCluskey's paintings, Blue Bella, a young woman sprawled naked in a field of the flowers, one small bunch covering her modesty. The story went that the model hadn't retained them for long enough for McCluskey to finish the painting. It had been completed from his imagination.

Dan added his piece to camera, telling the viewers about the details on some of the messages. It was poignant, he thought. And in a big story it was only right he should appear.

He finished the report with some of last night's pictures of McCluskey's house and the police activity around it, recapping on how the artist had been found dead in suspicious circumstances. Adam talked about the investigation continuing and appealed for anyone who knew anything that might help the police to come forward. It was straightforward and took Jenny an hour to cut.

The second report was longer and needed more time. They used the material Nigel had shot of the Death Pictures, with slow, artistic mixes between the paintings. Dan added few words of his own. The story didn't need them. It was almost all McCluskey talking about his life and how he wanted to be remembered. As Dan sat at the computer, entering the details of the two reports into the *Wessex Tonight* running order, he felt the excitement of the day ebb and his tiredness return. He stifled a yawn.

He thought about the Waterside Arms and how welcome a few hours there would be. It'd been a hell of a week. He needed some recharging time. A lie in bed, a Dartmoor walk with Rutherford and a few beers would be ideal for the weekend. Then the memory of tonight's unwanted date with Kerry intruded, like an uninvited guest. He slapped the computer mouse, spilling the remnants of a cold cup of tea. There was no way out. He'd have to go.

It was a powerful report he thought, as he sat at home on his great blue sofa, Rutherford at his feet. He'd done McCluskey justice, whether he deserved it or not. Dan realised he still wasn't sure about that.

On the coffee table in front of him lay a copy of each of the Death Pictures. He missed the rest of the programme as he leafed through them, looking for clues to the solution. Still nothing came. It was only a phone call from his parents that snapped him back to reality. 7.20, time to get in the shower. Could he summon up some enthusiasm for seeing Kerry? He tried, but felt nothing except a desire to stretch out here alone, drink some beer and study the pictures. It was going to be a long night.

Detective Chief Inspector Breen was going to be plain Adam and Dad tonight. He was due round for dinner with Annie and a game of football in the park with Tom, and he was damn well going to make it. They were his family. They needed him and he needed them. He wasn't running the rape inquiry any more, so he could afford to spare some time. The Assistant Chief Constable had made it clear, despite his protests.

'It's not negotiable, Adam. Get on with it.'

'Sir, with respect, this rapist could strike again at any moment.'

'As could McCluskey's killer.'

'It's a totally different scenario. We don't even know he was killed. And if there is a killer – if – we've got nothing that suggests he'll do it again. It's a simple case. This bastard rapist is different. He might as well have taken out an ad in the paper telling us he's going to attack more women. It should be our priority.'

'Other officers can handle it.'

'Other officers could handle McCluskey.'

'DCI Breen, let me make this even clearer. The eyes of the world are on us. You will find out what happened regarding the death of Joseph McCluskey. End of discussion.'

OK then, that's the way it would be. Or at least, appear to be.

Anyway, McCluskey was effectively on hold until he got the results of the forensics and fingerprinting on Monday. Suzanne was in charge of tracking down the rapist, but with strict orders to call if there were any developments. She understood that didn't need to be mentioned to anyone else. So for now it was time for his family. He hadn't managed to see them over these last few hectic days. If he was ever going to escape that cold and detested flat then some relationship repair work was needed.

As he drove the five minutes from Charles Cross to Peverell, he tried to force himself to think like a family man. He concentrated on Annie and Tom, imagined their faces smiling to see him. He trapped the spinning football, sent a shot at Tom, the boy diving to block it. He poured a glass of wine for Annie, chopped herbs next to her in the kitchen. She scooped them up, dropped them in the casserole, planted a kiss on his cheek.

But a dark, silhouetted figure lurked in the background. A

figure without a face. A shape that breaks into women's homes and attacks them as they sit watching soap operas. Rapes and traumatises them.

Adam noticed the car's speed creeping up. His hands were gripping hard at the wheel, the fingers whitening. He'd get this man, whatever his bosses told him about priorities. He'd get him, even if he had to DNA test the whole damn city.

Surely the McCluskey case wouldn't take long anyway? It looked straightforward enough. Verdict: McCluskey had committed suicide. He had cancer, was in pain and didn't have long to live. It made perfect sense.

That attempted break in was just a distraction. It could have been some hopeless drug addict trying their luck, or a burglar who'd been frightened off. Perhaps even someone trying to find a clue to the riddle. It was a coincidence, nothing more.

He turned the car around the corner into Rosslyn Park Road. Careful though, careful, he thought. You're a professional. Don't prejudge, don't want the case to be over before you've looked at it thoroughly.

The real concern was what Abi McCluskey had said. She was sure Joseph wouldn't have killed himself without telling her. But could they rely on that? She'd have to be interviewed again, and in detail. She was distraught and couldn't tell them much so far. They knew Joseph had other women, something she admitted herself. Did she really know him that well? It looked as though he'd deliberately chosen a time when she'd be out to take his life. And that he would be found by a friend rather than her. To minimise her distress perhaps?

Adam inched the car into a space, trying not to nudge the van behind. Curtains were twitching. They always did in this neighbourhood. It was pleasant but nosey, classic middle class. He grabbed the bottle of red wine he'd brought, locked the car and turned to catch Tom as he bounded down the path. Annie stood in the doorway, smiling.

Enough of work. All that was for Monday. For now, it was football in the park and when Tom was in bed, dinner. And perhaps a romantic night too, depending on how it went. Perhaps.

*　　　*　　　*

'You're a selfish bastard arsehole.'

It wasn't quite a scream, but her voice was loud and acidic and heads were turning.

'Kerry, can you just keep it down a bit please,' Dan pleaded. Her face darkened and her lips thinned further, just red lines now. 'Please,' he repeated.

'What, so you can hold on to your reputation as a nice guy, eh? So people don't start talking about that bloke off the TV, and how he had a row and his woman went storming out on him. Is that all you care about? Well bollocks to you!'

Dan looked around him. They were getting glances in that sly way people have of being irresistibly interested, but not wanting to look.

The ground floor of Etrusco's Tapas Bar wasn't full, but there were still about 30 people dining. Worse, it was one of those places where they cram diners in to maximise profits. Their window table was separated by only a couple of feet from their neighbours, a polite and now increasingly embarrassed-looking older couple. The only opportunity to have a private conversation in this place was the new lovers' way of leaning forward to talk cheek to cheek. There was no chance of that. They were at the opposite end of their relationship. Both sat stiff and upright, arms crossed, faces set hard.

Kerry's finger jabbed out at him. 'You're a selfish, selfish bastard. And you're screwed up too. I was stupid enough to think I could help you. I don't know why I bothered.'

The woman next to them cleared her throat, got up and headed towards the toilet. Dan caught a look from the man. He thought he saw a fleeting wink of sympathy.

'You just used me, didn't you?' Her voice was growing louder again. 'The other night I mean? You never had any intention of us getting back together! You just wanted a shag!'

'Shhh', he said hopefully.

'No I will not fucking shhh! It's about time more people knew what you were like. A shag's OK eh? That's fine. But not a relationship. You haven't got the guts for that. It's OK

107

when you fancy a quickie, but any form of commitment's totally beyond you isn't it?'

The waitress arrived and hovered uncertainly. She was a young woman, perhaps nineteen or twenty, possibly a student working her way through her degree. She probably hadn't been through any break ups like this yet. Well, her time would come. 'No sweets, thanks, just the bill,' Dan said as politely as he could. She disappeared gratefully.

Still, at least he'd got the timing more or less right. He knew he was going to have to pay and he wanted to enjoy his meal before the outbreak of hostilities. So he'd told Kerry just as they were finishing their fajitas. The result was predictable. It was just as well he didn't fancy a pudding.

'Look, I'm sorry, but it's the way I feel,' Dan managed as soothingly as he could. 'I tried my very best to give it a go, but it just hasn't worked for me. I might as well be honest about it.'

'It didn't stop you giving it another go last week, did it?'

He knew he'd come to regret that. It wasn't the first time he'd got himself into such trouble. But what man can't say that? And anyway, wasn't there some hypocrisy here? It wasn't as if she hadn't wanted to see him. He could feel himself starting to absorb her anger.

'Hang on!' he growled. 'I didn't exactly force you! You seemed pretty keen!'

There was a sharp cough from the woman next to them. Newly returned from the toilet, she looked as though she wished she'd stayed there.

'I thought we were getting back together!' Kerry's voice was louder now, on the verge of a shriek. It was carrying beautifully across the whole restaurant. More heads turned.

Dan lowered his voice to a whisper, hoping she would quieten too. 'I never said that.'

'Oh no, you wouldn't would you?' Kerry shouted. 'Because it'd spoil your fun, wouldn't it?! Well fuck you!' She scraped back her chair, sprung up, and stamped out of the door, her shoes crashing an angry rhythm on the wooden floor.

Everyone was looking at him now. I wouldn't be surprised

108

to be featured in the *Standard*'s gossip column tomorrow, Dan thought resignedly. Other people's bust-ups were such good entertainment.

He squirmed a little in his seat, sighed, and gave a mental shrug. What can you do but tough it out? He glanced around the room with what he hoped was his best sheepish half smile. There were some looks of amusement and sympathy from the men, some accusing glares from the women, and some stares of bafflement. But then – thankfully – after what felt like hours, the interest began to wane and the diners returned to their food and conversations. The show was over.

The bill arrived, the waitress looking more relaxed now he was alone. She was cute when she smiled. Fifty-four pounds. Expensive for a public humiliation he thought, as he gave her his credit card. Dan added a good tip to compensate for her embarrassment and managed to stop himself from asking for her phone number.

So, what to do now? Part of him said go home, have a whisky or two, watch a film and relax. The other part said he was in town now, so why let Kerry spoil the evening? Find some friends and do some drinking.

It was an uneven contest. He drew back his chair as quietly as he could and slipped out of the restaurant. He began walking down towards the honey-pot of bars on the Barbican. He'd find sympathetic company and drinking mates there.

Dan typed out a text message as he walked under the streetlights of Royal Parade. 'If anyone's out on the beer in town tonight, and doesn't mind a wandering journalist for company, please say now. DG.'

He forwarded it to all possible accomplices in his numbers list. Within five minutes, three responses came back. He decided to go to Bigwigs bar, just down from the law courts where a group of barristers were having what they called a quiet drink. Dan had never seen lawyers have a quiet drink in their lives. The cheering and shouting he could hear from a hundred yards away confirmed his suspicion. It would suit him perfectly. He was feeling bloody-minded and in a mood to drink himself into surrender.

He woke the next morning with a throbbing head and the flat heavy with the smell of a greasy kebab. Bad news. He had two measures of being drunk. If he started to think he could dance, or if he fancied a kebab, he knew he should go home. The thought that he'd ignored his own rule cheered him. He smiled, then winced as his headache pounded with renewed enthusiasm. It felt like a pneumatic drill hammering in his mind.

He got up to find some tablets in the bathroom and slurped gratefully at the cold tap as he swallowed them. His mouth felt painfully dry. The TV was on in the lounge so he switched it off, retrieved his shirt from the back of the door, noted the beer and chilli sauce stains and threw it in the washing bin. He let Rutherford out into the garden, then went back to bed. It was only nine o'clock. He was planning to get to the Waterside for mid afternoon. El would join him later.

He suffered a nudge of guilt for the thought, but he felt liberated and light with relief. Kerry was a good woman, just not good for him. He slept on with a smile.

Chapter Eight

DAN HAD NEVER BELIEVED in an afterlife. He'd been brought up without religion and was young enough not to have thought seriously about it. He tended to see it as something older people did, often more in hope than belief.

He could understand why. It was a chance of something where otherwise there was darkness, void, silence and vacuum, simply cold, frightening nothing. But as he sat in the Waterside Arms, a pint of ale in hand, he found himself hoping there was an afterlife and that Joseph McCluskey had settled in comfortably. Because if there was, he would be rocking back and forth in a fine chair and laughing himself stupid, at him, Dan, and the thousands of others he could watch hopelessly trying to solve the riddle of the Death Pictures. The joke was very much on them.

He'd been going through the prints for an hour now and his progress was summed up by the sheet of paper on the table in front of him. It was optimistically headed, 'Death Pictures ideas,' but apart from that it was blank.

There were clues in there, he was sure of that. McCluskey had promised it and Dan believed him. But he'd hidden them amongst a mass of distractions and deviousness, and one pint in Dan had no idea what the answer could be. The numbers kept nagging at his mind. Why else would they be there? But he couldn't see any hint of a pattern in them. There was just one thing to do. A time-honoured solution. Another pint.

Barry the landlord stood behind the bar. Dan settled on one of the wooden stools and reached out to stroke the weatherbeaten black and white cat curled up on the neighbouring seat.

'Any ideas what McCluskey's picture in here means?' Dan asked.

Barry grinned as he pulled the pint. It frothed darkly into the welcoming glass. Dan wasn't planning to have such a feisty beer so early, but his brain was being sullen and unforthcoming and needed a kick.

'Not a clue,' replied the landlord. In one way I wish I did have. I wouldn't mind that picture. In another I'm glad I don't and hope no one else does either. I can't count how many new customers we've had come in ask that very question. It's been great for business.'

Dan sipped an inch off his beer and wandered over to the dartboard. Picture five, a double two, a nine, a 13 and a bull's eye. Three cherries on the fruit machine next to it. Some hints that something here would be a winner? He stared at the board, aware a couple of people in the pub were watching him and smiling. Locals, they'd seen this routine more than a few times no doubt.

Assume the bull's eye means this picture is on target, so take that away. A double two then, could that mean 22? Or just four? Then the nine and 13. Or could it be the whole lot, making 224 913? That was more like it. It sounded like a grid reference, but for where? And what? Some landmark? A place something was buried or hidden? He'd have to check the office Ordnance Survey maps when he got back to work. He sat back down at the table, glad at last to have one idea to mark down on his paper.

Back to the start, picture one. Who was the flame haired woman? That was one for El, they could talk about it later. And why was she riding a mobile phone? Was it a confirmation that numbers were important, that they would carry you somewhere? And what about that number on the phone, the Plymouth code followed by 225? Another part of a grid reference? Or could it mean Plymouth, two to five? What could that indicate? Postcodes? PL2 to PL5? Perhaps that could link in with the grid references to give a location? He noted the idea down, with an admiring glance at the beer. No one could ever tell him it wasn't inspirational stuff.

Picture two then. That would take a bit more work, as it seemed to show a place. Dan was sure it was somewhere on the west of Dartmoor, the scene an annoyingly familiar one. He still had friends among the Rangers in the National Park Authority from his days covering the environment. He could ask them. But what about the symbolism in the picture?

Could the vicar indicate some religious connection? Dartmoor was full of ancient sacred sites. There was even a church on the top of Brent Tor. Why was he pointing at that plane? Goodbye number one... Could that simply be a reference to Abi, a way of saying farewell? Or did it mean remove a one from some numbers in the picture? But there were no numbers in this one, so the previous picture perhaps? And what did the digging dog indicate? That something was buried on the moor? In that location, or somewhere else defined by the grid references he might have uncovered? Ideas, ideas... Dan knew he was flailing around, but at least he had some ideas.

The street in number three didn't look familiar, but he was willing to bet it existed somewhere in Plymouth. McCluskey had planned his little game carefully. Could that mean it was important? And if so, how the hell to find it? Could the postcodes from picture one help? There was a jumble of letters and numbers on the cars. Did they mean anything? And what of the chough? It was the symbol of Cornwall, so perhaps a clue that the answer was in the county? Could that tie in with some of the numbers, another indication of a grid reference?

Dan wondered if the child lifting the manhole cover was symbolic of discovery. But discovering what? Surely it'd be too literal for something to be hidden under that cover? He jotted the thoughts down for more research when he got back to work.

Number four reminded him of Salvador Dali's painting, The Persistence of Memory. Was that deliberate? A cryptic way of saying forget it? Again he saw grid references, the snake perhaps signifying an S, the 9.15 on the clock giving the number. If so, where was the other half of the coordinates? In one of the other pictures? Dan sat back from the table and shook his head. Talking of puzzles, his glass had mysteriously emptied itself. Thinking was thirsty work.

'Getting anywhere?' Barry asked, scratching his balding crown.

'Not that I can tell,' replied Dan thoughtfully. 'The man

knew how to set a puzzle.' He tasted the beer. 'Mmmm, excellent.' He had another sip. Better take it easy, he wouldn't make the evening at this rate.

'You could help me with something, though,' Dan went on. He walked back over to the table, returned and showed the landlord the pictures of the two women, the redhead and the blonde. 'Any idea who they are? My mate's trying to trace them.'

Barry shook his head. 'A couple of his women?' he said. 'McCluskey used to come in here every month or so, but he was always on his own. I've no idea I'm afraid. It's a pity, I wouldn't mind seeing ladies like that here.'

Dan couldn't help but agree. There had only been a pitifully small rash of guilt from last night with Kerry, and it had cleared up already. His brain had obviously adjusted to being back on the market. He imagined himself with a 'For Sale,' sign around his neck. Or perhaps 'To Let,' might be more appropriate, given what she'd said about his attitude to commitment.

On to painting six, the blonde woman. More numbers here, the bingo ones. Grid references again? But there were seven numbers. Was it meant to read 222 to 739? That would be a hell of a spread. Or was it a six-figure reference, with one of the numbers designed to mislead? And then there was the 'It's a Fiddle', headline. A clue the answer wasn't here? And what about the boat? Did the 98 refer to a page number? But a page of what? The bible was the classical answer when dealing with codes designed around books. But religion and McCluskey? It didn't sound likely. Well, it was worth a look. He'd have to check when he got home.

Abi dominated painting seven, crying for the loss of her husband? Key 09 on her shirt was interesting, perhaps another page number? Or more cunning than that, how about Quay 09? How many quays were there in Plymouth's harbours? Or one quay with a mooring number nine? And was there a boat there with a number 98 on it? He liked the sound of that idea, probably his best yet. Mind you, there wasn't a great deal of competition.

Dan drummed his fingers on the table and stared at the sleeping cat. He was about to get up to visit the toilet when his phone rang. Adam.

'Dan mate, just a quick call.' He was whispering, his voice echoing. It sounded like he was talking from inside a tin box.

'Where are you?' Dan asked, pressing the phone closer to his ear. 'The signal's awful.'

'I'm in the toilet at home. I mean old home, Annie's. Listen, I've only got a few seconds so I wanted to let you know. There's been another rape, the same guy. He left another witch's hat.'

Dan grabbed his notebook. 'Where? When?'

'Plymouth again, this morning. It's a different area this time though, down in Stonehouse. A couple of miles from the others. It's another young woman with a kid. The boy was away spending the weekend with his dad, thankfully. Suzanne's handling it. I've got to go mate. Call me Monday morning.'

There was the sound of a toilet flushing, then the line went dead.

Dan rang the newsroom and passed on the details. They could cover it. He deserved some time off after last week. Besides, there were only very short bulletins on a Saturday, he'd had a couple of beers, couldn't drive and didn't want to be handling a story like that without a clear head. Well, that was what he told them and the excuse seemed to work. It was lucky Lizzie was on holiday for the weekend or he'd never have got away with it.

Another rape. That was three of six then, the man half way through his mission, despite the efforts of the police. The women of Plymouth would be in a state of fear, jumping at every creak in their own homes. They'd have to get this guy, and soon. Just what Adam was thinking no doubt, sat secretly in the toilet at Annie's, trying to coordinate the investigation while pretending his attention was devoted to his family.

How had the man managed to strike again, evade the extra police patrols? Simple. He'd chosen a different area of the city this time and carried out his attack when most attention was on

115

McCluskey's place and the possibility of him being murdered. What to conclude from that? Simple again. He'd planned his attacks well. He must have known the police would be putting officers into the area where he'd struck twice and so he'd moved on to somewhere else.

He'd had some luck too, taken advantage of the McCluskey distraction. That was, if he was nothing to do with McCluskey's death. The police hadn't ruled that out, had they?

Enough of work, this was the weekend and he had some beer to drink. Dan got up, walked across to the bar and pondered the pumps. He asked for a pint of water as well; the beer was going down too fast. He needed something to check its befuddling passage into his head.

Back to the Death Pictures then, while he could still think reasonably clearly. Three more to go.

Number eight was baffling. There was no other word for it. What was a goldfish tank to do with anything? Some symbolism of it being a world and McCluskey fishing around in it? And those soldiers? Was he looking for a castle or stately home with some kind of military history? Dan let out a long sigh. Under the heading Picture 8 on his piece of paper he wrote 'no bloody idea'. At least it was an honest answer.

Number nine was equally impenetrable. Numbers again, it all seemed to revolve around the numbers. The clock said five to ten. Was that supposed to mean 5210? Could that be some kind of combination, or PIN number? If so, to what? Something hinted at in one of the other pictures? But what? And why was there no 11 or 12 on the clock? A pointer to some place where there were no such numbers? A street perhaps? But where? What kind of street would have numbers 11 and 12 missing? One preserved with the bomb damage of the war?

There were such places in Plymouth he knew, but couldn't remember where. And what did the chessboard mean? Some sort of game? Or just McCluskey's playing with the rest of the world? Dan took another deep draw of beer and, with an afterthought, some water too. The cat stretched, hopped down from the stool and slid out of the pub's back door.

So to the last picture. Good job he thought, he'd had enough of McCluskey's riddles. It was clear there were two self-portraits here and there was another clock too. Indicating time was running out on him? It said five to 12. Did that mean 5212? Another possible combination? But again, to what? And what did the planets below the young McCluskey and above the older version mean? Symbolism of the passage of time, one day the world at his feet, the next it's beaten him? And what did that river of numbers at the bottom of the picture indicate? He couldn't see any patterns in there at all.

Dan pushed the pictures away. He sat back on his chair and drank some more beer. Enough.

Had he made any progress? He had one or two ideas, but… The word no kept coming back to him. It was joined by an annoying vision of McCluskey reclining in a Sedan chair, at a fireside in a warm and comfortable heaven, looking down at him and laughing helplessly.

Enough. Time for some easier puzzles, like what beer to have next and what pie from the excellent home cooked menu. Probably the minty lamb he thought, and with chips too. It was the weekend after all. Maybe even a pudding to follow. He didn't get one last night after that screaming match with Kerry. His brain needed fuelling after all this thinking, however ineffectual.

Every boat trip brought back a hated memory. Dan had been on a brief school holiday to France when he was ten years old and it still ranked as one of his top five worst experiences. The seas were mountainous and the eight hours on the water had all been spent vomiting. The deck was freezing cold and soaked in rain and sticky sea spray, but he'd had no option other than to stand there and wait for the next bout of retching. It'd taken days to recover and was still a living memory, more than a generation on. But he enjoyed the water taxi ride back from Turnchapel to the Barbican. It helped sober him up.

It was coming up to eight o'clock and the sky had dimmed to an inky velvet. Green and red jewels of navigation lights shone and shimmered in the oily water. The boat chugged in its acrid fog of diesel fumes. Two swashes of waves from its prow cast a cone of white in its wake. Dan registered the handful of other passengers pulling coats up around their necks, but he didn't feel cold. Beer was a wonderful insulator.

Two tower blocks of flats shone with chessboard patterns of window lights at the Barbican's southern edge. He stood up from the boat's hard wooden bench and gazed out across Plymouth Sound. The silhouette of Drake's Island rose like a dark fist breaking from the steely water. A sleek warship slipped menacingly alongside, as if guarding the harbour. The rocky cliffs of the Hoe towered behind it, topped by the blunted obelisk of Smeaton's Tower lighthouse.

A change in the easy wind ushered away the engine's diesel cloud and the air around them was filled with the tang of salt. They were near the Barbican now, and Dan could hear the scrapes of uncertain stiletto heels on the cobbles and shrieks of laughter. Above, the wheeling gulls joined in with their mocking cries. He breathed in deeply, then again, leant over the side of the boat and trailed a hand in the caressing water. Its sudden chill made him shiver.

El was waiting in The Seafarer's Arms. He'd sat himself on one of the benches opposite the bar and cuddled a fresh pint of beer along with what looked like a double whisky. He must have realised Dan had been out for a while and was making a noble effort to catch up.

'Evening, mate,' said Dan, pushing his way through the crowd. He was pleased at how steady his voice sounded. 'You got a thirst on?' He pointed at the two drinks, 'or are you celebrating something I should know about?'

El produced his usual sleazy grin. 'It's kind Mr McCluskey. He's been very good to poor El. First there was that little unauthorised snap I got of the last Death Picture. That was lucrative.' The grin widened. 'Then he did me the favour of dying in a dodgy way! The national papers loved it. The pictures at his place made me some very good money.'

'And what about the women you've got this commission for?' shouted Dan over his shoulder, as he made it to the haven of the bar. 'You want another drink?'

'Whisky and beer,' came back the reply. In the same glass, wondered Dan? El would be wasted by nine at this rate. He quietly bought himself a shandy.

Billy the landlord was on his usual stool at the far end of the bar. Dan caught his eye and he nodded. The Seafarer's was famous as a spit and sawdust place, but trouble was rare. Billy was a landlord with countless years' experience. He could sense a fight coming and it was dealt with quickly. Dan had seen it. It wasn't pretty. The Seafarer's was a pub where most of Plymouth's Commando officers drank and an unwise place to start trouble.

There was a good crowd in tonight. Already the bar was packed. Beer was being spilled onto the ever-sticky stone floor, and voices rose as they competed for attention. All sorts drank in the Seafarer's. By the bar stood a line of muscled men with short hair and tattoos peeking out from beneath tight T-shirts. Every time the door opened their eyes snapped to it. Military, probably, Dan thought.

In the corner a knot of men leaned together in a huddle around their pints. The table was almost full of empty glasses. Some wore waterproofs, others thick woollen jumpers. All looked ruddy and weatherbeaten, their hair untended in spraying styles. Fishermen, celebrating a good week's catch most likely. A couple tucked into plastic trays of chips.

There were a few younger lads in loud shirts, their weekend best, jeans fashionably faded, hair spiked and gelled. They were edging imperceptibly towards a group of young girls, all dressed in a uniform of figure-hugging tops and short skirts. The girls had formed a protective circle, just like in the old Westerns, Dan thought with a grin. Draw the wagons up in a ring to try to keep the enemy at bay.

Dan pushed his way back to El, who was aiming a vacant grin all around.

'What's the plan for tonight then, El?' he shouted.

'Drinking,' said El simply. Dan gave him a look that said he wanted more detail. 'Heavy drinking,' he added helpfully.

'I got that bit from the state of you already. What I meant was are there any plans to go anywhere else?'

'Oh yes,' said El. 'I've got a naughty little idea you might just like.'

Dan woke on Sunday morning feeling slightly thick-headed, but remarkably well considering the two nights running on the beer. Those couple of shandies and the water had kept an angrier hangover at bay. And he'd only had a couple of bottles of lager in the lap-dancing club. He didn't know whether to feel ashamed or amused. How had El got him in there? He'd become caught up in the moment and the beer had yet again oiled his path to another fate he shouldn't have known.

So what, he thought? They'd agreed to work together on the Death Pictures riddle and El was the kind of man to have on your side. He knew how to get things done. Dan had no idea how he planned to find the two mystery women from the pictures, but El clearly did. He'd been cryptic as ever, and what did he want with a fancy dress shop?

Yes, it'd been a fun night and he had all day to recover. A Dartmoor walk would be good, he'd been neglecting Rutherford lately. A walk, combined with some research. He fumbled the lead out of the darkness of the hallway cupboard and Rutherford whirled circles around him, jumping up and yapping in that puppy-like way of his. He'd never grown up, that dog. Perhaps it was something to do with his master's influence?

They passed Merrivale Quarry, a deep granite scar in the rising emerald moorland. Death Picture two lay next to him on the passenger seat. They rounded a corner and there it was ahead, Vixen Tor, the tall, multi-layered, grey granite stack. Dan checked the picture again. It was unmistakeable. His guess had been right. He indicated and pulled in to a small car park hollowed from the hillside. They crossed the road and headed down onto the open moor.

Dartmoor was awakening from its winter hibernation. Above him a brown speckled skylark fluttered and trilled, an eager invitation to a mate. We're not so different, us humans and the rest of the animal kingdom, Dan thought, revisiting last night, the lap dancer and his pompous chat-up lines about being on television. 'I wish you better luck than me,' he called to the bird.

Gorse sprayed the grass with flashes of yellow, the hillsides were freckled with contented white sheep. A thin worn track wound through the thorns of the jabbing bushes. He followed it, his boots slipping on the occasional emerging plate of glassy granite. Above, the sky stretched a dull white, a benevolent covering of cloud. Ideal walking weather. Dan took deep lungfuls of the pure upland air and felt it fill and relax him. It reinflated him with life. The residual headache waned.

A leat gushed ahead of them, gorged by April's showers. He found a narrowing to jump, steadied himself and leapt, one foot slipping into the freezing water. Rutherford watched, then plunged into the icy, frothing torrent, wading upstream against the current, then turning and letting it carry him back down the hill. He found a stick stuck firm into the muddy bank and head shaking, growling, wrestled it free. He clambered out of the stream and ran for Dan who jumped instinctively back, tried to reach a safe distance, but the dog was too quick. A rain of droplets sprayed from his coat as he shook himself into a spin.

'No tea for you tonight hound, and you can sleep in the garden too,' he shouted, laughing and wiping the water from his face.

Dan took the picture from his pocket and unfolded it. 'Over that hill,' he called to Rutherford, pointing ahead. He found himself panting as the gradient wound against them. Could the answer to McCluskey's riddle really be here, he wondered? Surely it wouldn't be as simple as where the dog was digging? And what was the meaning of the vicar and the plane? And the banner with 'goodbye number one' written on it? Real clues? Or more iron pyrites, as the infuriating artist had put it?

Dan scanned around him. It was classic Dartmoor. Tumbled granite boulders, pyramid tors, grassy hills, winding streams, defiant gorse, squelching mud and pervasive bracken, an abstract canvas of green, silver, yellow, grey and brown. The road ran behind them, the tiny dark blocks of a couple of farmhouses on the horizon. There was nothing to suggest any link to the second Death Picture.

'He's taking the mickey out of us dog,' Dan panted to Rutherford. 'I bet you any amount of dog biscuits the answer's not here.' But we'll keep looking, won't we? he thought. Because McCluskey's got me hooked up in his riddle in exactly the way I said I never would be.

They reached the top of the hill and Dan stopped and breathed out heavily in gratitude. He loosened his coat. The sun had forced her way through the clouds, warming the moorland. Rutherford sniffed around a pile of rocks, then sat down on a flat granite slab. Dan was glad to see the dog was panting too. He fumbled the print from his pocket, but before he could study it, a noise from down in the valley stopped him.

He walked on a little, topped the hill, then stopped again. A Dartmoor ranger was surrounded by a group of a dozen people. Ugly brown scores marked the green spread of the moor grass around where they stood. Dan checked the picture. Yes, this was the spot, as near as he could tell. He looked up at the thinning clouds. Why did he have the feeling McCluskey was laughing himself stupid again?

He walked over to the crowd. Some held mud-coated spades in their hands. They were getting a stern lecture on how it was illegal and immoral to damage the fabric of the moor and how they were too late anyway. The Rangers had been patrolling constantly since Death Picture Two was revealed. They'd turned dozens of people away as they came to dig in the same spot as the dog. There was no answer here.

Dan slipped the lead over Rutherford's head and put the print quickly back into his pocket before anyone noticed. He kept walking, past the group, pulling the dog to heel. It was only when they'd climbed a tor and reached a safe distance that he burst out laughing. Even Rutherford seemed to find it funny. He had that mouth open, tongue hanging out look that Dan always thought of as his smiling face.

The image of the group searching Dartmoor to dig for the answer to McCluskey's riddle kept him amused for the rest of the day. Even come Monday morning, his most detested time of the week, he was still smiling at the thought. But the smile died quickly when a man was arrested on suspicion of murdering Joseph McCluskey.

Chapter Nine

THE STORY BROKE AT ten past six. Dan felt his body tense with a flush of adrenaline and annoyance. Perfect timing to maximise the stress for his poor heart. Just 15 minutes to find something sensible to say for the programme.

Adam phoned him with the tip off. 'This didn't come from me, but I thought I should warn you. I know you're on air in a mo. It'll go on the force's website in the next half hour anyway. There's a limit to what I can say, but this evening we've arrested a man on suspicion of murdering Joseph McCluskey.'

Shit! 'Who?'

'I can't say.'

'Kid?'

A pause. 'Might be.'

'How might?'

Another hesitation. 'This didn't come from me.'

'OK, OK. I got that. It never does.'

'A lot might.'

A hasty scribbled note. 'Why?'

'Some new evidence.'

Dan checked the clock. 6.15. Shit.

'What evidence?'

Another pause. 'I've got to go.'

'Adam!'

'OK, strictly not for broadcast, right?'

'Yes.'

'Strictly.'

'OK!'

'The knife that killed McCluskey had Kid's fingerprints on it.'

Shit! 6.17.

Dan hung up, dropped the mobile on his desk and ran down the stairs. He leapt the last couple and barged in to the broadcast gallery, panting hard. They were rehearsing the headlines. The red glowing clock above the wall of television screens ticked on. 6.20.

'Really!' exclaimed Eddie, the director. He looked round accusingly from his bank of flashing buttons. 'So unprofessional! We're preparing for on air you know…'

'Shut up!' cut in Dan. 'Monica… Monica… urgent one,' he puffed, struggling to get the words out. 'There's been an arrest in the McCluskey case.'

'What?' She swivelled in her producer's chair. 'What?! Can you do something?'

'Yeah, just give me a minute to think. Let's get a cue ready, then I'll go into the studio to do a live bit.'

'OK,' she said, opening a file in the computer. 'You'll be the top story. Dictate, I'll write it in.'

'Some breaking news for you as we go on air tonight,' Dan said quickly. 'Within the last few minutes, a man's been arrested on suspicion of the murder of the famous artist Joseph McCluskey. Our Crime Correspondent Dan Groves is here and can tell us more. That'll do. Now I'll go work out what to say.'

6.23. Dan's mind spun with what he could report. He strode into the studio and sat down heavily at the desk with Craig, the presenter. No more running, he had to save his breath for the live broadcast. Jerry, the floor manager clipped a microphone onto his tie, wiped the sweat off his forehead and began dabbing some powder on to his face to stop him shining under the banks of lights.

6.24, four minutes to on air. He could feel his heart pumping, his brain racing. Dan grabbed his notebook and started scribbling some words. Careful, must be careful, he warned himself. You've got to tell the story, but an arrest means the case is legally underway. We're at risk of committing contempt of court if we say anything that could prejudice the investigation. Jerry filled a glass with water and Dan took a grateful swig, let its coolness calm him. He carried on writing, fast.

6.26. Just two minutes to go now. A couple of engineers slid the cameras into position to take shots of him and Craig together at the desk. Lights above them flared and died as

Eddie checked they were both evenly lit. Dan crossed out a couple of sentences on his pad, added some other words. He took another gulp of water. 'What do I ask you?' said Craig calmly.

Dan looked up from his notes. 'Two questions. First, what more do we know about what's happened. Second, what's the background to it?'

'Thirty seconds to air. Stand by,' called Jerry. Dan scanned through the words he'd written for the last time. They'd do. They'd have to.

The opening titles of the programme played and Craig came in.

'Good evening, and welcome to *Wessex Tonight*, with me, Craig Watson. The headlines...' A pause, waiting for Eddie's cue as the pictures rolled.

'Tourist tax shock; charge condemned for putting visitors off.' Another pause, another cue. 'In urgent need of a bypass; when will Cornwall's biggest bottleneck be eased?' Another second's wait, the pictures changing again. 'And the Dorset hamster who can play cricket...'

The rest of the titles ran, artistic images of some of the region's most recognisable landmarks. An aerial shot of the Advent Project, the St Ives lifeboat crashing through waves, Dartmoor's Hay Tor, Land's End, the lonely Isle of Portland stretching into the sea. The music faded and Craig picked up with the cue Dan had dictated a few minutes before.

'But we begin tonight with some breaking news...' Dan didn't hear the words, was concentrating on going through his lines. Deep breath. Don't gabble, sound rushed or excited. Just keep it calm and professional. He could feel a sweat spreading from the base of his back.

'Craig, I can tell you that detectives have arrested a man on suspicion of the murder of Joseph McCluskey. He is Lewis Kiddey, widely known as Kid, who is also a famous artist from Plymouth.'

Dan had been tempted to go into the colour of their relationship, that they'd had a feud until the reconciliation prompted by McCluskey's terminal illness. But he knew that would be pushing his luck. It could be prejudicial, imply a motive to kill. He stuck to safer ground.

'Mr Kiddey was friends with Mr McCluskey and his wife Abi and often used to visit their home. It was he who found Joseph McCluskey's body on the night he died. Now, as we know, the police weren't sure whether Mr McCluskey had committed suicide, so they began an investigation. That inquiry has just taken a dramatic turn with the arrest of Mr Kiddey.'

That'll do, Dan thought. It told the story without being legally dangerous. That bit about Kid going round and finding the body was slightly dodgy, but it didn't in any way imply guilt, so he thought it'd be OK.

'And what's the background to what happened?' Craig asked.

Safer ground now, he could relax a little. 'Joseph McCluskey was terminally ill with cancer. When he discovered he was dying, he began painting what became known as the Death Pictures, a set of 10 works containing a riddle. They've become very famous, but so far no one has solved it. The last picture was unveiled only this week. Mr McCluskey clearly did like to create a stir and a mystery and he succeeded. Now, even though he's gone, another mystery surrounds him. Exactly how did he die?'

'Dan, thank you,' said Craig, turning from him to the camera to read the introduction to the next report. 'Other news now, and plans for a tourist tax in Torbay have caused uproar today...'

Dan walked slowly back up to the newsroom, getting his breath back, letting his heart settle. He noticed his hands were shaking. Lizzie stood by her desk, her eyes on the door, waiting for him. An eyebrow was raised like an arch.

'Are we really saying he could have been murdered?' A three-inch heel ground into the carpet. 'What the hell's the point of killing someone who's going to die in a few days anyway?'

'The very question the police are asking themselves,' replied Dan, sitting on the edge of a desk opposite her. 'And I don't know is the answer.' She gave him one of her looks. 'No, really, I don't. I don't think the police do yet.'

'Then you'd better go find out, hadn't you? I want wall-to-wall coverage on this.'

She was off, into full flow. It didn't take long. Nought to breathless in a couple of seconds, he thought.

'I couldn't have created a better story myself,' Lizzie fizzed. 'It's got everything. A famous artist, dying, sets an unsolvable mystery, apparently kills himself and then the police find out it's actually a murder. The viewers will love it.'

The heel got to work again. 'They'll be glued to their sets. Glued! Absolutely glued! So go on then, what are you waiting for? Go join their investigation, like they asked. I want all the inside track. I want every in and out. I want each little detail. I want a story a night, if not more.' She paused, raked him with another machine gun stare. 'But remember, you're a hack, not a detective. I want stories. I don't want you disappearing for days like you did in the Bray case. Stories are what you're paid for, stories…'

Dan turned and headed for the door.

Suzanne Stewart sat in the MIR, staring out at the ruined church and thinking back over the day. Had she been talking to the rapist? Was it Will Godley? Should she have arrested him? No, of course not, not yet anyway. They had no evidence. So he didn't have an alibi and wouldn't take a DNA test, so what? That didn't mean it was him. But it did make him their main suspect.

His attitude had made her suspicious from the start. 'Mr Godley, I'm sorry to disturb you, but it's only a couple of routine questions.'

'Don't disturb me then. I don't like you slaves of the stinking State and I don't like women and you're both.'

She'd had a moment to study him as he made a cup of tea at his office in the dockyard. Yes, he just about fitted the description. Medium height, the women had said, probably about five feet nine or ten. Godley was a little taller than that, but she knew from long experience the descriptions given by traumatised people were often only vaguely accurate. Stocky build? Well he wasn't fat, but he was going that way. That was all they had. That, and the faint smell of tobacco. And here was Godley, rolling himself a cigarette.

'What do you want me for anyway? Haven't you got a rapist to catch?'

Godley talked with a sneer, the ever present hint of an impending outburst of anger. She backed off a little, warily. Suzanne had come alone. They didn't have enough detectives for them to double up and she thought there'd be plenty of people around in the dockyard. But it was lunchtime and there were just the two of them in this Portakabin office. She tensed herself, ready to fight or flee. But he just sat down on a desk and glared at her.

'That's exactly what we're trying to do Mr Godley.' She kept her voice level, firm but reasonable. 'Please understand, this is just a routine inquiry.'

'It's that Fathers for Families who put you lot on to me, isn't it?' Suzanne said nothing. 'Well I've had a guts full of them,' Godley went on. 'Them and their pathetic pantomime dressing up and waving banners. It'll take a lot more than that to change the system.'

She couldn't help herself. 'A revolution?'

'Yeah, something like that.' For the first time, Godley looked surprised. He got up from the desk to stub his cigarette out and throw it in the bin. 'Two sons I've got. Or had, I should say. I'm lucky to see them twice a year now.'

He stared out of the window at the stooping cranes, swinging supplies and stores to a sleek grey frigate, F98 stencilled black on her bow.

'The court gave me weekends, once a fortnight,' Godley spat. 'The standard shit. Once a bloody fortnight! But even then, every time she's got some excuse. Some sickness, some emergency, something from work comes up that means it can't happen. Sometimes they're just not in when I call round. And when I get so pissed off I go back to court, you know what happens?'

He turned to stare at her, his eyes wide, clenching and

unclenching his fists.

'The judge calls her in and tells her she must make sure I can see the boys. That's it. And then I get to see them the next week, and after that, it's back to the same thing again. Pathetic.'

She had to get back to the point, didn't have time to debate the workings of the family courts. Suzanne knew them anyway. Adrian and his battles to see his young daughter, an ex wife lonely and jealous that he was happy in a new relationship, Tasmin the only remaining weapon she had to hurt him. Yes, she knew what could happen. She'd seen the frustration, even despair in Adrian. The courts never punished mothers because it could harm the children. Yes, she could understand what made men so embittered. But this wasn't the time to talk about it. Three rapes so far. Three witch's hats from a pack of six. Three more rapes planned. DCI Breen on the phone every hour.

Suzanne tried again. 'Mr Godley, I appreciate it must be difficult...'

His fist slamming into the wall silenced her. 'Difficult!!' Godley's voice was hoarse with rage. 'Have you got kids?' She shook her head. 'Then don't tell me it's difficult.'

His voice fell, quieter now, but each word spat out. 'It's not difficult. It's impossible. It's torture. Those boys are growing up strangers to me. My sons!! And you know what she's telling them? She's telling them I hate them and don't want to see them. She's telling them I hate her and used to beat her. I'm an evil man. God knows what she's telling them.'

His knuckles were clenched white, his breathing loud. 'So... please... don't... come in here... and tell me... it's... difficult.'

'I'm sorry Mr Godley, I didn't mean to upset you,' Suzanne said, as soothingly as she could. 'But we have an investigation to conduct and it would help if we could rule you out. If you wouldn't mind giving us a sample of your hair or saliva for a DNA test, that would be the easiest way.' He stared at her, shaking his head a little now, as if in pity. 'And if you could tell me where you were when...?'

'No,' he interrupted, the word quiet but emphatic. 'I can't remember where I was whenever it was and I'm not giving you any sample of anything. No one from the so-called authorities helps me. I'm not helping them.'

What would Adam Breen have made of it, she wondered? He would have treated Godley in his usual calm but clever way, spotted any little evasions or signs that he was lying. Or would he have been so calm? Wasn't something about this case getting to him? What about that brief conversation they'd had earlier?

'How's it going Suzanne?'

'OK, sir. We've got some leads and we've eliminated quite a few people, so we're making progress. Did you want a briefing?'

He'd smiled then, but not with any humour. 'No Suzanne, you handle it. You're a fine detective, you'll get him. Just make sure you do. The High Honchos are all over me with the McCluskey case. I think they're worried about the media coverage and they want it settled. Well, that's their priority. But it's basically a murder inquiry about a dying man. Whereas what you're doing…'

She'd thought he was going to say something else then, and wondered what it was. He'd turned away, tapped a hand on the felt boards and pictures of the victims. 'Well, I'm fully behind you and any help or resources you need, I'll make sure you get them.'

That gave her an idea how she'd handle Godley. If he wanted to be awkward, fine. They could be awkward too. Time for a little pressure. Some very obvious surveillance, so in his face as to be bordering on harassment.

Plymouth's finest fancy dress shop is on Ebrington Street, just outside the centre of the city. Silver racks of clothes of all materials, colours and periods of history fill its walls, hats and helmets hang from the ceiling, shoes and boots scattered on the floor. It feels like the debris from an explosion triggered by the impossible collision of so many countless eras and lifestyles. That Monday afternoon, Dirty El picked his way

131

carefully through to the counter, only once tripping over a thigh length fisherman's wader that snaked out from under some boxes.

Under his breath, he hummed a tune and ad-libbed a limerick.

'A snapper can need lots of faces,
As he goes through his paces,
So he dons a disguise,
To avoid watching eyes,
And fills up the tabloids' blank spaces!'

They knew El well here. He was a frequent and loyal customer and they even had a couple of cuttings he'd inspired on the wall. The manager's favourite was the one about the black suit and tie he'd borrowed. It was designed to be part of a Blues Brothers outfit. El had used it to dress as an undertaker, hired a black estate car and talked his way past a gullible constable on sentry duty to get access to the scene of a double murder in Cornwall.

The pictures he took had made most of the national papers and paid for a fine holiday in America. The grateful photographer had sent them the articles. One was gruesome, from the *Gazette*, it had a series of El's pictures and a story about the killing. The next was from the *Western Daily News*, about the police investigation into how the photographer got to the scene.

'How can we help you, El?' asked the manager, shaking his hand warmly. 'A doctor's white coat and stethoscope too if we've got one, eh? Yes, that shouldn't be a problem. They're popular with stag parties and we've got a few in. Yes, I think they're pretty convincing. Do you want a fake name badge as well? How long will you need it for?'

Dan lay on his great blue sofa that night, Rutherford at his feet, a glass of rye whisky on ice on the table in front of him. He didn't often drink spirits, but after that panic to get the arrest story on air his nerves needed calming and he didn't think beer would be strong enough to do the job. Plus whisky always sent him to sleep and he could do with a good night's rest. Tomorrow would be busy. He was joining Adam on the McCluskey investigation.

The Death Pictures surrounded him. Some were spread out on the coffee table, some on the sofa, some on the floor by Rutherford. He'd had a chance earlier to check the grid references, any possible PIN numbers or harbour quays, but hadn't come up with anything. The idea about the Bible being the key to a book code hadn't worked either.

There'd been no time to research the streets with missing houses, so that was the next job. In the meantime, another look at the pictures could always prompt some new ideas. None came. Dan knew he wasn't concentrating. He was staring at the pictures, but thinking about McCluskey and whether he could have been murdered. Why kill a dying man was Lizzie's question, and as ever she'd hit the target in one. Why?

Dan checked through the briefing notes on Kid and the stories he'd printed off from the News Library. One thing was sure. The man didn't look like a killer. Far from it. But then, as Adam always said, you never knew.

The first mentions of him were brief, as a pupil of McCluskey's with a 'budding talent' according to one article on an exhibition he'd contributed to in Exeter. It didn't sound too promising for the start of a career. Given a journalist's tendency to hype anything they covered to try to get readers interested, it was more like damned with almost imperceptible praise.

There were a couple more articles in which he won a few lines about works being shown at various galleries, nothing of real interest. Then a turn of the page and a surprise.

'Plymouth Artist Arrested in Dirty Water Protest,' ran the headline in the cutting from the *Standard*. Kid had led a group of anti-poverty protesters to daub the government offices in the city with a delightful mix of their own urine and excrement. Then they'd waited around to be arrested. They were pictured with banners, sitting outside the once pristine office.

"This is to remind our government that millions of people in this world have to drink water which is horribly polluted,"

Kid was quoted as saying. "So we thought we'd give our beloved government some specially polluted water of our own."

Interesting Dan thought, putting down the papers and lying back, stretching out his neck. So the man had a criminal past. But it wasn't exactly anything violent, was it? Nothing that would suggest he could become a killer.

He rubbed Rutherford's ear and was rewarded with an appreciative whine and yawn. Dan picked up the notes again. There were a couple more *Standard* cuttings, smaller stories this time, both on poverty protests featuring Kid. In one they'd poured maize into the fuel tanks of some cars in the dockyard, apparently to make the point that a handful of grain was all many people had to live on. Another had been an egg-throwing incident at some visiting government minister, a protest so unoriginal it only merited a few lines of copy.

Then came the big story. Dan had to read it, then re-read it, then put it down and read it again, so extraordinary was the headline.

"US President Attacks Plymouth Artist"

A journalist on a local paper doesn't get to write that very often he thought, as he wandered out to the kitchen to refill his glass. It was one of those perfect headlines that meant you just had to read the story underneath. Settling back on the sofa, savouring the golden whisky, he read the report. It was the story of how Kid became famous.

An economic summit of the world's most powerful leaders was being held in London and the government had launched a competition for artists to produce a work to mark the occasion. Nice idea, but they had, thought Dan, made one very obvious error. Instead of getting some tame and reliable civil servant to choose a winner, they'd left it to a popular vote. And Kid had won.

There was a picture of what he'd come up with. Dan stared, then laughed out loud, swallowed some whisky and had to run choking to the bathroom, holding onto the sink, still laughing and trying not to be sick while his throat burned. Rutherford padded after him, watched in what he was sure was a concerned way. 'I'm OK, mate, really I am,' he reassured the dog breathlessly, patting his sleek head.

Dan sat back down on the sofa and looked again at the picture. He couldn't stop chuckling. It was full colour, a good quality image, but what it couldn't convey would have been the smell.

Kid had created a ten feet high replica of the Statue of Liberty, but made it from cheeseburgers. The story explained how they were held together by metal rods running through the sculpture, but that it was designed to rot. The picture made very clear it was doing just that. Red sauce congealed as though frozen, some still dripped, stringy lettuce dangled brown and bread greened at its edges, like organic verdigris. The one part that hadn't rotted was the statue's arm, gold-sprayed metal, aloft. But instead of holding a torch of freedom, there were two insulting fingers.

"I wouldn't go too much into what it means. I think you can work that out for yourself," Kid said in an interview to celebrate his success. "But look at it this way. At a time when America is spreading its so-called culture everywhere and using up as much of the planet's scarce resources as it wants without any consideration of what it might be doing in the way of climate change, somebody needs to point that out."

A great story in itself, but here was the snow on the summit. The US President is asked about the sculpture in a press conference. He calls it 'an irrelevant and pathetic attempt by a nobody artist to smear the reputation of a proud country.' My, he must have been in a bad mood, thought Dan. From that moment on, Kid's fame was assured.

After that there were many more mentions, but no more arrests. He spoke at rallies, led marches, donated money to good causes, but seemed to be devoting his efforts to peaceful protest. Kid continued painting and his fame made the works desirable and his profession lucrative. But he stayed in Plymouth – the old 'close to his roots, won't let it change me story' – and continued campaigning against poverty.

Dan sat back again and closed his eyes, tried to imagine what could have turned someone like that into a killer. What was the feud between him and McCluskey, and what could have happened in the house to make Kid kill him? That question again, the one that had no answer. Why murder a dying man?

Adam seemed certain Kid was the killer and he'd know soon enough now. The detective had called earlier, sounded jaded.

'Did you get it on air?' Adam asked.

'Yes, just about. Thanks for the tip.' Dan didn't mention he'd only just started to relax again. 'What are you up to now?'

'I'm going home. There's not much point questioning Kid tonight. I'd prefer a decent, uninterrupted session with him tomorrow. I'm going to leave him in the cells to sleep on it and have a nice think about things. It might soften him up a little.'

'When you say home, that's...?'

'The flat.'

'So no...?'

'No. Not yet anyway. We had some good time together at the weekend, but it was difficult with this rape case going on. I think Annie could sense I wasn't quite there with her. So I'm going to stay in the flat for now and we'll see how it goes.'

A pause, then a comical moment. 'I was wondering...' both said at the same time.

'Go ahead,' continued Adam.

Dan was tempted to say 'no, you,' but thought it would sound like a teenage romantic.

'You know you said I could come and join the inquiry again? How does tomorrow suit you?' he asked.

'Funny, I was going to say the same thing myself. The Assistant Chief Constable asked me unsubtly about our 'media strategy' earlier. I think they're desperate for some good publicity. So you're in. Charles Cross at nine tomorrow? It'll be good to have you back along. I'll be interested to see what you make of Kid. I'm not sure I understand you creative types. You might give us a way in to the man.'

Chapter Ten

DAN DROVE IN TO the entrance to the police station at just before nine the next morning. He stared up at the familiar five-storey grey block and remembered the first time he'd been here, on the Bray case and how nervous he'd felt. Now it was very different. He couldn't suppress a growing excitement and anticipation at joining another investigation. The metal-rung gate ground up and he was about to park the car when he was surprised to see Adam come striding out to meet him. The detective opened the passenger door and climbed in.

'Let's go,' was all he said.

'What? Where?' asked Dan. 'I thought we were interviewing Kid?'

'Later. We've got to see Abi McCluskey first. She had another attempted break-in at the house last night and she's got something she wants to tell us. She wouldn't say any more on the phone. She said it had to be in person. I want to get this one wrapped up and sorted. I had a nightmare that bloody rapist attacked Annie last night. I can feel him out there, waiting to strike again.'

Dan turned the car round and headed past the ruined church, up the hill and out of the city centre. They drove through Mutley Plain and on to Royal Gardens. The traffic was slow and lethargic coming in to the city, but thin the way they were going. Adam stared sightlessly ahead, his fingers drumming on the dashboard.

'Any more you can tell me?' Dan asked hopefully.

'Not much,' he replied. 'We were called to her place in the early hours. She reported a downstairs window had been smashed. She went to investigate and says she saw a figure running away across the lawn. We sent a car straight round. It looks like the window was hit with a jemmy or metal bar of some kind. We didn't find any prints again.'

'The rapist?' asked Dan. 'Or something to do with McCluskey's death? Or connected with that other attempted break-in?'

'Or all three,' said Adam, checking through a pile of notes on his lap. 'Whatever, something odd's going on. Let's go find out.'

A young police family liaison officer opened the door. He had one of those thin, comical moustaches that young men grow to try to give themselves more authority. 'She's in the lounge, sir,' he said quietly. 'In quite a state.'

'Thanks, Mike,' said Adam. 'Would you mind getting us some tea and coffee?' The man nodded and disappeared into the kitchen, taking off the cap he'd donned in anticipation of the arrival of a senior officer.

Abi McCluskey had curled herself up into a ball in the corner of her sofa. Her legs were tucked under her, her arms folded and she was leaning forwards on them. The room was full of 'With Sympathy' cards, or deepest or most sincere sympathy, as though trying to outbid each other in their grief. A series of McCluskey's paintings hung on the walls. Dan nodded as he looked around. He'd made a bet with himself the artist wouldn't have other painters' works here.

'Hello again, Abi,' said Adam, sitting on a chair. 'You know Dan, don't you?'

'Yes.' Her voice was faint and trembling. She didn't ask what he was doing here.

Adam explained. 'Dan's been attached to the investigation into Joseph's death to help the media provide accurate coverage. I hope that's OK with you?'

'Yes. Fine. Whatever.'

Dan sat down on a chair in the bay window, out of the way. Best leave this one to Adam, he thought. He wasn't good at dealing with emotions, particularly when it came to women. A quick jabbing thought of Kerry and the scene in the restaurant surprised him.

'I know it must be a very difficult time for you, losing Joseph, then our investigation into his death, then this attempted break-in,' said Adam in a soft voice. She nodded, picked hard at a toenail.

Adam studied a sheet of paper, then spoke. 'I've got your

138

statement about what happened earlier. Is there anything else you can add?'

'No.'

'You didn't have any sense of what the person was like? A man or woman? Big or small? Young or old? Even a smell they might have left? Like tobacco for example?'

'No. I just saw the broken glass,' she gestured through the door and to the dining room, 'and this shape running across the lawn.'

Adam noted that down. Dan knew if this had been an ordinary attempted burglary, the report would have been filed and forgotten, no hope of any progress. But not here, not with the suspicious death of a famous figure, the prospect of a reward worth more than a hundred thousand pounds for the person who solved his riddle and a serial rapist on the loose.

'Abi, I can see you've got some of Joseph's pictures on your walls. But is there anything else here someone might be desperate to steal?' Adam asked. Dan could see he was following the same thoughts. Not for the first time, he found himself reflecting how the job of the journalist and detective weren't so very different. 'Is the answer to the riddle here?' Adam continued.

She shook her head slowly. 'No. It's in the safety deposit box in the bank. The only copy.'

Dan had expected that and saw Adam had too. McCluskey would have suspected someone might try to find a short cut to the answer. If it hadn't been for the fruitless hours he'd spent trying to solve the man's riddle Dan would have respected him even more.

Abi McCluskey drew her legs closer. She looked pale, exhausted, eyes dark, no make-up, no jewellery, wearing just jeans and an old T-shirt. It had 'The Waterside Arms, Beer Festival 2002' printed on it. Dan would love to have asked… could he ask? Was it something to do with the Waterside? Just a little clue…

He checked himself. He was here on trust, in a murder inquiry. It was scarcely the time to start asking about McCluskey's riddle. But still, as he was here, it was too good an opportunity to miss.

Abi's attention was on Adam, so he subtly – he hoped – scrutinised the room. There was nothing that seemed to be a link to any of the numbers or places. The only obvious well-known book was an Oxford English Dictionary of quotations by the fireplace. Still, it was an idea. He had one at home, the same edition. What was on page 98? He got out his handkerchief, pretended to dab at his nose, then tied a knot in it. It would remind him later.

'Abi, we've almost finished disturbing you.' Adam lowered his voice. 'But there is one more thing I've got to ask.'

She stopped picking her toes and looked up at him. Suddenly frightened, Dan thought. Her eyes certainly looked wary, flicking from Adam over to him, then back again. What was she scared of?

'You said you had something else to tell us,' continued Adam. 'What was it?'

Her eyes were back on her feet. Remarkably tiny, thought Dan, perhaps size four. A soft pink varnish on the nails.

'Was it to do with Joseph's death?' She nodded, not looking up. 'Abi,' said Adam, his voice more urgent. 'Was it to do with Kid?'

She nodded again, but said nothing. Dan waited, Adam too, used the pressure of silence, pushing her to fill it. They could sense the words were near. She was gathering herself to tell them. It was important, they knew that now.

'He was going to let him know.' Her voice was so soft Dan had to strain to hear, but he didn't want to move forwards, risk breaking the moment. 'Sorry, Abi, who?' asked Adam. 'Who was going to let who know?'

She looked up and her voice was stronger. 'Joseph... Joseph was going to let Kid know.'

Another pause, then Adam prompted, 'What? Let him know what?'

'Let him know that he... he had to... he had to say it.'

'What? Say what Abi?'

'To get it off his chest... to clear it up... before he... before

140

he died.'

'What? Say what? How?'

'He was going to record some talks about his life… Joseph was… the story of his life… and he was going to tell Kid… tell Kid he'd have to put it in.'

The door opened and the police officer walked in with a tray of mugs. He was about to speak when he caught Adam's look, hurriedly put the tray down and left again.

'Sorry, Abi,' continued Adam gently. 'What was Joseph going to tell Kid?'

She stood up from her chair, took one of the cups, blew on it, then sipped at the steaming liquid. She stared out of the window for a few seconds, then turned back to Adam, the words coming in a rush.

'You have to understand that Joseph was well aware he was a great painter, Mr Breen. He knew many people would want to study and read about him when he was gone. He knew his life had often been controversial. So much had been written about him, he wanted to put his own side of everything before he died. He was going to record it all in a series of tapes, for whoever might want to use them after his death. He was determined every word had to be the truth, no spin, nothing like that, a full and honest account of all that he'd done and why.'

Adam stood up too. 'I understand Abi. But what was it that he was going to tell Kid? What was so important?'

Abi McCluskey put down her drink, then breathed out a long sigh. 'I have to tell you, Mr Breen. I know I do. It's not easy, but I know I have to tell you.'

Adam let the silence run, then prompted, 'What is it Abi? What do you have to tell me?'

She nodded slowly, closed her eyes for a second, then spoke.

'Kid copied him. He copied Joseph's idea. For the sculpture. The sculpture Kid did that won the national competition. The one that made him famous. The rotting burger one. The Statue of Liberty one. That was Joseph's idea… Joseph's… and Kid copied it.'

141

*　　*　　*

Will Godley sauntered out of his terraced house in the Coxside area of Plymouth to find a police car parked on the road outside. A smartly uniformed, middle-aged officer was leaning against the bonnet smiling. 'Good morning, sir,' he said cheerily.

'Morning,' replied Godley gruffly, getting into his Escort.

'That your car is it, sir?'

A colourful range of sarcasm and abuse filled his mind, but Will Godley had a feeling it wasn't a good idea to upset this man. 'Yes, officer,' he said, getting back out of the car. 'Is there a problem?'

'No, no problem, sir,' the man replied. 'I've checked your tax and tyres. They're all in order.' He ignored the frown that produced. 'No, it's just that I've been given this new beat to patrol and I like to get to know the people here, their cars, that sort of thing. It's always good to know the people you're looking after.'

'I quite agree, officer. That's how policing should be, just like the old days.' Godley got back into his car, wound down the window. 'Well, if you'll excuse me, I've got to get to work.'

'Of course, sir. Have a good day now.'

Godley was about to drive off when a thought surfaced. 'So can we expect to see a lot of you, officer? Where is this new beat of yours then?'

'Just here, sir,' said the policeman, still smiling. 'Just right here.'

There were plenty of pretty nurses and one or two with blonde bobs, or flame hair, but they weren't the ones he wanted. He'd paid them close attention though and they'd seemed to enjoy it.

It was funny he thought, how the clothes you wore brought a different reaction to what you did. With his usual fat-lensed camera slung around his neck, and his jeans and battered body-warmer, he'd often produce anger and sometimes even violence in those he was trying to snap. But put on a white

142

coat and a stethoscope and your attentions were suddenly much more welcome. No camera on show of course. He had a small digital model in his pocket, ready to whip out if the moment came. That was all he'd need, the one lucky break.

The oncology ward was his target, but he knew he couldn't hang around it for too long. He'd done a couple of sweeps and that would have to be enough for today. He reckoned that, given the various shift systems, four visits at different times over four or five days should cover just about all the staff without raising suspicion. The place was full of doctors, coming and going. Look like you knew what you were doing and you just blended in. No one ever questioned you. He'd learnt early in his career how powerful a bluff could be. And he'd done it so many times now he was an expert. A Professor of Bluff. Or, in this case, a Doctor.

It was just a hunch of course, but he'd played them before and they'd paid off. It was certainly worth a go. Where else was McCluskey likely to meet someone he could become so close to that he'd want to paint them? And what was he talking about anyway? Close? Sex was what he meant, and sex was what the papers wanted, why he'd been offered such a lucrative pile of cash to snap McCluskey's last lovers, immortalised in the Death Pictures. Sex sells, it was as simple as that.

He didn't intend to miss out on such a juicy prospect. He could feel the sun on his face as he lay in the deck chair on the beach sipping a pina colada, in... Where would it be this time? Greece? Spain? Somewhere more exotic? The Bahamas? The money that was on offer would fund the break easily and leave plenty left over too.

He walked back along the tiled corridor towards the lift and exit. That was enough for day one. OK, he hadn't found her, but there were plenty more chances ahead. Patience, that was the watchword of the paparazzi. Patience. His time would come.

Dirty El looked down at his name badge as he got into the lift. The fancy dress shop was right. It was convincing. Dr McCoy he'd decided on for himself. It was a slight risk, but he liked that little touch, couldn't resist it. What was life for without a bit of fun? He could almost hear Captain Kirk calling him.

'There's your motive,' said Adam, as Dan drove them back to Charles Cross. He stretched out in the passenger seat and straightened his tie. He looked annoyingly relaxed now, a transformation of his earlier mood. 'I think you'll have another good story tonight. Yesterday an arrest, today a murder charge.'

The traffic was crawling through Mutley Plain, down to one lane because of a delivery to a bar. They passed the Old Bank pub, a window cleaner working hard at the glass, fresh white suds sopping onto the pavement. 'There might even be time for a celebratory drink tonight,' Adam continued, following Dan's look. 'The High Honchos will be delighted and I can get back to the real business of catching the rapist. Everyone happy.'

'Mmm,' mused Dan. Something was bothering him, but he couldn't see what. Was it that the image he'd built up of Kid didn't make him feel like a killer? 'Tell me how you imagine it, then,' he asked.

Adam closed his eyes. 'Kid goes round as arranged. He's expecting just to have a couple of drinks and a friendly chat. They'll talk about the last Death Picture. One artist to another, as it were. But as we know, McCluskey was into clearing up his unfinished business. Taping talks about his life is part of that, as Abi's just told us. I'm guessing McCluskey told Kid he was going to record the thing about the sculpture being his idea. Kid panics. He's about to be exposed. It'll be revealed that his most famous work wasn't his own idea. You know what these arty types think of plagiarism. In one moment, Kid's reputation was going to be destroyed. So he killed McCluskey and made it look like a suicide.'

'Mmmm,' said Dan again, tapping a finger on the steering wheel. 'How did he do it, then?'

Adam shuffled his notes, found the page he was looking for. 'We know McCluskey was very close to the end of his life. The cancer was taking its toll. He was on big doses of morphine and weakening fast. The autopsy found lots of the drug in his bloodstream, along with some alcohol. Abi told us he liked a few drinks in the evening. That combination must have made him very weak. I don't know exactly how it happened, but Kid grabs the knife and either threatens McCluskey with it, or forces him upstairs somehow. Then he runs the bath, pushes him in and cuts his wrists. McCluskey dies quickly because of his condition and the drugs and booze.'

It sounded convincing enough thought Dan, but... but what? It was fast thinking on Kid's part, wasn't it? Fast and extremely cunning. To invent a plan that would make murder look like suicide in just a few seconds. Could he himself have done that? Probably not, but then Adam had warned him never to be surprised by what desperate people could do.

'Wouldn't the autopsy have found some marks on McCluskey if he was forced to do all that?' Dan asked. 'And wouldn't Kid have blood on him?'

Adam nodded sagely. 'There were marks. Bruises on McCluskey's wrists, arms and knees, as though he'd been dragged upstairs. There were bruises on his shoulders, as if he'd been kept pressed down in the bath. It wouldn't have taken that much force to get McCluskey to move. He might have been so weak it needed hardly any. And as for blood, when you cut someone's wrists, it doesn't spurt out. It just flows, and fast if the body's hot as it would have been from the bath. It's the old classic way of committing suicide. Kid wouldn't have had blood on him if he did it carefully. Then he just sits there, makes sure McCluskey doesn't try to escape and watches him die.'

Dan found himself still struggling to imagine it. 'What about Kid's prints on the knife? Were they conclusive?'

'Absolutely. The knife handle had been wiped, as you'd expect. Criminals know to do that. They're not stupid and they've seen it all on TV. But sometimes they miss something and I think that's what happened here. McCluskey's prints were on the knife, but there was also one other clean and clear print too, right up by the blade. We'd taken Kid's prints as a matter of routine because he found the body – or claimed to have. It's a perfect match. I reckon Kid wiped the knife, then pressed McCluskey's fingers around it so his prints would be there and it would look like suicide. But he missed that tell tale one of his own. The one that tells us it wasn't suicide, but murder.'

Dan had to admit it sounded like a good case. There was just one more thing nagging at him. 'So where does the attempted break in the night McCluskey died fit in? And the other one, come to that? And the rapist?'

'No idea,' said Adam as they turned into the police station. 'Maybe they don't at all. Maybe the attempted break ins were just someone trying to get in and find a hint about the solution to the riddle. A painting worth more than a hundred grand is a pretty powerful lure. Or they could just have been mundane attempted burglaries. And as for the rapist, I doubt very much it was him. His attacks have been carefully planned. He goes for women, alone with their kids. He wouldn't have picked McCluskey's place to try to get in. It just doesn't fit with his targets.'

Unless that's what we're meant to think, said Dan to himself, too quietly for Adam to hear.

The interview room was the same one they'd solved the Bray case in. A low grey concrete ceiling seemed to loom oppressively just above Dan's head. The whitewash of the brick walls was slapdash, smeared with vague streaks of faded colour, tinted green by the buzzing strip light in the centre of the ceiling. At the end of the room, a tiny oblong barred window allowed in just a hint of the world outside. It was always cold, whatever the weather, and echoed with every word or movement.

Kid was sitting at the table and jumped up when Adam walked in, Dan following.

'What the hell am I doing in here?' he shouted, gesturing wildly. 'I demand to be freed. I've done nothing. This is outrageous...'

146

Adam ignored him, let his anger blow itself out as he settled himself on one of the two chairs on the side of the table nearest the door. Dan stood behind him. The plastic chairs were uncomfortable and besides, on the television, one cop always stood while the other sat.

'Good morning, Mr Kiddey,' said Adam pleasantly, looking up at him. 'Why don't you sit down?' Kid stared silently at him, then did.

He was in his early 40s Dan guessed, neither fat nor thin, about five feet ten tall. He ticked off one question on his mental list. Kid would certainly be strong enough to force a dying McCluskey into a bath and hold him there.

He wore a flamboyant shirt that looked like its pattern was simply random sprays of bright colour. It reminded Dan of Loud. His face was long and thin, his hair blond and cropped short, almost a crew-cut. His skin seemed pale. Naturally so, or because he knew he was a killer about to be uncovered, Dan wondered? He wore a small silver stud in his left ear and another on the left side of his nose. Kid's hand trembled over an ashtray full of a pile of discarded roll-up cigarettes. He still didn't look like a murderer, but Adam was right, you never could tell. When he'd mentioned the man's campaigning against poverty and charitable work to Adam in the car, the detective was entirely unruffled. Look at all the doctors who became killers, he'd said.

'I'd like to ask you about what happened when you went to see Mr McCluskey,' began Adam, fishing a piece of paper out of his case.

'You know what happened. You've taken a statement.'

Adam leaned forwards and stared into the man's eyes. 'Tell me yourself. I want to hear it in your words.'

Kid stared back at him, then looked down at the table and shifted in his chair. 'Can I get a coffee?'

'When you've told me what happened.'

Kid took a deep breath, fiddled with his earring. 'It's just like I said. We'd arranged that I was to go round on Thursday night.'

'Who arranged?' interrupted Adam. 'Why?'

'Joseph invited me. He said he wanted to see what I thought of the last of the pictures. He also said he had something else to talk to me about, but wouldn't say what. Just that he was sure I'd be interested.'

The plagiarism of his idea, thought Dan. Adam's theory is holding together. He shifted towards the door a little to get a clearer view of Kid's face.

'OK,' said Adam, scribbling down a note. 'So what happened that evening?'

Another deep breath. 'I've told you all this.'

'Tell us again.'

'Are you sure I can't get a coffee?'

Adam's look made him continue.

'I went round there at about 7.45, as we'd arranged. I knocked on the door, but there was no answer. So I pushed the door and it was open. I went in and shouted that I was there.'

'Was that unusual? Not getting an answer and the door being open?'

Kid shook his head. 'No, it's happened before. They used to like sitting in the garden at the back of the house. They couldn't hear a knock there.'

Adam scribbled another note. 'Go on.'

'I stood in the hallway shouting for a minute, but there was still no answer. So I went into the lounge and looked out into the garden, but there was no sign of either Joseph or Abi. I started to get worried in case something had happened. You know his condition?' Adam nodded. 'So I had a look around. I thought I heard something upstairs so I went up. The door to the bathroom was open and that was where I saw...'

Kid's words faded and his chest heaved. He lifted his head up, stared at the blank, low, ceiling. He seemed to struggle to breathe.

'What did you find, Mr Kiddey?' Adam wasn't giving him a second to think. 'What?'

Another heave of the chest. 'You know.' His voice was shaking now. 'You know damn well what I found. You saw it.'

'Tell me.'

'I found Joseph McCluskey lying dead in his bath! That's what I fucking found, all right? I found him dead, and blood everywhere. All right?!'

Adam looked down at his papers, scribbled another note, let the silence run. Kid's face was glowing. He couldn't stop fiddling with his earring.

'Did you see a knife?' snapped Adam.

'What?'

'A knife.'

'Yes.'

'Where?'

'On the bathroom floor. Next to…'

'Did you touch it?'

'What?'

'Did you touch it?'

Kid stared at Adam as if he was a fool.

'Of course I didn't touch it! I just ran downstairs and called you.'

'You're sure about that? You're sure you didn't touch the knife?'

'Yes! Of course! Quite sure!'

Adam stared at him, let the silence run again. Dan could feel his heart pounding. He could sense the trap closing.

'You're absolutely certain you did not touch the knife?'

Kid slapped the table. 'Yes! Of course!'

Adam nodded, stared into him, waited, waited, waited for the moment.

'Then how come that knife has your fingerprint on it, Mr Kiddey?'

Kid's eyes widened. His mouth moved but no sound came out.

'What?' he gasped.

'How come the knife which cut Joseph McCluskey's wrists had your fingerprint on it, Mr Kiddey? Can you explain that?'

Kid sat there, gazing at Adam, shaking his head. His mouth opened and closed. Dan thought he could hear a faint, 'No, no, no, no, no, no, no…'

'Later today, Mr Kiddey, I'm going to charge you with the

murder of Joseph McCluskey,' said Adam, getting up and walking towards the door. 'Nothing will change that. But I'm going to leave you to have a little think. Because if you tell us what really happened – about what Mr McCluskey said to you regarding the idea you stole – and how you rowed and killed him, then I can tell the judge that in your favour. And that'll mean you'll get out of prison in – oh, shall we say – 15 years or so? Wouldn't you say Dan? 15 years?'

From the safety of his wall, Dan nodded. He knew what was expected, could play the part. 'Yes, about 15 years I'd say. Roughly 15. As opposed to, well at least 20 if we have to go through a trial.'

'Oh, at least 20,' said Adam pleasantly, as a uniformed policeman slipped in through the door to take Kid back to the cells. 'At least. Judges don't like the victim's family and friends having to go through the ordeal of re-living their murder in a court. It's almost like committing the offence all over again. No, they don't like it at all. And they hate jealousy as a motive, absolutely hate it. They think it means the murderer could easily do something similar again, you see. They don't like to see people like that released back into the community. In fact, forget your 20 years. It could easily be a whole life tariff.'

Chapter Eleven

SUZANNE RANG THE BELL, heard its metallic buzz echo inside the house. She kept her face towards the door, but slid her eyes to the right, onto the window. The faintest nudge ruffled the net curtains. Like a fisherman getting a hint of a bite, she thought. Another sound, this time a creaking floorboard, but the door remained shut.

A crash echoed along the bricks of the alley by the side of the house. It sounded like a door being flung open. Another noise, this time a voice, shouting, in pain.

'Ow, get off you bastard. Get off!'

That's two prime suspects now thought Suzanne, as the smartly uniformed and usefully muscular police officer bundled him up the alley. He wasn't exactly resisting, but he wasn't cooperating either. He was dragging his feet, making himself a dead weight as he was pulled along. There was a sneer on his face and he managed a couple of half-hearted protests and some light abuse, but the words were tinged with fear.

No more interviewing possible rapists alone, DCI Breen had said, no matter how tight resources were. Never underestimate what these people are capable of when they're cornered. She'd taken Charles Cross's bodybuilding guru, PC Colin Samson, with her and stationed him at the back of the house, just in case. He wasn't renowned as clever, but he was certainly big.

So, there was one basic question that needed answering, and she asked it. 'Mr Freeman, why did you run from us?' Or try to, she thought.

He sipped at the cup of dark canteen coffee and Suzanne took the opportunity to study him. Five feet ten or so, stocky build, yes, it could be him from the description they had. No sign yet he smoked though, and suspects who did usually wanted a fag to ease their nerves as they sat here in the interview room. He could have guessed the police would know their man was a smoker, couldn't he? But was he that bright? He didn't seem so, but you never knew. Clever people could hide it well.

His hair was short, dark, circling a bald ring on the top of his head, his nose flat and wide, as though a flying fist had squashed it. He seemed to peer suspiciously through narrow eyes. Or was that just her imagination? He certainly had the physical power to be a rapist. Did he have the motive and the means? There were those couple of previous convictions, both for assault. It didn't make him a rapist. But it did show he could be violent.

Beware starting to believe this is your man, she told herself. Beware. Work through the evidence and come to a conclusion. Don't guess, assume or prejudge. But the one piece of evidence that would give them a definitive answer she didn't have, and had no right to get. DNA, the golden gift to detectives was only his to give, not hers to take. She couldn't see him volunteering a sample. That scowl said he wasn't in a cooperative mood.

'I thought you'd come 'coz I wasn't paying. I thought you was the bailiffs.'

A man of few words, Suzanne thought. He'd said almost nothing since they'd brought him in. He'd confirmed his name and address, but hadn't even asked why he was here.

His voice was thin and oddly high-pitched, almost a whine, as though it had never truly broken. A clue there? He'd know he had a distinctive voice – would no doubt have been teased about it often enough – so was that why he'd stayed silent with the women he'd attacked?

She checked the file she'd taken from the CSA. Steven Freeman, 34 years old, taxi driver by trade. Married to Julia for 5 years. One son, bitter divorce, maintenance awarded, none received. None at all according to the records. That was the problem with self-employed men, the CSA manager had told her. If they get a salary, we can take the contributions straight out of their pay. But if they've got their own business, making their own money, that's where the system breaks down.

How to play it? He looked worried, kept tapping his feet on the concrete floor, shifting in his seat and checking his watch. Nerves? Or just thinking about a taxiing shift he was planning to put in?

She hadn't told him yet why they'd brought him in. Just a routine suspect to start with, another from the CSA's list of possible woman-haters for them to eliminate. But his attempted get-away had made him much more interesting. Maybe he did think it was because of the missing maintenance payments, but then again... So, take it gently or surprise him? She studied him for a moment, came to a decision.

'I'd like to talk to you about rape, Mr Freeman. A series of rapes in fact.'

His head snapped up and those narrow eyes widened. His feet stopped tapping. Surprise at the accusation? Or shock at being caught? He said nothing, just looked at her. Suzanne sensed the advantage.

'Where were you last Tuesday, Wednesday and Saturday?'

'I never done no rapes.'

'That wasn't the question. Where were you?'

'I never done no rapes.'

'Answer the question.'

He thought for a moment.

'Dunno.' The whining voice was higher now, more strained. 'Taxiing probably, or at home.'

'Can anyone confirm that?'

'Nah.' A fast answer she thought, too fast? 'I live on me own. I drive alone.'

An idea grew in Suzanne's mind, making her hesitate before her next question. They hadn't found a connection between the three women. What if they'd taken a taxi in the last few weeks? What if the driver had been Mr Steven Freeman? A little bit of harmless chat to find out if they were attached, if there was a man in the house. A note of the address to come back to. A drive past once or twice, just to check. Wait a while, let the memory of the flirty taxi driver fade, then strike. But was he a woman hater?

'How do you get on with Julia now, Mr Freeman?'

Suzanne asked.

The eyes widened again, but this time she could see what was in them. He couldn't resist the bait.

'She's a bitch,' he whined, and for the first time the words came quickly and easily. It was something he'd said many times before. 'She left me. Threw me out. Took my kid away. Then she wants my money. She's a bitch.'

Time to think for a moment, pretend to jot some notes, a trick she'd learned from Adam Breen. Means, motive and opportunity, they're all there. His record says he can be violent. He's a bitter man. The taxi link could be a good one. They'd have to check with their victims, then come back to Steven Freeman. But there could be a short cut, couldn't there?

'Mr Freeman, that's about all I need to know for now. But I must just ask if you would provide us with a hair or saliva sample for a DNA test, so we can rule you out of our inquiries?'

'No,' he whined quickly.

It'd been a busy afternoon thought Dan, as he drove them back to Charles Cross, and it could get busier yet. He hadn't believed Kid was the killer, but now he had to admit Adam's theory was looking persuasive. If he was charged before 6.30, it would be another burst of stress and panic to get the news on air. If it was later, he'd have to stay around for the 10.25 bulletin. Well, whatever, that was his job. And it would mean he could have some time off tomorrow morning to have another go at the Death Pictures.

First, they'd seen the McCluskeys' neighbour, Mr Jarvis. He'd been a pleasant enough old chap, but a classic nose. Out in his garden all hours. Keeping it pristine, yes, but also forever on the look out for comings and goings and the tantalising prospect of a titbit to talk about.

Dan and Adam had admired the newly shaped hedge as directed – topiary he'd told them proudly, that was his hobby – and made all the right noises about the colours and variety of the plants he'd bedded in.

Dan had managed to stifle a laugh when Jarvis had told them about his daughter's impending wedding at Kitley House, a local stately home. His pride was bursting – his son-in-law-to-be a merchant banker you know, top London firm, old money – but the sums it was costing, oh the money. He was determined none of her desires would be spared. She would have the dream wedding she wanted. Money wasn't the point where happiness was concerned, was it?

Dan had to stifle an aching urge to puncture the pomposity with a question about who would be taking the wedding photographs. No doubt a famous London photographer, not one of those sleazy local paparazzi types? But Adam was alongside, needed questions answered, and they couldn't afford to alienate someone who could be an important witness. Shame. It would have been so enjoyable.

Abi McCluskey had left the house at 7.15, Jarvis told them. Yes, he was quite sure about the timing. He rolled up his sleeve to show off a new looking silver watch, a birthday present from his wife. He had two watches, one for everyday wear and one for smarter occasions, and he always knew exactly what the time was. Dan looked ruefully down at his own watch. One day he might buy an accurate model.

She'd said goodbye to Joseph. Yes, he was sure about that, had heard quite clearly from the garden. He might be getting on, but there was nothing wrong with his ears. No, he couldn't swear to the exact words – and looked crestfallen for it – but they were something like 'back in an hour or so darling,' then a pause, then 'no, I won't forget the milk.' She'd left with their Boxer dog, Darwin.

No, he hadn't seen anyone else arrive – crestfallen again, he'd gone inside for his tea – until the police at just after eight. Then there was all that fuss with the ambulance and the detectives and the media. And then the terrible news about Joseph. Terrible, thought Dan, but enough delicious gossip to see this scrutineer through the rest of his natural days.

Abi McCluskey's story had checked out. Into the corner shop to buy some milk at about 7.30, confirmed by the owner who knew her well. 'She often comes in around that time as she's walking Darwin.' Then just up the road to pop in on a friend for a chat. 'We wanted to talk about a guided walk on the coast near Torquay,' the woman had told them. Abi left at about eight.

Abi had been re-interviewed too. Adam had only one question for her. Was there any possible way that Kid's fingerprints could be on a knife in your house?

She'd thought about that, long and hard, acutely aware just what difference her answer could make to a man's life.

'Yes,' she'd said finally, making Adam stop tapping his fingers on the arm of the chair. He leaned forwards towards her as she sat on the sofa, curled up in the same corner as before.

'How?' Adam asked slowly.

She thought again, closed her eyes for a moment. When she spoke she was careful with her words.

'Kid has been round for dinner a couple of times. In fact, that was the first thing Joseph wanted to do when they'd made their peace, have him round to eat. He was very proud of my cooking and I think it was a symbolic thing for him.'

Adam had smiled indulgently but his voice was tense. 'Go on.'

She was picking at a toenail again. 'Well, that's it. He came round for dinner a couple of times. I can't remember exactly what I cooked, but we usually put whatever it is out on the table and serve it from there. I think it's much more civilised that way. Then your guests can see what they're going to eat and have as much or as little as they want.'

Adam held his encouraging smile.

'So you have the knives out too?' he asked.

'Yes.' Abi nodded, but didn't stop picking at her feet. 'If we're carving a joint then we'll have the knife out. Or if we're cutting bread we'll have a knife for that too. And for cheese of course.'

Adam noted that down, much more slowly than usual.

'Abi, this is important,' he said. 'I know it's difficult, but please try to remember. I know you realise how important it is. Can you recall Kid ever using a knife here?'

She closed her eyes and the skin on her forehead bunched into lines of concentration. 'I can't remember,' she said finally. 'I think he might have, but I just can't remember for sure.'

Adam nodded and shifted in his chair. 'I understand. It's not the sort of thing you notice or that sticks in your mind. But can you help me with this? Can you remember when he came round?'

She got up from the sofa. 'Yes, I can tell you that exactly.' By the phone in the corner of the room was a small black diary. She flicked through the pages. 'The last time was…' she found the page she was looking for. 'March the fourth.' She nodded to emphasise her certainty. 'Yes, March the fourth. Just under two months ago.'

Dan saw Adam relax, lean back in his chair, straighten his already pristine tie.

'Abi, just one more question before we leave you alone, and it's going to sound like a silly one. But it is important too,' said Adam. She stayed by the phone, waited, tilted her head slightly to one side. 'What would have happened to a knife you'd used for dinner?'

'It'd just go straight into the dishwasher.'

'And that would be the case every time you used it?'

'Yes.'

'And you don't have any special knives you only get out for certain occasions?'

The question didn't surprise her. She knew exactly what Adam was thinking.

'No.'

'So any knife you'd used for a dinner two months ago would have been through the dishwasher...?'

'Scores of times.'

Dan thought Adam looked smug.

Did they have a breakthrough? The elusive link between the victims?

They might, thought Suzanne. They just might. All three had been re-interviewed and yes, all three had taken black cabs

157

in the past three months.

'Are we going to arrest him?' Claire asked. She was keen, had worked hard, efficient and precise. Suzanne couldn't tell if it was because they were hunting a rapist – she'd felt the extra impetus herself – or if her mind was on her career. Claire seemed driven, but then she always worked hard on her cases.

She hadn't liked Claire at first. There was no particular reason for that, or at least none she wanted to think about. But she knew, if she was honest with herself. Claire was everything she wasn't. She was beautiful, what men called a head-turner, and that could help in a male dominated career. All she'd had over Claire before was rank. And then came her promotion...

But she prided herself on being fair and honest, a good policewoman, and Claire hadn't put a foot wrong. Far from it. They'd even reached the cusp of becoming friends, that telling moment when they'd talked a little about their private lives. During one late night, going through alibis in the MIR, Claire had confessed to the loneliness that so often came with the job. How coping with the case would be so much easier if there was someone to go home to.

Suzanne had listened and almost told her about Adrian. Almost, but not quite. They weren't that close yet, though it could come she thought. Claire had been a friend where Suzanne had expected a rival, and she was grateful.

So were they going to arrest Freeman? On what basis? He'd run from them, but he had a plausible explanation for that, good enough for many juries at any rate. Plenty of people ran from the police. He didn't like women. He wouldn't give a DNA sample. He had a record for violence. He drove a black cab, and all three victims had used one in the months before they were attacked.

But that was all circumstantial, wasn't it? None of the women could remember a taxi driver being unusually interested in them. Yes, they were men – black cabs seemed to be a man's game – and yes they thought they could recall a bit of chat. Yes, on a couple of occasions the driver did ask about partners or husbands, but that wasn't unusual. Being in a taxi, alone with a man, it was an easy opportunity for them to work a bit of charm, test the temperature of the water, try their luck.

A couple of the journeys had been late, getting home from town after a night out. That made the memories so foggy as to be almost useless. The others had been shopping trips, meetings with friends on rainy days, mundane events that didn't stay in the mind. None of the women could remember anyone like Freeman driving them. One said she did have a driver with a bit of a high voice, but nothing out of the ordinary. It could have been him, but... But it could also have been anyone. As solid evidence, it meant nothing.

So what to do? What would Adam Breen do? The attempt to trace the witches' hats had come to nothing, but she'd expected that. They could try an identity parade, but she knew it would be hopeless. The women's memories of their taxi drivers were vague at best. And the rapist had always made sure he was well disguised.

How about some surveillance? They were tailing Godley. Why not do the same for Freeman? They wouldn't expect to catch their man carrying out an attack. Of course not, that wasn't the point. Both suspects knew well enough now of the police's interest in them. If one was the rapist, he would hardly go out and try to strike again. The tail was there to put the pressure on, the unspoken hope that the man would lose his temper, take a swing at the officer. Then you've got the grounds to arrest him, bring him in and take his DNA. Second best, at least it would stop him attacking again.

So was it worth tailing Freeman? Why not? But how do you follow someone who drives a cab? It'd take a patrol car for a whole shift, and despite what DCI Breen had said about making the resources available, she couldn't imagine getting that. Still, it was worth a try. They didn't have much else at the moment but suspects. Suspects, but no evidence.

First though, they had to finish the list and see the last of their possible woman-haters.

It was six o'clock. Munroe would be back from his case at the Crown Court by now. Edward Munroe, eminent barrister, highly successful, all the biggest cases, hired by anyone with

159

enough money to afford him. Keen seeker of loopholes in the law and discrediter of good evidence. Known quietly amongst the detectives in Greater Wessex police as the Devil's Advocate.

Dan drove them back to Charles Cross while Adam made a couple of phone calls. As he listened to one half of the technical, forensics and autopsy discussions he found his mind again drifting to the Death Pictures. They wouldn't leave him, seemed to hover permanently on the edge of his consciousness, calling for his attention.

The knot in his handkerchief reminded him that tonight he'd look up page 98 in the latest Oxford English Dictionary of Quotations. Then he'd go through the pictures again to see if it could mean anything. It was cheating of a sort, but only very mildly he reassured himself. And who would ever know if he did solve the riddle? He'd tell the world it was down to a flash of realisation. Genius even, perhaps? He couldn't help but like the sound of that.

'Great!' Adam's near shout roused him from his thoughts. 'I think we've got him. Fingerprinting say a dishwasher would get rid of any prints in a couple of cycles at most. And that knife would have been through scores. A defence barrister might make a play of it, but our technical people reckon we can do a simulation that would destroy any holes they'd try to knock in the case.'

Dan checked the car's clock. Almost six. No chance of a story on the 6.30 programme. It looked like a long night beckoned. 'Are you going to charge Kid then?' he asked.

'No, not yet.' Adam wound down the window and stuck an elbow out, breathed in the air. 'I want to put it all to him in an interview first. But basically yes, I think we've got enough to charge him. I just want to see if he can come up with anything we might have trouble with at the trial.'

Dan was almost convinced. Almost. But there was still something nagging at him.

Was it the man's character? Someone who'd always tried to do what he saw as good in the world? Was it the speed of

160

thought needed to invent the plan Adam was convinced he had? Or that basic question that was still bothering him. Why kill McCluskey if he was going to die in a few days anyway?

Ah, maybe Adam was right. Maybe it was talk of being exposed as a plagiarist that panicked Kid. What did he know? He was only a journalist. But he had helped to solve the Bray case, hadn't he?

The traffic ahead slowed and stopped. Road works on North Hill by the University. Gas and electricity supplies for new halls of residence, another wave of students for the city. A pneumatic drill thudded. Dan pulled on the handbrake.

He looked over at Adam. 'While we're stuck in this, take me through it again.'

Dan realised he hadn't managed to keep the doubt from his voice. Adam sighed.

'With pleasure,' he said heavily. 'Let me try to convince you. Abi leaves the house at 7.15, verified by nosey neighbour, annoying but impeccable witness. She says goodbye to Joseph, yes, I will get some milk, something like that. Kid arrives about 7.45 by his own statement, but I don't believe that. We get the emergency call just before eight. We arrive, Kid's there, McCluskey's dead. There's one of Kid's prints on the knife that slit McCluskey's wrists.'

Good start thought Dan. I'm beginning to be convinced. 'And the post mortem evidence?'

'Death from heart failure, brought on by blood loss due to cuts to the wrists. He was very weak as we know, so the doctors estimate it would have taken less than half an hour to die. There's the bruising on his body, on the knees, the lower arms, the top of the shoulders and the back of the neck. They're consistent with being pulled up the stairs and then held down in the bath.'

Dan shuddered, imagined a man holding another down, someone who was a friend, cutting his wrists, watching him slowly die. 'So you're saying…'

'It's simple,' Adam snapped. 'McCluskey tells Kid about revealing the secret of the statue idea in those tapes he's going to record. Kid panics. He imagines his reputation disappearing

161

in a flash. He sees the knife on the side in the kitchen and the plan comes to him. He forces McCluskey upstairs and gets him into the bath, then holds him down and cuts his wrists. He waits for him to die, then calls us.'

'But there was no blood on Kid or the phone? Or anywhere else in the house?'

'You wouldn't expect to find any. I told you, the blood flows from the wrists, it doesn't spurt. So none gets on Kid's clothes. And when McCluskey's dead, Kid can wash his hands and then make the 999 call. Flush plenty of water down the sink and there's no trace.'

The traffic trundled on, past the road works. They were almost at Charles Cross. Dan was starting to believe Adam's theory. It seemed to have all the answers.

'And the timing?' he asked.

'Abi told us Kid was due at 7.30. He says he was a bit late and it was 7.45 when he got there. But we have no evidence at all to back that up. I'm guessing he arrived at 7.30, they had the row and he called us when McCluskey was dead, just before eight.' Dan pulled up in the police station and they got out of the car. 'Convinced yet?' Adam continued.

Dan thought for a moment. He couldn't see any holes in it.

'Just about.'

'I'm delighted to hear it,' said Adam sarcastically. 'Let's go put it to him and see what he says. Then we can charge him and get down the pub in time for a celebratory drink. I always like to toast catching a murderer.'

Chapter Twelve

SUZANNE STARED OUT OF the windscreen as the intricate black iron gates swung open. Claire put the car into gear and they drove slowly up the crunching gravel drive. Both said nothing. Their conversation had faded as they approached the house. Abstract shapes of bronze sculpted forms slipped by as they followed the sweep of the drive, past a mirrored pond, a willow bending subserviently before it. Blocks of light shone from the house, half hidden beyond the dark, tapering curves of a line of trees. Even in the gathering darkness, Suzanne could sense the grounds were impeccably kept. She noticed she felt tense.

Edward Munroe had done well from his work. His house, just outside Modbury, half an hour from Plymouth in the classic Devon countryside of the South Hams could more accurately be described as a small mansion. She and Claire exchanged looks as they parked next to a new Jaguar. They got out of the car and knocked the heavy black iron ring.

Suzanne had expected him to keep them waiting and he did. On the phone he'd said he'd be delighted to help the constabulary, in that resonant and commanding voice juries so loved. But she thought she could feel a sneer – or was it just amusement? – that the well- publicised break-up of his own marriage and subsequent custody battle could possibly make him a suspect in this terrible case. But he was always on the side of the law he said, and would help them as much as he could. She'd had to turn a sarcastic laugh into a cough.

They were about to knock for the third time when the door groaned open. An elderly lady dressed in an apron appeared from behind it. 'Mr Munroe will see you in the library,' she said in a soft Devon burr and led them into the house.

They followed her along a stone-flagged corridor to another heavy wooden door. Stag and fox heads snarled down at them from the walls, along with birds frozen in death in their polished glass coffins. Suzanne counted off a thrush, buzzard, blackbird, heron, barn owl and bittern. The woman knocked reverentially, waited, then pushed it open.

Edward Munroe stood by a stone-arched window, peering into at a leather-bound book. He put it down, walked over and shook their hands but didn't introduce himself. He was wearing the lawyers' uniform of a navy blue, chalk pinstripe suit and dark blue tie, but Suzanne was surprised to see slippers on his feet.

He followed her look. 'Sporting injury,' he said gruffly. 'I run to keep fit.'

Or from slipping, when running away after breaking into a woman's home, she thought. Suzanne didn't need to check. She knew him well enough from her days in the witness box, but his build was right for the man they were hunting. His courtroom experience meant he'd know exactly what the police would look for as evidence too, useful if you wanted to cover your tracks. And in the ashtray were a couple of discarded cigar butts.

'So, how can I help you?' He didn't offer them one of the red leather chairs, but stayed standing by an antique wooden desk. His dark hair was swept back, greying at the temples in a way he'd obviously decided was distinguished and becoming. Suzanne was sure it would have been dyed otherwise. He had a shadow of a beard which he ran his hand over while they talked. A less likely rapist you couldn't imagine she thought. But experience had taught her you never knew.

'Mr Munroe, please don't think this is anything other than a routine inquiry. But we're looking at anyone in the area who could have had a reason to dislike women so much he'd want to attack them.' His smile said he'd heard that before. 'Rape them in fact,' continued Suzanne, quietly satisfied that made the smile disappear. 'And your name came up in our inquiries with the Child Support Agency as someone who...'

She searched for the words. Adam Breen had warned her to be diplomatic. The man had powerful friends, he'd said. '...someone who had a dispute over maintenance payments for their child. The family courts also told us of your challenge over custody.'

He nodded dismissively. 'I quite understand officer. You must do your job thoroughly of course. Yes, there was a dispute with my ex wife, but it's been resolved now.' He looked her up and down, a lofty stare. 'I should of course add that it was entirely within the bounds of the law. I was – shall we say not best pleased – at the way we parted and so was in no mood to surrender to her all that she wanted. It was she who left here after all.'

Suzanne nodded. The news of the former Mrs Munroe walking out to live with her fitness instructor had made all the papers. It was interesting he'd mentioned it though. She could hardly ask if he hated women, but she knew now he hated at least one. And that could have been the start.

She wondered if it was the loss of his wife or the blow to his pride which had hurt more. So there was a motive. And there was no alibi for any of the attacks. They'd already discussed that on the phone. Appearing in court in front of a judge counted as an unshakeable alibi to her. But he'd been at home, or shopping, or out for a run when the attacks took place. And no he'd said, no one could verify that. He'd been alone.

So, one question remained. How to phrase it? He'd picked up the book again, glancing at its pages as though already bored with his visitors. There were more important demands on his time, clearly.

Suzanne coughed loudly. 'Again Mr Munroe, please don't think this anything other than a routine inquiry, but could we take a sample of your hair or saliva for a DNA profile?' The book landed back on the desk with an echoing thud. 'It would help rule you out of the investigation,' she added quickly.

He stood and stared at her. Had he turned a little pale? What was he thinking? Feign anger? Throw them out? He'd never been so insulted... Or was he really angry? Would he try calm reason and excuses? Whatever, she was suddenly sure she wouldn't be getting that sample.

'Mr Munroe?' she prompted gently.

'I'm sorry officer. I was just debating with myself.' There was a smile, but it was one of the thinnest Suzanne had ever seen. A lawyer's smile, she thought.

'You've put me in a very difficult position, you see. Very difficult,' he continued. 'Of course I want to help you and I understand the need for a sample. But I'm an active supporter of Liberty. You know, the civil rights group?' Both Suzanne and Claire nodded. 'And I do quite a lot of work for them. My position of principle is against a DNA register of innocent people. I believe it to be an infringement of civil liberties.'

He paused, turned a couple of pages of the book lying on the desk.

'No, officers, I'm afraid I can't do that. It would go against my principles. I'm sorry.' The tenuous smile again. 'You'll just have to take my word for my innocence I'm afraid.'

'You realise that will make you a suspect for the attacks sir?' Claire got the words out before Suzanne had a chance to stop her. But well done, she thought, well done. You've hit the target. For the first time, either in court or here, in this interview, Edward Munroe's famous cool was faltering. His face had turned puce.

'Yes I appreciate that, officer,' he snapped. 'But I'm shocked you could even consider it. Quite shocked.'

'I'm sorry, sir, but we all have our jobs to do,' continued Claire. 'Don't worry, I'm sure you're as innocent as your clients.'

'Mr Kiddey, I don't think you appreciate how serious your position is.' Adam stopped pacing and leaned over the man sitting at the table in the interview room, his head bowed.

'It doesn't come any more serious than this. It's murder, Mr Kiddey.' Adam thumped the table, making Kid look up. 'Murder!' continued the detective. 'And you know what follows murder?' No response. Adam leaned closer and lowered his voice. 'Life in prison is what.'

'I can't believe this is happening.' Kid's voice was breathless, his mouth hanging open. 'I can't believe it. He was my friend. He was my mentor. He was my friend and now he's dead. And you think… you think…'

'I don't think,' Adam interrupted. 'I know. I know exactly

166

what happened, Mr Kiddey. I've got the evidence to prove it. And I'm going to charge you with murder now and recommend to the judge you spend the whole of your life in prison, unless you start telling us the truth.'

He paced over to the door and the uniformed officer there, whispered in his ear. The man slipped out, returned quickly with a bottle of water. Adam took it and swigged. Kid looked up longingly, but said nothing.

Dan checked his watch. Just before nine it said, so probably ten past. An amber halo of street light was spreading from the small strip of barred window, high up on the interview room wall. It made for a Hallowe'en mix with the harsh green glow of the fluorescent strip light.

Adam sat down opposite Kid, who stared at him but didn't speak. 'So, for the last time Mr Kiddey, this is how it goes. This is your last chance to tell us the truth. Are you ready?'

Still the man said nothing. 'You went round there at half past seven...' began Adam.

'No! No, I've told you that.' His voice was thin, panicked. 'It was more like ten to eight.'

'Mrs McCluskey told us you were due to go round at half past seven and that you were usually on time. So round you go...'

'It was ten to eight... ten to eight.'

'And you have some wine and you have a chat. And Mr McCluskey tells you the little thing he wanted to get off his chest. That he's going to reveal all, about you copying his idea for that sculpture of yours...'

'No! No! No... No...'

'...and it panics you, doesn't it? You panic, because you thought it'd all been forgotten about. And you can see yourself ruined, your precious reputation destroyed. So you come up with a plan. Was there a knife on the sideboard in front of you, Mr Kiddey? In the rack in the kitchen? Was that what gave you the idea?'

'No! No, I didn't. No there wasn't, no...'

'So you grab the knife and force poor Joseph upstairs. It's not too difficult, is it? He's a very weak man. But you have to

167

pull him, and he stumbles a couple of times. We know, Mr Kiddey, because we found the bruises. They tell the story. You pull him upstairs, then you force him into the bath. You cut his wrists and hold him there…'

'No!' Kid jumped up off his chair, and stood trembling. Adam stood as well, the two men facing each other over the table. 'You held him there while he died, Kiddey, didn't you? We know, we found bruises on his shoulders and the back of his neck, the bruises where you held him as you watched him die...'

'No! No! No!' Kid backed away from the table, shaking his head. His eyes were wild, darting around as if looking desperately for an escape from this place. 'No! No!'

'And then you wiped the knife handle, didn't you? You wiped it clean of your fingerprints. Then you held it in a towel and pressed poor Joseph's hand around it so it looked like he'd killed himself. And then you called us, didn't you? You called us to tell us of your shock… your horror… at what you'd found.'

Kid backed away to the cold brick wall, his palms flat against it as though he were pushing, trying to get as far away from Adam as possible.

'No, no… I went round... I found him... I'm a peaceful man... He was my friend...'

'It was a good plan, Mr Kiddey,' said Adam, sitting down, his voice calmer now. 'A clever plan. But you made two mistakes. Just two, but enough for us to know the truth. Abi was devoted to Joseph you see. She told us he'd never kill himself without telling her. Without having her there in fact. But just on the strength of that, you might have got away with it. A good barrister could have convinced a jury that people change their minds. It can happen. Especially people who are very sick, delirious perhaps with morphine and wine, who don't want their loved ones to have to go through the trauma of watching them die. You might have got away with it.'

Adam's voice grew quieter now, the words spelt out slowly. Dan leaned forwards to hear.

'But you made one very big mistake, Mr Kiddey. You

missed a fingerprint, high up on the knife handle. It's what they call the killer fact, isn't it? How appropriate here, eh? The killer fact that convicts the killer. Just the one print, and right up on the very edge of the handle. Not much of a mistake, but enough. It's that print which will have you sent down for murder, Mr Kiddey. It'll see you spending the rest of your life in jail.'

Kid stood, back flat against the wall, his palms still spread out against it. His mouth hung open, but he said nothing. His chest was heaving.

Adam waited. Dan held his breath, knew what was coming. The room was silent, still.

Ten seconds crawled by, then twenty, thirty. Finally Adam spoke. 'Lewis Kiddey, I'm charging you with the murder of Joseph McCluskey...'

Dan got home just before eleven. He was too tired to do anything but slump in front of the television with a cup of decaffeinated coffee and a chunk of badly buttered bread. The spread stood out in random yellow lumps, like icebergs at sea. It was only when he started to eat he realised he was hungry.

Rutherford padded over to nuzzle him and he cuddled the dog, telling him about his day as he always did. 'We're like an old married couple, my faithful friend,' he said. 'Well, we got it on air. I didn't get back into the building until 10.15, but we managed to get it on. That bloody Adam Breen is doing my heart in.'

Rutherford stretched out on the carpet in front of him. Dan rubbed his ears and told him how Lewis Kiddey had been charged with murder, how he'd had to run into the studio to do another live report. The dog looked up and yawned. Dan chuckled, then yawned too. 'Am I boring you? But good idea. It's time for some much-needed kip. First though, a little stretch out here on the sofa to unwind.'

Fatal he thought, as he woke just after one with a throbbing pain in his neck. Never 'just close your eyes for a few minutes.' You're guaranteed to flake out into the blackness of sleep. 'Come on dog, proper bedtime,' he said.

Dan let Rutherford out into the garden and began cleaning his teeth. He turned on the little bathroom portable radio to hear the news. It was covered in toothpaste stains. He must get round to cleaning it some time, he thought. The whole flat could do with a good clean, but when did he have a chance? The charging of Kid was running as second story, behind a political row about pensions.

Perhaps he would get a cleaner in. He was sure he'd seen an advert for a local firm who did good hourly rates. But would they take him on with Rutherford here? The dog was soft as putty, but could look intimidating if you didn't know him.

Dan put the toothbrush back in the cracked mug by the sink. Then he saw it, sitting on the little rack of books beside the toilet. The Oxford English Dictionary of Quotations. He'd almost forgotten in all that had happened today, but now it came back to him. Sitting in McCluskey's living room, looking around for clues. Could the book contain a hint about the solution to the riddle?

He sat down on the edge of the bath and leafed through the pages. Auden, Bacon, Bible, Browning. Page 98, the first author listed there. Robert Browning.

Did it mean something? It could do. Maybe even had to. He checked Browning's first quotation on the page.

'Burrow awhile and build, broad on the roots of things.'

And the last one too.

'I find earth not grey, but rosy.'

He stared at the lines until the words, blurred, lost their meaning. Dan blinked them back into focus. Surely that had to mean something? It couldn't be a coincidence. The book prominent in McCluskey's living room, and two references to burrowing and earth on page 98. So could it mean dig somewhere that the pictures made reference to? Or even that something was built there? It had to, surely?

Dan let his mind run through the Death Pictures. So what building? Or dig where? He tried to focus on the images, but his brain was vague with fatigue. Tomorrow, he could work on it tomorrow. He felt a nudge of excitement. At last, he had a lead. But for now he needed to sleep.

He was about to go to bed when a scrabbling at the door reminded him Rutherford was still outside. 'Sorry, old friend, I got a bit over-excited there and forgot about you,' he said, swinging it open.

The Alsatian padded lightly past him and into their bedroom. That was the great thing about dogs. They didn't bear grudges, no matter what. Their love was unconditional. They were always there for you, wouldn't one day decide your relationship was over and up and leave. Unlike some women he'd known. One woman in fact. The woman. Thomasin.

The thought shook him, like an attack from a mugger waiting in a hidden corner of his mind. It was always in the lonely hours of the night that her power was greatest. He'd done so well not thinking about her lately, the excitement of work and the Death Pictures chasing her memory away. But in the darker moments, the quieter moments, she was always there. Always there, ready to ambush him.

He suddenly felt the dragging, sucking pull of the swamp of the depression that had always stalked him at the edge of his consciousness. It did that. It waited its moment, then struck, no warning, just an enveloping cold emptiness. Work, friends, excitement, fun, walks with Rutherford, nights out drinking, all could hold it at bay but never banish it. The swamp waited patiently for its moment and it would always come. He felt it weighing every limb, slowing his body like a leaden suit, fogging his mind with numbing apathy. All in one instant, its irresistible debilitating power unleashed.

Dan got into bed and closed his eyes, but slept only fitfully, despite his tiredness. He kept fighting it, trying to push it from his mind, thinking of where he should be digging and wondering what the last of the Death Pictures would look like on his wall. But the swamp slept contentedly with him and was there waiting, refreshed and renewed when he woke up the next morning.

Chapter Thirteen

STEVEN FREEMAN CHECKED THE mirror. Had it gone? The taxi's diesel engine grumbled up the hill and rounded a bend. No, there it was, the police car just fifty or so yards back in the traffic. It had picked him up as he drove out of his street and been with him for the whole first hour of his shift. How long was it going to tail him? Not all day surely?

He felt a sweat tickle his forehead, his eyes nervously flicking to the mirror as he joined the back of the rank in the city centre by the Co-op. There were half a dozen cabs in front of him. Not bad that, it meant a fare in the next 15 minutes or so. The town was busy today, the sunshine bringing people out. Behind him the police car stopped at the edge of the roundabout, not in the rank but with a clear view and in place to follow the moment he drove off.

Did they think he was stupid? Did they think he hadn't noticed? Surely not. They could have put an unmarked car on his tail if they'd wanted. That would have been much harder to pick up, although he prided himself on keeping a careful eye out when he was driving. And not just when he was at the wheel. He had to, a man in his position.

So what were they up to? It had to be deliberate, designed to make him notice he was being followed, to put pressure on him. To force him into a mistake? That must be their idea. Well, they wouldn't, and he'd tell them so.

A tap at the window roused him. 'Are you free?' A young woman struggling with some plastic bags of food and clothes, pretty too. Blonde, crinkled hair, about twenty years old and a size eight in those tight jeans, his expert eye reckoned.

'For a girl like you, anytime love. Hop in.'

She giggled. 'Stoke please.'

He didn't do the old Plymouth joke about it being a long way up north, just put the car into gear and it rumbled off, onto the roundabout and out to the west of the city. The fluorescent stripes of the police car slid into the traffic behind him. Good.

He didn't want to have a word in the town with the other taxi drivers around. A quiet street in Stoke would do nicely.

The traffic was light, usually was on sunny days. People didn't mind walking or getting the bus when it was warm and dry. Until they were laden down with shopping of course. Good taxiing weather.

'Been treating yourself love?'

Another giggle. 'Just some nosh and something for the weekend.' She fished in the bag and brought out the tiniest black thong he'd ever seen. It looked like it was made from two pieces of cheese wire. She certainly hadn't bought it to keep herself warm.

'Lovely! You'll make someone a very happy man!'

Another giggle. 'Cheeky!'

He could have gone on, given it some more banter, been in there even, but not this time. It was easy to pull when you were taxiing. The ladies liked the charm and chat and sometimes they were lonely, had a few drinks, didn't want to go back to their homes on their own. But not this one, pretty though she might be. He was going to have a word with that copper and what if they wanted to talk to his fare? It wouldn't look good, this woman telling them he was flirting with her. There'd be others when he wasn't being escorted.

First though, was there anything they could get him for? He didn't think so. He'd half expected something like this, had checked the cab thoroughly. Tyres fine, tax fine, licence fine, everything fine. He was safe from any chance of arrest, and worse, much worse, the possibility of having to give a DNA sample.

The cab pulled up halfway along Devonport Road. 'Here we are love, number 133. That's four forty, call it four quid to you... ten per cent off for showing me your thong.'

Yet another giggle. She manoeuvred herself out of the back, not easy in those constricting jeans, he thought. She wiggled up the path, one look back over her shoulder and a smile. He waved.

Now to business. He checked the mirror. Yes, there was the cop car, parked about twenty yards behind him. He killed the

173

engine, got out and walked over.

'What's the problem, mate? Why's you bleeding following me?'

The policeman looked up from the clipboard and sheet of paper he was filling in. Steven Freeman had time to see it was a list of where he'd driven this morning. Minute by minute.

'There's no problem, sir. It's just a routine patrol.' PC Samson heard the whine in the man's voice, just as he'd been briefed.

'What, following me around?'

The officer smiled. 'Not following, sir. We're just checking you were OK. I'd hate to see you suffer any pretty young ladies forcing themselves on you. I know what they can be like around here.'

'Ain't you got better things to be doing?'

'Like what, sir?'

'Like catching this bloody rapist?'

'Just what we're trying to do, sir.' The smile vanished from the officer's face. 'Just what we're trying to do.' He pointed to a small plastic jar on the seat beside him, sealed in a forensics bag. 'Care to give a DNA sample to rule yourself out? Then you'd be able to go about your cabbing in peace, eh?'

Steven Freeman glared down. He felt like grabbing this policeman by his collar, pulling back his fist and... he clenched his teeth.

'How long you gonna be following me for?'

The smile slipped back onto the officer's face. 'How long are you planning to be out for?'

Detective Chief Inspector Adam Breen had done his job, as he'd been ordered. He'd done it thoroughly and professionally. Now he could get back to the real business.

The criminal psychologist's report on the rapist had arrived on his desk. The doctor was known in Greater Wessex Police as "Sledgehammer" Stevens, because he didn't care for subtleties or nuances, and clearly suffered a mortal fear of the slightest risk of being misunderstood. He had a habit of underlining or printing key phrases in capitals, so there could

174

be no doubt whatsoever about the learned doctor's findings.

"Consider attacker HIGHLY DANGEROUS," the report read. "Clearly a severe MISOGYNIST – that is, someone who hates women…"

'Thank you doctor, I know what a misogynist is,' Adam muttered under his breath.

"…CLEVER and CALCULATING. Obvious and extreme SOCIOPATHIC tendencies. Bent on REVENGE. Desire to MAKE A STATEMENT. In conclusion, this man WILL NOT STOP until either COMPLETES MISSION or is CAUGHT."

Not for the first time Adam reflected, the doctor's report told him nothing that didn't already seem obvious. But that didn't make the case any less worrying.

He hissed through his teeth. A recurring nightmare was taunting him. He'd been shocked awake early this morning by a vision of the man's hands around Annie's throat, Tom coming downstairs to find his mother sprawled on the floor, screaming and sobbing. His pulse was racing and he hadn't managed to get back to sleep. It was time to get this rapist.

They had their suspects. Now to push one into a mistake.

The McCluskey case was sorted. Kiddey had been remanded in custody by the magistrates, committed for trial in the Crown Court at a date to be fixed. All the evidence was there to convict him. They'd probably have to borrow that dishwasher and get the Eggheads scientific division to prove that a couple of cycles would destroy any fingerprints. But apart from that it was all over. He'd worried he was cutting corners on the investigation, wishing it away in his desire to get back to hunting the rapist, but the case stood up. A simple and straightforward one.

Abi McCluskey would make an excellent witness, as would that nosey neighbour Jarvis. Kiddey was still protesting his innocence, but they all did that. With a bit of luck, when he saw the evidence against him and had the benefit of some good legal advice he'd change his plea and save them a trial.

There were only those attempted break-ins the defence might make something of. But neither had been successful, had it? And he was sure they weren't connected. Just a

175

coincidence.

He didn't believe in coincidences – few detectives did – but on this occasion there was a good explanation. The lure of winning the last of those Death Pictures could easily prompt someone to try to break in to the McCluskeys' home in the hope of finding a clue to his riddle. And as for a connection with the rapist? Well, the defence could raise it, try to confuse the jury, but it was a pretty thin hope. There was no evidence to back it up. If there was a trial, it should be a short one, maybe only a week or so.

So that was the McCluskey case sorted. The Assistant Chief Constable had been on the phone this morning offering his congratulations. He'd also liked the media coverage. 'So good for the force, so very positive. A big story, a fast result. Excellent work, Adam! I knew it was right to put you on the case.' He'd managed not to say anything in reply.

Dan's report last night had been picked up just about everywhere. It was in all the national papers and had been on the radio and TV this morning too. Adam straightened his tie. Yes, a good result. So now back to the rapist. He picked up his coffee and walked up the stairs from his office to the MIR.

Dan awoke slowly, lingering hesitantly in the half-life between dreams and the light. He wasn't surprised to find tears in his eyes when he opened them. It often happened when the pull of the swamp was strong. Morning seeped through the curtains and he shrunk from it. He felt like pulling the duvet up over his head and taking refuge in its safe, enveloping darkness. He wanted to curl up into a ball, lock the flat's door and wait for the world to pass.

He'd suffered it so many times before. The hopeless fatigue. The listlessness and lethargy. The washing of colour from a world that turned grey all around him. The evaporation of hope. The fear of venturing outside into a happily hostile society where everyone else was content, relaxed, talkative, energetic. Everyone except him.

The doctor he'd finally turned to had clicked his tongue a couple of times, scribbled a note on his file and suggested mood-stabilising drugs. But no, he'd never resort to that. An emotional sticking plaster was no solution. He had his own ways to fight it, with friends, drink – too much drink sometimes, he knew – work, walks, his beloved dog, something, anything to hold onto, to look forward to, to believe in. Something to grab on to, he needed something to make him get out of this bed or he'd just lie here, lost.

The Death Pictures. Come on, the pictures. We've got a lead. We're ahead of the game. We've got a chance to solve the riddle. We've got to give it a go. Come on, come on, come on. But first a run with Rutherford. That always helped. No, first a phone call to a man who can provide an insight into McCluskey. We need to know much more about his life to find out what a reference to the earth, burrowing and building could mean.

Dan picked up the phone beside his bed. Yes, Professor Hughes was in, said the receptionist. Yes, he could have a word. Yes, the man himself could spare an hour or two between lectures. It would be a pleasure to catch up and help. Excellent, down to the university later then. But first his beloved dog, a guarantee to raise his spirits.

They ran over to Thorn Park, the weather, so kind recently, now turning its mood to match his. The sky glowered a slate grey and a mist of drizzle dampened the air. A cool wind ruffled in from the east. The children on their way to school had restored the coats they'd discarded at the first signs of the coming summer, the running and shouting of their sunny days dowsed by the rain. The roads ran busy with commuter traffic, hundreds of blank morning faces framed in the windscreens, crossed back and forth by the squeaking sweep of the intermittent wipers. The pavements shone wet and slippery, alive with the reflections of passing feet. They jogged slowly down the hill, across the main Mannamead Road and into the park.

Dan released Rutherford from his lead and the dog bolted away, unsure as ever which of the intoxicating array of scents to investigate first. He sniffed his way joyously along a hedge, then turned and sprinted back to Dan, sending a grey and white cloud of pigeons fluttering, cooing, into the air. 'Just a few laps, dog,' he puffed. 'I've got lots on this morning.' Running was hard going today, but he'd expected that. The swamp always sapped his energy.

Rutherford exploded into a burst of barks and shot off towards an oak tree, a blur of ginger streaking up its side. 'Leave that cat alone,' Dan called, trying not to laugh. 'Here! Come here!'

The dog refused to move, sat solidly at the base of the tree, head fixed above. Dan jogged over. Up in the crook of a branch sat an utterly unconcerned-looking cat, gazing pityingly down at them. 'Shhhh,' he said to the dog, calming his barks. 'Come on, you've taught him a lesson. Look how scared he is. Come on, mighty warrior. Let's go.'

In the shower, he noticed he felt better for the run. He dressed, gathered his notes and prints of the Death Pictures and caught a bus down to the university.

Professor Ed Hughes had been known as Ted when he was younger and just a Doctor of academia. But the rise to fame of his poet namesake had forced him to amend that. He hadn't done so graciously. Any mention of the other Ted Hughes would prompt a quizzical look.

A tall, stooping man in his early sixties, he'd worked his way up to become Devon University's Head of Art. Dan knew him from a couple of exhibitions they'd both had invitations to. He'd been attracted by the Prof's delightful lack of tact. 'Dreadful dross,' he'd said, when Dan had been introduced and politely asked him what he thought of one artist's offerings. 'I could do better blindfold.'

The university had applied some gentle pressure on Ed to consider retiring, but he'd resisted it. Dan helped by including him in a story on how much older people had to offer and how it was wrong they were expected to retire at a fixed age. They'd also discovered they were fellow Liverpool Football Club supporters, both having family links to Merseyside. They'd long been promising a trip up to see a match, but it had never materialised.

His office was almost standing room only, littered with

books and stacked with the canvas submissions of his students. Dan looked for a space to manoeuvre a chair into, but was stopped by the professor's check of his watch. It was after eleven and that meant the offer of 'a more creative place to go'.

They walked down the stairs to the campus bar, busy despite the early hour. Dan bought a couple of pints of beer, marvelling at the low price.

'We've seen you on TV plenty,' said Ed, quaffing a third of his pint in one go. 'You're doing all that death and disaster stuff now, aren't you? Not environment any more. How are you finding it?'

Dan had given up pretending he didn't miss the countryside, coast and moors of his old job and that it was his idea to switch.

'The bosses moved me. To keep me fresh, they said. Confused would be more accurate. I didn't like it to start with, but now I'm getting into it. It is fascinating being involved in police investigations.'

'That's how you come to want to know about McCluskey then?' Dan nodded, sipping at his beer. Good and fresh, barrels never lingered long enough to grow stale in student bars. 'After his prize, are you?'

'Not much gets past you, does it, Ed?' Dan couldn't help smiling. 'Yes, that's a lot of why I wanted to know more about him. But it'll also help me in reporting the trial too. I'd be interested in anything you know about Kid as well.'

'Well, fire away. But as you know, there's always a price in this life.' He looked meaningfully at his almost empty pint glass.

'Planning to be a bit hazy for this afternoon, Ed?'

'I've got some tedious admin stuff to do and a session with some of my dullest students. It'll help. Plus it's a fact of history that some of the finest artists work best with a bit of creative fuel in them.'

Dan got up and went to refill their glasses. He was glad he'd had the foresight to leave a note at work saying he was going to have today off to claim back the extra hours he'd worked recently. The swamp was still there, on the edge of his consciousness. He could feel its invisible pull. But a few beers would help fight it off. For now… He sat back down.

'Shall I start at the beginning and tell the story in its proper way?' asked Ed, leaning back in his chair and steepling his fingers together in a parody of a classic academic. 'Or shall I do the tabloid version? The shagging, rows and heartbreak?'

Dan picked up his notebook.

Adam listened while Suzanne told him about the interview with Edward Munroe and his refusal to give a DNA sample.

'Interesting, very interesting,' he mused, straightening his perfect tie. 'So we've got three prime suspects now?'

'Yes sir.'

'And that's the whole list done. The Family Courts, the CSA, Fathers for Families? Just these three we can't eliminate?'

'Yes, sir.'

Adam looked out at the sheet-grey sky and the grazes of drizzle etching diagonals on the windows. A pigeon was asleep, head under wing on the ledge by the flagpole where the Greater Wessex Police crest limply hung.

'And we're tailing Freeman and Godley?' he asked 'And now you want to tail Munroe too?'

'Yes, sir, but I appreciate that's a sensitive one.'

'Yes, it is,' Adam said thoughtfully. He was a powerful man, friends with judges, other barristers, senior police officers too, no doubt, far more senior than himself. Someone who could pull the hidden strings that connected the leaders of men. But he was a suspect and he'd refused to give a DNA sample. And he was the Devil's Advocate. None of them would say so, but he knew the detectives would all be thinking it. How pleasant to bring some tension to his life. And it wasn't a time for diplomacy. How long before the rapist struck again?

'I think it's a question of fairness and the public interest, Suzanne,' Adam said slowly. 'If we're tailing the two other suspects, we should do the same for him. Imagine if he was the rapist and we hadn't warned him off. What would the press say?

He mentally rehearsed the arguments for the call he knew would come from the High Honchos after they got a ring from the no-doubt morally outraged Edward Munroe. The thought of an uncomfortable Assistant Chief Constable didn't even register as a deterrent.

'Get a car onto him straight away,' said Adam. 'If there's any flak, I'll handle it. Let's make all three of them very sure we're after them.'

Professor Ed closed his eyes as he relived the memories.

'He was self-taught, you know. That's the first remarkable thing about Joseph McCluskey. He didn't go to any art school. He picked it up himself. His early works showed lots of potential, but that was all it was at that stage. Just potential. He did mainly portraits then, to keep the money flowing in really. They got quite a bit of attention. There was marvellous life in his brushstrokes and a lovely grasp of detail. It was clear he had a talent. It was just a question of how it would develop.'

They were starting on their third pints. Dan checked his watch. It said 12.20, so it was probably around half past. He wondered if he'd missed out in life, should have become an academic. He rarely had a chance for lunch, and if he did it was usually a tasteless petrol station sandwich, gulped down in the car whilst driving to the next interview.

'Well, his talent developed nicely,' went on Ed. 'He moved into doing a few abstract bits, surreal even, but then came back to figures. He seemed to like figures, particularly women's. Liked them too much in fact.' He looked at Dan knowingly. 'More of that later. But his work was still largely local. He hadn't been picked up in London at all. Then he got his break. Do you remember the story of Russell Reid?'

Dan nodded. High-flying Labour MP for the Plymouth Tamar constituency in the early 1970s, prominent in the shadow cabinet. Party lost an election, suddenly he was the leader. Brief great hopes but defeated again. Never became prime minister, left politics, disillusioned.

181

'Well, he needed an official portrait done and he was very keen to do the man of the people thing and play up his local roots,' continued Ed. 'He'd seen McCluskey's work and asked him to paint it. He did and it was a fine job. It went down very well except for one thing. Just one little detail.'

Ed took another sip of beer. Dan knew he'd heard this story, but couldn't remember exactly what had happened. It was well before his time. 'Go on,' he said.

'His tie. His tie was a blazing conservative blue. He'd worn red for the sittings, but bloody McCluskey had painted it Tory blue. The press saw it and there was a hell of a row. McCluskey wouldn't comment. No artist worth his salt does. It's the mystery thing we like. It sells. But the papers went into his background and found out from his friends that McCluskey was a lifelong Labour man who thought the party was moving too much to the right. So that was how the picture was interpreted. A Labour man from the look of him, but Tory inside. It was a great story. And that was what made McCluskey famous. After that he could paint a dog's bum and it would sell for thousands.'

Dan chuckled into his pint. He didn't know if it was the beer, Ed's company, or the fascination of McCluskey and the Death Pictures, but he was feeling better. Mood swings, a classic symptom of the swamp. Beware the mood swings, he thought. After the light comes the dark, just like day and night, only faster, so very much faster.

'And he used – some say abused – his fame beautifully.' Ed had begun chortling too now. 'He was still young and a handsome bugger. He would meet women he liked the look of and offer to paint them. They would be flattered and accept. And he would paint them – amongst other things. Then later he took on students as well, and the word was that some of the women were taught in two ways. Horizontally and vertically.'

Ed's tone changed, more serious now. 'Then he met Abi and he did seem to fall in love with her. They settled down happily. For a while there was no talk of any affairs. Then it started, just one or two and much more discreet than before, but they were definitely there. You know how gossipy and bitchy the art world is. From what I've heard, the affairs went on up until he died.'

The two mysterious women in the Death Pictures, Dan thought. It must be. Were they important to the riddle? They'd certainly be important to El. And did Adam know this? Could they have something to do with McCluskey's death? He still wasn't quite convinced Kid did it, was he? He didn't know why. It was just a feeling, but he'd learned never to ignore them.

Dan jotted a couple of notes on his pad and asked, 'Ed, what did Abi think about all this?'

The professor considered, swirled the remains of his pint. 'It's difficult to tell. They were a very private pair and I didn't know her well. All I can say is that she always stood by him. She seemed very loyal and was obviously totally devoted. He certainly loved her. For what it's worth, my guess is she accepted his little failings and indiscretions. Many women do you know. It's one of the great differences between the sexes.'

Dan felt his mind race. What if Abi hadn't accepted it? What if she was growing more and more jealous and angry? Could she have killed her husband? But then, how did that fingerprint of Kid's get on the knife? And didn't she have an alibi? And then that question again; why kill him right at the end, after so many years of affairs when he was about to die anyway? He'd have to talk to Adam, and El too. It was time they compared notes on their research.

'What about Kid?' asked Dan. 'How did he and McCluskey know each other? And what was their falling out about?'

'Many questions you have,' replied Ed. 'That's three in one go. I'm off to the loo. It'll probably help me form my answers if I have something to stimulate my mind when I return.' Dan got up and made his way back to the bar.

'So then, Kid,' said Ed, settling himself back down and sipping at his pint. Dan felt relieved to see it wasn't going down as quickly as its predecessors.

'Kid was one of McCluskey's pupils, and a talented one too. Probably the most talented of the set and they were a

183

pretty good bunch. McCluskey only took on a very few and they had to be good. Kid was, very good. It was obvious from the start he was going to make it big. He had a great eye for colour and form. A bit more abstract than McCluskey, but a very fine painter. And he did sculptures too. Not as many as his paintings, but the sculptures were very good. You know about how he became famous, with the burger sculpture? That was a corker.'

Dan nodded. Ed sat back and smiled, waved at a student in another corner of the bar.

'How close were they, Kid and McCluskey?' Dan asked.

'Very close. McCluskey used to talk about him in terms I never heard him use about anyone. He had no children you see, and I think Kid was like a son to him, if you'll excuse the pun. Yes, they were very close.'

'So how did they fall out?'

'It was never entirely clear, but this is how the story goes. McCluskey had another pupil, Joanna someone. I can't remember the name. She was talented too, maybe even as good as Kid. McCluskey was very fond of her, perhaps even had designs on her. Who knows? I wouldn't have put it past him. But Kid was fond of her as well, too much so. They got it together, as I believe the saying goes, and became a couple. It lasted a few years, but then Kid dumped her for some other woman…'

The professor's words faltered, and Dan sensed he remembered something unpalatable, was debating whether to reveal it. He felt his journalist's instinct activate. It was the sensitive ground, the dark land of secret regret which was where the best stories were always found.

He let the silence run, then prompted, 'Go on.'

Ed sighed. 'Well, there was talk of… violence too. That Kid had a nasty temper. Would occasionally… lose it. And take it out on Joanna. But that was just the talk, all right? I've got no evidence to back it up.'

Dan held the professor's look, nodded. So, perhaps Kid wasn't the peaceful man he'd claimed to be. Maybe he was capable of murder… killing Joseph McCluskey by slitting his wrists, just as Adam believed. The information would be no use to the inquiry – it sounded like pure gossip, no evidence to substantiate it – but it was certainly an interesting insight.

'Anyway,' Ed continued, 'Joanna was besotted with him and stuck with it, whatever the relationship was like. And when Kid left her…. she was distraught. McCluskey and Abi looked after her for quite a while, but the word was she never got over him. She stopped painting and moved away. I don't know where she went. That was what caused the split. McCluskey blamed Kid for ruining her and destroying her talent and they didn't talk after that. Well, not until McCluskey knew he was dying and they had that much publicised reconciliation.'

Dan noted all that down. 'What did she look like, this Joanna?'

Ed swirled his pint again and screwed his eyes shut. 'I don't really know. I met her once I think, but it was a long time ago and I can only vaguely remember it.' He paused, took a drink. 'The one thing I do remember is her hair. Vivid red it was, really striking.'

A flame-haired woman. The one riding the mobile phone in the first of the Death Pictures? It had to be. So did that painting take on new significance? Was she one of McCluskey's lovers, or just someone he wanted remembered? And what did the mobile phone mean? Dan felt an urge to get away, to start looking at the pictures again, but he had another couple of questions first.

'Ed, you must have looked at the pictures and thought about the riddle. Any ideas?'

The professor shook his head. 'Not a clue. I did work through them, but I couldn't make any sense of it. I'm an artist, not a bloody magician.'

Dan studied him. No, he wasn't keeping anything back, he was sure of it. Almost sure anyway.

'Was there anything in his life that McCluskey built? Or helped to build, like some project he was involved in? Or anything to do with digging? I know they sound like odd questions, but I'm wondering if there's a hint about something like that in the pictures.'

Ed finished his beer, gave a wry smile. 'You think you're on to something?'

'Maybe. I don't know. I've thought that before and got nowhere, but it's worth a try.'

'Well, there was only the Advent Project that I can think of. He supported and helped in the marketing and even did a couple of pictures for it. He was a great advocate of Advent. He thought it was a wonderful idea.'

Advent. Advent! The garden of the world captured under plastic domes in an old Cornish china clay pit. That had risen from the earth. And there was the chough in one of the pictures, the symbol of Cornwall. Dan felt a stirring of excitement. Could any of the numbers relate to something at Advent?

'There is one thing you should know if you're going to go hunting for McCluskey's prize.' Ed hauled himself up from his seat and put out his hand. Dan shook it warmly. 'Thanks for the drinks, by the way,' the professor added. 'But I really should go and do some more mundane work now.'

'Go ahead,' replied Dan, also getting up and trying to ignore the slight dizziness the effort brought.

'Remember this about McCluskey. He was basically a good man and if he says the answer to the riddle is in his pictures somewhere, then it is there. But he was also a little sod. He loved to tease and get one over on people and he was incredibly vain. He thought his way was the only way. What he believed was right was right, and he also thought he was cleverer than anyone else. Remember that. It might just help you.'

Outside, Dan took a series of deep breaths and decided to walk home to sober himself up. He wanted to look through the pictures again and needed a clear head to do it. It should take 25 minutes from the University he thought, but it's uphill most of the way and I bet it'll be more like 35 carrying the weight of these pints.

He rang El on the way, but got a response he'd never had before. The photographer's phone was turned off. He stared at

186

his mobile in surprise. Yes, it was the right number he'd called. There it was in the phone's address list. There was no answer machine service – El didn't need one, he prided himself on being available at all hours – so, baffled, Dan left it. He could call again later. What would El possibly be doing that meant his phone was off?

He made it to the top of Mutley Plain and gathered his strength for the final hill to Hartley Avenue when his mobile rang. El? No, it was a withheld number. Bad news, that usually meant work. Should he answer it? He'd better. He already felt guilty about sneaking a day off. He fumbled the phone from his pocket.

'Dan, Lizzie.' Her voice was sharp, fast. 'Where are you?'

'I'm on Mannamead Road, just up from Mutley. But I can't drive anywhere. I've had a few...'

'Keep walking. Nigel will pick you up.'

'What's going...?'

'Wessex airport. Plane crash. Need you on it.'

Chapter Fourteen

A LANE OF SOLID traffic loomed motionless in front of them. Red brake lights formed an unbroken line up the hill. Nigel didn't hesitate. He swerved the car onto the empty oncoming carriageway and headed past the queue, up to the road block. Dan closed his eyes, then opened them again when he started to feel sick. He grabbed the bottle of water Nigel held out to him and downed as much as he could. With an afterthought he splashed some on his face.

A police car was parked diagonally across the road, blocking it. A uniformed officer held up his hand. Nigel pumped the brakes and they stopped. Dan stuck his head out of the window. There was no time to negotiate. Every second was vital in a big story. He checked the man's shoulders for signs of a rank. Just a constable, good.

'Officer, Dan Groves, TV News. We're here to meet Chief Inspector Breen.'

The name-dropping did its work. The policeman jumped back as if pulled by an elastic band and waved them through. Nigel accelerated towards the airport. 'Nice bluff,' was all he said. Ahead they could see a knot of fire engines and ambulances, blue lights flashing through the grey gloom of the day. Beyond them a thickening plume of angry black smoke stretched towards the sky. Suddenly Dan felt very sober.

His mobile warbled. El. His phone had given him a missed call message.

'Hi mate, just wanted a chat, but I think you'll want me now,' said Dan quickly. 'There's a plane crash at the airport. You'd better get here. Where are you? The hospital? You OK? Then what are you..? Oh never mind, we'll talk later.'

Nigel pulled the car up on the grass verge by the terminal and leapt out. He ran to the boot and grabbed the camera. Dan took the tripod and microphone and they strode into the building. The doors to the runway were open so they jogged through, then stopped suddenly at the sight.

188

It was a twin propeller aircraft, the type he'd flown on many times to London. Instead of sitting upright, it rested pathetically on the remnants of its left wing. The engine was gone, looked as if it had been ripped off. The remaining wing was just a stump, reduced to blackened, melted plastic and spindly, twisted wire. The right wing was untouched and stretched up into the air. The plane's passenger doors were open and an inflatable gangway bridged the drop to the ground. Some survivors then, at least some…

The side of the fuselage closest to them had been licked a charred black where the hungry flames played along it. The white tail fin was scorched too, one of its rudders warped by the blaze's heat. Fire engines surrounded the plane, jets of water directed onto it. An acrid smell of scorching plastic stung the air. Tiny streams of running foam stretched out from the wreckage like tentacles.

Nigel hoisted the camera up on his shoulder and began filming. Dan stared on, shaken. Where were the passengers? About 30 people would have been inside. They weren't still in there, surely? What chance would they have had? He sensed a movement to his side, spun around.

A group of people walked slowly from the side of the terminal building. Some had their arms around each other, a few wore orange blankets over their shoulders. Survivors. Just what he needed. The golden rule in a disaster; always interview the survivors and eyewitnesses first. The police, fire and other uniforms will hang around to talk. The victims just want to escape.

'Nigel!' he hissed. The cameraman turned, saw the group and they ran over to them.

'Out of the way please,' said a small man in a dark blue uniform who was leading them. 'They're upset. We need to get them to hospital.'

No chance, thought Dan. Not a hope. I'm the only journalist here and I'm not missing this scoop. Just a few seconds, that's all we need. Just got to stop them for a moment.

Dan pulled Nigel in front of the group. The cable linking

the microphone he carried to the camera made an effective barrier. The little man's arm went up but Dan pushed it aside. Behind him, the survivors stopped.

'I'll have you arrested,' the man gasped.

'In a minute,' said Dan, thankful he was slight and easily held off. 'Just a word first.' He pushed the microphone under the nose of a young-looking man, a good bet for being composed enough to want to talk.

'What happened?' asked Dan quickly

'Shit, it was terrifying.' His voice was shaking. 'We were coming in to land normally. Just before we hit the runway, this voice came over the intercom, shouting brace, brace, brace!! Undercarriage failure. So we all tucked our heads down between our knees like you're supposed to. The plane hit the runway and tilted horribly on its side. We were catapulted forwards. People were screaming. There was this sickening screeching, grinding sound. I smelt burning and smoke and I thought we were all going to die. It seemed to go on for ever. Then the plane spun round and stopped and I looked up. There was smoke everywhere and I could see flames coming out of the side. People had stopped screaming. They were just whimpering now. No one knew what to do, but the stewardess was wonderful. She calmly said to everyone to walk towards her slowly. Then she opened the door and we jumped down onto this bouncy thing. There was smoke all around and the plane was on fire. I think we all got out, but Hell, it was a close thing. I thought my number was up.'

Brilliant thought Dan. But another one would be even better. Just one more, a woman if possible. The little man was pushing hard at him and he could see other uniforms approaching fast from the terminal. They only had a few seconds.

He spotted a middle-aged woman in the middle of the group. She was nodding at what the other passenger had said. 'What did you see?' Dan asked quickly.

'Everything was going normally,' she said. Her voice was thin and breathless, her face pale. 'We were about to land and then the pilot told us to brace. I was so scared... so scared. I

190

just kept my head down and said my prayers. There was smoke and flames everywhere. There was so much noise, horrible, screeching noise. Then we all had to jump out of the door onto this mattress thing. It was the most frightening thing I've ever known.'

Wonderful. The key to the story. Two fantastic interviews with the survivors and even better, not a sniff of another hack. Some great pictures too. The golden secret to television cracked in just a few minutes work. People and pictures always made stories and he had the lot.

Now just the rest of the details to get. What happened, how many were on the plane, did they all survive, that sort of thing. He was so lost thinking about it he hardly felt the arms on his shoulders and the police officer telling him and Nigel they were under arrest.

Dirty El ran as fast as his lumbering frame would allow, across the hospital grounds to his car. His eyes were fixed on the smoke in the sky just to the north.

He was about to jump in to the driver's seat and roar off when he had a thought. The airport was only five minutes away, but there was just one road in. It would be closed and heavily patrolled. He didn't stand a chance of talking his way through. The police knew him too well now and would delight in stopping him after all the tricks he'd pulled on them. There was a mug shot of him on the wall of the cop stations in Plymouth, alongside the wanted criminals.

El let his panting subside while he thought. He was in a hospital. And what had he just seen gathered here that could help him? He dumped his white doctor's coat, got his camera out of the boot and jogged back over to the Accident and Emergency Department. It was more exercise than he'd had in months, but it would be worth it. Plane crash pictures sold.

A line of three ambulances stood waiting, all empty. Discharging their patients no doubt. He tried the back doors of the nearest one. They were open. El climbed in, shutting them softly behind him and slid under one of the two beds. It was a gamble. What if he ended up at some school football match watching a twisted ankle being treated? But it was this or nothing. He'd never get to the airport any other way. He stroked his camera for luck.

It was only a couple of minutes later that two paramedics leapt in, flicked on the emergency lights and siren and sped away. El crossed his fingers and lifted his head to look out of the windscreen. His chubby, freckled face relaxed into a grin. Off up the road, waved through the police cordon and into the airport in no time. This was the way to travel. He waited until the medics got out to talk to some firemen, then slipped out of the back, walked over to the terminal and began taking photos.

The snaps were wonderful. A wounded and charred plane, striking and dramatic. The local papers would certainly take them and probably some of the nationals too. He could hear the cash register ringing. With what he'd managed earlier in the hospital, this was turning out to be his day.

He hummed a little tune to himself as he clicked off a big close up of the melted wing, and improvised one of his limericks.

'It can be a disaster,
Needing more than a plaster,
A fire on a plane,
Usually brings pain,
But for El it can mean earnings vaster!'

The paparazzo thought he might even push his luck and buy a lottery ticket on the way home.

'Officer, I hate to be pedantic, but trespass is a civil offence. You don't actually have the power to arrest us,' said Dan, as he and Nigel were marched back to the terminal.

'We'll see what the Inspector has to say about that, sir.'

'Well, OK, but I'm just trying to give you a friendly warning. You're going to make a fool of yourself.'

'We'll see about that, sir,' said the officer determinedly.

Dan exchanged a look with Nigel. Officious constables were a hazard of the job. It wasn't the first time they'd been arrested. The last occasion was when they'd filmed a big crash on one of the South-west's few dual carriageways. There was

192

a five-mile jam, so they'd taken some back lanes and found a farm that neighboured the road. The farmer had been happy for them to cross his land. But the constable they met when they emerged on the road had decided he didn't want the accident filmed. It was too shocking to be shown on TV, he said.

It's a matter for us what we show, Dan had tried to explain, not you. We won't broadcast any distressing pictures, but we need something to explain to the viewers what happened. We'll use less intrusive wide shots of the wreckage and an interview with some of the eyewitnesses. How's that for a compromise?

The officer didn't seem to understand the concept and had tried to confiscate the camera tape. Dan stopped him and they'd been arrested. They were released an hour later after Lizzie scrambled a solicitor to Police Headquarters with a writ citing the Chief Constable for wrongful arrest. A written apology had followed. Dan kept a copy of it in his bag for occasions such as today.

'Do you want to see where you're acting outside of your authority?' he asked the constable, offering the sheets. 'It's right here.'

'Shut up, please, sir,' the man snapped. 'Sit there.' He pointed to a line of seats. 'I'm going to book you in with the Inspector.'

Dan and Nigel watched as he walked over to a police van and disappeared inside.

'Two minutes it'll take,' whispered Dan.

'Five,' said Nigel. 'Shall I see if anyone's about in the canteen and get us a coffee?'

The constable emerged from the van. Dan checked his watch. 95 seconds. He thought the man looked paler. He tried not to smile as the officer walked back over to them.

'You're free to go, sir,' he said heavily. 'But please keep behind the cordon we're going to set up.'

They walked out of the front of the airport to the gathering media scrum. The journalists and photographers were standing behind some newly strung out blue-and-white police tape. Dan

193

and Nigel ducked under it and joined them. Loud was there, moaning to a radio reporter about the cost of a dentist's appointment. He was wearing a shirt which boasted parading peacocks. Not great for a plane crash thought Dan, but better than it might have been. He seemed to have a memory that Loud owned at least one shirt patterned with aircraft taking off into a sunny sky.

'They want loads,' he grunted. 'A big report and lots of live stuff. I guess we'll be busy. And I was supposed to be going to a wrestling match tonight.'

Dan didn't know what to say to that. He couldn't quite see Loud screaming and shouting as a couple of half-naked men twisted each other's bodies into submission.

A man in a black suit strode out of the airport and made for the pack. Cameras were hoisted onto shoulders and microphones offered. He stood in the middle and faced them.

'Ladies and Gentlemen, I'm Phil Webber, Deputy Director of Wessex Airport. I've got a statement for you and then I'll take questions. Is everyone ready?'

There was a good-natured chorus of 'yes'. A big story always cheered the hacks, despite the cool drizzle that was moping from the leaden sky.

'At 1.31 this afternoon, a twin-engined passenger plane en route from the Channel Islands to Plymouth suffered a failure in its undercarriage whilst landing. The structure supporting the left wheel failed to lock and collapsed on contact with the runway. The plane skidded along on one wheel and its wing, which then caught fire. When the plane came to a halt, the cabin crew put the emergency procedures into place and evacuated the aircraft. I'm pleased to say all 24 people on board were unharmed. They were shaken but unhurt. They were taken to hospital for a check up, but all have now been released. The airport's emergency plan was put into action, with fire engines and ambulances scrambled. The fire was put out, but, I'm happy to say, apart from that they weren't needed. An investigation into what happened has begun. The airport was closed for a couple of hours this afternoon, but has now fully reopened. I must stress, incidents of this nature are extremely rare and flying remains a very safe form of travel. Thank you.'

There was a second's pause for the hacks to digest that, then the questions poured in.

'Did the wet weather have anything to do with it?'

'No. We don't think so.'

'How long will the investigation take?'

'We don't know yet.'

'Are any of the passengers or crew available to speak to us?'

'No.'

Dan signalled the cut throat motion to Nigel to tell him to stop recording. This wasn't worth taping.

'Mr Webber, Dan Groves, *Wessex Tonight*. Are you available to be interviewed here live tonight?'

'No.'

Can't blame him, Dan thought. The story wouldn't exactly look good for the airport. It would just be himself appearing then, but that was fine. The report was much more important than any interview. And how sweet to hear that none of the passengers would be interviewed by the other hacks.

Dan climbed into the outside broadcast van beside Loud.

'Ready in a minute,' he said. 'Just got to call the newsdesk for instructions.'

Lizzie answered the phone. Not unusual that when a big story was unfolding. She liked to know everything first. Dan explained the details. An editor with less of a sharp nose for news might have thought the lack of deaths softened the splash. Not Lizzie. She had an almost supernatural ability to sense an angle.

Plane crashes were always a big story, but what you could usually guarantee was people being killed. And based on the classical theory that the definition of news is that which is out of the ordinary – not dog bites man, but man bites dog – a crash with everyone surviving ranked even higher in a good editor's esteem. There was a final blunt but winning point in the debate. Survivors could tell their gripping accounts of what happened. That wasn't exactly an option in a normal plane crash scenario.

Dan sensed her thoughts, and just managed to get his words in first. 'I reckon we go for a miraculous escape-type story.'

'My idea exactly. It's extraordinary. Great tale. Do it. I want lots. I want people. I want pictures. I want shock. I want power. I want emotion.'

They started editing. Loud put down a couple of pictures of the wrecked plane, a wide shot first, then a detailed close up of the charred wing. Dan added his commentary, just a few sparse words. He wanted to quickly get to the survivors' accounts. They were the important part, the drama.

'24 people were on board the plane when the undercarriage collapsed on landing,' he intoned. 'There was a fire and extensive damage, but all were evacuated safely.'

Ideal, two lines just to set up what happened and see the damage the crash had caused. The viewers would be in no doubt how lucky the passengers were to escape. Then it was into the interviews, the young man first, then the woman. He used all they had to say. The power of their story needed no embellishment.

After that, they put down some general shots of the airport. Dan talked about it being closed for a couple of hours and an investigation launched, the reason for the undercarriage failure unknown. Then it was into some clips of the fire service and the airport's Deputy Director. Lastly came more pictures of the crashed plane and the pay off piece of commentary, not exciting but necessary. The basic details of where the plane was from and going to next.

They watched it back. Not a bad piece of work, Dan thought. Three minutes worth and it flies by. Time for the live report.

He squeezed his earpiece in and hopped out of the van. Nigel had set up the camera with a view back onto the runway and the wrecked plane, now covered in a quilt of blue and grey tarpaulins. This time they wouldn't do an opening live link. The newsreader back in the studio would introduce the report. It was better to get straight onto the pictures and hear from the survivors, not have Dan standing waffling for 30 seconds to set the scene.

He came in after the report with some details of the normally good safety record of the plane and the airport, important for context. They got the all clear from the broadcast gallery and Dan said goodbye to Nigel and Loud, jumped into a waiting taxi and was away, back to the flat for a quick wash and change. He hadn't had much time to talk to El in the media scrum, but they'd arranged to meet at eight in the Old Bank for a couple of beers and a debrief. El's beaming grin said he had something interesting to tell.

El was in his usual alcove opposite the bar. Like a spider lying in wait, Dan thought. His grin hadn't dimmed and he had a whisky on the table in front of him next to his pint.

'Another?' asked Dan.

'The pint's still OK, but I wouldn't mind a nice spirit. Surprise me.'

Dan strolled over to the bar. He ordered himself some ale and was tempted to get El a Campari and soda – that would certainly surprise him – but he opted for vodka instead. Neat.

'What are you grinning about, then?' Dan asked, taking his coat off and sitting down.

Outside, the drizzle had turned into persistent rain. He sipped the beer. It tasted good, very good. With El in this sort of mood, it could be a long night. He hadn't lost the taste for beer after that excellent lunchtime session with Ed. The plane crash had taken his mind off it, but he was pleased to find it lingering. Even more pleased that the excitement of the crash had forced the swamp back, for now at least.

'I got some great snaps of that plane before they covered it over with tarpaulins,' said El. 'No one else did. Ta for the tip. They'll bring me a few quid. The papers are going for it as an extraordinary escape story.'

'Yeah, that was the line I took. It's a good tale. But you sounded like you were up to something before that. So come on, what is it? McCluskey?'

El's grin stayed fixed, but he shook his head. 'You said you'd found out something. You go first.'

Dan didn't bother arguing, told him what he'd learned from Ed about McCluskey's life and possible hints regarding the solution to the riddle. The photographer's eyes widened when Dan explained about Joanna and how she could be one of the women in the Death Pictures. El leaned back, joined his hands behind his head and sighed.

'I knew it was my day,' he said happily.

'Come on then, what have you found?' asked Dan.

'I've found the other one.'

'The other what? The other woman?' El nodded, beaming. 'How?'

'Well, it's like this. You know I went to the Fancy Dress shop?'

'Yeah... I did think it odd for a while, but then knowing you...'

'I got myself a very convincing doctor's white coat and stethoscope because I was following a hunch. I reckoned this. Where would McCluskey be more likely to meet a nice young lady who he'd become attached to than in the hospital where he was being treated for his cancer? So I staked out the oncology unit over a few days and guess who I should bump into? A beautiful blonde woman with glasses. A Dr Rebecca Sanders, cancer specialist. I asked her why she looked familiar. Had I seen her in some picture somewhere? She didn't say anything, just blushed and hurried off. I took that as a yes and after the passage of a couple of bottles of malt whisky to the all-knowing hospital porters, Dirty El discovers it's the talk of the ward. I've got a few lovely snaps of her.' El's grin widened. 'That's one down and one to go. And we've got a good lead on the other one too, so I reckon we're well on the way.'

El held up his vodka and downed it in one. 'Here's to Joseph McCluskey. Cheers!'

Chapter Fifteen

HE SWALLOWED TO KEEP the anger down and flinched at the burning in his stomach. No one did this to him. No one. Fellow barristers, solicitors, even judges might try it on. But he could always better them. No dull-headed, fat and ugly woman plod was going to get away with it.

The police car had followed him to his chambers again this morning and his fellows were starting to notice. Notice, and have a joke at his expense, and no one did that to Edward Munroe. No one. You didn't become a Law Lord by being a figure of fun on your home circuit. He rubbed his stomach. The humiliation was giving him heartburn.

'Morning Edward! The police recognised your talents need safeguarding, eh? They've been told to keep a future Attorney General under close protection no doubt. Don't want the future of the British legal system imperilled in any way...'

That, from a fellow barrister, was just about bearable. But from the lowly chambers' clerk, no more than a jumped-up bloody bookkeeper...

'Good morning sir,' the obnoxious little man had chirped. 'Have you become a master criminal over the weekend? What was it, doing 32 in a 30 limit? Or you haven't been riding a bike without lights again have you? And you, a bastion of the law...'

He'd had to hide his clenched fists in the pockets of his bespoke suit. This nonsense had been going on quite long enough. It would stop.

He knew what it was all about. His refusal to give that DNA sample of course. They were trying to intimidate him. Utterly disgraceful and totally unacceptable he would call it, to hound a man because of his beliefs. He swiped away a pile of papers on his polished teak desk and caught a glance of his reflection in the shining wood. He looked jaded he thought, a little sweaty, not his usual clinically composed self, and it was all because of the stupid damned idiot police. It was the kind of behaviour more befitting a tin-pot dictatorship, not a fine and free democracy like the one he was so proud to serve.

The very words he would use, the very words. And he'd add a little snipe about the dreadful waste of scarce resources too, when such a dangerous criminal as this rapist remained at large.

He slid some personal headed notepaper out of his drawer and poised his fountain pen above it. Having that dullard of an Assistant Chief Constable as a dining companion was a most useful asset sometimes, even if it meant hours of suffering the man's stupefying anecdotes. A letter first, then followed up with a phone call.

'Dear Brian,

I am so sorry to trouble you, but you should be aware of some most unacceptable events which are unfolding within your constabulary. It is my unfortunate duty to have to complain in the strongest of terms...'

Edward Munroe felt himself relax as he wrote. He bet himself a box of Havana cigars that his escort would be gone by tomorrow.

He didn't know whether to rage, be shocked or feel sick. So they thought he was a paedophile.

Will Godley had seen the neighbours gossiping in the street. Little gangs of two or three chatting, sly and secretive, pointing over to his house, the patrol car outside, the policeman sometimes sitting inside reading a book, sometimes leaning on the bonnet.

It was the man's cheerfulness that irritated him most. Always that bloody 'Good morning, Sir!' or 'Good afternoon, Sir!' or whatever. And it was the sarcasm too. 'Just doing my rounds, sir...' his rounds which consisted of Will Godley's home, or outside the dockyard while he was at work, or even the pub when he fancied a pint.

He could have handled it if it hadn't been for the graffiti he'd found sprayed on his wall this morning. Yellow paint, appalling handwriting and even worse spelling, but the message very clear.

'PEEDO'

He could hardly believe it. He'd had to sit down on the wall to look again. Surely they didn't think? They couldn't think..? Him, a devoted Dad to his kids, a man who'd be even more dedicated if the bloody courts and system would give him a chance. Him!

But he could see how it would add up to the locals. Some here knew he had kids but didn't get to see them much. He'd moaned about that enough down the boozer. And then there was this police watch on him. Yes, he saw how it could look.

He knew what it was all about, of course, but he wasn't giving them that DNA sample. Sod them. He owed the system nothing – it owed him – and he wasn't going to help them, not in any way whatsoever. Why should he? He'd done nothing wrong. Quite the opposite. Sod them.

He wasn't putting up with this. It was harassment and he knew just what to do about that. No point in complaining to the cops, they were all in this together. But he knew a better way, to embarrass them and force them to leave him alone.

He took a can of lager from the fridge, lit a cigarette and opened the packet of writing paper he'd bought from the corner shop. Letters of protest to *The Wessex Standard*, the *Western Daily News* and the TV. They'd love a story about a waste of police resources at a time when they should be devoting their efforts to catching the rapist. That would do it.

Steven Freeman scarcely bothered checking his mirror for the police car. He was content it would be with him, like the guardian angel it had become. And yes, there it was, a couple of cars back in the traffic.

He'd relaxed now, worked out they had nothing on him, nothing at all. Otherwise they would have arrested him, wouldn't they? They were just trying to push him into a mistake. Well, they were out of luck.

They were taking the piss out of him, so he'd decided to turn their little game around and take the piss out of them. Night shifts were always the most lucrative in taxiing. The turnout from the pubs and clubs left the city awash with fares.

Working ten at night to four in the morning could make you a pretty penny, but there was a price.

He'd stopped doing them, got sick of the aggro. The rows about the fares, the threats and fights, the people who sprinted off without paying. But now he was back on nights and raking in the cash without any hassle at all. He turned the radio up as the guitar of T. Rex's 'Get it On' rang out. Good driving music. It was amazing how well your passengers behaved with a police escort right behind you.

One of the modern wonders of the world it was often called, and Dan couldn't disagree.

He hadn't been to the Advent Project for more than a year and was amazed how it had grown. As Environment Correspondent, he'd seen it rise from a sludge-filled china clay pit in an overlooked part of Cornwall to become one of Britain's finest attractions. Every time he visited he wondered at the huge bubble domes, their plastic skin and the lightweight silver metal web that anchored them together. Inside thrived a living and ever-changing theatre, the bursting trees and plants, towering into the air, a spectrum of dizzying colour in leaves and blossoms and blooms.

Dan hardly noticed the jungle of the tropical zone crowding around him. His interest wasn't what was on show, but what could be hidden. The answer to McCluskey's riddle. He sat down on one of the tyres – part of the rubber display – and looked around, wondering if the solution could really be here.

To his side, a waterfall cascaded and crashed from the rock face fifty feet up at the peak of the dome. Its cooling spray split the sunlight into floating rainbows and wafted a welcome relief from the cloying humidity of the air. Wax-leaved plants waved contentedly and spots of vibrant red and yellow flowers crept up the cliff. A slow snake of people trundled past, pointing, touching and talking, all struggling to take in the spectacle.

So McCluskey was a big advocate of Advent. It meant a lot to him. So what? Was there something here that would help? Was the answer here? Dan leafed through the prints of the pictures and his notes, more covered with question marks than anything else.

The grid references he thought might have existed in the pictures didn't mean anything in Advent, or anywhere near it. Nowhere at all in fact. He'd wondered if the PIN numbers might have something to do with the range of interactive exhibits they had in the visitor centre, but nothing tallied. On a whim he'd even checked the pay phones for numbers containing 225, but found nothing. So he sat, stumped again. Still, it was a beautiful place to be baffled in. He wiped some of the waterfall's drifting spray from his face and tried to force his mind to find the elusive inspiration.

What about symbolism in the pictures? Was he taking them too literally, looking for grid references and PIN numbers? Possibly, but he'd always had the feeling the answer was in the numbers and he'd learned never to ignore his hunches.

Hang on, picture four. What was picture four? Dan fumbled it out. The drooping clock in the desert landscape. The next dome was the Mediterranean zone. And that looked like a desert. It was worth a try. It had to be. He picked up his papers and made his way towards it.

A very different feel to this dome, he thought. The air was drier and the plants less lush, built to survive, not flourish as they had in the tropical zone. Spidery fronds against the sandy earth, bare rock faces with only splashes of dry green clinging on grimly. He checked picture four again. It did look similar. He felt another growing excitement and checked himself. Don't get too enthused. OK, it looked similar, but it was still a huge area he was facing here. Where to start? Where to look? And what for? Did he expect the answer to be here, or just another clue? Or anything at all?

Dan walked slowly up a path, past some copper sculptures of grazing goats. His feet crunched on the sand and gravel. There was a snake in the picture forming an S shape, but no goats. He looked around. What could the S signify? Just ahead was a children's interactive exhibit, a board with letters on, letters you pushed to light up an area on the display. A possibility? He hurried down.

A couple of children stood pressing the buttons and he felt an urge to push them out of the way, but resisted it, waited. They quickly got bored and wandered off. Dan reached out and pressed the hexagonal S key.

A display lit up, a message. S is for sand. It looks difficult to live in, but some manage. Cacti love it and snakes slither across it.

He stood back, pressed it again. Cacti and snake, just as in the picture. It had to mean something. He stared at the board, pressed the button again.

A voice rose behind him. 'Excuse me?' Dan turned. A youngish man holding a boy's hand, waiting politely. 'Do you mind if we have a go?'

Dan mumbled an apology and stood aside, still staring at the board. McCluskey had to have been thinking of this place when he painted it. He was sure of it. Was there anything on the board that could help? He followed the alphabet. Animals, Burrowing, Cacti, Desert. No, nothing he could see. So what else was in the picture?

It was the simplest of the ten. Was that significant? Was McCluskey saying the answer was simple, that it was here, that all the other pictures were diversions? Dan hissed in exasperation.

Cacti feature in the picture, two of them together. Dan walked slowly around the dome. There were cacti everywhere, but only one place where two stood close together, almost intertwined like new lovers. He felt another surge of adrenaline and checked around. No attendants. Dan hopped over the low wooden fence, bent down and quickly examined the ground. No, nothing buried here. He stood up, his eyes running over the firm green of the plants' flesh and their angry needles. Nothing written here, nothing attached to the cacti. Nothing at all as far as he could see. Cursing he rejoined the path, ignoring the curious looks of the other visitors.

A little further along there was a pond, a big one, more like a small pool, plants dangling thirsty fronds into its still waters. And there was a pool in the picture... He walked over and stared at it, slowly scrutinised the area around, but could see nothing. No obvious S shapes, no numbers, nothing. Even the displays about how water was a precious commodity in the Mediterranean climate didn't offer any hope.

Dan sat down on a wooden bench in the middle of the dome and looked around him, then down at his prints of the Death Pictures. Nothing. Not a bloody thing. It was tantalising though. It couldn't be a coincidence, that some of the features here matched the pictures, could it? If the answer wasn't here, McCluskey must have been thinking of Advent when he created the riddle. There could be a clue here he was missing, or… He remembered what Ed had told him. McCluskey loved getting one over on people. It could just be an intricate joke.

What were his instincts telling him? He knew he believed there was something here. But what? Or was that just wishful thinking? Hoping his journey wasn't wasted. But it wasn't wasted, was it? He hadn't been for a while and it was a good day out.

Dan smiled knowingly, shook his head. He could con many people, but never himself. He stared up at the silver spider's web of the dome's supports and felt a tug from the swamp. It was still there, lurking darkly on the edge of his mind, waiting for its moment.

No, not now, he could hold it off. He had this quest to complete. He was here to find the answer to McCluskey's riddle and he was sure there was something in Advent somewhere. But where? He waited, tried to think, but the stage of his mind remained obstinately empty, no matter how hard he worked to usher ideas onto it. Well, if all else fails, have an ice cream and a wander.

Dan ambled down a sandy hill to the little wooden stall in the corner of the dome and checked what was on offer. A vanilla tub would do nicely, good brain food and fresh, Cornish produce. They were strong on that at Advent, always tried to source their food and drink locally.

He queued behind a couple of old ladies, wearing raincoats despite the dry heat. Then he saw it. A number 559, tiny, ingrained on the base of one of the dome's metal supports. He'd never have noticed it if he wasn't so close to the edge of the structure and part of the number hadn't been flecked with green paint.

Dan strode over and checked the next support. 560 was etched on it. So each was individually numbered. That made sense. He remembered from reporting on the building of Advent that all the supports were different lengths and shapes, depending on what part of the quarry they were designed for. The whole thing had been built from a kit of parts, like a giant model.

He felt his pulse quicken. The ice cream forgotten, he checked picture four. A three-figure number in here? Where? Nothing obvious, it had to be the clock. The drooping hands on a quarter past nine. 915…

He'd been feeling good this morning. The weekend with Annie and Tom had gone beautifully. The whole day together on Saturday, to the beach at Bigbury and blessed with spring sunshine, a kick about in the sand, some rock-pooling, then lunch and a drink at the pub on Burgh Island. Perfect family life and for once his pager hadn't bleeped its disruptive electronic burble.

The McCluskey case was sorted. The rapist case was… on hold? In the process of being sorted…? Well, whatever, they were doing all they could. His family was keeping it from his mind and he had a chance to try to repair and rebuild the relationship. He hardly dared to believe, but it seemed to be working.

He'd stayed at home – his old home – on Saturday night. He'd cuddled up with Annie in the enveloping, king-size bed, their first joint buy when they moved in together, and tried to forget that cold and lonely one-bedroom flat he was forced to rent.

They'd looked in on Tom before they'd gone to bed. The boy's hair was sprayed out on his pillow, as always. Adam smiled. His dad's influence that. His hair could be impossible to shape up in the morning. And that sleeping smile on his son's face, he saw so much in it. The smile of a contented boy, knowing his father was there to love, help and protect him. In that moment, holding Annie's hand, them looking at each other, he resolved to make his wife and son his priority. Not his job. Not any more. It was just like the time when Tom was born. He could only remember it as a valium haze of family contentment, centred on that tiny, wrinkled face. Nothing mattered except Tom and Annie.

He'd lain awake thinking about it, Annie's soft breathing next to him. He'd said it before. Did he mean it now? It felt like he did, but what would happen the next time he was scrambled to a murder or rape? Or if the man they were hunting now struck again? Would it take him over? And what about Sarah? Could he justify it to her now? He was surprised to allow himself to let the thought slip away in his sleepy contentment.

The warmth had lingered until he'd got into work this morning and the call from the Assistant Chief Constable.

'What the hell's going on with the overtime budget, Adam? It's soaring. And uniform are moaning you keep nicking their officers to sit around and do nothing.'

'The rape case is staff-intensive, sir. We need uniform back-up.'

The phone line burst with a splutter. Brian Flood wasn't a patient man.

'Back-up yes, but not the whole bloody Plymouth division! You've got three cars out following people day and night. It's costing a fortune.'

He'd expected the call, knew he wouldn't get away with it for long.

'They're the prime suspects we're following, sir. And we're getting results. There hasn't been another attack since we started following them.'

'But you haven't caught him, have you?'

'We're working on it.'

Another splutter. 'Well you're going to have to work on it some other way. We can't afford the manpower or cost. Today is the last day of your triple surveillance operation, understood?'

'But sir…'

'Understood?!'

Adam knew from long experience it wasn't worth arguing. He'd been amazed it lasted as long as it had. 'Yes, sir.'

He told Suzanne as he stood with her and Claire in the MIR. She said nothing. Claire turned and mumbled something under her breath.

'Enough, Claire. He's the boss and that means what he says, goes.'

'Sorry, sir.' Her face flushed and she fiddled with one of the buttons of her white blouse.

Adam waited for a moment, then said, 'So, where are we at the moment and where do we go?'

Suzanne walked over to the felt boards. 'As was, really, sir. We still have three prime suspects, but no evidence against any of them apart from the circumstantial that they have motives, don't have alibis and won't give DNA. And that there have been no more attacks since we've been following them.'

A thought hit him. Or since Kid has been in custody... Where did that come from, Adam wondered? They had that hint Dan had passed on, that Kid could have been violent towards a previous partner, the Joanna woman, but that didn't make him a rapist. It was only talk, just gossip, it meant nothing as evidence...

No, there couldn't be a link between the rapes and McCluskey's death. That was only Dan putting a journalist's fantasies into his mind. But he'd better be ready for it in the trial, just in case. Desperate defence barristers resorted to incredible arguments to fog the evidence.

'Have we got any more on their backgrounds?' he asked thoughtfully. 'Anything interesting?'

'Yes sir,' said Claire quickly.

Adam ran a hand over the stubble already gathering on his cheeks. A good officer, Claire, he thought, she was going to go far. Cute too, he knew at least one man who was very soft on her. Dan had asked him if she was attached, made that comment about her having the rare combination of looks and intellect. 'She's single as far as I know,' he'd replied. 'And you leave my staff alone!'

It wasn't even a half jest, Adam thought. An intertwining between Dan and one of his officers... he didn't want to think about the possible consequences.

'Freeman and Godley have been checked as you know, sir, and you know about the previous convictions for violence we found for Freeman,' Claire continued, checking her notebook. 'Godley is clean. I also checked Munroe. He's clean too and he does indeed work for Liberty on a regular basis. He charges only his costs apparently.'

Adam tried to think better of the man, but failed. The current government would surely be impressed by such good work when looking to appoint new judges.

He considered for a moment. 'So we've hit a wall then, haven't we? I don't intend to sit around waiting for the rapist to make the next move. We all know what that means. So what do we do next? Any ideas?'

A sullen silence. Both Claire and Suzanne shook their heads. In fairness, he couldn't think of anything either. That idea about taking DNA samples from Freeman's, Munroe's and Godley's kids had been vetoed by the force's solicitors. Too many legal and moral problems, the potential for a young child to effectively convict its father. So no evidence, no reason to take DNA, no chance of a search warrant on what they had, and to look for what, anyway? Witches' hats in their wardrobes? Not a chance. These attacks were carefully planned. The rapist wouldn't leave any evidence lying around at home ready for the police to find if they happened to come calling.

It was the DNA issue that was most frustrating. They had evidence to prove who the attacker was, but nothing to check it against with their suspects. Could they get some DNA from the men? They'd need just a little hair, blood, skin or saliva. How could they get that without their permission? The only ideas were the stuff of books. Break into their homes while they were out, steal coffee cups from their offices. All impossible in the real world.

'OK then, let's think about how this guy works,' Adam said. 'The attacks are planned, we know that. He intends to carry out six, he's managed three. Any ideas what we should be looking for?'

Another silence. They looked at each other. 'I think we're stuck, sir,' said Claire finally. 'I reckon he's already planned all six and knows exactly who he's going to attack next. If he's prepared it as we think, he'd know there'd be a big operation going on to get him after the first couple. He wouldn't want to be out looking for new victims during that.'

Adam nodded. 'I agree. And we've got no way of knowing who his next victim might be. We've still found no connection between the women, Suzanne?'

'No, sir. Other than that they got those taxis, which may or may not have been driven by Freeman.'

'Or it could just have been Munroe or Godley surreptitiously tailing a woman home, then building up his plan from there,' added Adam. 'Or it could be some connection we haven't seen.'

'Or it could be a totally different man who we haven't even had a sniff of yet,' added Claire gloomily, toying with her blouse again.

The door swung open and a cleaner shuffled in, emptied the bins into a black plastic sack and left without a word. They watched the door close again.

'Listen,' said Adam. 'We'll have to work on the basis it's one of the three, because it's no help to us at all imagining someone else out there without any way to find him. So let's concentrate on what we've got for now.'

He pointed to each of the pictures on the boards, the three victims. 'How long have we got before we get another broken face up here?'

'If it is one of the three,' said Suzanne slowly. 'I reckon we've got a few days. First he'll see we're not tailing him any more. Then he'll think we're tailing him covertly. He'll keep a look-out. Then he'll realise we're not. By that stage, the rapist story will have died down a bit and women will be relaxing and perhaps leaving windows open again. That's his chance and that's when he'll think about striking.'

Adam drummed his fingers on the felt board above the

picture of Rachel Bloom. 'I agree. So, we've got just a few days.' He blinked hard to blot out the looming image of the silhouetted man lurking outside a window, his fingers reaching for the latch… 'That's a few days to come up with a way to stop him.'

Dan jogged up to the support with 892 etched on it, then hit a dense patch of scrub. He was sweating again, a dark stain reaching up the back of his shirt. There was a notice about how important scrub was in preventing erosion in Mediterranean farming, but he didn't see it. Surely he wasn't going to have to push his way through that lot? The leaves looked dense and tipped with angry needles.

He took a look around. No attendants and only a few visitors. It wasn't a busy day in Advent and the tropical dome tended to attract the most people. Was he really going to have to wade through those bushes? They looked like nature had designed them to stop an idiot like him trying any such move.

Was the answer in there? That it was difficult and probably painful to get to made him suspect it was. Knowing McCluskey, he could imagine the man standing here and laughing, thinking of the person who cracked his riddle and what their final ordeal would be. At least he was wearing jeans and not the shorts he had half considered when setting off from home. Dan took another look around. There was no one about.

It wasn't quite as bad as he expected, but it still hurt. The heavy denim of his jeans blunted most of the thrusting needles, but some found a way through, jabbing into the soft skin of his thighs with sharp pricks. He swore quietly to himself and kept wading on, almost at the line of metal supports now, the edge of the thicket.

A needle stabbed hard at the top of his thigh. Another needle, penetrating just beside the kneecap, making him gasp, bringing a hot desire to kick out at the belligerent plant. He kept going, kept pushing. Then he was through, at the edge of the dome, by the supports. He was at number 909. He followed the line around. 910, 911, 912, 913, 914…

211

There it was, the one he wanted, just in front of him. He bent down to examine it, looking for a note pinned there, a picture perhaps, some kind of sign he'd finally cracked the riddle. There was nothing, nothing at all. He stood up and checked again. Still nothing. He bent down and stared at the support's number. It was 001.

Dan waded back out of the thicket, this time not noticing the jabs in his anger. He sat down heavily on the bench, threw the pictures onto the sand by his side and got himself an ice cream. He deserved it and this time he would eat it, regardless of what thoughts came to him.

When he'd calmed down and stopped cursing McCluskey, he picked up the pictures and his notes again and looked through them. There was a funny side, he could see that, but he didn't feel like laughing. Why did he have that sense that McCluskey was yet again watching, holding his sides to contain his hysterics?

The man had a malicious sense of humour. Clever though, he had to give him that. He'd foreseen all this happening, someone looking at his life, seeing what he'd done, what was important to him, matching that up with the pictures and coming here. He'd been here too and had planned it all. Dan wondered if he was the first to try looking in Advent. He couldn't see any sign that anyone else had.

On Dartmoor, the National Park Authority had stationed a ranger to stop any more digging. Here there was no attendant, so perhaps he was ahead of the rest in working through what the pictures contained. A comforting thought, but no use if the answer you'd come up with was wrong. The swell of his excitement and anger had waned and he felt the tug of the swamp again. It was stronger now, pulling harder. He wondered whether to give up and go home, take Rutherford out and drown his frustration in a few beers.

Hang on though, what if it was a double bluff? Given how devious McCluskey was, what if the number of another support was hidden in the pictures? How would he feel if he read next week of someone solving the riddle, the answer on a metal pillar at the Advent Project? Dan checked the pictures again, his enthusiasm returning in an unexpected wave, pushing the swamp back out of his mind. Mood swings he thought, beware the mood swings.

Only two possibilities struck him. Number nine, from the key in picture seven, and 225, from the phone in the first picture. Surely that was the most likely, the most obvious? Nine was easy to check, it was just here. He examined it, found nothing. 225 then. That would be back in the tropical dome. Dan finished the ice cream and set off.

He'd expected it, but was still irritated to be right. 225 was well protected, hidden behind a dense thicket of bamboo. There were too many people around to take this plunge slowly. What the hell, he thought. He'd tell them his car keys fell off his belt and he was looking for them if they called an attendant, something pathetic like that. He wasn't giving up now. And if it was the answer, he'd just tell them the truth. They'd love the publicity.

He hopped over the low wooden rail and started pushing his way through the trunks and stalks. They were smooth, springy, resistant, pushed right back at him, but this time at least they weren't thorny. There were a couple of shouts of 'Oi!,' but he was through the first thicket and almost at the edge of the dome now. One pole jumped back at him, glancing off his shoulder. He hardly noticed. Just another push...

A foot slipped on some moss, but he kept going. He could hear shouting, 'What you doing? Come out of there!' and feet tramping from behind him, but he kept pushing, kept pushing. He almost fell as he reached the clear space of the concrete foundations of the supports.

Dan looked down at the one nearest him. 221. He moved on quickly, aware of the flailing behind and more shouts. 222, 223, 224, 225. Could it be here? It was certainly a good hiding place, he couldn't imagine anyone finding it by chance. Shit! There was a small envelope taped around the bottom of the support, coloured grey to match the metal, invisible unless you were looking for it. His heart raced. Shit, was this really it? He reached down and ripped it off.

'Here! You! You! What the hell are you doing?' A middle

aged man dressed in the white Advent polo shirt of the attendants appeared behind him. He stopped, studied Dan, his face slipping from angry to puzzled. 'Here, blow me. Aren't you that bloke on the TV?'

Of all the times to be recognised, Dan thought as he stood panting. Of all the bloody times.

'Yes,' he managed breathlessly. 'I'm sorry. But I was looking for something,' he gasped. 'Something important.'

The man stared at him, baffled. 'What?' He pointed to the envelope. 'That?'

'Yes, that.' Dan was getting his breath back now, but could still feel his heart pounding. Sweat dripped from his chin and he reached up a hand to wipe it. There was no point lying. 'I'm looking for the answer to the Death Pictures riddle. You know, Joseph McCluskey, the artist?'

'Cor, yeah I do.' The attendant's face changed again, flashed with excitement. 'And you reckon it might be in that?'

'I certainly hope so,' said Dan. 'It's taken enough bloody effort. You want to find out?'

The man walked over, stood alongside. 'Yeah, you bet.'

Dan leaned back against metal support 225 and started to tear at the envelope. He noticed his hands were shaking, but he couldn't stop them. An image of the final Death Picture on his wall at home filled his mind. That or a lovely holiday somewhere on the money he'd make from selling it.

The envelope ripped open and a small piece of paper fell out. He grabbed at it, but missed and it fluttered down onto the grey concrete. Dan stared at it, hardly daring to look. Was this it? Not another clue surely... He couldn't take another clue.

He bent down and picked it up, unfolded it. There was writing on it, handwriting. This had to be it... Just two words there, only two. What did they say? 'Well done'? 'It's yours.' 'My congratulations?'

No. Nothing like it.

'Sorry. Wrong!'

A BREAK. A BEAUTIFUL break at last. Adam almost raised a fist to the sky in jubilation. By tomorrow they could have their man. He straightened his impeccable tie.

'So Freeman got into a fight?' Adam asked.

'Well, to be fair to him, I don't think it was his fault.' Suzanne smiled, not a common sight. 'He had some guy in the back who was drunk. He was sick in the cab and Freeman stopped and told him to get out. He refused, Freeman tried to grab him and there was a bit of a punch up, quite a vicious little one apparently. Both men were bleeding. We were lucky that it was on a main road and there was a patrol car going by. They were both brought in and the custody sergeant recognised his name. Interestingly, Freeman didn't want to give a DNA sample, but as he'd been arrested on suspicion of actual bodily harm we could take one. It's being analysed now.'

She checked the clock on the wall. 'The lab has promised the results will be ready by this time tomorrow morning.'

Dan was beginning to feel as though life was conspiring against him. A button had pinged off his favourite blue work shirt this morning and he couldn't find it. It had probably rolled far under the bed or into a dark corner behind the wardrobe, somewhere way out of reach. After ten minutes on his hands and knees looking, he'd given up. Anyway, that was almost a relief. He hated sewing. He'd changed into another shirt, but it was new and itching his back.

The cold tap in the kitchen had started dripping a monotonous, tinny beat. He'd have to find a plumber to fix it, but when would he have time? He'd discovered it at about four o'clock this morning. He hadn't slept much before that and not at all afterwards. Try as he might, he couldn't shut out the sound. It echoed through his brain.

The only time he managed not to notice was when he

thought about the Death Pictures, but that made him tense with irritation. His notes on the riddle had been consigned to under the bed where they could gather dust, not to come out again until the solution was revealed. He'd wasted enough valuable time on the bloody thing.

Dan was getting seriously worried about himself. Not even the morning run with Rutherford had lifted his mood. The swamp was thick and greedy, sucking him down into its lifeless depths. Its sticky tendrils wrapped around him, slowing him, sapping his energy and spirit. It felt as though he would never free himself of its grip. The world outside the flat's windows looked a hostile and menacing place. If it went on like this, maybe he would have to see that doctor for the drugs he had offered.

He'd managed to force himself into the car and driven to work. He hadn't been surprised to find a traffic jam in his way after a minor collision between a car and a motorbike. He waited for quarter of an hour, scratching his back the whole time.

'I've got a story for you,' called Lizzie from across the newsroom when he finally made it to the studios. She waved an envelope in the air as though beckoning. It was ten to nine and he hadn't even had a chance to sit down at his desk yet. He felt like shouting, slamming his bag down, but he controlled it, ignored her, took his notebook carefully out of his satchel.

She came bustling up, her heels high today, maybe four inches. Not a good time to pick an argument.

'Yes?' Dan asked in as neutral a tone as he could manage.

'Did you have a nice day off?'

'No. I could do with another one to make up for it.'

'Tough. I need you on a story.'

'Am I the only person who works here?'

A stiletto grated into the carpet. 'No,' she snapped. 'But you're the one who's supposed to be the expert in crime. And here's one for you. A crime by the cops themselves.'

'Look, I've got other…'

Lizzie cut in. 'We got this in the post this morning.' She

slapped the envelope down on his desk. 'It's a complaint about the police harassing this guy. He says they think he's the rapist and are following him just because he won't give a DNA sample, something he's entirely entitled to do. He says it's a shocking waste of resources which should be devoted to catching the attacker. He also says it's led to his neighbours thinking he's a paedophile. It sounds good.'

Bad days rarely get better, Dan thought. Trouble has a momentum of its own. Adam's going to love hearing from me on this one.

'Are you sure it's worth doing?' he asked. 'One guy who might be the cops' prime suspect moans that they're watching him. Surely we'd expect them to do that?'

'Are you sure you're not getting too close to your detective friends?' she shot back. 'Anyway, I'm not saying that's all the story. What I'm thinking is we haven't done anything on the hunt for the rapist for a while, and it's time we had an update. This – and the lack of an arrest – makes me think the cops are struggling.'

'I'm sure they're doing their best…'

'As am I,' Lizzie interrupted again. 'Doing my best trying to report the news. My job… and yours.'

He was going to say something, but curled his toes in his shoes and kept quiet.

'Get on to it then,' she added briskly. 'I want to interview this chap. I want to talk to the cops. I want to put it to them they're stumped. Oh, and I want it on for lunch as well.'

'OK,' Dan mumbled, getting up wearily from his chair and itching his back.

'And another thing,' Lizzie continued. He tried not to grimace. 'McCluskey's funeral is tomorrow. We've just had notification. Hundreds of people expected. You're the expert on him as well now. I want you to cover it.'

She was away before he could argue. Great, a funeral, just what he needed in the mood he was in. That should cheer him up nicely.

Dan's mood brightened a little when his mobile rang and El's name flashed up on the display. Nigel was driving them down to Charles Cross to interview Adam about the state of the rape investigation and the harassment complaint. When Dan phoned to arrange it, the detective's reaction had been baffling. First the irritation and defensiveness Dan had expected. Then he'd gone off to think about it, then a call back 15 minutes later when he sounded strangely keen.

'Hi El. How's the hunt for the mystery woman going?' Dan asked.

'Nowhere. That's why I'm calling you.'

'And you tried the electoral register, art galleries, all that?'

'Yep. Not a sniff of her.'

'So what you going to do now?'

'That's why I'm calling you. You're the hack. You got any ideas?'

Nigel manoeuvred the car into a tight gap between a badly parked police van and a wall. Dan thought for a moment.

'I've got an idea,' he said slowly as his mind ground into gear. Not a bad one either, he mused. 'If we can't go to her, let her come to us.'

'What?' said El. 'What you talking about?'

I'm as bad as McCluskey with my riddles, Dan thought. No wonder I can't honestly find it in me to dislike the man that much.

'We've just had word that McCluskey's funeral is going to be tomorrow.'

'And?' El sounded highly unimpressed. 'Might be worth a snap, but...'

'It'll be well attended, won't it?' interrupted Dan. 'I imagine anyone who thought highly of him will want to be there. And particularly anyone he may have taught. Anyone he may have comforted when they were upset. Anyone who thinks they owe him something. Anyone like your mystery lady...'

A uniformed officer showed them up to the Major Incident Room. It was empty, so they sat on a couple of desks and waited. Unlike Adam not to be here, Dan thought. But he was

218

busy with the case. He must be under stifling pressure, with no result so far. The High Honchos on his back and the media scrutinising mercilessly. Still, it was odd.

The door opened and Suzanne Stewart walked in, wearing a dark and weatherbeaten trouser suit. Her usual attire. She looked genuinely pleased to see him. That was strange too. She normally thought he had no place here and wasn't shy of showing it. What was going on?

'Hello, Dan,' she said pleasantly. He tried not to look surprised. 'Mr Breen wants a word before you do the interview,' she continued.

Stranger still, but OK, he probably just wanted to discuss what questions he'd be asked. It was a sensitive subject, the force being criticised for hounding an innocent man. He got up from his desk, as did Nigel.

'Erm, not you, if you don't mind,' Suzanne said to the cameraman. 'Mr Breen needs to see Dan alone.'

She escorted him down a flight of echoing stairs and into Adam's office, a room Dan had never been in before. It was small, just a wooden desk, computer, phone and a couple of chairs for visitors. There was only one window and it was small and dark, looking out onto the 60s, grey-sided tower block of Plymouth Art College. Still no sign of the Detective Chief Inspector. Suzanne didn't leave, but sat down on the chair next to his. She was still smiling. What was going on?

'Suzanne, do you mind me asking…?' Dan began, but was interrupted by the door opening.

Adam strode in, shook Dan's hand and slid behind the desk. He didn't say anything. He'd closed the door, but Suzanne got up and opened it again, looked out, checked there was no one around, then closed it once more. She stayed standing in front of it, like a sentry.

'Er, what's going…' asked Dan.

'Right,' interrupted Adam. 'Sorry about the MI5 bit, but I don't want any chance of anyone overhearing this conversation. Right,' he said again, looking Dan straight in the eye and adjusting his already perfectly straight tie. 'You've helped us before and I need your help again. What I'm about to ask is illegal and must remain entirely between us three. It breaks all police rules and no doubt whatever dubious code of practice you journalists work by too.'

He managed a smile, but it was tight and fleeting. 'So just between us three, OK?'

Dan nodded. He felt suddenly nervous. 'Yes, sure.'

Adam held his look. 'This is crunch time and I need your help,' he said. 'How bad are you prepared to be in the interests of justice?'

Chapter Seventeen

DAN GROVES, TV CRIME Correspondent, senior and experienced reporter, proudly cool and hardened professional hack was feeling shaky. More so than in a long time he thought, perhaps since he was interviewed for his first job as a junior TV journalist, 15 years ago. A persistent sweat ran its sticky fingers up his back, making the new shirt itch even worse. He stretched his arm around for another scratch.

'You OK?' asked Nigel. 'You seem tense.'

'Fine,' lied Dan. 'I just didn't sleep too well last night.'

He took a steadying breath, reached out and knocked at the frosted, double-glazed glass of the door. It quickly opened.

'Mr Godley?' Dan asked. A nod from the head poking around the door. 'Hello. I'm Dan Groves, the reporter. This is Nigel, the cameraman.'

He stood back to let them in, ushered them through. 'Thanks for agreeing to see us at such short notice, Mr Godley,' said Dan, struggling not to chip the cream hallway walls with the tripod he carried.

'No problem, no problem at all,' the man replied. 'It's important this sort of thing is exposed. There's too much police harassment going on. I'm glad to talk to you about it. And please call me Will.'

They made it to the living room. Nigel took the tripod and began setting up the camera.

'Mr Godley... sorry, Will, please excuse us getting a move on, but my editor wants this story on the lunchtime news.' Dan glanced at his watch. Just after 11.30 it said, so probably more like 11.45. 'Which means we have to shift.'

'No problem. I want to get back to work anyway.'

Will Godley seemed pleasant enough. He certainly doesn't look like a rapist, Dan thought. I hope Adam knows what he's doing or we're all in trouble. Deep in it. I couldn't go on doing my job if word got round I'd been acting like a police stooge. Lizzie would sack me instantly. His back prickled again at the thought.

When to do it then? When to do what Adam wants? Not yet, build up some rapport first. Break the ice, establish a little trust. Do it after the interview, when we're de-rigging the kit or it'll look suspicious.

'Nearly ready,' said Nigel, checking the camera's focus and exposure.

'Will, we'll sit you on the corner of your sofa, if that's OK?' He nodded and sat where Dan was pointing. 'I'll be by the side of the camera. When I ask you the questions, just talk to me. I know it's easier said than done, but ignore the camera and think of this as a chat between the two of us. Try and keep your answers fairly short, we're looking for little sound-bite-type chunks of 15 to 20 seconds. It's not live, so if it goes wrong we can just do it again. Is that OK?'

'Fine.' Godley looked composed and relaxed, even enjoying the moment. His revenge on the police no doubt. We'll see, thought Dan. It's a good job you don't know what I do. You could have offered them the ammunition to shoot yourself with.

Godley shifted on the sofa, crossed his legs. 'Before we start, can you tell me what you're going to ask me?'

'Sure,' replied Dan. All interviewees wanted to know that and he had a well-rehearsed answer. 'I'll ask you to tell me your story, what's happened to you to bring us here to interview you. So, in this case, it's about the way you've been treated by the police. Then, after the facts, I'll ask you for your opinions, about what affect it's had on your life and what you think about it. OK?'

'Sure.' Godley's face warmed into a smile. Dan could see he'd been rehearsing what to say. Many interviewees did that too, especially when it was something they felt strongly about, a message they wanted to get across as best they could.

Nigel clipped a small personal microphone to Will Godley's shirt, then retreated. 'Ready,' he said from behind the camera.

'OK, Will, we're off,' said Dan gently. 'So first of all, tell me what's happened with the police following you?'

222

He was fluent, relaxed, a good talker. He told Dan about the officer outside his home, outside his work, even outside the pub and how it had led local people to believe he was a paedophile. Good stuff.

'What effect has it had on you?'

A brief hesitation, the man's eyes closed momentarily, then the anger flared. 'It's wrecking my life. Wrecking it,' he spat. 'The police following me has made me feel paranoid, like people are out to get me. I don't know what I'm supposed to have done. I'm just an ordinary, hard-working man. I don't know why they'd want to pick on me. I used to get on well with the people round here. They don't talk to me now. They think I'm some kind of criminal. And the people at work are asking questions about what I've done and I just don't know what to tell them. I don't know what I have done.'

Good stuff, thought Dan. Very good. The man's either innocent or a fine actor.

'Finally, Mr Godley,' Dan prompted, 'What do you think about the way you've been treated by the police?'

Colour flushed in his face. No pause this time, the answer instant.

'I think it's a disgrace. I've done nothing wrong. I've got no criminal record, nothing. I'm an ordinary, honest man and I'm being persecuted on a whim. And I can't believe they're doing this to me at a time when you'd think every police officer should be out on the beat trying to catch this rapist. It's a disgrace.'

Dan couldn't help but be impressed. Good interview, he thought, very good. An intelligent, articulate man this, no bumbling inadequate or raging misogynist, the picture Dan had always had of a rapist. Did Adam really believe this could be their man? He couldn't see it, those words sounded genuine. But we need to know, Adam had said. We desperately need to know. This morning, we can clear or convict two of our three suspects. All we need is a tiny helping hand from you... and just a little illegality and immorality involved... all in a good cause, of course...

'That's it, Will, as simple as that,' Dan said. 'Thanks for

223

seeing us, we appreciate it. We'll leave you in peace now. We just need to do a couple of pictures of you outside where the graffiti was sprayed, but that'll only take a minute.'

'Sure. Was the interview OK?'

'It was great. Really good. Wasn't it Nigel?'

The cameraman nodded. He was coiling up the microphone cable. They were almost finished. Now, Dan thought, he had to make his move now. He itched his back again.

'Excuse us if we dash along, Will, but, as I said, we've got to get this on the lunchtime news.'

'Sure, no problem. I appreciate you coming to see me.'

Now, it had to be now. One chance, just one. Now. Once they were outside it would be much more difficult to come back in. Dan felt his heart pounding, controlled his voice.

'Our pleasure, Will. Just before we go outside, could I borrow your loo? I haven't had time this morning, it's been so busy.'

'Sure.' No pause, no searching look, not a trace of suspicion. 'It's at the top of the stairs.'

Dan tried to walk nonchalantly upstairs and into the bathroom. He closed the door and locked it, checked it twice then leaned against it. He took the tiny plastic sample jar Adam had given him out of his pocket and looked around. There, on the windowsill, a comb. Carefully he pulled half a dozen hairs free and placed them in the jar. His hands were shaking. He sealed the lid and breathed a deep sigh of relief. He even remembered to flush the chain before walking back downstairs, still itching hard at his back.

The lunchtime news edit was tight. By the time he got back to the studios it was 12.50. Just 40 minutes until the bulletin. Dan jogged up the stairs and into the edit suite. 'Slash and burn time then,' said Jenny, taking the tape.

She laid down some shots of Will Godley pointing to the wall outside his house where 'peedo' had been sprayed. Then they edited in the last part of Godley's interview, calling his treatment by the police a disgrace.

After that it was pictures from the library of officers on the beat at night time, looking out for the rapist. Dan recapped on the crimes, the extra patrols and the operation to try to catch the man. Then it was the interview with Adam, some of the most extraordinarily candid words he'd heard from a senior police officer.

'I hate to admit it, but basically we're stumped. This man is clever and has been leading us a dance. He's way ahead of us and I can't see much chance of catching him, not unless we have a real stroke of luck. I can only hope we've scared him off and stopped him committing any more of these dreadful crimes. All I can do is to warn women out there to be careful and watchful.'

Dan scratched away at his back as he heard the words again. Extraordinary. But Adam had insisted on using them.

His mobile warbled. Adam, as if on cue. Great timing. The edit suite clock said 1.24. Six minutes to go and his report was the lead story. Lizzie was pacing the corridor outside. He could hear the ominous beat of her stilettos on the floor.

'Adam I can't talk, I've got to finish the report,' Dan said quickly. A fast sentence burbled back from the phone.

'Yes, yes I did get them,' he replied. 'Yes, they're safe and sealed. Yes, I understand they've got to go to the lab straight away. Yes, you can come up now and get them. Got to go.'

Lizzie knocked on the door. 1.27. 'Two minutes,' called Dan. 'Just the pay off to do.'

His back was itching worse than ever. No time for anything clever. He scribbled some quick and obvious words about the police still wanting to hear from anyone who might be able to help with their investigation and signed off in the standard way: Dan Groves, *Wessex Tonight*, Plymouth. 1.28 now. Jenny laid down a shot of police on patrol to cover his words, rewound the tape, ejected it and dashed it into the transmission suite.

Deadline beaten by a minute Dan thought, scratching his back. Tight, but not the worst by any means. He'd known tapes go in as the newscaster read the cue to the story.

'Good report,' said Lizzie after the bulletin. 'I'll be happy with the same sort of thing but a bit longer for tonight. That was amazing what that copper said, wasn't it? It looks like they're completely stumped. That'll send a shiver through the women of Plymouth.'

Dan walked back to his desk and put down his satchel. He realised he was hungry. The morning had been so busy he hadn't had time to think of food. He headed towards the stairs and the canteen. Lizzie held up a hand as he passed her desk.

'Before you slope off, are you across McCluskey's funeral tomorrow?'

'Yep,' he lied. 'One hundred per cent. Got it all sorted.'

At least it wasn't his first lie of the day. Far from it. He didn't like lying, but sometimes there was no choice. Like when you were hungry, or, as Adam had said, in the interests of justice. He just hoped his friend was right. They'd know by tomorrow.

Chapter Eighteen

THE MAN COULD HAVE been the definition of acting suspiciously. His coat was too thick for this warm, spring morning, the clear sky full of the golden promise of a beautiful day. The baseball cap was pulled down too far over his face. He was blatantly nervous, his eyes flicking around the shop. And he was sweating, his neck shining with the glistening moisture.

It was just after eight o'clock. Adam had stopped in to the shop on the corner of Peverell Park Road to get some headache tablets. He hadn't slept well, restless with the anticipation of that call from the lab today. At worst, two prime suspects could be ruled out of the inquiry, leaving Mr Edward Munroe, the Devil's Advocate, firmly in their sights. Not bad for the least appealing outcome. At best, they'd have their man.

He could feel the gathering of a dull, bass pain in the back of his head and wanted to stop it before it gained momentum. He'd dropped in to the store on the way to Charles Cross and checked through the painkillers. He wanted something powerful, but which wouldn't make him drowsy. Then he'd noticed the man, lingering at the DVD section, pretending to read through the films.

Adam slid to the side of the shop and busied himself checking the magazine rack. He picked up a copy of *Devon Society* and turned to an article about the Dartmoor Folk Festival. Morris dancers were frozen in a leap, sticks crashed together. He turned his back to the man, watched him in the mirrored strips at the side of the rack.

He was looking around again, feeling nervously at his coat, up by his chest. Adam was sure there was a bulge there. He kept his head down, intent on the article, his eyes angled to the mirror.

A young man with wild blond hair finished buying cigarettes. The woman assistant called a cheerful goodbye and he was out of the door. There were just the three of them in the shop. And now the man was moving, striding over to the till. He was still looking around him, one hand up by his chest. Adam kept his head fixed down, stared into the mirror, but took a couple of sideways steps towards the counter.

The man fumbled under his coat. A flash of tapering steel split the air and the woman behind the counter stepped back, her hands flapping to her mouth. Adam couldn't hear any words, but he could see the blade. A chopping knife, a foot long, held in a shaking hand, just a couple of feet from the woman's chest. She reached for the till, opened it and the man leaned hungrily over to the blue and brown notes, grabbed for them.

Adam moved, three quick strides. One of the man's hands was fumbling in the till, the other held the wavering knife. Adam grabbed it at the wrist, twisted hard, pulled it up behind his back in an arm lock. The knife clattered to the tiled floor. He used his weight to ram the man into the counter, bent him over it, forced his face into the unyielding wood.

'I'm a police officer,' he said calmly to the woman. She was standing back, open mouthed, looked ashen. 'Call 999 and ask them to send a car. Tell them Adam Breen's caught an armed robber in the act.'

She nodded and reached for the phone. The man shifted slightly as though testing for resistance and Adam gave his arm an extra twist. He yelped, then groaned.

A good omen for the coming day, Adam thought.

Dan was surprised to find himself enjoying the funeral. He'd expected the swamp to inflict its full draining weight, but when he woke that morning it had gone. He wasn't surprised. It was like that, as familiar as an unwelcome acquaintance. Fickle and whimsical, it would come calling when the world was running for him and he should be happy. It could stay away when life was against him and he should be miserable. He ought to know better than to try to anticipate it.

It was a beautiful morning for a run and they'd both delighted in it. Rutherford had on his tongue out, smiling face.

For once, Dan had even managed the twenty laps of the park he'd set himself. Why did he feel so much better, he wondered? Was it because he couldn't shake off the buzzing feeling that today he might at last make some progress into McCluskey's riddle? That he might finally get one over on the infuriating artist and find out who the woman in the first picture was? He grimaced about admitting it, but when he woke he'd got the Death Pictures notes out from under the bed and worked through them again.

He hadn't even had to put on the black jacket and tie he kept in the car. He'd called Abi, and she'd said no dark clothes and no sorrow. That was the request to all who were coming and it went for the media too. And they had come, in their hundreds.

He'd caught a brief glance from El, who'd shrugged, then gone back to his scanning and weaving in the crowd. With his black sunglasses he reminded Dan of an American Secret Service man, always searching for a threat. No sign of a beautiful redhead so far and it wouldn't be easy finding her in this throng either. Especially as it was a sunny day and many of the women were wearing hats.

Trinity Church on Mannamead Road, local for Abi. A beautiful building, much favoured by marrying couples. No spire, but one tower, flat-roofed, its black arched windows resonating with the clamour of the calling bells. The proud stone was local, tinged yellow from the invisible assault of traffic fumes and with elegant fluting curves arching upwards like stretching trees. A necklace of green grounds surrounded it, sprays of bushes and trees, ideal for wedding photographs. A rainbow of dots flecked the grass. It was one of the few remaining places that didn't ban confetti.

Inside a mighty organ dominated with its pyramid of wooden pipes. Ranks and rows of dark stained pews stood in lines like well-drilled recruits. The church was warm with that mellow, technicolour spectrum of soft light from the aged stained glass windows. The still air filled with contemplation.

What would McCluskey have made of the attention, Dan wondered? There were all the local great and good here and

229

hundreds of his fans, come to pay their respects. The front of the church was already ringed with flowers, many bluebells again, lots of bunches with prints of the Death Pictures attached. Five camera crews and countless photographers worked the crowd, the interest from the local and national media so great that a pool facility was being operated inside the church. Only one cameraman was allowed in, Universal TV's, one photographer and reporter, both from the Press Association.

It was the same arrangement they made for Royal Visits, to save an unseemly gaggle of hacks cluttering the regal way. Dan couldn't help but think McCluskey would be laughing again, up there in the clouds, looking down and holding his sides. The same arrangements for him as for the Queen…

More people were converging on the church in knots and lines. All were dressed in the summer colours Abi had requested, no hint of black. The crowd was growing, spilling out onto the pavement and into the Mannamead Road, one of Plymouth's main routes. The traffic stopped and began to tail back up the hill. A couple of police officers made vain attempts to herd people out of the way, but there were too many and they were too intent on the church. It was like trying to herd cats.

Nigel crossed the road away from the church to get a wide shot of the people and congestion. Dan stood behind him, watching his back. It was always dodgy filming in crowds, particularly with cars around. He thought about doing a couple of interviews with the mourners, but there was no point until after the service. Touching as it was now, it would be much more emotional then. An occasion like this demanded public tears.

'Oi, seen her yet?' Dan spun around. It was El's voice, but where was he? 'Oi!' he heard again.

It was coming from above. He looked up. El was sitting in the bough of a chestnut tree in the front garden of one of the houses facing the church. Like a mischievous spirit, Dan thought.

'I haven't had a sniff of her yet,' El shouted. 'This sun's

the bloody trouble. Loads of the women are wearing hats.'

'Then you'll have to pray for the weather to change,' Dan shouted back. 'But I wouldn't have thought the Lord would be particularly entertaining of your requests, the sins you get through.'

There was a flash of the El grin. 'The devil looks after his own though, doesn't he? Keep an eye out for her will you? Drinks on me if you see her. And lots of 'em.'

A fine incentive, Dan thought. They crossed back over the road for Nigel to get some closer shots of the flowers and tributes. The police had managed to clear the crowd and the traffic flowed again, a couple of good-natured blares of horns as the cars trundled past. The bells had subsided, the air now rumbling with excited chatter, huddles of friends and strangers all comparing memories of McCluskey.

Dan eavesdropped on a couple of the conversations. Sexy, rogue, brilliant, annoying, arrogant, teasing, wonderful were some of the words he heard. Everybody had a passionate view. Joseph McCluskey had certainly made his mark.

The babble died away as the service began, relayed on loudspeakers to the crowd who couldn't get into the church. They stood in respectful silence. Nigel filmed close-ups of some of the faces around them as they listened. Tears and smiles for the poignancy and humour in the address. Even a laugh when the vicar told the congregation he'd checked the church for any clues to the riddle of the Death Pictures and had found nothing, so they didn't need to waste their time looking.

El bobbed back, the grin gone. His habitual body warmer was tied around his waist and he wouldn't stand still, his head flicking from side to side, scanning the crowd.

'Still no bloody sign of her and the service is almost done,' he groaned. 'They'll all be off in a minute and that'll be it, my one chance gone. Goodbye to all that money. All that work for nothing. Bloody weather,' El growled at the sky.

The organ exhaled the thunderous chords of a final hymn, a modern one Dan didn't recognise. The congregation began slowly shuffling out. He grabbed the microphone and did a few short interviews. Uplifting was the consensus. Yes it was sad he was gone, but he'd given the world so much. This was a time to remember that and celebrate, not just mourn. Dan understood, but wasn't surprised to see a couple of people in tears, Nigel zooming the camera in on their faces. That would be the headline shot, the golden picture that summed up the story.

'Quick,' hissed Nigel urgently, taking the camera off his shoulder and striding towards the church's arched doorway. 'Over there.'

Dan looked up, then moved fast after him. They pushed their way through the crowd to where a group of journalists had surrounded Abi McCluskey. She was wearing a floral dress and straw hat, looked relaxed, not at all tearful. Well spotted Nigel. They'd almost missed the most important interview of the day. Above him, Dan was aware of a darkening in the sky. The sun was being dowsed by the razor edge of a front of silver cloud sweeping in from the west.

'It was a beautiful service,' Abi was saying. 'Quite beautiful. I think it struck just the right note. Joseph didn't want his funeral to be gloom and darkness. He enjoyed his life and lived it to the full. We all miss him, of course. We miss him terribly. But I want to remember him for the good times. The service will be part of that.'

A couple more questions from the reporters, the usual stuff, her reaction to the number of people turning out here and what she would like to say to them? She was delighted, flattered, would like to thank everyone, as she knew Joseph would. Then a cheeky one from a journalist Dan didn't recognise, from one of the national papers probably.

'The riddle still hasn't been solved. Do you have any clues for the people who are trying?'

Her face changed in an instant. 'It's not a day for that,' she snapped, glaring at the man. 'Forget it. There are still months left to work it out. Maybe when we get nearer the deadline.'

Interesting, Dan thought. He reached into his satchel and made a note in his diary to call her again in a few months. A clue would be big news if the riddle still hadn't been solved.

The cloud had covered the sky now and gathering gusts of wind swirled around the church, ruffling the bluebells and pictures. The crowd fragmented. Some moved away, others stayed in little groups, chatting amongst themselves. Reporters checked the messages left with the flowers, took down notes for their stories, thoughts, bits of colour, comments overheard. El sped amongst them, sweating heavily. From his urgency, Dan knew he still hadn't found the woman.

'What next chief?' asked Nigel, resting the camera on the ground but standing over it protectively. 'I've filmed lots of good stuff. Are we done here?'

'Pretty much,' said Dan. 'I don't think there's anything else worth getting. I'll do the report chronologically. It'll start with the crowds outside and talk about how much interest the funeral attracted. We'll have a bit of traffic disruption too. Then we'll cut to the service from the Universal pooled pictures – they're being fed back into base in a while – then we'll have the people coming out and some of the interviews with them. We'll have a bit of Abi talking, then finish with some pictures of the flowers outside the church and I'll mention the riddle still hasn't been solved.'

Dan considered for a moment. 'Perhaps I'll conclude with some thoughtful line like, "Joseph McCluskey may be gone, but he's left behind an enduring and enticing puzzle which will ensure he won't be forgotten," ' he added. 'How about that?'

'Beautiful,' said a wry-looking Nigel. He was well used to Dan's lyrical flights. 'I just hope my pictures are as moving as your words.'

They set off for the car when Dan saw a flash of emerald green floating by just over the stone wall surrounding the church. It triggered something in his mind, a vague memory of a woman he'd once taken out on a date. Nothing had come of it, they didn't really click, but it was more than that. There was something else his brain was telling him was important. What was it? What had stirred his subconscious?

Another memory surfaced. That was it. He didn't like her dress sense. Green. He had a powerful vision of green. She wore a bright green top, did so because it went best with her hair. Redheads always wear green, he remembered her saying. Always green. It goes best by far with the hair.

'Come on, quick,' he said to Nigel. They jogged round to the gate and out into the road. There she was, just ahead. A green hat, she was wearing a green hat and dress. No sign of any hair though. Whatever colour it was, it must be pinned up under her hat.

'El,' Dan shouted, waving. The photographer was still standing by the church, hands on hips, staring down at the ground. He looked round, shrugged, then came ambling over. Dan waved for him to stay back. He didn't want to scare off his prey.

'Madam, excuse me, madam,' he panted as they caught up. She turned, stopped walking, looked at him in surprise.

'Sorry, don't worry. I'm not stalking you, much as you're very worthy of it,' Dan gasped with his best winning smile. Some charm never hurt. 'We're from *Wessex Tonight*, the local TV News. We're looking for people who were inside the church to interview. I noticed you coming out and wondered if you'd mind having a word?'

She stared at him for a moment, almost knowingly he thought. Or was he imagining that? Wishing it? 'Of course,' she said pleasantly. 'He was a great man. I'm happy to talk to you about him and the service.'

Dan studied her while Nigel hoisted the camera up onto his shoulder. His memory for faces wasn't good, but he thought it was her. She was beautiful, a finely drawn pale face, lovely cheekbones, good full lips. He still couldn't see her hair though and that was the real test. Just one way to check. From the corner of his eye he could see El sneaking around the side of a car towards them.

Nigel hoisted the camera onto his shoulder. 'Ready,' he said.

Here comes the moment, Dan thought. We have to see her hair. How to do it? How to do it subtly and not lose this chance. If she doesn't agree, I can scarcely pull her hat off, can I?

'Just before we do interview you,' Dan said, trying to make his voice sound light, 'Would you mind taking your hat off please? It casts a shadow over your face which makes the picture difficult to expose properly. Doesn't it Nigel?'

A quick tap from the side of his foot into Nigel's ankle prompted the right answer. 'Yes, oh yes, it's very difficult,' said the cameraman. 'A nightmare of light and shade.'

She stared at him again. Was she going to do it? Did she know what he was up to? Suspect it? Would she walk away, or play along? His heart was thumping again, an odd thought wandered through his mind that it had done too much of that recently. To his side he could see El sneaking closer, caressing the long lens of his camera like a sniper in a battlefield.

Her head tilted coyly. 'Of course,' she said at last. 'I wouldn't want to not look my best for the television, would I?'

Slowly, so slowly, she slid the hat off her head. It was pinned up and shorter than in the first picture, but her hair was vivid and red. Dan was sure now, quite sure. He couldn't see it, but he knew El was behind him somewhere, the camera motor whirring, the lens zoomed in on her. The radiant trademark grin would be back on his face at the thought of mission accomplished and his fattening bank account.

Deep breath, he had to go through with the interview now. And El had what he wanted, so he could ask, couldn't he? Might even get a scoop out of it. Might even get a clue about the riddle.

'So what was it like?' Dan began.

'It was wonderful.' She had a deep, husky voice with a hint of the Devon burr. 'It was a beautiful service, a great tribute to a great man. Everybody knows what a brilliant artist he was, but not everyone knows what a great man. I was lucky enough to know him personally. He was simply wonderful. He was kind and caring and so generous and he'll be sorely missed. A great man.'

He knew it was her now, knew it, knew he was safe in his next question. A simple one.

'It's you, isn't it?' Dan asked quietly. She looked at him, a smile crinkling the edge of her mouth, another coy tilt of her head.

'You who?'

He knew it was, and she knew he knew.

'You, in the first of the pictures?'

The smile spread, but Dan thought he saw a misting in the green of her eyes.

'Yes. Yes, it is me.'

She didn't need to say anything else, but he had a couple more questions to ask. The first was one of the oddest he ever had, he thought later. The second was a risk, but he'd try it when he saw how she responded to this one.

'Err… why are you riding a mobile phone?'

She wasn't perturbed at all. 'Now that I'm afraid I don't know. I have no idea. He was a great man, but his imagination wasn't always the most predictable. That was part of his genius. He saw and thought things that other people couldn't.'

Dan nodded, tried an understanding smile. He had the sound bite he needed for his report. It was safe to try the difficult question.

'What do you think about Lewis Kiddey being arrested for his murder?'

She stared at him for a second and he couldn't read her expression. Then she turned, walked quickly away. Dan went to follow, but she waved him back.

'Joanna,' he called. 'Joanna!'

She hesitated, almost looked around, then kept walking, faster now, her head bowed. He thought he heard some words, but her voice was wavering and she was breathless. It sounded like, 'Never, never… never. He could never do it.'

Chapter Nineteen

ADAM EXCHANGED GLANCES WITH Suzanne, a look they'd shared countless times this morning. He checked the clock. Only another couple of minutes had ground by. Claire's chair scraped through the silence of the room as she got up and asked again if anyone wanted tea or coffee. No thanks. He'd had enough tea this morning for a week. Suzanne didn't want anything either and he was sure Claire herself didn't. She just wanted to puncture the tension. Escape this room.

He glared at his mobile. Nothing. Silent. There was a signal, a strong one. The battery was fully charged. His phone was working perfectly. Nothing wrong at all.

He'd called the lab three times this morning. They were used to detectives doing that in big cases, but even their patience could fray. We'll call you as soon as the results come through, the technician had said. The very second we hear, we'll pick up the phone and call. The machines are crunching the samples. They're immune to being hurried and we'll call you the very second. Don't worry, we will. But you calling us is just interrupting all the other work we've got on. We'll call you as soon as we know.

He was tempted, but he knew he couldn't ring them again. It would achieve nothing, they would call when they had the results, but it was tempting anyway just to have something to do. He, Suzanne, Claire had all tried to work on other cases, go through files, think about alibis and lines of investigation. But it was a charade. They were all thinking about, and waiting for, the results of the DNA test on Will Godley.

Still, at least they'd solved one crime, Adam thought. Not an investigation he knew anything about, anonymous people in a far away place, but at least they'd cleared it up. Sussex police had been grateful enough.

Steven Freeman's DNA profile had come through, with mixed results. Are you ready for this, the technician had asked? Adam had managed not to lose his temper, but only just. Of course he was bloody ready. He'd been waiting by the phone to hear, hadn't he?

'He's not your man. Not yours at least.'

'What? Explain?'

'He's not your rapist. Totally different DNA pattern. Sorry.'

'You're sure?'

A very audible and pointed sigh on the line. The scientist's way of telling a Detective Chief Inspector not to annoy him.

'Yes, we're quite sure thank you. Quite sure,' said the piqued voice.

He felt an instant deflation, had to sit down on a desk, shook his head at the other detectives in the MIR. Some gritted their teeth, a couple turned away in frustration. Others mouthed and uttered oaths. One banged a fist on a table, a pounding resonance in the echoing room. It summed up their feelings. Chance gone. No go. The rapist still free and probably preparing his next attack.

'Hello? Hello?!'

The voice on the line again. Adam composed himself, loosened his tie.

'Yes, sorry, I'm still here,' he managed.

'I said he's not your man, but he is someone else's.'

'What? How come?'

'Your Mr Freeman is wanted on suspicion of grievous bodily harm in Sussex. Brighton in fact. Some sort of fight outside a bar. A bloke got badly beaten and put in hospital. He's suffered permanent brain damage and needs 24-hour care for life. A sample of blood taken from the scene matches Freeman's. We've alerted Sussex.'

Adam couldn't convince himself it was anything other than a consolation prize. He'd spoken to a Detective Inspector Rawson in Brighton and he was grateful, would be here later to talk to Freeman. Not much talking needed really. That was the great thing about DNA. Little room for doubt.

So that was one crime cleared up at least, and a serious one too. And it explained why Freeman didn't want to give a sample. But it was no comfort, was it? It wasn't the crime, the one he was chasing. No comfort really. Not when you still hadn't caught the man who'd carried out three rapes here in your patch, and planned to carry out three more.

Now they were down to two then, two suspects. It was one of those, or... He didn't want to think about the or. The fact that it could be someone else entirely, someone they hadn't even had a sniff of yet. Not a thought he wanted to entertain. It would mean their inquiry had got precisely nowhere. Wasted time, wasted effort, no leads. Nowhere.

Nowhere that is apart from the damage it'd done to his career. That conversation with the Assistant Chief Constable, the second he'd had in a couple of days, that wasn't pretty.

'Adam, what the hell are you doing appearing on TV saying we're stumped? And why are you tailing Edward Munroe?'

'He's a suspect sir.'

He'd expected the call, but that hadn't made dealing with it any easier. First accused of wasting resources, now blundering in scaring the public and making the force look inept. That and persecuting innocent pillars of the community. It certainly wasn't pretty.

There'd been an explosion of snorted disbelief on the line. Adam held the phone away from his ear.

'First things first,' growled the voice. 'What are you doing telling a bloody journalist we're stumped?'

'The truth, sir.'

'Yes, but can't you be a bit more bloody diplomatic, man? Say something like 'we haven't got him yet, but we've plenty of lines of inquiry to pursue and we are confident of a result.' Something a bit more reassuring for the public? It makes us look like we're no-hopers otherwise.'

'Yes, sir. Sorry, sir. I will in future.'

What else could he say? He knew that interview would cause trouble, but he'd thought it was worth the risk. He could hardly talk about what he was really thinking.

That seemed to calm Flood a little and distract him. Important that he was distracted, Adam thought. He wanted to close down this part of the conversation, didn't want Flood asking too much about why he'd said what he had in the interview and certainly not going into what else he was up to in the inquiry.

The phone buzzed again. 'And what about Mr Munroe?' Adam noted the mister, not many people accorded that accolade. The movers and shakers dining network in action. He could see them, dressed up in their dickie-bow ties, passing the claret, swapping power stories.

'He's a suspect sir.' Adam tried to keep his voice neutral. 'He wouldn't give a DNA sample, he has a reason to dislike women and he has no alibi.'

Another snort. 'And he's an eminent local barrister with friends in high places.' Like you, Adam thought, but didn't say anything. 'You can't possibly tell me you think he could be the rapist,' Flood continued. 'That's absurd.'

'He's a suspect, sir and we have to treat him just like the others. We have to be fair.' No response. 'Imagine what the press would say if it did turn out to be him and we hadn't been following him as we had the other suspects.'

Another pause on the line. Adam could hear his boss's brain working. The media, that was the one thing always guaranteed to worry him, the prospect of a savaging in the press. Bad for the force, bad for Flood's hopes of one day making the top job.

'Well, now we're not tailing the others, I take it you'll be leaving Ed... err... Munroe alone.'

The slip made Adam feel better. He could see almost hear the little chat his Assistant Chief Constable and the pillar of the community had had before this phone call.

'Yes, sir, of course,' he replied.

'Right, well, that's enough for now then. But try and keep it together more will you? You're a senior officer, one of our best. I expect better from you.'

He wouldn't be applying for any promotions in the near future, Adam thought as he put down the phone. Not unless his little plan came off. And even then, he wouldn't be telling Flood how he cracked the case.

He wasn't sure he wanted promotion anyway. A Detective

Superintendent he'd be then, yet more big cases to supervise, yet more of a workload. What would Annie make of that? He didn't have to imagine. They were on the verge of getting back together and he applied for a job that would mean even more pressure.

He glared at his mobile again. Still mute. Suzanne was drumming her fingers on the board with Rachel's picture, looking at the notes there but not seeing them. Claire was staring out of the window, over at the city and Plymouth Hoe, the red and white hoops of the lighthouse of Smeaton's Tower lofty above it.

Adam's mobile rang and he jumped, grabbed it, then swore. He shook his head at Suzanne and Claire, who lapsed back to their drumming and staring.

'Hi Dan, not a good time,' said Adam into the phone. 'I'm expecting an urgent call. No, we've no news on the DNA yet. I'll let you know as soon as I do.'

What would they do if there was a match, he wondered? What could they do? That little scheme of his to get Godley's DNA was a sharp one, and Dan had done his bit in stealing the hair. But, whichever way it went, if there was or wasn't a match, that just left them with a whole new set of problems.

If there wasn't, that left Mr – in the Assistant Chief Constable's words – Munroe as their prime suspect. How the hell would they get anything on him? He was clever, knew they were suspicious and that they'd already been warned off him. He didn't like to think of Brian Flood's reaction if Munroe complained again.

If it was a match they had their man, but then what? Godley wasn't stupid. He'd seen their interest in him and wouldn't go out trying to rape another woman in a hurry, if at all. The DNA evidence they had was utterly inadmissible in court. And he didn't want to go telling his bosses how he'd got it, either. So what would they do if it was Godley?

His mobile rang again. Suzanne and Claire's heads both snapped round, stared at him. A withheld number this time. Hopeful, that could be the lab. All police numbers were withheld.

'Hello, Adam Breen.'

'Adam, Keith at the lab.'

A shot of excitement kicked his mind. He stood up, started pacing, nodded to Suzanne and Claire. They both edged towards him, staring expectantly.

'We've got the results of that sample test you wanted,' the technician went on. 'The one on, what was his name? Hang on... I've got it here...'

'Godley,' said Adam quickly. 'Will Godley.'

'Yes, that's it. Will Godley. Yes, we've got the results here.'

Adam thought he was holding his breath. Was the man being deliberately exasperating? 'Yes?' he prompted.

'It's a... hang on, I've got it here.' For Christ's sake! 'Hang on... it's a... match. A match.'

Adam sat down heavily on a desk, gave Suzanne and Claire a thumbs-up. They stared, then hugged each other.

'You sure?' Adam asked breathlessly. 'A hundred per cent?'

'Ohh, now, we never say a hundred per cent,' the voice replied. 'You should know better.'

Adam was glad the technician wasn't in the same room. He could imagine his hands around the man's throat, squeezing.

'How good then?' he asked. 'Ninety-nine per cent?'

'Oh, we can do rather better than that.' The man sounded miffed. 'It's a very good match. If you pushed me, as I expect they will in court, I'd say ninety-nine point nine nine nine nine per cent.'

Adam thought for a moment, did some swift mental calculations.

'So effectively it's a million to one chance that Godley isn't the rapist?'

This time the response was instant.

'Oh, at least.'

Chapter Twenty

FRIDAY NIGHT HAD DELIVERED its sweet release from the cares of the week and Dan was heading down to the Old Bank to meet El. He didn't want to think about it too much, just in case, but he was feeling good. The swamp hadn't returned, and although he knew its mercy was only ever temporary, he was savouring the moment.

Mood swings were part of the mountainous territory of depression. But if you had to suffer the troughs, you might as well enjoy the peaks. It had been an important, productive, and even enjoyable week and he had a good drinking session to look forward to tonight funded entirely by El, his reward for finding the red-headed woman.

So much had happened. Policing, professionally, even a hint of a new romance. It'd all been stirring. Dan thought it through as he walked down the hill to Mutley Plain. He barely noticed the cars swishing by, the laughing groups of weekend revellers or the luminous full moon rising above the city.

He picked some fluff from the shoulder of the new polo shirt he'd bought. A shopping trip was a sure sign he was feeling better. It was dark blue, with a diagonal red stripe across the front and a number nine on the back. Smart, in a casual way, he thought. Just one of the positives of the week.

There was that article in the *Daily Gazette* the morning after the funeral. A full page they'd given it. A great story.

'The Mystery of the Death Pictures Revealed' ran the headline, almost making him drop the paper. Him and thousands of others, he thought, exactly as the smart sub-editor intended. Some spluttering over their breakfasts, others swearing out loud on commuter trains. It was the brackets underneath which made him relax. 'No, not that one,' it read.

Half of the article was devoted to a report on McCluskey's funeral. There were quotes aplenty from the mourners and quite a few from Abi too. The other half was the mystery El had solved, the two previously unknown women featured in the pictures. One of El's snaps of each was positioned next to the corresponding painting for the readers to compare. The likenesses were striking. The text held a few words of explanation about how the women knew McCluskey and was full of none-too-subtle hints about the nature of their relationships.

Dan had called El to congratulate him.

'Well done, mate, great splash. It looks really good. You must be delighted.'

'I am, Dan. It's one of the best stories I've ever done. I'm going to have it framed and stuck up on me wall. And thanks for your help too, I couldn't have done it without you. The drinks are on me.'

He'd managed to dissuade El from hitting the town that evening. Work-night drinking tended to finish him off for the rest of the week and Lizzie wasn't a sympathetic boss at the best of times. Self-inflicted illness made no headway whatsoever into her understanding. They'd agreed on Friday night. El wouldn't say how much he'd made from the pictures beyond that it was quite a few thousand pounds.

Dan had covered the funeral in roughly the way he'd outlined to Nigel, but added a sequence at the end of the Death Picture containing Joanna and some of the interview with her. They were the only media who had the angle, sending Lizzie into the closest she came to unbounded delight.

'Very well done. That was a great exclusive,' she'd said at that evening's post-programme meeting. 'I knew it was a good move putting you on the story.' News editors, he thought. Their strategy in brief; claim credit for all successes, disown any failures.

The Death Pictures were out of sight under his bed again, but still playing on his mind. He'd got them out again a couple of times this week and studied them closely, to see if he could make any more headway. He could sense thousands of others doing the same. He had that familiar feeling McCluskey was laughing at him, but he did it anyway. What was there to lose?

He'd gone to the library, looked up streets with missing house numbers and found what he expected. Canterbury

Street, just off the city centre, a section in the middle left flat and undeveloped as a memorial after the Blitz of Plymouth. There was a photo, but it was an old one and Dan couldn't tell if it was the street in Picture Three. He had promised himself he'd go to the supermarket after the library, but a familiar growing excitement overrode that. He jogged down the stone stairs into the street, got into his car and set off.

As he pulled into the street, he knew straight away it was the one. McCluskey's work was scrupulously accurate. There was no chough, but apart from that it was the same. And there was the manhole cover, half lifted in the picture, now flat in the road. Dan felt his excitement grow. He parked the car untidily – more abandoned than parked really, he thought – got out and walked quickly over to it.

The street was quiet, so he stood on the pavement and stared at the cover. Was he really going to have to get down on his knees and lever it up? A memory of the embarrassment at the Advent Project intruded sharply into his mind. Not again, surely not again. Was McCluskey trying to humiliate him? But what would he think if he read in the paper next week that the solution had been found here and he'd given up? He couldn't risk it.

Dan walked back to the car and found a couple of hefty steel spanners in the boot. He checked up and down the street. No cars coming, no one about. He kneeled down and began levering up the metal slab.

It was heavy, but after a couple of hard pushes, it gave. Panting, he sat back and took hold of the edge with his fingers. But he was sweating and it slipped. He dropped it again and swore. A crashing metallic clang echoed around the street like a discordant cymbal, but still no one came to see what he was doing.

Dan got back up, counted to ten and prized it open once more. He bent down and looked inside the drain. There was nothing. No note, no envelope, nothing taped there at all, just the darkness and pungent rotting smell of sewage. He checked again. Nothing.

He was about to drop the cover back into place when he

245

looked at it. Sprayed on its inside face in small but neat yellow letters was a word. 'No!' Dan stared at it for a second in disbelief, swore again and glared angrily up at the sky. That bloody man McCluskey.

That had been bad enough, but just as he was about to hurriedly leave, an old man had emerged from the door of a house on the opposite side of the road.

'Ere, boy!' he'd called in a pure Plymouth accent, waving a stout walking stick. 'You's the twenty-third arsehole to do that now. We's been counting and we's thought you should know.'

Dan could smile now, walking down to the pub on a spring weekend evening for a free night out, but he didn't at the time. No, he certainly didn't. There was plenty more cursing of bloody Joseph bloody McCluskey, a good run with Rutherford and a couple of tins of beer before he calmed down.

The pictures were back under his bed again.

He was almost at the Old Bank and stopped at the bank next door to get some money from the cashpoint. He shouldn't need any if El was true to his word, and he usually was. But there was just the one potential complication tonight. A very pleasant one too.

He'd dropped in to Charles Cross to see Adam, but the Chief Inspector was busy with a call, so he'd waited. He only wanted a coffee and a chat, an update on how the rapist investigation was going. Given what they'd agreed, Dan wanted to talk to Adam in person, not even risk a telephone call. The word his mind wouldn't let go of, that he could imagine a barrister spitting out in court as the two of them stood trial, was conspiracy.

'This conspiracy, members of the jury, to try to entrap a man for the crime of rape... this conspiracy between two men who are supposed to be upholders of the truth...'

Dan sat in the MIR and waited. Claire Reynolds was the only officer there. She'd asked him about how he'd seen the solution to the Edward Bray case and they'd got chatting.

They compared notes on the places they went out in Plymouth. Roughly similar: the less raucous, more upmarket ones. They were getting on well, he thought. He was applying the old Groves charm and it seemed to be working. She wore no ring, wedding or engagement. And she had such a lovely smile.

But Adam had warned him off, hadn't he? And Dan could see the danger. How could he miss it? No, it was best not to go there, Adam was quite right.

'So how come I haven't seen you out, given we go to the same places?' he asked, noting he'd completely failed to listen to his own good sense.

'I'm not out that often,' she'd said. 'I get really tired after work some weeks and I don't know all that many people here yet either. But I do like a good night out.'

She hadn't mentioned a boyfriend. Surely she would have by now? It was the standard female defence if they suspected unwanted attention.

'Yep, I know what you mean,' Dan replied. 'Something to relieve the tension of the week. A good blow out.'

'Yes... I often wish I knew more people so I could go out more often.'

That was a hint surely? It had to be. And her body language was good. Lots of smiles, she'd angled herself to face him, no sign of folded arms or defensiveness. But Adam had warned him off. And he was usually right. Oh, what the hell, it was an opening and he liked her. Get on with it. Deep breath, best smile, try to appear nonchalant...

'Well, if you're at a loose end, you're always welcome to join me and some of my friends for a drink one evening.'

Some of my friends? What was he talking about? Would it be one of those 'come out with me and some of my friends' nights, when mysteriously the friends failed to show up? They'd happened before, sure enough.

'Thanks, I'd like that,' she'd said, still smiling. 'Take my mobile number and give me a call or text me when you're out.'

Shit, she was interested. She was! He'd had to curl his toes hard in his shoes to stay calm.

He'd sent her a text earlier to say he was going into town with a friend for a few beers, and would she like to join them later? The answer had been quick. Not a brush-off he thought, just honest. 'Busy at mo with big job on, but could be out later. Do fancy a drink. Will let you know. x'

He liked the kiss at the end, Dan thought, as he walked into the Old Bank. So a possible complication tonight, but a welcome one.

Dan looked around and spotted El in his customary corner with what looked like a bottle of champagne in front of him. Almost worth a photograph in itself. El produced a sleazy grin and waved his glass.

Claire Reynolds wondered if she'd have a chance to wear the new top she'd bought yesterday lunchtime. It was midnight blue, a good colour for her, a few subtle spangles around the neckline to add some life. It was tight too, flattering her figure, stomach in, breasts out, especially if she wore one of her new bras.

She'd told herself she wasn't shopping to impress, just needed some new bits with the summer coming on. And she'd been working hard, it was time she spoiled herself a little. But she did like that reporter, didn't she? Not the best-looking guy she'd ever known, but he had that knack of making you laugh, and that went a long way.

He said he'd text or call when he was next out. She couldn't risk it being that weekend and her not having anything new to wear. And then he had texted her, and here she was, stuck in this cold and cramped parked car again. Waiting and watching, not a hope of any partying later and not much of catching their man either by the look of it. Just waiting and watching.

They'd kept Godley under surveillance since they knew he was their man. If they couldn't arrest him, they could do the next best thing. It was unauthorised and illegal, but she was confident it was right. She was proud to have been taken into DCI Breen's confidence.

'How do you feel about the law, Claire?' he'd asked over a coffee in his office. An informal 'how's the promotion going' chat, Mr Breen had called it. 'It's our master, but do you think it sometimes restricts us too much?' he continued. 'Should we always obey it to the letter?'

She hadn't quite known what to say. It felt like one of those impossible questions from a job interview. 'It depends on the circumstances, sir,' she'd replied. 'I joined the force to do what was right.'

She'd tried to read his expression, but Adam Breen's face was set. Then he raised a hand, tightened his tie and she knew she was on target. He'd got up from behind his desk, checked the office door was securely shut and no one was around, then explained.

She didn't know where that DNA sample had come from, but she did know Godley was the rapist. That was all she needed. Now it was just a question of getting the evidence against him. Subtly and discreetly, or just plain deviously. It didn't matter.

It was only the three of them and it was taking its toll. Adam wouldn't allow her or Suzanne to watch Godley alone, so they were both sitting at the end of his street, in the inconspicuous old CID Astra, waiting and watching. Mr Breen one shift, she and Suzanne the next, strict orders to call him if they were onto something. How much longer could they keep it up? She felt leaden with fatigue. She stifled a yawn, prompting a smile from Suzanne.

'Have a sleep if you like, Claire. I'll keep an eye out. You don't need to be awake, just so long as you're here.'

She cuddled up into her fleece and rested her head back on the seat. She knew she wouldn't sleep, but at least she could close her eyes. It was half-past eight, darkness encroaching slowly over the land. She thought of Dan, out having a drink, enjoying himself, talking to other women, no doubt. He was a charmer. She wondered where he was. Leaning against a wall, sipping at a pint, laughing, telling some of those anecdotes of his.

An urgent whisper from Suzanne interrupted her thoughts. 'Claire!'

She sat up. Suzanne was pointing ahead. A dark figure was leaving the house. Godley. Was it her imagination, or did he look furtive, sinister? No, it must be wishful thinking. He'd been out many times while they'd been watching, to the shop, the pub, or just for a walk. But she scrambled out of the car, walking well back on the opposite side of the street. It had to be her doing most of the tailing. Godley had met Suzanne, would recognise her straight away, even in the dark.

Suzanne started the engine and prepared to follow. They'd swap intermittently. Claire tailing him for a while on foot, Suzanne going past in the car, safe in its anonymity, Claire resuming the trail. He mustn't spot them. He'd be warned off, then they'd never get him. If he saw them, it was all over. That was, if he went any further than the corner shop this time.

When they'd started tailing Godley he'd been suspicious, continually stopping, looking over his shoulder, switching direction. Not so much now, he'd relaxed a little, but they still had to be careful. Claire followed quickly, her trainers soundless on the pavement, all thoughts of a night out and new clothes evaporating in the heat of the hunt.

Nine o'clock and he was feeling light-headed already. It was that bloody cheap champagne. And there was no respite either. They'd taken a taxi into the city centre and made it to the Exchequer Bar, next to St Andrews Church. El had ordered cocktails. Not a cocktail each, that was far too restrained. Before them stood a towering jug of technicolour pina colada. He was glad he'd bought those headache tablets when they'd passed a garage earlier. He suspected he'd need them, come the morning.

'To warm me up for a little holiday I've got planned,' El said gleefully, running a hand along the side of the jug. 'I'm going to take a last-minute flight from Exeter to Spain and lie on a beach for a week. I reckon I deserve it.'

'You sure do,' shouted Dan above the music and the chatter. It was a crescendo, voices competing about the noise, the mix ever-rising. 'Have you got any other dirty little projects lined up at the moment?'

El shook his head. 'A job like the Death Pictures doesn't come up very often. I've got some commissions for pics of hoodlums who are up at the crown court, but it's all the usual stuff. You?'

'Nothing work-wise.' Dan thought for a moment. 'Well, sort of work-wise I suppose. I'm trying to find the answer to the Death Pictures riddle.'

El looked interested, sipped the rest of his pina colada and poured them both a top up.

'Getting anywhere?'

'Not so's you'd notice, no. I thought I had a couple of leads but they've come to nothing. There were other people who'd seen the possible clues too and were well ahead of me in fact. I don't suppose you've seen anything that might help?'

El thought for a moment, stirred his drink.

'I did have one idea, but I didn't think it was up to much so I didn't do any more about it.' His grin widened. 'Thinking's not my thing really. I leave that sort of stuff to you.'

'Come off it, El, you're not daft,' chuckled Dan. 'And you know lots of gossip that might be useful. Let's hear it. I could do with some help.'

El wasn't listening. His eyes escorted a pair of young women as they wiggled their way to the bar, short and tight skirts, strappy high heels. A good show thought Dan, but... But what? What was bothering him about it? He was becoming too much of a detective, just as Lizzie had said. He could sense there was something wrong in the picture and wouldn't let it go.

So what was it? He sipped his cocktail. The tan, that was it. They were both wearing fake tan to compliment their skimpy outfits and it almost convinced, but not quite. Understandable though, spring was an unattractive time of year. The inclination to don cooler and more revealing clothes as the world warmed, but the skin underneath still starkly pale from the dark winter months.

'I don't usually come in places like this,' said El, still looking at the women. 'But it has its advantages.'

'Indeed it does,' replied Dan, thinking of Claire and why he hadn't seen her out before, wondering if perhaps he would tonight. 'But come on, what was this you were saying about the thought you had?'

'Oh, it was only a little thing. You know that first picture, with the woman I snapped and the phone between her legs?'

'Joanna? Yes.'

'Well, the phone's got 01752 225 on it. Or put another way, Plymouth 225.'

'Yeah, so what?'

'It just made me think of Plymouth Street. Or just Plymouth as it's known by the locals, and the Post Office too I think. Letters sent there just get addressed something like 17, Plymouth and they get there. To number 17, Plymouth Street, Plymouth.'

Dan had never heard of it. 'The mind boggles. How do you know that?'

'I did a photo of it for some 'Where I Live' feature for a magazine. Anyway, the only reason I mention it is because I thought McCluskey used to live there once, in Plymouth Street. But then I reckoned that was silly, and didn't think anything more about it.'

Claire stopped on the street corner, knelt down low and peered around the jagged line of red brick wall. Godley was looking over his shoulder, then disappeared into a forecourt surrounded by garages. A metallic grinding noise echoed through the air. She crossed the road and walked quickly on, casting a glance over as she passed. A garage door was open, but there was no sign of Godley. She waited until she was past, then called Suzanne. He was up to something, she was sure of it. They didn't know he had a lock-up. And anything could be hidden in there, anything. Suzanne called Adam.

'Sir, I think we may be onto something.'

'What?' Adam sounded tired but eager.

'He's gone into a lock-up. We didn't know he had a garage, did we?'

'No, no idea. Stay on his tail. I'm coming over.'

Suzanne waited in the car, turned off the engine and slid down in the seat, eyes fixed on the garage door. Twilight now, ideal surveillance time, changing light and shadows to hide in.

She eyed the clock. Five minutes, six, seven ticked by. A head poked out of the garage, looked around, then back in again. Another minute passed, then another. Finally he emerged, closed the door, walked off quickly.

Claire stayed following on the opposite side of the street, still well back, whispering updates into her phone. White headlights loomed behind the Astra. Adam pulled up, got in and took the phone from Suzanne.

'Make sure he doesn't see you Claire, keep well back. We're behind you and we'll take over in a minute,' he whispered.

Adam turned to Suzanne. 'Back in a sec,' he said, opening the car door. 'I need that off-licence.'

He emerged with a four pack of lager and a bottle of wine. 'Disguises,' he said. 'You carry the wine, I'll take the beer. And here,' he added, passing a baseball cap. 'Stick your hair up, he won't recognise you in this.' Adam opened a tin and took a drink. 'Thirsty work and the ideal disguise.' He walked up the road to take over from Claire.

It was quiet on the streets, the time of night where people had mostly got to where they wanted to be. Godley kept walking, but to where? He was heading up the hill out of town, towards the old village of Higher Compton, long since subsumed into the city. He hardly looked back over his shoulder now, seemed satisfied he wasn't being followed.

Had what he'd said on the television, about them being nowhere near catching him worked, Adam thought? Had it flushed him out, convinced him it was safe to attack again? If it was, he'd take that mauling from Flood as a price well worth paying. If...

Ahead, Godley had stopped and was kneeling, pretending to tie up a shoelace. But he was looking around, head scanning back and forth. Had the man seen him? He couldn't take the risk and stop or hide, had to keep going, act naturally. Adam took a swig at the tin of lager and put on a gentle sway as he walked, just another good-natured drunkard off to a party.

He was yards from Godley now, getting closer by the step, the man still pretending to fumble with his shoes. What to do?

Look at him or not? Say something? A big moment, get the gamble wrong and it could send him scuttling home. What to do? It wouldn't be natural not to say anything, would it?

'You alright down there, mate?' Adam tried to slur his speech a little, roughen it. 'You OK?

'Fine, yes thanks. Just got a loose shoelace.'

'Cheers then.'

Adam walked unsteadily on, spilt some drink from his can and managed a loud burp. He didn't look back, but saw in a car's side mirror that Godley was up again and off into the street he'd stopped by. He was sure he'd seen a bulge in the man's jacket, sure of it. He whispered into his phone for Suzanne to join him. Was it time to call in reinforcements? Not yet. They couldn't be sure yet, didn't have the damning evidence they needed. And they had to be sure.

He stood, watched Suzanne walking towards him, past the road. A quick glance down it and she carried on, beckoned to him.

He ran over.

'He's gone up there,' she whispered urgently. 'The alley there between the houses.' She pointed and they walked slowly up the street together. There was no sign of Godley.

'Come on,' hissed Adam. It was almost dark, the last light seeping away fast. They mustn't lose him, not now. They crept slowly up the alley and found two identical gardens either side of them, both with metal gates. Lights were on in the downstairs of the house on the left, a hint of a TV's burble, all dark on the right.

They waited, silently. Nothing, no sound or movement. They waited. A plane droned by overhead. Then, suddenly, a shadow of a figure in front of the lit windows.

Suzanne started forwards, but Adam reached out an arm, held her back.

'Surely we've got enough now, sir,' she whispered. 'He's prowling, about to break in. We've got plenty of evidence.'

'Not if he doesn't have that witch's hat with him. Wait. Let's wait and get him game, set and match.'

'You're gambling with the safety of whoever's in there,

sir.'

Yes, he was, he knew it. And it wasn't the first time. Together they could stop Godley, arrest him, but what if he had a knife, knew he was about to be caught? Managed to get into the house and took a hostage? A woman? Her young child? Cornered people could find unnatural strength in desperation. He knew that from those days long ago on the beat, their legacy in his crooked nose.

But they still didn't yet have the evidence they needed. They couldn't be sure of a conviction. It had to be right, to wait to see what he did. Be sure they had him, had enough to see him locked up for long years to come. But what if it was Sarah in that house, what would he do then? Or Annie…

'We wait Suzanne. He's not going to hurt anyone and he's not going to get away. I promise you that.'

They ducked back in the garden. A cat slid by, sniffed at them, rubbed against Adam's legs. A car passed in the street, music thumping a bass beat from its open windows. The silhouetted figure froze, waited, then moved again. A sudden sound, a complaining creak followed by splintering.

'Go!' whispered Adam. They bolted forward. The figure turned, but before he could move Adam had him, around the waist, wrestled him to the floor. He struggled but it was hopeless against the detective's venting anger. Adam had one arm, pinning him down, knees on the man's chest as hard as he could, winding him, knocking the fight from his body. Suzanne gripped the other arm, twisted it.

An outside light clicked on, flooding the garden with stark whiteness. A key turned and a door opened, a young woman in a dressing gown, hair in rollers, stared down as Adam handcuffed the struggling man.

'Here, what the hell's going on?' she shrieked. 'I'll have the police on you.'

'We are the police,' grunted Adam. Suzanne fished a warrant card out of her pocket, waved it. 'But I'd be grateful if you'd call 999 and tell them Adam Breen said to send a car here. Tell them we've caught the rapist.'

'Oh my God!' A hand flew up to her mouth. 'Is he..? Was

255

he..? I mean, was he coming for me..?'

Adam didn't answer. He stared down at the man, hiding his face in the grass, but there was no mistaking. It was him. Suzanne pulled open his jacket. Out fell a child's witch's hat, innocent gold stars and moons stuck to its small black plastic cone. It lay on its side on the floodlit grass.

Adam stared at it, felt a surge of rage rip through him. He could feel Sarah, standing there with him, tearful and wretched, her life wrecked, then Rachel, the same, then the others, all watching, all waiting for their justice. He could feel the ecstasy of his fists beating into the man's face, time and again, pounding and pummelling, his feet stamping, grinding, despatching him into bloody annihilation.

He controlled himself, breathed deeply, pushed the fantasy away, focused on his job. He was panting, breathing fast, his mind racing and his eyes wide and wild. Duty, at last he could do his delicious duty.

He leaned forwards, next to the head pressed into the grass. He couldn't stop his voice from shaking. 'Will Godley, I arrest you on suspicion of rape...'

Chapter Twenty-one

DAN REACHED FOR THE headache tablets through the slits of his eyes, ignored the flashing, stabbing daggers that split his vision, made a guess at the size of his hangover and popped four from their plastic wrapping. Champagne, cocktails, beer and whisky. A toxic combination. Four seemed about right. He gulped them down with some water, concentrated on not retching and closed his eyes again.

He woke again a couple of hours later with Rutherford's insistent wet nose in his face. This time, opening his eyes wasn't the cue for fireworks to begin their flashing and crashing in his brain. He waited tentatively for a wave of engulfing sickness. Nothing came. Encouraging.

He swung himself out of bed and was relieved to find no sweats, shivers or shakes. In fact he felt remarkably well. Good stuff, those tablets. He'd have to remember them.

'Toilet time hound?' he rasped in a voice he only barely recognised. It was amazing how a night of drinking could turn you into a soul singer. Rutherford yelped and Dan opened the front door, watched the dog scuttle around the corner of the flat and down to the garden. The gust of cool air from the outside world tasted fresh and rejuvenating.

It had been a fine night. El was true to his word and paid for everything, even that ill-advised decision to go to the Moorings Club to do some dancing. He should have known better. When he thought he could dance it was definitely time to go home.

The only disappointment was not seeing Claire, but then, given the state he was in, that was probably for the best. He wouldn't exactly have made a good impression on a sober woman, more likely blown it in a new record time. She'd been kind enough to text him to say work had kept her late and he'd no doubt soon find out why. Some other time she hoped. There was another kiss too. He'd saved the message, kept looking at it throughout the night.

What did that mean, about finding out why she'd been busy? She was working on the rapist case, he knew that. Some developments? He sensed a story, but then it was the weekend and he wasn't feeling up to investigating, not yet anyway. He'd call Adam later to see what was going on. Work could look after itself for a while. It'd had its pound of flesh – more like a whole limb in fact – for the week.

There was a stale smell of meat in the flat so he checked the kitchen. Ah yes, the familiar remains of a kebab, how delightfully predictable. He tasted the chilli sauce and flinched, then quickly downed a glass of water. Good job he had the benefit of numbing drunkenness or his taste buds would have melted. There was a note in the kitchen too, in very bad handwriting. Puzzled he leaned over to check who'd been in the flat. It took a good few seconds before he recognised the writing as his own.

Dear handsome fella, (it read)

I thought I'd better remind yer about Plymouth Plymouth and number 225, as El said, coz you've been drinking and won't remember in the morning otherwise, you pissed idiot.

Go get that picture big boy!

Love, yer biggest fan,

Dan.

PS. You dance shite.

He leaned back against the cool white of the fridge freezer and shook his head. What went on in his mind was enough of a mystery when he was sober. Drunk it was even worse, and it seemed to be deteriorating. He couldn't remember ever leaving notes for himself before.

A scrabbling at the front door interrupted his musing and he let Rutherford back in. The dog looked meaningfully at the cupboard where his lead was kept and sat down in front of it. As subtle as his master, that dog.

'OK, mate, I get the hint, no decent walks for a while. We'll go in a minute. I could do with clearing my head.'

He looked at the note again. What rubbish was he talking anyway? Plymouth Plymouth and 225? Then it came back to him, El's guess at a possible solution to the Death Pictures riddle. He felt the familiar, creeping excitement branching out through his body. His hangover forgotten, he rummaged through his bookshelves and found the A to Z of Plymouth. There it was, Plymouth Street, a couple of miles away down towards the embankment.

'Come of dog, we're off for a new run,' Dan rasped. 'Call it a journey of discovery. Hopefully anyway.'

It was a horribly tough call. But he'd made it and he knew it was right. Now though, now the guilt was burning and he wondered how much damage he'd done. But he had to be there to interview Godley. He had to.

'Annie, there's no easy way to say this, but I can't make it today.'

'What? What?! But it's Saturday! We're supposed to be taking Tom to the worm-charming festival! He's so looking forward to it, and seeing you.'

'Annie, I'm really sorry…'

'And you couldn't make it round here in the week either, that bloody surveillance operation you said you had to run.'

She was angry, very angry, his phone distorting with her firing words.

'Annie, I really am sorry, but I was trying to catch this rapist. And now we have got him, I have to question him today, and charge him…'

'What? It's the same thing all over again, isn't it? Your work coming before your family! Christ, it was bad enough you not turning up in the week, but weekends! Haven't you got anyone else who works for the police force? Are you the only bloody one?'

He knew how much trouble he was in when he heard her swear, even such a mild word.

'Listen, Annie, I'll make it up to you and Tom. I will, I'll take us all…'

'Oh yeah, you'll always make it up, won't you? That is until something important comes up, then you drop us. Just like that.'

'Annie, please, this is important.'

'And we're not?'

Shit. Why had he said that?

'No, no, of course, it's just…'

'It's just we're always the thing in your life that can give, aren't we? We're always the expendable ones, your wife and your son. And just when I thought we were on the verge of getting back together and making it work.'

He'd felt his temper bite then, couldn't hold it.

'Maybe you should feel proud of me, eh? Has that occurred to you? That your husband has caught a man who was terrorising women in this bloody city? An evil bastard of a rapist! That he's got to interview him to make sure the case against him is watertight so he goes to prison for a long, long time? Maybe you should think of that!'

She'd cut the call and wouldn't answer when he'd rung back. Hadn't answered all morning, mobile off and no one at home. He hoped she'd taken Tom to the worm-charming at Blackawton, hoped too her anger had calmed and she'd been kind, told him Dad was ill, or had been called away. Not that he didn't care, or other things were more important to him. Please not that.

Maybe she had a point. He was here, at Charles Cross, wasn't he? Not in the quaint Devon village of Blackawton, buying ice creams, explaining to Tom about the mystic art of worm-charming, holding Annie's hand, laughing with her at the contestants' bizarre antics.

But it was the right decision. He knew it was. It had to be. It was his case. He was the senior officer and it was up to him to make sure they did it right, that Godley couldn't be freed for a long time. He wanted to enjoy the man's face as he charged him with the rapes, wanted to see Godley led down to the cells.

Suzanne and Claire could have handled it, but Godley was a woman hater. Adam wondered if he would even talk to them. He had to be there, had no choice. But still he thought of Annie and Tom, watching those wonderful idiots pouring their potions into the ground, or playing trumpets or singing into it in their ludicrous attempts to entice as many worms as possible from the safety of the warm and quiet earth. Sometimes a worm's life could seem so very appealing.

They jogged down through the Deer Park, towards the embankment. Dan couldn't stop his mind filling with hope that the answer could lie in Plymouth Road. He was prepared for disappointment after what had happened before, but he couldn't suppress that resurgent swell of excitement and anticipation. And anyway, what was there to lose? It was a beautiful day. He could do with a run and Rutherford was enjoying his exercise. Checking out El's hunch could just be a part of it. That was a good safety net for disappointment.

The mud track they followed was dry and flashes of bluebells lit the hedges as they ran past. A pair of magpies hopped across the rough tarmac of the road next to them, chattering to each other, circling, dancing, showing off their ink and white wings. A car slowed as it approached the birds, but they took no notice, went on with their embrace, oblivious. The driver hooted his horn and they flapped off to the roof of a red-brick house to continue their courtship.

The mating season, Dan thought as he puffed up a gentle hill. Springtime and the world is feeling determinedly frisky, not interested in the impertinent distractions of cars and people. On the subject of which, what would he do about Claire now?

She seemed keen to see him, and he wanted to see her. He could wait until next weekend. That would be the cool thing to do. But why wait? Follow the example of the magpies perhaps and flutter his wings, take her for a drink this week? For dinner even? He was a messy eater though, wasn't he? That's what comes of living alone and heating up the fridge's contents, rather than cooking. Maybe just a drink then.

Rutherford had found a fascination in a hedgerow, his head half buried in the leaves, his tail wagging fast, a black and brown blur in the spring air. Just as Dan was almost upon him, the dog yelped and jumped back, turned to his master, whimpering, jerking his head from side to side in spasms of pain.

Oh no, what's he done this time? Dan thought. Rutherford was a serial victim of curiosity-induced injury. In the last year, he'd managed to badly cut his nose on an old tin can and poke himself in the eye with a tree branch when chasing a stick. Both required expensive trips to the vet. It was worse than being a parent. At least with kids you had the NHS. No such help for a stupid, disaster-prone dog.

'Come here boy, come here,' Dan soothed, and cupped the dog's head in his hands, checked his eyes, nose and mouth. Nothing obviously wrong, though his nose was dripping. He didn't seem to be in real pain now. Maybe just the shock of a poke from a protruding stick?

The hedgerow rustled furtively and the dog looked round, but didn't plunge his nose back into the undergrowth.

'So you do learn lessons then?' said Dan, trying not to chuckle with the relief of finding Rutherford wasn't badly hurt. He leaned over carefully and looked into the grass and leaves, moved some aside with a tentative hand. A snarling fox? A growling cat? A movement made him flinch back, but then he burst out laughing. Curled up at the bottom of the bank was a hedgehog, two black eyes peering suspiciously from within its ball of spines.

'There's your conquering foe, you pathetic hound,' he said. 'Seen off by a hog eh? I don't know, what use would you be against a burglar?'

Dan knew exactly what had happened, had seen it before. The hog had got fed up with the dog sniffing at him and had sprung upwards, spiking Rutherford's nose. It was a shock, but nothing serious.

'Come on then, you great warrior,' he called to the dog, jogging on again. 'Let's leave the victor in peace.'

They ran on down the hill and into a maze of streets. Dan stopped to check the map, wiped the sweat from his face with a sleeve. Just on the left here he thought. They turned a corner and came out into Plymouth Road.

It was a long one, probably one of the city's earlier streets, busy until the dual carriageway embankment was built to usher the rushing traffic in and out of the city centre. There

262

were houses down both sides, long lines of terraces. The River Plym sparkled behind, a ribbon of diamonds in the sunshine. The tide was low, black dots of birds pecking busily at the wizened mudflats. Dan put Rutherford back on his lead and they walked along, counting down to number 225. His excitement was growing again, he couldn't help it. Hope was irrepressible. Maybe this time.

Godley hadn't asked for a solicitor, a good sign, thought Adam. He wanted a confession, a signed statement, no need for a trial. He didn't want to see those women in the witness box, reliving their ordeal, listening to the defence counsel suggest they'd given Mr Godley the come on, that they'd lured him into doing what he did.

Offensive, repellent, so hard to sit there quietly and take, but that was what they did. Godley couldn't very well deny he was the attacker. They had all the evidence they needed. But if he was the misogynist Adam thought, he would enjoy his day in court, his one last triumph over his victims. He could delight in their distress, savour the wounds he'd inflicted. And there was always the chance the trauma would be too much for the women to continue with their testimony and the case would collapse. That had happened before, too many times. He couldn't risk it here.

Most suspects they had in this interview room sat slumped over the table, looked defeated, sullen. Some sat upright, tense and angry, silently stiff with defiance. With a few it was hard to stop them talking, so relieved were they to finally confess their crimes, a lancing of the toxins that had festered within them.

Will Godley was none of those. He sat on the plastic chair, legs crossed, humming a tune, looking relaxed and writing a couple of notes on a piece of paper. Adam pressed the record button on the tape machine and sat down opposite him. Suzanne stayed standing by the door, alongside a uniformed officer.

'So, Mr Godley, what have you got to tell us?' asked Adam, as neutrally as he could.

263

'I'll tell you exactly what I'll tell the jury,' the man replied, calm and easy, looking Adam in the eye.

The look of a rapist, he thought. Authors would tell you the eyes were cold, emotionless, cruel. That you could see his crimes in them. They'd tell you the hardened detective shivered at the sight. Nothing like it. His eyes are perfectly normal, if anything sparkling with amusement. The beautiful imaginings of his fists pummelling Godley's face roared back, ricocheted around his mind.

He pushed them away, calmed himself, thought of the worm-charming at Blackawton. It had become a family tradition for them to visit. The insanity was wonderful. That man he saw last year, the one with the little drum kit, beating out an insistent rhythm on the earth, imploring the worms to come to him.

The distraction blunted his anger and cleared his mind. Adam focused back on Godley's smug face. He knew he had to stay as calm as the detested man he was facing.

'And what would that be, Mr Godley?' he asked. 'What are you planning to tell the jury?'

Number 225, semi detached, next to a playground patch of hilly grass covered in dry mud tracks and with a lopsided football goal at the far end. The house first then. What was there about the house?

A strange thought came to Dan of it being like something he used to draw at junior school. There were four windows, two up and two down, and a door in the middle with a crazy-paved path leading up to it. It was whitewashed, with a grey slate tiled roof and there was nothing in any way remarkable about it. The garden was grassy with a few pink roses and other plants he didn't recognise colouring the earth beds around its edges. It was absolutely ordinary.

Dan stood back and again looked it up and down. Rutherford sat patiently at his feet, tail thumping on the ground. Still nothing came to him. He looked through the notes and pictures he'd brought, crumpled now and with the odd trail of sweat sliding off them, but still clear.

Could any of this refer to the house? Nothing in the numbers that he could see, and nothing in the imagery, no matter how devious he encouraged his mind to be. Nothing at all. Try a hard learned trick then. Walk away for a bit, let the power of your subconscious chew it over and see if it spits anything out. Let's try the playground.

He kept Rutherford on the lead as there were kids about and climbed up onto one of the grassy mounds. A couple of young lads wandered carefully over from the football goal.

'Is this your dog mister?'

Tempting, oh so tempting, but it was a lovely day and the kids were pleasant enough. No need for sarcasm. 'Yes, he's mine, and no he doesn't bite. So yes, you can stroke him.'

They looked at each other in amazement.

'How did you know we was going to ask that?'

Dan was going to tell the truth, that it's what every youngster asks, but why spoil the illusion of genius? He didn't get to experience it very often.

'Because I can read minds,' he said in his best mystic voice.

'Cool.' They weren't listening, were too busy rubbing Rutherford's head and patting his back. The dog tolerated it, as he did.

Dan looked around again. Was there anything here that could possibly relate to any of the pictures? Could the paths in the play area resemble a snake? He knew it was hopeless even as he thought it. He couldn't see anything that could possibly be a clue. Oh well, another futile attempt he thought, but a pleasant run anyway and at least my hangover's cleared.

'Cheers, mister!' shouted the kids, running back to the goal. The goal... Could the goal be his goal? Tenuous, but worth a try.

He followed them, stood watching the kick about, dodged the odd badly directed shot and knocked the ball back to them. Dan thought he made a nonchalant but thorough job of looking round the posts, but he couldn't see anything useful at all.

Time to give up, jog back home and have a shower. The sun and his sweat were a potent combination. Better get home before I start to smell.

Then he saw it. The back garden of number 225, small and neat and next to the bird table a metal figure of a red-legged, red-beaked bird. A chough.

His heart started up again and Dan walked across to the wooden fence, looked over. Yes, it was certainly a chough, frozen as though hopping over the earth beneath it. Earth that looked like it had been disturbed recently. Had someone else found the answer? Or was it evidence that it was buried here?

He looked around. No one about. He could hear a radio playing in the house. So there was someone in. He couldn't very well hop over the fence and start digging, could he? Certainly not with Rutherford to keep an eye on. So could someone have buried the answer here? Why not, if they did it at night? The garden was easy to get into. His heart was still pounding. So how to check? He wasn't going home now without at least having a look.

He didn't like to admit it, but this time the honest and obvious solution was going to have to be the one. Dan pulled Rutherford alongside and walked up the paved path. He stared at the door for a moment, then knocked.

Adam sat still, breathed regularly, didn't fidget. He kept his eyes on Godley, stayed focused. From behind he heard a scrape as Suzanne ran a shoe across the concrete floor, but he remained motionless, eyes locked on the man in front of him.

'You see, Detective Chief Inspector, I know women. I've always been good with women. I've always known what they're thinking.' The man was talking easily, as if telling the story of a relaxing fishing trip he'd just returned from. 'And I know what they want. Some women like playing a part you see. I like playing a part myself. So when we get together, it can have very pleasant consequences if you know what I mean?'

Godley smiled, knowing and understanding, one experienced man of the world to another. Again, that image screamed in Adam's mind, the fists he was clenching under the table beating into Godley's face, Sarah watching, nodding approvingly. Calm it, control it.

'I'm not sure I do… sir.' Neutral tone again, the best he could manage. 'Please, explain it to me.'

Godley's smile grew. He stretched out an arm on the table, spread his fingers, yawned.

'Then perhaps I have more experience of life than you, Chief Inspector.' Godley paused, waited for a bite, but Adam stayed silent. 'Some women like it rough, you see. Some women have the oddest fantasies. And they're more common than you think.' He paused, scratched an ear with a well-trimmed nail. 'And do you know what one of the most common is?'

Again that image, Adam's fists pounding into the man's face. Push it away, calm, control.

'I'm afraid I don't,' he managed. 'Do… please… tell me.'

'Well, it's like this,' Godley continued smoothly. 'And don't be shocked here, Chief Inspector. I was a little when I first found out, but you get used to it. I came to enjoy it in fact. I was glad to help them.'

Again he smiled, waited for a reaction. Still the detective remained impassive.

Godley nodded gently, then spoke. 'Some women have this fantasy about sex with a stranger you see. And not just as simple as that. Oh no… nothing quite so easy. They like a little bit of security to go with the excitement. So they want to do it in their homes. And you know what makes them even more excited? If they pretend to themselves they don't know the man's coming and he has to break in to get to them. They just love that. It really… gets them going. Oh, it gets them going so much.'

Again the smile, again a pause waiting for the reaction that Adam knew he couldn't give. Godley leaned forward across the table and dropped his voice, a whispered confidence between old friends.

'And do you know what they like most of all? The icing on the cake, as it were? They like to pretend they didn't arrange it all, they didn't want to do it, that they were forced to. And they like to get the police involved, to give their little fantasy

267

that delicious added reality.'

Godley sat back on his chair. He crossed his legs again and beamed at Adam.

'Strange, isn't it? But it's true, so very true. And I help them with it.'

A balding man in his mid 30s opened the door. He was wearing a green Plymouth Argyle football shirt and tracksuit bottoms, flecked with white paint.

'Yeah?' he said suspiciously, looking from Dan to Rutherford. 'Can I help you?'

For once in his life, Dan was at a loss to explain what he wanted. 'Errm, yeah,' he said, but was interrupted by a peroxide blonde older woman joining the man at the door.

'Here!' she exclaimed. 'Aren't you that guy off the telly?'

An opening, Dan thought. Being recognised could be useful for once. 'Yes. Yes I am.'

'Well, come in. Bill, don't keep guests waiting on the doorstep. I've told you about that before. And yes, bring your dog in too. We love animals.'

Dan was ushered into a kitchen which looked out over the garden, and was given a cup of tea. It was old-fashioned, but tidy and clean. An African grey parrot sat on a perch in a silver cage on top of the fridge. It eyed them balefully. 'One nil to the Argyle,' it squawked and cackled. Dan tried not to stare.

'Quiet, Jake,' the woman said. 'So what do we owe this honour to?' she asked as Dan blew steam from his tea. 'Are you going to put us on TV?'

She was doing all the work here, he thought.

'You know, I just might,' he replied. 'It rather depends. May I ask you an odd question?' They both nodded. 'Has anyone come knocking at your door, asking to dig up part of your garden?'

From their obvious bafflement, Dan knew he was the first. Another kick of adrenaline hit him.

They stood in the garden beside the chough, Dan and Bill both with spades in their hands. He'd explained, they'd grown excited, then businesslike. After some bartering, they'd reached a deal. If the answer was here, they'd be interviewed for the TV news and get five thousand pounds.

The one thing that was worrying him was whether someone had beaten him to it. Bill and his mum said no one had come asking to dig up the garden, but what if it had happened at night? The earth looked like it had been disturbed, but Bill said he'd probably done that when he was gardening.

First Dan checked the chough. Nothing, not a hint of a clue. Then they started digging up the ground beneath it, each shifting a spadeful of earth at a time. If there was something important here, he didn't want to damage it.

It was only a couple of minutes work before there was a dull metallic clank and Bill's spade stopped abruptly in the earth. He'd hit something. 'Shit!' he hissed, falling to his knees, scrabbling the soil away. Dan watched, stroking Rutherford's head, tried to contain his excitement. He thought back to Advent and then the manhole cover, tried to prepare himself for disappointment. But couldn't resist kneeling down to look.

They'd uncovered a small metal box the size of a biscuit tin. It was covered with faded flowers. Bluebells, Dan thought with a shock. Bluebells as in Blue Bella. This had to be it.

Bill pulled the tin from the ground, shook off the loose soil and stared at it. He went to lift the lid but his mother slapped his arm.

'He should open it,' she said, in a tone which allowed no argument.

Dan was annoyed to see his fingers trembling as he reached for the lid. He found an edge and lifted it. It opened easily. Inside was a piece of paper. 'Five grand. Come on five grand,' Bill repeated in a hushed voice. 'Five grand…'

Dan unfolded the paper. There were some words, handwritten, McCluskey's writing again. He recognised it now. This time, surely this time. It had to be… Come on, stop shaking fingers, give me a chance to read it. His throat had gone dry. He turned the paper round. What did it say?

'Not here either!'

*   *   *

Adam was amazed at how level he managed to keep his voice.

'So you're going to tell the jury that these women secretly wanted you to come round and have sex with them, then tried to cover it up afterwards by saying it was rape. And that they added to their fantasies by calling the police in?'

'That's it,' replied Godley warmly.

'Despite all three giving us sworn statements saying they were attacked and raped in their homes by a man unknown to them? Despite all three of them being willing to testify to that in court?'

'Well, they would say that wouldn't they? You know what women are like. They'll say anything to get themselves out of trouble. They just want to make themselves look good.'

Adam didn't rise to it, knew what Godley wanted.

'No jury in the world will believe you.'

'We'll have to see, won't we? It'll be an interesting trial. I'm certainly looking forward to it.' Godley rolled a cigarette, beamed that infuriating smile.

'I'm planning to defend myself, you know,' he went on chattily. 'I'm sure the ladies will be excited to see me again. I'll be close to them too, just a few feet away. Probably close enough for them to smell me, just like they did before. I'll be able to ask them all about what it was like when we had our little moment of ecstasy together.'

Godley tapped the cigarette on the table, tilted his head. 'The one thing I haven't decided yet is what to wear. I think it'll have to be the same clothes I had on when I popped round to see the ladies. I'm sure that little touch will excite them even more.'

It took all of Adam's self-control not to blaze his fist into that smug, leering face. His mind ran to the trial. Godley would be convicted, yes, of course he would. But that would be little consolation when the women broke down in court. When they collapsed and sobbed and screamed in front of the judge, barristers, jury and the packed public gallery. Godley himself, watching with that smile on his face. Not to mention the risk of the trial collapsing… There must be some way to

270

shake him up, get to him, make him admit to his crimes.

Adam breathed deeply. 'Mr Godley, I'm going to outline the evidence against you one more time, just to see if it makes any difference to what you've told us.'

Godley smiled again, opened his arms in a friendly way.

'Go ahead. I love hearing it, and the spin you put on it.'

Adam gritted his teeth.

'These three women were attacked in their own homes by a man they didn't know and had never met. Attacked and raped. Your DNA matches the samples we've taken. So it was you, you don't contest that?'

'Not at all. I wouldn't dream of contesting it. I'm here to tell you the truth Inspector. It was me, doing what they wanted. I think all that evidence tallies. It just depends on which way you look at it to see what story it tells.'

'And you made this arrangement with them when?'

'Oh, when I met them in town, or in a bar. That was part of it you see, they wanted the element of surprise. They didn't want to know when I was coming. They gave me their addresses, told me they were alone in the house and would love to see me. More than love to in some cases. The timing was up to me. It was much more of a thrill for them that way.'

Adam stared into the man's eyes.

'They say that's rubbish,' he growled.

'Well, it's just my word against theirs then, isn't it? We'll have to see what the jury think. I'll be surprised if they don't see it my way, especially if there are plenty of men on there. I'm sure that's what I'll be looking for. A jury nice and full of men. I only need three to understand, and I can't be convicted, eh? There aren't many men who haven't suffered at a woman's hands, are there? Have you, Inspector?'

That image again, his fists, pounding Godley's face. The hard heels of his leather shoes stamping on it, grinding...

'I think you followed them home,' hissed Adam. 'You checked the place out to make sure there was no man around. Then you came back and struck.' He couldn't resist it, had controlled himself for too long. 'Just like the coward you are, Mr Godley. The pathetic, inadequate coward.'

271

Godley's smile didn't flicker. He shook his head, but sadly now, as if indulging an idiot.

'I'm shocked you could think that. Shocked. Have you suffered at a woman's hands, Inspector? I'm getting that feeling from you.'

Adam ignored the bait. 'I think you hate women because your wife left and took the kids,' he said. 'I think all this was your attempt at revenge.'

'Officer, really!' Godley sounded amazed. 'That's absolute conjecture on your part. I still see my kids when I can, the courts permitting of course. And as for revenge, it never crossed my mind. I was just doing what the women wanted. Providing a service if you like.'

Was there any point in going on with this, Adam thought? Godley was going to stick by his story. He was determined to have his day in court, but he would go down. Hold on to that, the man was going to prison, for many long years.

'What about those witches' hats?' Adam asked. 'They're clear evidence about what you think of women.'

Godley shook his head, the smile still fixed.

'Not at all Chief Inspector. You're reading that all wrong. The ladies told me they longed to reveal their dark sides and they wanted me to leave them a souvenir when I'd gone. They wanted something to remind them of such a wonderful experience, they said.'

Behind him, a sharp breath from Suzanne. This was pointless. The man was set on his story and would force them to go to trial. That was… unless…

Just one idea. One chance. Nothing he should be doing, but he'd broken the rules on this one already, hadn't he? Several times. And before, on those two other rape cases. Once more wouldn't hurt. Adam turned to the door.

'Suzanne, would you mind getting me a coffee please? And John, would you help her? You know what those stairs can be like.'

Suzanne stared at him for a moment, then nodded silently and left. The uniformed officer followed behind her. The heavy door clunked shut.

'Interview suspended 12.20 pm for a refreshment break,' Adam said and reached out, stopped the tape. He saw Godley stiffen. His eyes widened.

He thinks he's going to get a beating, Adam thought. Tempting, so tempting. But no. Nothing so obvious, but there's no harm keeping it in his mind. He stood up, walked over to the whitewashed brick wall behind Godley, making the man shift uneasily in his chair and crane his neck to look round.

'Right, then,' Adam spat. 'There's one thing we haven't talked about which I'm going to mention now. Prison.'

'That's if…'

'Forget that crap. This is between you and me now.' Godley turned on his chair, faced Adam but didn't get up. 'We both know you're going down. I'll be amazed if the jury even have to retire before they bring in the guilty verdict. You just want to have your final sick bit of fun in court.'

'I resent that! I'm an innocent man, I…'

Adam strode across to the table, slammed his fist down on it. He leaned over, his face an inch from Godley's. He could smell the cigarettes, just as the man's victims had.

'There's one more twist, Godley, and it's this. I'm going to give you a chance, which is more than you deserve. A lot more.' The man looked at him, silent at last.

'You're going to have a rough time in prison as it is. You know how sex attackers get treated in there.' Godley didn't react, kept his eyes on Adam's. 'There's only one type of person who gets it worse inside than a rapist, Godley. Do you know who that is?'

'Tell me.' The words were heavy with contempt, but he was listening, at least he was listening. That sickening smile had finally faded.

'Paedophiles, Godley. Kiddy fiddlers. You know what happens to them inside, don't you? They're lucky to get out alive.'

Godley sprung up from his chair. 'I'm not a…'

Adam grabbed his shoulder, pushed him back down hard, enjoyed the feeling of the man's body giving under the force.

'The only thing that saves them is the watchfulness of the warders,' hissed Adam, his mouth next to Godley's ear. 'But they're only human. They have lapses. They can't be everywhere all the time. Especially when they get word from someone outside that it's time to have a lapse.'

Godley glared at him, but didn't try to get up again. 'What are you saying, you bastard?'

He was scared now and Adam sensed it. Sweet fear, he relished it.

'What I'm saying is this, Godley. Your neighbours already think you're a "peedo". Isn't that what they wrote on your wall? That's a good start. So when it comes to court, all it needs is for the Detective Chief Inspector in charge of the case to voice his belief that you aren't just a rapist, but a paedophile too.'

Godley snarled at him, but his face had changed colour. He'd turned pale. 'Fuck off! You wouldn't... you bastard!! Fuck off!'

'What I shall say, Mr Godley, is this.' Adam straightened up, breathed out slowly. He stared at the tiny window of the interview room, as though rehearsing his words for the witness box.

'I shall say that it's too much of a coincidence for me that there were young children in the houses you broke into. I shall have to tell the jury, and the judge, and all those reporters in the press gallery that I suspect you had it in mind to sexually abuse them too, but were frightened off before you could do so. It won't take long for that to get into the papers and around that lovely prison you'll be heading off to.'

Godley stared up at him, his face tight and twisted with hate. 'You bastard.'

'I'm not the rapist here, Godley,' spat back Adam. 'Now, are you going to reconsider the statement you've given us? Or shall we call it a day and get you back to the cells, so you can have a nice bit of peace and quiet to think about what's going to happen to you in prison?'

Dan was on his knees, sliding the box containing the Death

Pictures prints and his notes back under his bed when his mobile rang. He shuffled backwards to get it and banged his head on the wooden bed frame.

'Ouch!' he yelped. 'Bloody hell, McCluskey, isn't it about time you stopped tormenting me?!'

The phone was on the table in the hallway. He grabbed it before the answer machine kicked in. Adam.

'Afternoon, mate, how you doing?' Dan said, rubbing his head.

'Good thanks, very good.'

In the background came the sound of a trumpet playing, very out of tune.

'What the hell's that?' Dan asked.

A chuckle on the line. 'That is a man playing a trumpet at the ground, trying to charm some worms out of it.'

'Blackawton.'

'Spot on. You've been?'

'I went a couple of years ago, but found it so weird I had to get pissed to watch. It didn't help, mind. It was still very strange.'

'I'm down here with Annie and Tom.'

Dan heard the relief in his friend's voice.

'Going well?' he asked.

'Much better thanks, yes. Listen, this is just a quick call. I've nipped away for a minute to get some ice creams. You know how much Annie likes me thinking about work when I'm with her.'

'Sure, carry on.'

'You should know we've charged a man with the rapes in Plymouth.'

'What?' Dan almost dropped the phone. He jogged quickly into the lounge, grabbed a pen and some paper. So that was what Claire was talking about.

'It's one of the main suspects, Will Godley,' continued Adam. 'He's confessed to the crimes, so I don't think there'll be a trial. But obviously don't put too much detail into whatever you broadcast.'

Dan thought his way through the law.

'I don't think we'll be able to do much more than report the charge, Adam, just in case he changes his mind about the confession and it does come to trial. We can't risk prejudicing it. But thanks for the tip-off anyway, and well done. That's a hell of a good result. I'll call the newsroom and we'll get it on air. Plymouth will breathe a big sigh of relief. Now go celebrate! Have fun with the worms!'

'Will do. Oh Dan, just one thing. Any luck with the Death Pictures riddle? Annie's really interested in it.'

'Don't ask. Just don't ask.'

Chapter Twenty-two

AS EVER, THE SPRING and summer had passed too quickly and the autumn arrived too fast.

The ninth day of October, Hartley Park, just before eight in the morning. The leaves had begun to cascade down in determined herds. A gust of wind through the oaks and limes sent another set spiralling. The sky hung an ominous, leaden grey and the distant cars of the countless commuters sparkled with jewels of white and red, a trail of robotic routine heading to work.

The warmth that summer had infused into the world was ebbing away. It seemed to seep south Dan mused, as he jogged through park, down to the opposite side of the planet where eager people waited for it to banish their winter. All around him, autumn had elbowed rudely in and taken over the landscape. Nature was preparing for her winter hibernation. The trees looked tired and resigned to their fate. Even the usually boisterous birds had quietened. Their occasional song sounded forlorn.

Dan already had to wear a fleece to run in and Rutherford was growing his seasonal coat. The dog looked cutely dishevelled, his fur a barrage of tiny explosions of black, brown and grey. He'd better buy a winter coat of his own Dan thought, ready for wet and freezing days standing outside court for a few strangled words from a bereaved relative after a murder trial. That, or waiting around the familiar blue police tape at crime scenes for a detective to grace them with a statement about the latest atrocity. It wasn't something to look forward to.

Rutherford galloped up one of the grass banks covering the park's underground reservoir. He stopped at the top, looked around as though admiring the view. A whisper of wind ruffled his fur and he turned instinctively into it.

'Poser,' Dan panted. 'I'm not running up there with you, mate, I've got to go to work in a minute.' He jogged on towards the tarmac of the children's play area. Rutherford watched for a minute, then lolloped back down. He slipped and stumbled, catching and crossing his legs just as he had when he was a puppy, then managed to recover and sprinted after Dan. His mouth hung open in his smiling face.

A couple of crows scattered from the dog's path, their mocking calls making Dan think of McCluskey and the chough in the Death Pictures. The dusty memory surprised him. The box with his notes and the prints was still under his bed, untouched for months now. He hadn't solved it, hadn't even got close he thought, and no one else had either. The sum total of his discoveries amounted to McCluskey taking the mickey. The story had gone quiet, interest dimmed.

He had a note in his diary to call Abi McCluskey soon. It must be time the answer was revealed. And hadn't she said there might be another clue if no one had got it by now? He'd call her later, didn't have anything else on today. It might make a decent story. There hadn't been much strong news about recently. It would be good timing too. Wasn't it next week that Kid went on trial for McCluskey's murder? At least that would be an interesting one.

There were no children playing today. The dank and drizzle did that, dampened both body and spirit. It wasn't just an adult thing. You learnt early how the weather affected your moods.

They jogged one more lap, faster this time. Then, both panting, he put Rutherford on his lead and they dodged across the busy Eggbuckland Road and back to the flat. Dan gave the appreciative dog a quick brush, then slipped into the shower, enjoying its steaming, pummelling warmth.

His mobile rang while he was washing his hair, but he ignored it. At this time of day it had to be work. He could call them when he got out. The landline went, then the mobile again. He swore, stuck a towel around him, grabbed the phone from the hallway table and called in.

Lizzie answered, a sure sign something was going on.

'Dan! Get going! As fast as you can.'

Automatically he started towelling himself off. Like one of Pavlov's dogs, he thought with a tinge of annoyance, reacting

278

to his master. 'What's happening?'

'You remember Godley, the rapist?'

Of course he remembered. He'd interviewed one of the victims, hadn't he? A hospital room, a shaking voice, a shattered life. You don't forget that kind of anguish in a hurry. Adam had caught him though, before he could carry out the six rapes he'd threatened. He was safely in Dartmoor prison.

There hadn't been a trial. Dan had reported Godley's confession from the steps of Plymouth Crown Court back in the summer when he was sentenced. 17 years Judge Lawless had given him, and then with the proviso Godley could only be released if the authorities were sure he was no longer a threat to women. That could easily amount to life inside.

It had been a big story, particularly that juicy little exclusive Adam had fed him. Strictly didn't come from him of course, but powerful for Dan to include in his report. The police believed Godley to be not just a rapist, but a paedophile too, striking only at women who had young children. Fortunately, so fortunately, he'd been scared off before he could assault them as well. Yes, it had been a hell of a story. Of course he remembered Godley.

'He's dead,' yelped Lizzie.

'What?' managed Dan, who was trying to dry his feet.

'Dead. Beaten to death in Dartmoor prison by some other inmates. Retribution for his crimes no doubt. Get going. I'll get Nigel to meet you at the jail. I want a big splash. I want you to try to get inside the prison. I want to speak to the cops. I want...'

'I'm on my way,' Dan managed to interrupt.

Adam Breen pushed a ream of papers into his internal post tray and straightened the photo of Annie and Tom next to it. He'd finally found the belief to retrieve it from the drawer and the hope to expect it to stay out on his desk. He straightened his already impeccable tie. Life had changed.

That cold and lonely flat was a memory, one that only rarely intruded now. He couldn't bring himself to think about how glad he was. He didn't know if he could have faced another winter there. Instead of a microwave dinner and the TV for company tonight, he'd have fresh food, an effervescent son babbling about his day at school and a wife to sit and talk with.

He smiled at the photo of the two of them laughing together, the one taken at the Blackawton Worm Charming Festival six months ago. It was a symbolic picture. Not quite ranking alongside the sunshine of their wedding photos and the pink, wrinkled and screaming face of the newly born Tom, but not far off. It marked the real start of their reconciliation. The day he'd got Godley and felt free to rejoin his family.

He shuffled the pile of papers teetering from his in-tray and began checking a surveillance report on a gang who were suspected of people trafficking. A knock at the door came as a welcome distraction. He kept his eyes on the report and played his little detective's game. Such a deferential knock would come from a subordinate officer, certainly not an equal or superior. It sounded female in its politeness. He'd heard no footsteps, so not hard or high-heeled shoes.

'Come in, Suzanne,' Adam said, without looking up.

She looked flushed, he thought, but as smart as she had been these last few months. She wore a fine check trouser-suit, a little silver jewellery too, necklace and earrings, and even some make-up. The black, air-soled shoes were the same, but even they were regularly polished now.

It was quite a change from the old Suzanne. He hadn't said anything, but knew there had to be a man on the scene. It had changed her, made her relax, given her something to live for apart from her work. He wondered whether she'd noticed a change in him since the reconciliation with Annie.

'Sit down,' Adam said warmly. 'How can I help you?'

'Sir, we've just heard. You remember Godley, the Plymouth rapist?'

The warmth of his mood chilled. Of course I remember. Of course…

Adam could see him, sitting in the interview room, relaxed, smiling, telling him the women had arranged it with him, wanted him to attack them. The sick bastard. We got him

280

though. We got him and spared the victims a trial. Perhaps not in the most straightforward of ways, but justice was done. And he'd managed to add that little extra element to the reporting of the time. That delightful bonus to make sure Godley had a very unpleasant time in prison.

'Yes, of course I remember, Suzanne. Why?'

'He's dead, sir. Killed by a couple of other inmates in one of the prison wash rooms.'

Adam felt the breath leave him, stared silently for a second. His eyes wandered instinctively to the comfort of the photo of Annie and Tom. Dead? He could see Godley in the interview room, legs crossed, smiling.

A storm of thoughts broke in his mind. Had he killed the man with what he'd said? He'd meant for Godley to be abused. Even take the odd beating. He couldn't deny that. But murdered?

'Sir, I'm a little worried that…' Suzanne's words faltered. 'That…' she went on. 'That if there's a new investigation, then what we did will come out.'

What we did? Adam thought. What I did. It was all down to me. Telling Dan the man was a paedophile as well as a rapist.

'Sir? Sir?!' Suzanne urged. 'You know, that business with getting his DNA? And the unauthorised tail we put on him.'

Oh that, the least of his concerns. He'd almost forgotten that. Angelic by comparison, and easily justified. But labelling him a paedophile?

Adam tried to keep his voice level. 'I shouldn't worry too much about that, Suzanne. Only you, me, Claire and Dan know about that, don't we? As far as anyone else is aware, it was just good and dedicated police work on your part. You always had your suspicions about the man, so you followed him one evening when you happened to be out and saw him behaving oddly. It was just good luck and good policing.'

He knew none of their fellow officers or superiors believed a syllable of it, but that didn't matter. The story had just about held together. No one wanted to look too deeply. Godley had been caught, and that was enough.

Suzanne didn't look convinced. Her fingers fidgeted with her silver necklace. She deserved more reassurance, he thought. Worrying about how they'd caught Godley was a matter for him. 'But if you're concerned, I will give Dan a call to make sure it stays between us, don't worry,' he added.

And there was something more urgent to talk to Dan about too. The other matter, the one that might have led to Godley's murder. If that came out...

Dan changed down a gear, pulled out and accelerated the car around a tractor. You couldn't drive far on Dartmoor without getting stuck behind one, but it had only held him up for a couple of minutes. He passed the great granite boulder of Roborough Rock and the old Second World War airfield it guarded, now a stretch of tidy, well-kept grass. It was chewed down like a lawn by the herd of overweight ponies that lingered there and begged treats from passing walkers.

He crossed the roundabout and headed out towards Princetown. Another seven minutes to the prison. Not that there was a great rush. Godley would still be dead when he got there. Despite Lizzie's excitement, he couldn't convince himself the man's murder was a major story. Dan could imagine the viewers watching tonight with a shrug. There wouldn't be much of an outpouring of sympathy for a serial rapist who got himself stabbed in prison.

The road narrowed through a patch of trees at Burrator, then opened out again. He slowed the car to 30 miles per hour. It was a notorious village for speed traps. His mobile rang. A Plymouth number, but an unfamiliar one.

'Hello, is that Dan Groves?' crackled through the speaker of the car's hands-free unit.

He knew the voice, but couldn't quite place it. A woman, cultured, well-spoken. Teasingly familiar.

'Dan, it's Abi here. Abi McCluskey.'

Abi! She'd beaten him to it with her call. 'Hi there,' he replied. 'I was going to call you. Long time no speak. How are you?'

'Yes, fine thanks.' She didn't sound as if she wanted to

chat. 'Listen, I know you're busy, so I won't keep you. You remember at Joseph's funeral I said there might be another clue if no one had got the riddle?'

The road broke through the canopy of the tree line and opened out onto the moor, but Dan kept the car at just over 30. It was foggy up here on the high ground, he didn't want to hit a pony or sheep. Their road sense was hopeless.

'I certainly do.'

'Well it's six months next week, and Joseph said if no one had got it by now I was to give out a final clue before I revealed the answer.' Abi hesitated, seemed to struggle to go on. 'He wanted me to give the clue to you. He liked you, you know, particularly after that interview you did with him. Are you interested?'

Blimey yes, he thought, great story. It all comes at the same time, doesn't it? The old buses complaint holds true for news too. It's been a dull time lately, mundane stuff to keep us ticking over. Then two real stories in one go.

He thought of the Death Pictures again, his notes and prints lying undisturbed for months under his bed. He'd almost forgotten them, but couldn't deny the occasional wondering about what the answer might have been. Many nights with sleep elusive, he'd tried to imagine a way in to the riddle. Why was it suddenly back in his mind, bothering him again? Because the time was running out to crack the puzzle and he hated being beaten? Maybe it was time to get them out and have one final try…

'I certainly am interested, Abi. I'm on Dartmoor at the moment doing a story. Can I call you later? We can arrange something for tomorrow.'

'Fine. Tomorrow would be great.'

The road flattened out into Princetown. Dan realised he hadn't noticed any of the last five minutes of the drive. His mind was still awash with the Death Pictures. With one call, Abi had demolished the dam he'd built to hold them at bay.

He looked around as he turned off the main road towards the prison. Most of the lines of weatherbeaten houses were built from grey Dartmoor granite. The brooding rock gave the impression it would much have preferred to stay part of the land than be quarried out for construction. On a mist-lingering day like this, the village had a sullen air. Its centrepiece, the great Napoleonic prison was even more determinedly dour.

Dan pulled the car up outside the main gate, glad to see Nigel there. His was already filming.

'What've you got?' Dan asked, joining him and thinking how much colder it was up here on the moor.

Nigel curled a lip. 'Not a lot. Maybe a couple of useful bits. I got an ambulance leaving. I guess that was called in case the victim had any chance. It might even have had the body in. I also got some people coming in who looked like detectives, but then again they could have been anyone. Apart from that, I've knocked off a few general pictures of the prison for you.'

It was always the same with these stories. A lack of pictures was the problem. They'd dutifully called the Home Office to ask if they could film inside the prison and interview the governor. The answer had been fast, straight, simple and entirely what they expected. 'No.' It always was. In times of trouble, officialdom drew up the drawbridge.

That left him with the pictures Nigel had just filmed and some of the library material of the hunt for Godley. No interviews either, and not much in the way of reliable information. It wouldn't be a long report. Unless he could talk to someone who might know more of course... He left Nigel standing by in case anything else happened, retreated to the warmth of his car and called Adam.

'Hello, Dan. How can I help you?' The detective sounded subdued, sombre even. Unlike Adam. Annie and Tom problems? He couldn't be upset Godley was dead, surely.

'Hi, Adam. I'm up at the prison covering the Godley murder. You've heard I take it?'

'Oh yes. I've heard.'

'I just wondered if you knew any more. I'm having trouble getting any information.'

'I don't, no. All I know is that he was killed in a washroom, with a knife.'

That'll do for a bit more detail Dan thought, noting it

down. It's more than we're getting from the prison.

'You won't be put on this one then?'

'No.' Adam was still very quiet and Dan struggled to hear. 'I did the original case, so someone else will have to investigate what happened to him. Otherwise there'll be a concern I might be prejudiced from what I know about the rape inquiry.'

'Understood.' Should he ask? Adam was his friend, wasn't he? 'Mate, you sound really down. Are you OK? Is it Annie?'

A pause on the end of the line, then a deep breath. 'No, that's going fine. It's just...' Another pause. 'Listen, there is one thing you can do for me.'

Dan felt a jolt of worry. 'Anything,' he replied simply.

'As you'll remember, certain, err... things happened on the original investigation that weren't strictly legal. I'd appreciate it if I knew they'd stay absolutely between us. How I worked the case may well get looked at and if that kind of stuff came out...'

The DNA trick. Dan hadn't told anyone. It wasn't exactly the best impartial journalist's practice to get involved in an inquiry and help the police.

'It's just between us, Adam. No one else will ever know.'

'And any details about any information I gave you too please.'

What did he mean, Dan wondered? The inside track on the case? He couldn't think of anything Adam had told him which was particularly dodgy. And they'd caught Godley. Justice had been done. Surely that was what mattered?

'Of course,' said Dan. 'It's all entirely between us, as ever.'

The clammy mist turned out to be merely the support act. After half an hour, it gave way to an icy, persistent drizzle. Dan and Nigel looked at each other, then quickly took shelter in his car and waited for something to happen. Nigel read his book, a crime thriller. Dan went through the list of calls he had to make on the story. They kept the engine running to provide some welcome warmth.

It was a forlorn hope. The Home Office was referring all

285

requests for information to Greater Wessex police. The police press office read a statement, which said there were detectives in the prison interviewing inmates about the stabbing. That was all they would be saying and there would be no interviews. The only good news was the outside broadcast wagon's gearbox had burnt out, so they wouldn't have to stay here all day to do a live report. No interviews, very few pictures, a TV reporter's nightmare, Dan thought, staring at the prison's rugged walls. He sketched out a script, but it wouldn't be an award winner.

'Piece to camera time, mate,' he said to Nigel, who stirred reluctantly. He put the book down on the dashboard, climbed out of the car and took the camera out of the boot.

'I'll start the report with your pictures of the prison, the ambulance and those people who might have been detectives,' Dan said, rehearsing the story. 'I'll talk about lots of activity after the killing of Godley and the police investigation. Then we'll go into my bit to camera. After that I'll use some of the library stuff of cops out looking for the rapist to recap on what he did and the fear it created at the time.'

Nigel set up the tripod so the prison gate would form the backdrop to his shot and positioned Dan in front of it. The rain was starting to beat in now, and an aggressive autumn wind buffeted them. True Dartmoor weather.

'Rolling, go ahead,' said Nigel. 'And it'd be good if you could do it in one take. I'm freezing.'

The wind flapped at Dan's coat and he paused to allow it to die down. Then a van began reversing somewhere behind them and he waited for the grumbling diesel engine to stop too. It was always the way. The moment you needed to record an interview or your piece to the camera, an intrusive noise would start up. Pneumatic drills were the favourite, followed by passing aircraft.

'The Home Office are saying little beyond that the police are investigating what happened here,' Dan began, trying to project his voice over the percussion of the wind and rain. 'Greater Wessex police confirmed they have assigned a team of detectives to the case and they're inside the prison,

286

interviewing inmates. A source within the force tells me that Godley was killed with a knife in the washing room area.'

One take, as requested. Not a bad effort. Just about all the information he had and a bit of colour to spice it up. It would do. He took the tape from Nigel and drove back to the studios to edit the story for the lunchtime news. Just as he got into the car, the rain stopped.

'Decent stuff,' was Lizzie's verdict after the broadcast, a heel scraping in to the carpet. Low today, Dan noticed, only a couple of inches. 'Is there anything else we can do on it for tonight?' she added.

He shrugged. 'Not that I can think of. No one's saying anything and we haven't got any more pictures. I used just about everything we had.' And I don't want to go back onto Dartmoor in this weather, he could have added, but didn't. That would be an irresistible invitation for his return.

She studied him, an edge of her black, bobbed hair sliding across a cheek. He could see her weighing up what to do. Not an easy woman to mollify is Lizzie, even if she's in a relatively calm mood today. He'd have to find something to distract her. What about Abi?

'Plus there was another story I wanted to look at which I thought might interest you,' Dan added quickly. He explained about the call earlier. 'I could set that up for tomorrow, while keeping an eye on the Godley story in case there were any developments.'

'Done! OK then, we'll have roughly the same on Godley for tonight and if there are any developments, you can do a live report in the studio. You can cover the Death Pictures tomorrow. But not on the lunchtime news, I don't want all the other media getting tipped off about the story. I want full coverage. I want an exclusive. I want Abi. I want tears... And hey, I've got an idea...'

Her eyebrow gathered into an arch.

'Let's really build it up,' Lizzie continued, her voice rising. 'I want us to trail that we'll be doing something big on the Death Pictures on the lunchtime news. I want the actual thing live tomorrow night. The OB truck will be fixed by then. I

287

want you down in McCluskey's studio with the other pictures. I want you to interview Abi and let her give the clue out live on air. That'd be brilliant. The viewing figures will soar.'

He had to hand it to her, Dan thought begrudgingly. It was a hell of a good idea. But there was just that little tingle of annoyance that he'd wanted to hear the clue first. To see if it meant anything to him, just in case it gave him a head start in the final effort to solve the riddle.

The excitement was back. Suddenly he couldn't wait to get home tonight and go through the Death Pictures again.

He'd played World Cup football on the Playstation with Tom and been soundly thrashed, but he'd hardly seen a single goal. His son had been delighted with the victory over Brazil – he'd been England of course – but even he had noticed by the end of the match.

'You OK, Dad?'

'Yes, fine son.' Adam shook himself. Whatever he was feeling, it shouldn't impact on Tom. He'd learn about the agonies of adulthood soon enough. 'Come on, haven't I taught you the game's never over until the final whistle goes?'

A seven-year-old, spotting his Dad was preoccupied. How about that? He felt a nudge of pride. The boy could go on to become a detective. But he wouldn't know why Dad wasn't quite there with him. No one would.

He'd gone through it countless times today. Only Dan knew he was the source for the paedophile allegation against Godley. No one in Greater Wessex Police was aware where the story had come from. Dan didn't know that he had no evidence for it, that it was just his way of getting revenge on the man. And now that revenge had gone as far as it possibly could.

So he was safe, he knew that. His job, his reputation. He could trust Dan. And he'd done the right thing, hadn't he? The man was a cold and vicious rapist. And he'd caught him, and... The thought echoed in his head. And he'd sentenced him too, hadn't he? Sentenced him to death.

No. No, no, no. He had no idea why Godley had been

killed. It could just have been a fight between prisoners. It happened. It could have been because of his rapes. It could have nothing to do with the news that the man might have been a paedophile. But then again, it could...

A triumphant scream from Tom jolted him back to the living room. Final whistle, four nil. A drubbing. He reached out to shake the victor's hand, soothed by the smile of delight on his son's face.

If Godley hadn't been in prison, who knows what else he could have done? Attack Annie? With Tom here, asleep in his bed, woken by the noise, coming down to find...

Yes, he could live with what had happened. What other choice was there? He'd have to.

Chapter Twenty-three

DAN STARED AT THE ten Death Pictures on the walls surrounding him and tapped a foot on the stone floor. None showed the slightest inclination to give up their secret. He had to admit it. He was just as baffled as before.

He'd tried it on a little naughtily. He could probably justify it as research, but she was having none of it. He'd phoned Abi, arranged with her to cover the release of the clue and asked if she would tell him in advance what it was. Just to prepare, of course, he'd assured her. Just so they could have some graphics ready to illustrate it, to put in on their website when she revealed what it was.

No, she'd said firmly. It'll go out live on air, so everyone gets to see it at the same time. It's fairest that way. From there, everyone will have roughly a week, and then, if no one had got it, the answer would finally be revealed.

That had bothered him. Roughly a week? No precise deadline?' Her answer had been enigmatic.

'It depends on a few factors over which I have no control. You'll understand when all is revealed. Joseph gave me discretion about when the answer should be released, within certain parameters. I intend to remain absolutely loyal to what were effectively his last wishes. So all I can say at the moment is about a week.'

Dan had spent last night looking through the Death Pictures and his notes, wondering if there were any time references there, any reason why the answer would have to be given on a specific date. But he'd found nothing.

The clocks were the obvious candidates. He wondered if 9.15 might have referred to a date, but clearly not one in October. Five to ten could, though. The fifth? Was something supposed to have happened on the fifth? Or the twenty-fifth? But then, that would mean the date when the answer was revealed wouldn't be variable. He pushed his notes away in frustration and got himself a tin of beer and a biscuit for

Rutherford. The numbers, he still suspected it was in the numbers, but… there was no disguising it. After all these months of trying he still had no idea about the solution.

Dan didn't usually get nervous when presenting outside broadcasts, but he could feel a twist of tension in his stomach. Was it more to do with hearing the clue than the actual live television? He suspected so. And was that McCluskey he could feel chuckling away at him again?

Five minutes to on air. Enough musing. Concentrate, he told himself. Be professional. Last checks.

'This is how it'll go then, Nigel,' Dan said. 'Ready for a final rehearsal?'

Nigel hoisted the camera up on to his shoulder. 'Ready, mostly willing and passably able.'

'I'll start here by the first picture, then walk around the room, going past each of them in turn.' Dan started walking. 'I'll ad lib something about the long-running mystery, the answer contained in the pictures, thousands trying to solve it, something like that. Then, at picture ten, we'll find Abi who we'll ask for the clue. That OK?'

Nigel was standing in the middle of the room and had panned the camera around to follow Dan's walk. 'Works fine, very nice.'

'And you're OK Abi?'

She stood to the side of the last picture, arms crossed and looking composed.

'Fine, yes.'

'Ok then, standby. The next time we do it, it'll be for real.'

The opening music of *Wessex Tonight* played and Craig came in. 'And now, the moment you've all been waiting for…'

Dan stopped himself from smiling, knew the camera would be on him at any moment. That introduction was pure Lizzie, simply showbiz.

It was so unorthodox, starting the programme with a story like this, but she had a point. There wasn't much else going on, and it was the one that people had been talking about. Several had already walked in to McCluskey's gallery while they were setting up for the broadcast to ask what the clue was. Wait, you'll have to wait, Abi had told them with a smile. She was enjoying the moment, a tribute to her husband's gift for drama and suspense perhaps? Outside there was quite a crowd too, at least a couple of hundred. Dan wondered whether this was just how McCluskey had imagined it when he designed the riddle.

In his ear, Craig's voice was coming to the end of the introduction. '…we can cross live to Joseph McCluskey's studio and our correspondent Dan Groves. Dan…'

'Yes, here they are,' Dan said, gesturing behind him to the pictures and beginning his walk. 'The 10 Death Pictures – or prints, as we know – and contained in them is the answer to a riddle which, if solved, would mean the lucky winner being given the original of the last painting. It's a prize worth many tens, perhaps now even hundreds of thousands of pounds. No wonder then there's been such intense interest. Well, the hints in the pictures have been too difficult for anyone to find a solution so far, but help is at hand, right now. It's your final chance, so have a pen and paper handy.'

Dan reached the last of the pictures, stopped. 'So now, time for the clue to be revealed, live on air. And here with me to do it, is Joseph McCluskey's widow, Abi.'

He turned, Nigel panning the camera onto her. 'Abi, good evening to you, and please, give us the clue.'

It sounded like an American game show host, he thought. But she smiled at him, then turned to the camera.

'The clue is this.' Her voice was strong and measured, no faltering. 'Why are the pictures hanging here in the gallery prints and not the original paintings?'

She stopped, nearly catching him. He hadn't expected it to be so short.

'Repeat that for us will you please, in case anyone missed it the first time around?'

She nodded, still smiling.

'Why are the pictures hanging here prints, and not the original paintings?'

*   *   *

292

Dan spent that night going over what Abi had said. Even when he slept it was fitful, and always with the recurring question rattling in his mind. Why should it be that the pictures in McCluskey's own studio were prints?

The first reason was the obvious one. McCluskey had given the originals away, to make money for whatever causes he'd chosen at the time. But that wasn't an answer which could in any way solve the riddle. It had to mean there was some difference between the prints and the originals. But what could that be? They were the same in every way weren't they? That was the point of prints, given the power of modern technology. The detail and the colours were as alike as they could possibly be. He'd seen the original of picture ten and a couple of the others along with their prints, and hadn't noticed a single difference.

He'd had an idea as they were de-rigging the camera, cables and lights. What about McCluskey's signature? Each print was individually signed. What if there was some subtle difference in each, something he'd added or left out, some letter perhaps? Or a series of letters that spelt out a message.

He liked the idea, felt the familiar growing excitement, along with the equally familiar expectation of failure. He'd studied them, Abi watching him, that calm smile still on her face. Thousands of people had been in here before doing just the same, thousands more would follow over the next week. She was sure he wouldn't see anything, he could tell that. And she'd been right. He'd found nothing. All the signatures were identical. But while he'd had a chance, he'd examined each print, just to see if there was something in there that could possibly be a hint. Still he'd found nothing.

The only other idea he'd had was that it might be something in the canvas of the originals. But that was hardly a fair challenge. Then the riddle could only be solved by the people who owned or had access to the paintings, and they'd been dispersed to a range of organisations. So how could any one person find a pattern in them? Unless the answer was contained in just one of the originals, and Dan couldn't see that would be fair either. It didn't tally with what Professor Ed had told him. That McCluskey would have ensured the answer was available for all, but made it so cryptic that no one could get it and he would have the last laugh. Well, he was certainly doing so at the moment.

The thought that the answer must be somewhere in front of him had been both a comfort and an irritant. He'd checked through the pictures again. But still he found nothing, had no ideas, couldn't see what the answer might possibly be.

Across the country Dan imagined thousands of other people in their lounges and studies, at their work desks, all scouring the images. He wondered what conclusion they'd come to. The same as his? No idea... Not a clue...

His copies of the pictures and his notes had eventually been dropped grumpily back into their box and consigned to their home, underneath his bed. His excitement had evaporated and he felt deflated. He's suffered too many disappointments chasing McCluskey's riddle. He was sick of it.

Now, this morning at work, he'd got in to find Lizzie already at her desk and fizzing. Her honed fingernails flew over the computer as she checked news and gossip web sites for stories on the Death Pictures. Her search had thrown up tens of thousands of matches. A four-inch stiletto heel ground into the patchy carpet beneath her chair.

'We've generated massive interest,' she buzzed. 'Massive! What a scoop! We've broken the news of the clue. Now let's break the news of the riddle being solved. Someone must have got it. I want it first. I want the winner on the programme. I want Abi. I want art experts. I want the charities that have benefited from the pictures. I want...'

Dan trooped away and sat down at his desk, wondering where to go next. He made all the obvious calls. He tried Abi, who told him that thousands more guesses had come in, but none had been right. None even close in fact. That would do for a bit of the story, but he needed more.

He rang the places with the nine remaining original Death Pictures, a list of charities, companies, dealers and art collectors. He'd managed to speak to all of them. They'd been caught up in the mystery and were keen to say their bit, but it had led nowhere.

They'd all heard the clue and come to the same conclusion he had. It must be something in the canvas of the original paintings. They'd checked, but found nothing. They had also checked the frames – he hadn't realised they too had been chosen by McCluskey – but found nothing there either.

Lizzie was pacing the newsroom, casting occasional machine gun stares over at him. He got the message. A follow-up story was non-negotiable. He called Abi again, just after six o'clock for the latest information.

'We've had several thousand calls and emails now,' she said, sounding content. 'And I can tell you that none are right, and none are even close. As of tonight, the riddle remains unsolved.'

Dan asked her when the answer would be revealed, but she'd again said in a week or so, depending on factors which are still, and which will remain, out of my control. Will remain, he wondered? What did that mean? What could be happening to influence her timing? And if it was so important to Joseph McCluskey, how could she have no control over it? It was annoyingly bewildering, and he'd risen to it.

'Is that another clue?' Dan asked.

'If you want it to be.'

'Is it?'

'If you want it to be.'

'Meaning?'

'If you knew the answer to why it was out of my control, that would certainly help you with the riddle. It wouldn't give you the answer, but it would point strongly the right way.'

Dan had sat there, phone to his ear, baffled. He couldn't even think of a decent follow up question.

'Any hints?'

'None.'

The merciless clock ticked on towards broadcast time. He should hang up, get ready for the programme. Dan doodled a few squiggles on his notebook. One looked like the mobile phone from the first Death Picture. He should thank Abi and say goodbye. Where his next question came from, he didn't know.

'Why did Joseph want me to have the final clue? Why me?'

He wasn't sure whether to expect an answer, but he got one anyway. And it wasn't what he anticipated, not at all.

'He liked you,' Abi replied, her voice misty. 'He'd seen your news reports and said they were thoughtful and perceptive. He was interested in crime too, and he liked the way you seemed to understand criminals' minds. He'd heard you had an insight into people and he wanted to meet you in that obituary interview you did. He wanted to see if you'd have any idea about the solution to the riddle. He reckoned you had a decent chance. And if you didn't get it, he thought you were a fit messenger to give the rest of the world a go.'

Dan hadn't known how to react then, apart from to feel guilty for all the times he'd cursed Joseph McCluskey and his riddle. He had a bourgeoning sense the world was a far less rich and colourful place without the infuriating artist. He was surprised to find himself wishing he'd known the man better.

'You miss him, don't you?' Dan asked.

It was the first time he'd made Abi hesitate before replying. It was ten past six now, just 15 minutes until he was on air. There was no time for such questions, but he couldn't help asking it anyway.

Finally, she said, 'More than you can possibly know.'

Then one more question, just time for one more. Lizzie was hovering, glaring over at him, an icicle heel fraying the carpet. She wanted her follow-up, wanted him downstairs in the studio, ready for the programme. Hundreds of thousands of people would be watching, waiting.

'How do you think I'll feel when I know the answer?' Dan asked.

This time the reply was instant. 'You'll kick yourself, as I think everyone will. The one thing I can promise you is that it's been right there in front of you all the time. It'll make an extraordinary impact when the answer's revealed. You'll be amazed at what it'll do. The repercussions will be quite a show.'

Dan went on air feeling a mixture of irritated and lifted by the conversation. He'd told the viewers the riddle remained unsolved, despite thousands of guesses, and that only a week or so remained before they would all know. And he reported what Abi had told him, that no one should give up because she could guarantee the answer was there in the pictures, right in front of them. But there would be no more clues to help, and the time to see it was running out, and quickly.

Chapter Twenty-four

DAN STOOD WATCHFULLY ON one corner of the street, Sean, the Universal reporter on the other. Nigel and Pete, the two cameramen lingered by the court entrance, alert, waiting. El was with them too, pacing back and forth, occasionally stroking his long lens. There was one big problem with Plymouth Crown Court for journalists. There were two ways the prison van could bring the defendant in and they'd guessed wrongly before. Dan didn't want that to happen today, not at the start of a big case like this. The long awaited McCluskey murder trial.

They'd cut a deal, him and Sean. Each would stand on one street corner and shout to the cameramen when the van appeared. You could put rivalries aside and work together on court cases. It made sense. The only information you got was what was said in the trial. However great your guile, or however subtle and penetrating your interview technique, they meant nothing when all you could do was observe the words of the barristers, witnesses and the judge. All that distinguished was how you wrote the story, and Dan was confident his way would be better. At least he hoped so.

The ban on filming in court meant you needed all the pictures you could get. A shot of the prison van coming in with the defendant was the classic way to start your report. So here they stood, waiting for it.

Behind him, Dan heard a shout. 'Coming, coming!'

He spun around. Sean was waving, Nigel and Pete running towards him, hoisting their cameras onto their shoulders. Around the corner trundled the white van, a line of small, metal barred windows along its sides. El ran with it, held his camera up to the windows, let off a few flashes. It was a one in a hundred chance he'd get Kiddey, but worth a try. A shot of him being delivered to court at the start of the trial would be worth thousands of pounds. The barrier shielding the court car park shuddered up and the van was inside, parked safely around the back, out of sight. Good, thought Dan. One decent sequence of pictures for his report. Now for some of the people who'd feature in the case.

He checked his watch. 9.20 it said, so probably half past. The trial was due to start at ten. He stood with Nigel outside the front steps of the court, ready to film the judicial procession. Barristers, witnesses, police officers, anyone who could be useful to show the viewers when he was writing about what they said in court.

'It's the golden quarter,' hissed El. 'They'll all be here in a minute. Between 9.30 and 9.45, that's when they like to arrive. Not too early, they've got to be a bit cool, but still plenty of time to prepare. The sacred golden quarter.' El grinned as he polished his camera lens with a dirty looking sleeve. 'I've got another holiday booked too for after the case, courtesy of Joseph McCluskey and his women,' he added. 'Off to Spain again. Can't wait.'

He broke into a tuneless warble. Dan sensed a dreadful limerick coming, but wasn't quick enough to stop his friend.

'The death of poor Joe,
Made many feel low,
But for El it's a hoot,
It brought him some loot,
So now on his hols he can go!'
Even El had the decency to look ashamed at that one.

Adam walked around the corner, dignified and upright, wearing what looked like a new suit. Dark blue, his favourite colour, single-breasted, sober and smart. Just right for a Detective Chief Inspector. He always made even more of an effort than his usual impressive dress sense when he knew he'd be filmed. He nodded to Dan as he walked up the court steps. They never made a public show of being friends. People might start to suspect where some of Dan's stories came from.

A couple of barristers strode in, wigs and briefcases under their arms. They were always keen to be filmed, it was good advertising to be associated with a big case. The prosecution counsel, Tristan Wishart, even agreed to walk in again when Pete wasn't happy with the first shot he took.

Inside the court, the press bench was crowded with a line of hacks, all chatting to each other. Dan had expected it to be busy, so he'd nipped in earlier to see an usher whose son he'd taken out for a week's work experience. A reserved sign had duly appeared on the seat nearest the door. Always be prepared to leave fast if you needed to, in case the defendant's or victim's families made a run for it after the verdict. They were vital shots and interviews, jubilation or tears, depending on the outcome.

The public gallery was full too, no surprise there either. It was a big trial, a great story. A shame it wasn't scheduled to last longer, Dan thought. Just four days it was set down for, only a limited amount of evidence to get through, many of the facts of the case agreed between defence and prosecution. There was no dispute that Kid was at the house and McCluskey died there. The only issue for the jury was the central one. Was the evidence strong enough for them to conclude Kid did kill McCluskey, despite his denials?

'Court rise!' shouted the usher, and Judge Lawless stalked in. Everyone sat down and he glared around the wood-panelled courtroom, his greying wig and immaculate red robe symbols of his authority. The passing years had cultivated his face with the lines of a permanent scowl. A scary judge this one, icily sarcastic with ill-prepared barristers and no time whatsoever for journalists.

Dan had seen his fellows suffer the sharp end of the learned judge's ire when they'd reported a case in a way he didn't like. One journalist whose paper criticised a jail term Judge Lawless had passed in a domestic violence case was summoned to receive a three-page letter on the detail of sentencing law.

'I expect to see an article tomorrow about it,' the judge had said acidly, leering down from the bench. 'Criticism is appropriate when based on the rock foundation of sure knowledge. When built on the shifting sands of ignorance, it is folly.' The article had duly appeared.

It should have been a good joke, a judge called Lawless, but it was remarkable, Dan thought, that he couldn't remember anyone ever being inclined to crack it. Even if the judge was nowhere around, you'd be looking over your shoulder twitchily, feeling he was watching.

Kid sat in the plate-glass dock, his eyes flicking nervously around the court. He wore a plain black shirt, no tie. It was quite a contrast from the last time he'd seen the man, Dan thought, when he'd boasted that vibrant, multicoloured shirt. The silver stud in his nose had gone too and he looked pale and drawn, gaunt even. Not surprising, six months in prison on remand, waiting for the week that would decide whether he'd spend most of the rest of his life in jail, or walk free into the sunlight. Dan felt a flutter of nerves at the thought. What must he be going through?

Kid pushed a palm up to the glass of the dock as if he couldn't believe it was him that it incarcerated. He still didn't look like a killer, just didn't have that air of ruthlessness about him. Could he really have improvised a murder plan so quickly in McCluskey's house? And what about Joanna's words, that she was sure he couldn't have done it?

Or was that just him, allowing his imagination to expect the killer to be a Hollywood type villain? Adam had said so many times that murderers almost always looked absolutely ordinary. And the evidence was compelling, wasn't it? That fingerprint on the knife, what Adam had called the killer fact.

Dan wrote a heading in his notebook; 'Kid trial/McCluskey murder', and underlined it twice. It was going to be a fascinating case. Next to him, the other journalists had started betting on how long the jury would take to return a verdict. It was a tradition in big trials. Guilty in only a couple of hours was the emerging consensus.

In front of the hacks, the barristers, their juniors and solicitors, the police officers and the clerk to the court settled themselves. All had neat piles of lever-arch files laid out on the benches before them. Behind was the public gallery, bubbling with excited conversation. It was how Dan imagined an ancient tribal gathering.

Abi was there, dressed in a black trouser suit. She sat rigidly, eyes fixed forwards. Professor Ed was too, wearing a

301

white shirt and tie, the first time Dan had seen him dress so formally. The rest of the crowd looked like interested members of the public. Dan didn't blame them for coming. It'd be quite a show, and all for free. When he retired, if he was ever bored, he planned to pop into court for a couple of hours of enjoying whatever sordid or gruesome trial was being held.

Kid stood, faced the judge and the courtroom quietened. The clerk read the charge.

'Lewis Kiddey, you are charged with the murder of Joseph McCluskey on the fifteenth of April this year. How do you plead?'

'Not guilty.' His reply was instant, his voice strong, but Dan could see Kid's hands trembling behind his back.

Tristan Wishart QC stood, a line of ginger hair sneaking out from under the back of his wig. He smoothed his jet-black robe, waited for his moment. All the hacks sat with pens poised. The prosecution's opening statement was always one of the best parts of a trial, full of juicy detail and lurid allegations.

'Your honour, members of the jury,' he began. 'The Crown's case is a simple one. That this man, Lewis Kiddey,' he turned, gestured to the dock, 'took advantage of Joseph McCluskey's terminal illness and crippling weakness to murder him, then attempted to cover up his crime by trying to make it look like Mr McCluskey had taken his own life.'

What a line to start off with, Dan thought admiringly. Like many barristers, Wishart was a performer. Arms lofted in front of him to make a point, continual eye contact with the jury, playing them, convincing them of his trustworthiness, the truth of his case. He charmed and beguiled them into believing him.

'Members of the jury, what we say happened is this. That on a pleasant, spring evening, some six months ago now, Lewis Kiddey was invited around to the McCluskeys' house for a drink and to discuss the latest of Joseph's paintings.'

Dan had been scribbling fast, taking it all down, but now he paused. His brain hung onto Wishart's words, repeated them. Six months ago? It was, wasn't it? Six months ago that

McCluskey had died. And he'd said just before his death that it would be six months until the answer to the riddle was revealed. A coincidence, or something more?

He didn't believe in coincidences, especially not where someone as manipulative as Joseph McCluskey was concerned. So, he thought? So what? Did it mean something? What could it mean?

A dramatic fling of Wishart's arm brought him back to the courtroom. Leave those thoughts for later, Dan told himself. You've got an important trial to report. And with Judge Lawless presiding, getting any of it wrong isn't an option you want to explore.

'It was an innocent enough invitation, members of the jury,' continued Wishart, lowering his voice a little to match the mood of his words. 'A couple of friends, a glass of wine, a pleasant chat. We've all done it. And we believe that was exactly what Lewis Kiddey had in mind when he went round that evening, nothing more sinister than a drink and a chat. But then – then members of the jury – then... Joseph McCluskey said something which in a second changed Lewis Kiddey's intentions... changed them... to murder!'

You could almost hear the gasp run around the courtroom as Wishart emphasised that last word. 'Murder' boomed out and echoed around, bouncing, time and again from the wooden panels. Heads turned to Kid, to look at this man, the killer, already convicted now in many eyes. Judge Lawless glared down from his chair. He gave the barristers some leeway for drama, but not much. Wishart was treading on the borders of his tolerance.

He sensed it, shuffled some papers, carried on.

'This is what we say happened, members of the jury. We will produce evidence to show you that Joseph McCluskey was a very ill man. He had cancer and he was in the last few weeks of his life. When he was told his illness was terminal, some months before, he set about tidying up his affairs.' Another pause, Wishart's voice dropping again now, sympathetic and rueful.

'It was the noble endeavour of a deeply decent man. All

303

those he had arguments or feuds with he contacted and told them he would like to resolve their disputes, so he could leave this earth in peace. And they all responded, members of the jury. They all responded – for who could resist the heartfelt plea of a dying man?'

An imploring spread of the arms to the jury, another glare from Judge Lawless. But it was good theatre, thought Dan, excellent stuff for tonight's report.

Wishart took a step forward towards the jury, as if sharing a confidence. 'Lewis Kiddey was one of those with whom Mr McCluskey had his disagreements, and with whom he'd been reconciled. We will show you evidence that Mr Kiddey had visited the McCluskey house on several occasions before the fatal night, times when he ate and drank with Joseph and his wife Abi. All was well. The hatchet was buried and they were getting along fine, old friends together, preparing to say goodbye. Sad times, members of the jury. Poignant times.'

That thought kept resurfacing in Dan's mind. Six months on now, the murder trial starting and the answer to the riddle soon to be revealed. Events were converging. It couldn't all be a coincidence.

What about Abi's teasing words? She would give the answer in about a week, depending on events which were beyond her control. Could that mean the trial? How long it lasted? Was that what she couldn't control? But how could that be linked with the riddle?

Dan felt the familiar excitement returning, rippling through him, stronger now than before. He was onto something, he was sure of it. He forced his mind back to the humiliation of Advent, the manhole cover and the chough in the back garden, calmed himself. He never learned. But he knew he wouldn't be able to resist. He thought he was onto something. Tonight would be another night with the Death Pictures, a couple of beers to stir his brain, one final effort before it was all revealed.

'Then comes the evening in question.' Wishart looked down at his notes, as though scrupulously checking the tiniest detail. 'Lewis Kiddey arrived at the McCluskey house, we say at about half-past seven. We will show you evidence of that, although it's disputed by the defence. Abi is out, walking the dog. Mr Kiddey is invited in by Joseph, says hello, is offered a glass of wine which he accepts, you know the sort of thing. Just small talk. It's exactly the way it has been on previous occasions, but this time – this time, members of the jury – there's one key difference. A fatal difference.'

A pause, a long look into the twelve silent and rapt faces in the jury box. Another glare from Judge Lawless, the cue for Wishart to continue.

'This time, members of the jury, there's something Joseph McCluskey wants to get off his chest. We will produce evidence to show you that Lewis Kiddey's most famous work, the one which led to him receiving national acclaim, was not in fact his own idea... but that of Joseph McCluskey!'

In the dock, Dan noticed Kid shaking his head violently. His mouth hung open, his hands gripped the wooden ledge in front of him. His knuckles whitened with the pressure.

'It's this, members of the jury, this which we say leads to the murder of Joseph McCluskey. We will show you that Lewis Kiddey thought the issue had been forgotten, perhaps had even convinced himself that the idea was his own. But this evening – this fateful evening – Joseph brought the matter up again, to get it off his chest. He told Mr Kiddey that he'd thought about it, that it was something he needed to resolve with his conscience. And then, members of the jury, then comes the fateful moment. Joseph told Mr Kiddey he had decided he was going to reveal the secret in an audio diary of his life that he was about to record. The truth would be laid bare at last.'

Dan heard a faint sobbing from behind him, looked over his shoulder. It was Abi, and the tears were cascading down her cheeks, dampening her jacket. A black robed usher put a hand on her shoulder, passed a tissue.

Wishart lowered his voice again and Dan had to lean forwards to catch his words. Around him, others were doing the same.

'And what happened then, members of the jury? We say

this is what. Lewis Kiddey panicked. He thought it had all been forgotten. But here it was again, suddenly resurrected, a secret which could ruin him brought back to life. He panicked and in that moment he came up with a plan... a murderous plan.'

Wishart took a sip of water from a clear plastic cup. Nice trick, thought Dan. The barrister wasn't thirsty, just wanted to let the words linger, allow them to imprint on the jury. Even Judge Lawless couldn't admonish someone for having a drink of water.

Wishart put down the cup, continued, the pace of his words faster now, his voice more urgent, his argument gathering momentum.

'He spots a knife in the kitchen. He looks at Joseph. He's frail, full of cancer and the morphine he's taking to control the pain. It wouldn't take much to overpower him and use that knife... but how to disguise his crime? He has an idea. He grabs the knife and forces Joseph upstairs to the bathroom. He makes him run a hot bath and pushes him down into it. Then he cuts the man's wrists and stands back to watch his life's blood flood out of him. He stands there, members of the jury – he stands there – and watches Joseph McCluskey die. He watches his friend, Joseph McCluskey, die from the wound he himself has inflicted. Murder, members of the jury. Murder! Not a gunshot, or a beating, but murder nonetheless. Murder, plain and simple.'

Dan scribbled fast to keep up. Great stuff, this would make for a hell of a report. Behind him, Abi was still quietly sobbing. He'd add a line about that too, important colour and emotion. They had film of her arriving at court.

Then members of the jury, then it's time to cover his tracks,' boomed Wishart. 'Lewis Kiddey wipes the knife clean of his own fingerprints and presses it into Joseph's hand so his prints are on it instead. Oh yes, it's cold... calculating... ruthless. Then he waits. He waits until he knows Joseph is dead and he calls 999 to say he's found his body in the bathroom. Please, send an ambulance as quickly as possible, please... His friend has tried to commit suicide. But he's

306

waited long enough. He knows it's too late.. That Joseph is already dead.'

Another sip of water, the courtroom hushed. Everyone was looking at Wishart and then Kid, still shaking his head in the dock.

'But Lewis Kiddey made one fatal error, members of the jury.' Wishart nodded with his own words. 'One fatal error.'

A lone finger rose to emphasise the point. His voice fell, sorrowful again, the words slow.

'He missed one fingerprint. One print on the murder weapon. A print that matches his finger perfectly. A print which tells the story of what happened on that spring evening, six months ago. A fingerprint which sees him stand before you today, members of the jury, we say... as a murderer.'

Again he emphasised the last word, let it hang in the silent courtroom, his eyes running over the jury. Then he drew himself up and turned to the judge. 'Your Honour, we call our first witness. Abi McCluskey.'

She rose from the back of the court, dabbing her eyes with a tissue, walked slowly forwards. She kept her eyes straight ahead, careful never to slip a glance towards Kid in the dock. He leaned forwards, pressed a palm to the glass, seemed to mouth some words, but she didn't look, just walked on and up the wooden steps into the witness box.

That evening, Dan sat with Jenny in an edit suite and they put the report together. He started with the van arriving, talked about Kid being brought to court for the beginning of his trial for McCluskey's murder. There was a shot of Wishart over some of the quotes from the barrister's opening address, then the first of Dan's pieces to camera. He added more of what Wishart had said and some colour about the court being packed with journalists and the public.

They used some library footage of the police cars and cordon around the McCluskeys' home on the night of Joseph's death, while Dan recapped on when and how he'd been found. Then it was another piece to camera when he talked about Abi's evidence, going out, walking the dog, and her shock at coming back to find the police at her house, her husband dead. She'd also testified about how Joseph had planned to tell Kid that night about his audio diary and the secret of the statue. Dan added that she'd cried through much of the opening of the trial. He could almost feel the viewers hurting with her.

To end, he used a couple of shots of the court building, and the dull but legally necessary; 'Mr Kiddey denies murder. The trial continues tomorrow.'

'Great stuff, just great,' Lizzie fizzed after the programme, her eyebrow arched to a fine peak. 'I can sense the ratings shooting up. What a pity the trial's such a short one. But then, there are the Death Pictures too, aren't there?' The eyebrow arched further. 'We've got the answer to the riddle to look forward to as well. Why not see if we can get Abi to reveal it live on air too, like she did that clue? I want us to be the first with the answer. I want everyone tuning in to us to see it. I want us to be known as the Death Pictures station…'

Dan pulled a dubious face, but Lizzie's momentum was unstoppable.

'I know Abi's probably a bit upset at the moment, but she'll come round. It's wonderful stuff, such mystery, and violence and death too. I couldn't have written a better plot myself. The viewers will be loving it. Oh, God bless Joseph McCluskey.'

Dan lay on his great blue sofa that night, Rutherford at his feet, determined this time he would finally make some headway into the riddle of the Death Pictures. But he wasn't sure he believed himself.

He was interrupted just once, not by work as he'd half expected, but by Adam.

'You didn't put me on,' the detective said ruefully.

He sounded more cheerful. Dan wondered what had been wrong. Annie and Tom was the usual explanation, but he'd said it wasn't that, didn't seem to want to go into the reason.

He'd been worried Adam had found out about him and Claire. He'd have to tell him soon. He'd been waiting to see if the liaison came to anything – no point bothering him if it didn't – but they seemed to be growing closer and enjoying it, so he would have to know. Dan felt a nudge of concern. Adam could be very fatherly with his officers, and he knew only too well how good Dan was with women.

'You didn't give any evidence today,' Dan said reassuringly. 'Tomorrow you'll be on, worry not.'

The phone rattled with a chuckle.

'Now that gives me a dilemma. That was a new suit and tie and I wanted them to make their TV debuts. So do I now wear the same suit two days running, or change into something which I've already been on TV in?'

'That sounds agonising. I think you'll just have to wrestle with it tonight and I'll see what you come up with tomorrow. By the way, you're sounding chirpier. What's happened?'

'The start of the case. It's gone very nicely indeed. I thought Wishart did a cracking job. It shouldn't take the jury long to come back with a guilty verdict if it goes on like this.'

Yes, it had been a powerful opening, and the evidence sounded strong, but Dan still wasn't quite convinced. What was making him doubt Kid's guilt? Nothing he could identify, just one of those feelings.

'We'll see,' he replied, running a hand over Rutherford's head. 'If there's one thing I've learnt from all this crime reporting, it's never try to predict the outcome of a case.'

Dan took another gulp of beer and went back to the Death Pictures. He'd managed to convince himself the trial did have some relevance and he spent the evening looking for anything that could be a hint about the court building, or the law, or... well, anything. Three hours he lay there, three hours and four tins of beer, and what had he come up with?

Dan sat up and stretched. Nothing. He'd found nothing, and he'd started to disbelieve his idea anyway. How could Joseph McCluskey possibly have put any reference to the courts or justice in his pictures unless he knew he was going to be murdered? And clever and scheming though he was, he could hardly have predicted that, could he?

Chapter Twenty-five

THE GUILT WAS BACK. He'd woken to find it as fiery as before. The distraction of the first day of the trial had only dampened it. Had he slept much? He wasn't sure. If he had slipped into the blissful blackness, it was only a temporary respite before the remorse jabbed him awake again. Was he, a Detective Chief Inspector, responsible for a man's murder?

OK, so Godley was a rapist. And he couldn't be sure that what he'd leaked to Dan had led to the attack on him. But it felt that way. He'd have to do something about it, couldn't carry this around with him. He had to know.

Adam tried to think of something else, distract himself. But not even the usually pleasant dilemma of his wardrobe and the thought of standing in the witness box pushed it from him mind.

He needed something else to hang onto, like a drowning man clutching for help. His family, his life. It was all getting better. Annie was still asleep next to him, just stirring, he thought, her breathing growing lighter as it did when she rose close to consciousness. He was back at home. They were getting on well, rebuilding their marriage. There were still issues to tackle. He was working too many hours, as ever, but he didn't know if that would ever change. Wasn't it said you married the police force when you became a detective?

Annie seemed to be coping more easily now. He wondered if it was because she'd concluded it was better to have him around for most of the time than not at all. Tom was growing older too, would need them both in the difficult teenage years to come.

A fine boy and a handsome one. He could see trouble with many a heartbroken girl's father ahead. He imagined himself standing on their doorstep, defending the lad, just as his dad had done for him. At least that brought a half smile. Tom would be awake in a minute, demanding breakfast and the bathroom. He'd better get dressed, get sorted. It was an important day.

The new suit, it had to be the new suit again. He'd bought it specially, after all. It deserved its moment of glory. He could disguise its appearance two days running with a different tie.

The guilt hit him again, like an opponent who wouldn't lie down. It wasn't going to seep away. He'd have to call Jack and see how his investigation into Godley's death was going, see if they'd uncovered a motive yet. He could have called him sooner, but... but what? He knew what. He was frightened of what he might hear.

A plain burgundy tie, that would do.

Day two of the trial, and Adam would get his TV appearance. He'd given his evidence, how the fingerprint on the knife matched Kid's, how the artist had been arrested and questioned, the story he'd told. It was interesting, Dan thought, although nothing like as dramatic as yesterday. A shame. But it was still good stuff and Adam and his new suit would feature strongly. Nigel had filmed him walking into court this morning.

Dan shifted uncomfortably on the wooden press bench. He'd been sitting for three hours now and his legs were stiff. They were too long for this space, he couldn't stretch out properly. A break would be a relief. Could he risk nipping out for a coffee in the court canteen? Was this stuff worth listening to? It was one of Greater Wessex police's fingerprint experts, Neil Whelton MSc. Wishart had insisted on emphasising the Master of Science qualification to the jury.

Mr Whelton had been called so the prosecution could establish beyond all doubt the print on the knife was Kid's. Wishart seemed to have done that to his satisfaction and sat down. Edward Munroe, the defence counsel, stood to cross-examine the witness.

'Mr Whelton, you're sure it's my client's fingerprint, I appreciate that. But are you sure it's a contemporary print? What I mean is this. We've heard evidence from Abi McCluskey that Mr Kiddey had been round for dinner on several occasions and could well have used the knife in question to cut bread?'

Neil Whelton checked his notes, found a page. A tall, studious, stooping man, he wore a double-breasted dark blue suit, which looked like it only came out for weddings, funerals and trials. It was the fashion of five years ago, bought when he'd been heavier. It hung off, rather than embraced him.

'The knife had been through the dishwasher, sir, according to Mrs McCluskey, many times since Mr Kiddey last dined with them. We did some tests on how many washes it would take for the prints to be wiped off. We believe two at most. And that's at the very most. One would usually be sufficient. So I think it extremely unlikely the print could have been a residual one from weeks ago.'

Munroe saw his opening.

'Unlikely, but not impossible?'

Whelton considered this, like a computer running through an equation to reach an answer. 'Not impossible, no. Fingerprints can linger longer than people realise.'

Dan could see what would come in Munroe's closing speech. 'Members of the jury, to convict my client, you must be sure beyond reasonable doubt that he killed Mr McCluskey. But I put it to you, if it's possible his fingerprint on the knife came from a previous visit, you cannot so be sure...'

In front of him, Adam was shaking his head. He'd seen it too.

'Thank you, Mr Whelton,' continued Munroe. 'Before you stand down, may I ask you about one further oddity in this case, something yet to be explained satisfactorily. A trace of residue you found on the knife. Talcum powder, I believe?'

The fingerprint expert looked down again, found another page in his notes.

'Yes, sir. We found traces of talcum powder on the handle.'

'Odd again, Mr Whelton, wouldn't you say? Can you offer us any explanation for that?'

'No, sir, beyond that it was a bathroom and there could have been small, dust like amounts of powder on some surfaces. They might have been disturbed by the paramedics or police and got on to the knife.'

'An interesting theory, Mr Whelton, thank you. I'm grateful. But let me offer you another, if I may. It's this.'

Munroe waited, turned to the jury, let his eyes run over each of the silent faces.

'Criminals sometimes use talcum powder to help their hands fit into tight gloves, don't they? So they don't leave fingerprints at the scene of their crime?'

Whelton paused, then replied, 'Yes, sir, I believe they do.'

'So we could in fact be seeing evidence of some criminal intervention here. Some unknown intruder being the one who carried out the alleged attack on Mr McCluskey – if indeed there was one – and leaving only that little trace behind. And that would fit with the attempted break-ins to Mr McCluskey's home, would it not? There could be a powerful motive to break in if someone wanted to try to find the answer to the riddle he'd set?'

'That's your theory, sir, not mine.'

Adam shook his head again. Dan couldn't help but agree. He'd seen it before, defence barristers with little ammunition to defend their clients resorted to muddying the waters, trying to confuse the jury with false trails. Throwing skunks, they called it in the legal trade.

But that stuff about the talc was interesting. Why was it buzzing around in his head like an annoying summer fly? Did he believe there might have been some mystery assailant? No, he didn't think so, surely there'd have been some evidence of it? But the idea was still there, and his subconscious wasn't letting go of it. It did that when it thought there was something important going on that he'd missed, but wouldn't always tell him why. Leave it be, it would come to him when it wanted. Talcum powder...

The rest of the afternoon session was more forensics stuff, too scientific and detailed for his report. Dan did his pieces to camera, then Nigel drove them back to the studios and Jenny edited the story. Not so powerful tonight, Dan thought, and it only made third slot on the programme. But it was still interesting, and important. And he'd done as good a job as he possibly could with the material he had.

Tomorrow would be better. That was when the defence began their case. Kid would go into the witness box to tell the jury he hadn't killed McCluskey. The best of luck to him, Dan thought, it would have to be a hell of a performance. The evidence against him looked compelling.

That evening, Dan took Rutherford for a run, then, in a fit of energy, cooked some pasta for his tea. He even managed to fry some greening bacon and boil down a tin of tomatoes to make a passable sauce. Rutherford padded into the kitchen to watch the rare spectacle. Dan thought he detected a look of amazement on the dog's face. He ought to cook more often, he thought, not just unwrap and heat up. But then, there were lots of things he should do. He still hadn't managed to find a cleaner for the flat, despite months of telling himself to.

The thought about the talcum powder was still bothering him. Why? It couldn't be anything to do with the Death Pictures, surely? Of course not. How could it? But it wouldn't stop teasing his brain, so resignedly he did what he'd promised himself many times now he would never do again. He scrabbled under the bed, got his notes and the prints out and worked through them. He swore this time really would be the last.

What was he looking for now? A tin of talcum powder? Dan breathed out a deep sigh and shook his head. His ideas were getting ever more absurd, through desperation probably. He still thought the answer was in the cascade of numbers, but he couldn't see anything in the pictures which might lead him to it, talcum powder or not. He slapped the notes down on the coffee table. It was ridiculous.

His mobile warbled, a text message. He picked it up, glad of the distraction.

It was Claire. They'd said they might meet up later tonight if she could get away.

'Working late again, can't make it, very sorry. But look forward to the weekend, need a cuddle! x'

He didn't mind not seeing her, felt tired and knew how seriously she took her job. He liked and respected that. She was similar to Adam in many ways. He would have to tell his friend about Claire soon. He knew he wasn't looking forward to that at all. Perhaps over a beer, it was about time they went out for another drinking session. And beer always softened the impact of unwelcome news.

Claire's message lifted his spirits. It was something to look forward to, just what he needed. By the weekend, Kiddey's trial would probably be over and the answer to the Death Pictures riddle revealed. It'd be off his mind and he'd be free to relax and enjoy himself. About time too.

Perhaps he'd treat them, take Claire away for a night at an inn in Cornwall somewhere. If they found a dog-friendly place, Rutherford could come too. He always felt guilty about going off and enjoying himself and leaving his faithful dog behind. The three of them could do an energetic cliff-top walk, then reward themselves with a good meal and a few beers afterwards. Perfect.

Dan started to tap out a reply on his phone, then stopped, sat very still. He felt suddenly frozen by realisation. He sat rigid and stared at the mobile, kept staring until the letters blurred, lost their meaning. Nothing around him registered, apart from the phone. The phone... the phone... the phone... The first picture had a mobile in, didn't it? Of course it did, he knew them by heart now. And he always thought it was in the numbers, didn't he?

A memory flashed into his mind. The first time he'd met McCluskey, that interview in his studio. The artist's teasing answer to one of his questions.

"I'd consider the studio by far the best place to solve the riddle. All the information you need is here in front of you. If you were to buy some prints of the pictures elsewhere, it may not be. It may, but then again, it may not."

Suddenly the enigmatic words made sense. If this vision, this idea of how the puzzle worked was right, it would explain exactly what McCluskey meant. The one small but now so very obvious difference between the original paintings and the prints hanging on the studio's walls. The two tiny numbers inscribed on each... Shit, was this it?

315

He calmed himself. Steady. Take it easy. You've got it wrong enough times before. Steady. Prepare for more disappointment. Let the excitement wane. This is just another hopeless, useless guess. But he was breathless. He couldn't convince himself he was wrong again. He didn't think so, did he? His heart was racing. Calm…

Dan reached for a pen, knocked it clumsily off the coffee table, bent down to retrieve it. He was surprised to see how much his hand was shaking. He grabbed a piece of paper, anything, began writing, using the phone as a guide. He tapped out the numbers.

Dan swore under his breath. Could it really be a code? And so simple? Could it? Surely not, someone would have got it by now. But his hand was shaking badly, could hardly hold the phone.

The first letter made sense. Then the second. Then the third. It was working, making sense, the first four, five, six, seven. All ten. Shit! Shit, it all fitted. He'd got it. The answer was there, on the back of this beer-stained Indian take-away menu. It was there, staring at him. He'd got it. He'd bloody got it. Abi was right, it was there in front of him all the time. He'd bloody got it! Shit!

Dan flopped back on the sofa, his heart pumping and pounding. He reached up a hand to his chest to soothe it. He hardly dared believe it. He'd got it. He'd cracked the riddle. He'd got it.

He calmed himself again. Check once more, twice more, before you make a fool of yourself. But he knew it was right, knew it. He forced himself to go through the same process again. He checked it, came to the same conclusion, did it again.

He'd got it. He'd bloody got it. After all this time, all this thought and searching, all these humiliations, Advent, manhole covers, digging up people's gardens, he'd finally bloody solved bloody Joseph bloody McCluskey's bloody riddle.

He couldn't help himself. 'Yeeaahhhhhhhh!!!!!' Dan shouted, making Rutherford jump up in alarm. 'Sorry, old friend, sorry,' he laughed, giving the baffled dog a reassuring cuddle. 'See that space over there?' he said, pointing to the wall. 'I think we might have a very nice new painting coming there.'

He walked unsteadily to the kitchen and poured himself a generous glass of VSOP cognac, special occasions only. His hands were shaking so much he had to put the bottle down, try again.

He took a couple of gulps and calmed himself, leaned against the fridge and stared out of the window. The orange street lamps were lit, the road quiet, even the trees still tonight. He didn't see any of it. His mind was spinning around what he'd found, as if in a reckless orbit.

When the glass was empty and he'd relaxed a little, he realised his discovery meant much more than just a new and fine painting for his wall. Very much more.

Dan poured himself another cognac, resolved to take this slower, actually taste it. He popped a couple of ice cubes out of the tray, slid them slowly into the glass, didn't want the waste of any splashes. He swirled the liquid, took another deep sip, let his racing mind settle.

What he'd found was going to have profound implications for the murder trial tomorrow. How the hell was he going to explain it to Adam? Let alone Judge Lawless? And what would Lizzie say? Not to mention the hundreds of thousands of people who'd been captivated for months by the riddle of the Death Pictures. He could scarcely believe what he'd discovered.

There was no escaping it Dan thought, but he didn't know whether to feel anger or the awe of admiration. Joseph McCluskey has made fools of us all.

Chapter Twenty-six

'THIS IS EXTRAORDINARILY IRREGULAR,' hissed the court clerk over the top of her half-moon spectacles. 'Extraordinarily. I have never heard of anything like it. I can't just grant you an audience with the judge in the middle of a murder trial. It could be highly prejudicial. It could bring the whole system into disrepute. I simply cannot allow it.'

Dan and Adam stood in the empty courtroom facing her. He'd slept fitfully, called Adam first thing in the morning, as early as he dared. They'd met outside court and Dan had told his story. Adam had gone from being scornful, to interested, to reluctantly convinced. Now they both had to see the judge, to explain it to him and see what action he decided to take. That was, thought Dan, if they could get past the clerk.

He swallowed his annoyance and tried again. 'Look, I can't tell you what it's about. I can only tell the judge. It's that sensitive. But I can promise you it's something he must hear, and he must hear it before the trial resumes this morning. It's very important indeed.'

She still didn't look convinced, shook her head vigorously making her black robe flap waves around her. 'No, I can't allow it.'

'OK then,' growled Dan. 'If we can't see the judge in person, I'll make him aware by putting it out on the radio and TV. Then, when all hell breaks loose and he issues a warrant for my arrest and has me rushed here in a police car, sirens screaming, I'll tell him I did originally want to see him but you wouldn't allow me to. And I assure you, that's what will happen. It's that serious.'

They held each other's glares for a long moment, then she huffed. 'Oh very well then, I'll go and ask if he's prepared to see you. But I can't guarantee he will.'

'Nice bluff,' said Adam, as the door closed behind her.

'I wasn't bluffing. I hate jobsworths like that. The only way to deal with petty officialdom is to scare them with trouble

318

from their seniors.'

Dan leaned back against the witness box, stared at the empty dock where Kid had sat. What would happen today, he wondered? If his solution was right, it could turn out to be the most extraordinary day of his life. He noticed his hands were still shaking. They hadn't stopped since last night. He looked over at Adam. The detective was gazing down at his polished black shoes. Going through similar thoughts about what the day would bring, no doubt.

The door opened and the clerk beckoned testily.

'He will see you,' she said, her face set and stony. 'But he says it had better be very, very good indeed.'

'It is,' said Dan grimly.

Judge Lawless's chambers were effectively a grand office. Thick red pile carpet caressed Dan's shoes as he stepped hesitantly in. Dark stained wood panelling on the walls shrunk the space and created an air of intimidating magnificence. By the lead-paned stone window stood a large and antique looking wooden desk, and behind that the glowering judge.

His wig rested on a corner of the desk, facing the door, as if it too waited to meet them. It was the first time Dan had seen the judge's hair. Tightly cropped and silvery, it seemed to say the man beneath it would tolerate no prevarication. Small wonder journalists called here talked about how they shuddered. Dan suddenly began to have doubts about what he was going to say, and imagined the judge bawling him out for wasting his valuable time. Come on, pull yourself together, he thought. You're sure of your story and you're here to help.

The judge studied them for a moment, then spoke. His voice was quieter than in the courtroom, but just as acidic.

'My clerk says you have something extremely important to tell me. I sincerely hope it is. It is most irregular and, probably, highly inadvisable for a judge to have a private audience with a journalist in the middle of a high-profile murder trial.'

He didn't invite them to sit down on the stern-looking red leather armchairs, and he spat out the word 'journalist' as though it tasted rank. Not good omens, thought Dan. He slipped his hands into his pockets to hide their shaking, then thought the judge might find that disrespectful so put them behind his back.

'Judge Lawless, thank you for your time,' Dan began, trying to keep his voice steady. 'I think I can guarantee you will find what I have to tell you very important and that it will have a significant impact on the case.'

'I will be the judge of that.'

Dan took a deep breath. Thanks for making me feel so at ease, he wanted to say. Thanks for telling me to go ahead, do what I think is my duty, the right and just thing. He had no difficulty stopping himself saying it.

'Your honour, you're aware of the riddle of the Death Pictures, that Joseph McCluskey set before his death?' A slow nod from the judge, but a glance at the clock too. It was almost ten, the scheduled restart time for the case. 'Well, I've been trying to solve it, and last night I think I did,' Dan continued. 'I believe I've found the secret message contained in the pictures. If I'm right, it has grave implications for this trial.'

Judge Lawless studied him with that icy gaze. 'Go on,' he said slowly.

A hint of interest now, Dan thought, just a hint. 'Your honour, it would help if I could show you how I came to the solution.' He fumbled in his satchel for his notes and the prints. 'May I?'

Judge Lawless rose from his chair. He was taller than Dan expected. 'I'll come around there and you can spread your props out on the table,' he said.

Dan did, laid out the ten Death Picture prints in order. Adam stood back and watched, silent, arms folded. He'd seen it already.

Dan put a finger on the first picture. 'I worked through them many times without getting anywhere,' he said. 'But the key to cracking the puzzle came to me last night, when I was sending a text message on my mobile phone. You use a mobile?'

'Of course,' he said coolly. 'Just because I'm a judge, it

320

doesn't mean I'm entirely out of touch with the world. Don't believe everything you people write.'

Dan didn't know what to say. He shifted his weight from foot to foot.

'Well, your honour, you'll see that a mobile features prominently in Picture One. It's that which I believe is the key to solving the riddle. In the pictures there are lots of places and people and numbers, which could seem to be a clue, but I think they're all false leads. They're what magicians call misdirection, distractions from where you should really be looking. I believe the only clue you actually need is the prints. The numbers of the prints in fact. You can see them in the corners of this set of reproductions.'

Judge Lawless leaned over, peered down at the pictures.

In the cells below the courthouse, Lewis Kiddey was growing increasingly nervous. There wasn't a fingernail left he hadn't bitten down. It was well past ten o'clock. He should have been taken up to the court by now, should be in the witness box telling his story.

The police, warders, security guards, his fellow remand prisoners, no one had believed him. Over the past six months of torment, no one had believed a word. They'd all smiled and nodded understandingly. Yes, yes, that's right, you're innocent. We're all innocent in here mate. We're all wrongly accused, the victims of evil and intricate conspiracies.

The difference though was he truly was such a victim. Six months of his life, rotting away in prison, accused of the most serious crime in the land. The only compensation was that they'd allowed him to carry on painting, and his incarceration had freed something in his spirit, made his work more vibrant, poignant, filled with despair. The colours and shapes beseeched. It had given his pictures a soul.

If he ever got out of here, his prison paintings would cause a sensation amongst the critics. He knew it. That was how he consoled himself, lying in his wrongful cell at night. The thoughts of the exhibition he would stage, full of the pictures he'd painted in jail, the admiring faces, the acclaim, the telling and re-telling of his story. Interviews, papers, television and radio, all would flock to him when he was freed. If he was freed...

What was he talking about? He would get out, of course he would. He was an innocent man. He wanted to be there in court, in the witness box, telling the jury he was innocent. It was down to them, twelve of his peers, his fate in their hands. If no one else had believed him, surely they would. Surely. They had to.

Dan stood back and watched as Judge Lawless used his mobile phone to work through the code. It was way past ten now, but on the couple of occasions the officious clerk had knocked on the door to remind him, the Judge had waved her dismissively away. Dan couldn't resist turning a smile on her.

The Judge had almost finished, and Dan stood silently by. It was the only way to convince him, to let him see it for himself. He checked the penultimate picture, print 3/4, three presses of the number four key, wrote down an 'I'. Then the final picture, print 1/3, one press of number three. Judge Lawless wrote down the last letter, a 'D'. Then he stood back and read the words he'd written. All in capitals, as if to emphasise their importance, it was as though they shouted out from the paper.

I FRAMED KID

Lawless stared at the words for a moment, then stalked slowly back to his desk and sat down. He looked up at Dan and Adam as they stood, waiting silently, expectant. Dan felt his heart pounding again, was sure the judge could hear it in the quiet of his chambers. What would he say? Did he believe it? Did he think it was significant? How could he possibly not? He shifted his feet on the thick carpet, waited. Beside him, Adam waited too.

'I am going to adjourn the trial until this afternoon,' said Lawless calmly. Not a word of thanks, Dan noted. 'Mr Breen, I trust that will give you enough time to re-interview Mrs

322

McCluskey? That would seem the most obvious way forward.'

'Yes sir,' replied Adam. 'She's in court. I'll go and see her now.'

'Will you rejoin me here to tell me what you find, please? Then I will decide how we shall proceed.' He paused, stared at both of them. 'If indeed we proceed at all.'

Dan thought he saw it in Abi's face when they walked up to her in the court's waiting area and Adam asked for a chat in one of the private rooms. He thought he could see the realisation. No fear, just understanding, and was there some relief? He thought he could see her let something go, as if breathing out a secret that she'd held uncomfortably inside for long months. She followed them without a word.

Dan closed the door behind them. She sat down at the table, Adam opposite her. He stayed standing at the door, was only watching now. This part was up to Adam. But it was to him she turned and asked her question.

'You've got it, haven't you?'

'Yes,' Dan said gently. 'I've got it.'

'And he knows?' Abi asked, turning her head towards Adam.

'Yes, he knows. He knows everything.'

'Then it's all over, isn't it? The trial, the riddle, all of it. All over.'

'I think so.'

She studied him for a minute and Dan wondered what she would do. Then she released an unexpected smile.

'I'm glad in a way, I think,' Abi said, her voice faltering. 'I was never comfortable with it. It was Joseph's idea and he made me promise to follow it all through. It was his last wish and I had to be loyal to him for that. I hope you'll understand.' She gazed at him, her eyes misty. She was somewhere else, Dan thought. With Joseph perhaps? 'I'm glad it's all over now,' she added. 'Really, I am glad.'

He nodded, felt for her, returned the smile.

'I thought so. That was what I suspected.'

'Yes.' Another pause as she sat, looking at him. 'Joseph

323

said he thought you might get it. He reckoned your mind worked in a similar way to his and you might understand what he was trying to do. But he hoped the riddle would run for a while. He liked you very much you know.'

'I didn't, but thank you.' Dan suddenly felt flushed with an inexplicable pride. 'I thought he was a remarkable man too. And it did run, didn't it? I have to say, it was brilliant. The riddle, the whole plan. Whatever anyone might think of the morals involved, it was brilliant and almost perfect. And it ran for nearly the whole of the course you had planned, I think? Just a couple of days short?'

There were tears forming in her eyes now, a tightening of her face, but she was still in control. Just, Dan thought, only just. He could almost see the memories of Joseph surrounding her.

Abi's voice trembled. 'You guessed that too? About the verdict and what would happen afterwards?'

Dan nodded. 'Yes, I think so. Were you going to reveal the whole story a day or two after the verdict? That would be my guess.'

She flicked at a stray hair, rubbed her eyes. 'Yes, you're quite right. When the jury came back with their guilty verdict, I was to give Kid one night in prison. To think and despair, to feel his loss. Joseph said it would be just the same feeling he'd inflicted on Joanna. I was to tell the police the next day. And I would have.'

She nodded hard to emphasise the point, dislodging a tear from her eye. It slid a silvery trail down her flushed cheek. 'I would have. He's suffered enough. I hope he's learnt the lesson Joseph wanted to teach him now. That it's a terrible thing to take something precious away from someone, particularly someone you've cared about.'

Adam had been watching, listening carefully. 'Take it from the beginning,' he said gently, making Abi turn to him. 'I'm only a policeman and not privy to the leaps of creative insight that you and Joseph and Dan seem to go in for. Just tell me all that's happened.'

She took a deep breath, tried to compose herself. But the

tears were gathering force and she struggled to find the words.

'Joseph never forgave Kid, did he?' prompted Dan. 'He saw Kid and Joanna as the son and daughter he never had. Despite Kid's faults... even to the extent of him sometimes hitting Joanna...'

Abi said nothing, just shut her eyes as though trying to hide from the words.

'Don't worry, we don't need to go back over that,' Dan continued. 'So, Joseph doted on them, and when Kid broke Joanna's heart – and I'm guessing possibly even worse, destroyed her creative spirit – I'd say he was enraged and inconsolable. A dangerous mix. I know you both helped Joanna as much as you could. I imagine that time with her, seeing her suffering, ingrained Joseph's bitterness and feeling of betrayal about Kid. It made him more determined still to teach him a lesson?'

Abi nodded again. 'Yes, that's right,' she said hoarsely. 'Joseph couldn't have children. It was just one of those things. He used to say it was the way of the world. That he'd been given some great gifts, so it was only fair there was something he shouldn't be able to do. I think it was his way of coping. He managed to hide the pain, but I knew it was there.'

Adam checked his watch. Time was slipping on. Dan knew what he was thinking. He could sense Judge Lawless waiting, no doubt impatiently.

'What happened when Kid left Joanna?' asked Dan.

'I've never seen Joseph so angry, so hell-bent on revenge. It was frightening. He was never a violent man, but he raged about it for months. He felt betrayed by Kid, and he hurt for Jo. He was determined to teach Kid a lesson.'

'And that's where all this started?' asked Adam. She nodded again, dabbed at her eyes with a tissue. 'Was the whole reconciliation thing with everyone just part of the plan to get Kid?'

Abi looked surprised. 'No, no that wouldn't be fair. Not fair at all. He wasn't like that, not deceitful. He was an honest and good man who simply wanted to see justice done.'

Her voice grew stronger now, more sure. 'He wanted to

bow out with a clean conscience and no regrets, he said. But he saw a way he could do that, and with it teach Kid a lesson too. He thought of it as justice, you see. He was being just in making his peace with everyone, and in giving Kid a warning that if he didn't live a better life in future there would be a price to pay. It was only ever going to be a warning. He didn't want to destroy Kid, just change his ways.'

Adam scribbled some notes, the looked up and asked, 'So what did you do? How did you set him up?'

'It was easy, much easier than I thought it was going to be,' Abi replied. 'Joseph called him and told him he wanted to make his peace, to leave what had happened between him and Joanna behind. Kid responded happily. Everyone Joseph approached did. I think he knew it would be very hard to turn down an appeal from a dying man. That was part of his plan. So we had Kid round for dinner, on several occasions. During one of those, I put out a knife we'd cleaned thoroughly for any of our fingerprints, and Kid cut some bread with it. When he'd done that, both Joseph and I made sure we didn't touch the knife again. When Kid left, we kept it, safe in a drawer, with his prints on it, until...'

Abi's words faded. Adam was still writing, so Dan prompted her with the next question. He knew Adam well enough by now to know the detective would want to take the story chronologically.

'And you knew from the start this was what you were going to do? Hence the Death Pictures riddle?'

'Yes, that's right. Joseph had borne his grudge against Kid for years. When he was diagnosed with the cancer, he had the idea immediately. He wanted to go out with a bang he said, and settle some old scores at the same time. He wanted to make his death worthwhile.'

He certainly did that, thought Dan. Revenge on an old enemy, achieve your own idea of justice, secure enormous fame for yourself, your final works and the riddle contained in them, demonstrate your cleverness, your ability to con the entire world, lots of money raised for good causes and one hell of a story. It'll live long and be retold endlessly. Not bad for an epitaph, not bad at all.

Adam looked up from his notebook. 'And the Death Pictures gave him an opportunity to do all that?'

Abi smiled, the pride shining through her tears.

'Yes. He was an extraordinary man, Chief Inspector. He planned it all and predicted precisely how it would go. And he got it exactly right too, up until almost the last.' She turned to Dan. 'Up until you solved the riddle.'

'Tell me about the night of his death,' asked Adam gently. 'What happened there?'

Abi's face changed instantly, and Dan could see her loss. He wondered if it would ever leave her.

'Kid was due to come round at 7.45 and he was always roughly on time.'

'You told us 7.30?'

'Yes. That was a lie to fit in with the plan.'

She was being truthful. Both Dan and Adam could see it, there was no need to push her.

'So you went out with your dog at about 7.15?' Adam said.

'Yes. We knew Jarvis would be in the garden next door, he always was. You could set your clock by him. He was out at seven every day – just after the TV news – watering plants and pottering around. Then it was back inside at 7.20 to wash his hands and get ready for his tea at half past. So I shouted goodbye to Joseph, then waited, then said something else about some milk.'

'To create the impression he was alive and well inside?' asked Dan.

'Yes.'

'Whereas in fact..?'

Now Abi's voice dropped. 'Yes. He was upstairs in the bath… dying.'

She closed her eyes. Adam said nothing, waited for her to steady herself.

'Before I left, we said our last goodbyes.' The tears were back now, rolling down her face again and she made no attempt to stop them. 'Then I ran the bath and he got into it. He was very weak by this stage. He didn't have long left. I put

327

on some gloves and got the knife with Kid's fingerprints out, being careful not to touch the handle. Then I cut... I cut...'

'OK,' interrupted Adam softly. 'After that you pressed the knife into Joseph's hands to put his prints on there too, to make it look like a faked suicide. But you made sure you didn't touch where Kid's print was. I understand. You don't have to go through all that. Then you came downstairs and left the house. And as Dan said, the shouting to Joseph was an act to convince your neighbour all was well and normal?'

'Yes.'

'And you left the door on the latch? So when Kid came round at 7.45, he would have got no answer to his knocks and calls. He would have gone in, as he'd done before when you'd been sitting outside in the garden and not heard him. He'd have looked around and then found Joseph dead?'

'Yes.'

Adam nodded. It was just how Dan had imagined it.

'How could you be so sure half an hour would be enough?' Adam asked.

'Joseph had done his research well. He always did. The hot bath aids the blood flow. It's a classic suicide technique. He was already weak with the cancer and he was taking morphine too. Half an hour would be plenty. He also found out that fingerprints could linger for years if they're not disturbed. That was the basis of the plan.'

'And the bruises on his body?'

'Caused by me, pulling him upstairs, then pushing him down in the bath in the way that Kid would have had to in order to kill him. It was all part of Joseph's plan. He knew when suspicions were raised you'd have to do an autopsy and you'd find the bruises. He knew you'd be able to work out roughly when they were caused too, so he wanted them to be timed right.'

'And the attempted break-in?'

'The first one was done by me earlier that day, to give you a complication to make you suspicious. Joseph needed something to make sure you couldn't just conclude it was suicide and leave it at that. He had to make you look twice, otherwise all the work would be wasted. My story was part of that, telling you that I was sure he would have told me if he planned to kill himself. And then, later, to mention what he intended to say to Kid about his copying the idea for the burger sculpture. But he wanted you to have your suspicions before I told you that, so you would never consider I might be deliberately leading you somewhere.'

'And the other attempted break-in?'

'The other one I have no idea about. Perhaps someone seeking a clue to the riddle? Or just an ordinary burglar? I don't know, but it had nothing to do with me.'

Dan believed her, had guessed that was the case. It didn't seem to fit in anywhere. The rest of the plan was brilliant, he had to admit it. It was a work of criminal genius. And to do all that, and then leave the answer behind in the form of a riddle too, convinced you'd made it so cryptic that no one could solve it. It was brilliant.

'Did Joseph plan to take his own life at the end?' Adam asked.

'Yes, he did. He wanted to be in control, to decide when to go, when the pain and the weakness got too much for him. He thought it gave him some small victory over death, to decide his own moment. That was very him. He liked to be in control.'

'And I'm guessing he'd looked at murder cases in this area and seen how long they take to come to court? He'd have found about six months, and so put that time limit on the riddle?'

'Yes,' Abi replied proudly. 'It was the one thing he was concerned about in the whole plan, the delays in the justice system. But he even got that one right too, didn't he? Perhaps he deserved to,' she added falteringly.

Dan had to fight back a flourishing admiration for Joseph McCluskey. There were more questions he needed to ask.

'Abi, the talc? Knowing what I now do of Joseph, I don't think he would have left anything to chance. Kid's print on that knife was fundamental to the plan. Was the talc used to dust over it, to check the print was there?'

She looked at him, flicked at her hair.

'Yes. He sprinkled a little powder on the knife handle and it showed the print was there. As you say, he needed to be sure.'

One more thing was bothering Dan, one final question.

'That story about Joseph having the idea for the sculpture which Kid then stole. Was that true?'

'No. Joseph thought Kid was a very fine artist who didn't need his help. No, that was just a way of giving Kid a motive. It was another of Joseph's ideas to make the plot more secure. He knew you'd ask for a motive, otherwise there'd always be that question – why kill a man who was already dying? – so he gave you one. Kid would of course deny it when you interviewed him, but Joseph knew you'd conclude he was lying to cover up his crime. The fingerprint would give you all the evidence you'd need.'

Adam hadn't finished, clearly wanted this part of the investigation to be watertight. He looked flushed and Dan could feel his irritation and embarrassment at the case collapsing. Being conned in fact, if he was honest. But hadn't they all been? And not just them, but the people all around the world who'd been trying to solve the riddle of The Death Pictures. The moment someone cracked it, the framing of Kid would have failed. McCluskey must have been very sure of himself, very sure indeed.

'Abi, I'm bound to say that what you're telling us all fits together very neatly, but have you any corroboration for it?' asked Adam. 'I do have to question whether you in fact were the prime mover in this, and your story is just a device to cover you.'

Dan had expected an angry reaction, but a kindly smile returned to her face.

'Joseph expected that too, Mr Breen. He could see how it might look, with him not being here to talk to you. But he even found a way to do that. He said he'd make sure it would be clear the idea was his. You'll find, when we open that safety deposit box with the answer to the riddle inside, that there's also a letter from him detailing exactly how we went about framing Kid. The bank manager has signed a paper testifying when the box was sealed and what documents were in it – without seeing their contents of course – and he'll tell you it hasn't been touched since.'

'We'll have a look at that later then,' said Adam. His voice was flat, neutral, and Dan couldn't read what he was thinking. 'Well, I think that's enough for now,' the detective continued. 'I'll have to tell the judge all that you've told us, and Mr Kiddey will be freed from custody. I'm also obliged to warn you that you are facing charges of perjury and conspiracy, very serious crimes, Abi.'

'Yes, I realise that, Mr Breen. I've been through it in my mind many times and I've searched my conscience, but I'm content I did the right thing. I had to go along with Joseph's last wishes. He was my husband and a just man, Chief Inspector. A just and extraordinary man.'

Adam said nothing, surprising Dan. He'd expected some rejoinder, but none came. The detective looked as though he was drifting in his thoughts.

Abi got up from her chair.

'Just one final thing, if I may?' she said. Adam shrugged.

'It was to ask you something, Dan. What did you think of Joseph?'

His mind spun. What a question. What did he think? Incredibly clever, hugely talented, wonderfully vain, extraordinarily conceited, richly arrogant, but with something he couldn't help but admire so very much.

'I think he was an utterly remarkable man, Abi. A remarkable man who I wish I'd had the chance to know better.'

She smiled again, her face lifting and lightening.

'Thank you, Dan. Thank you. That would mean a lot to him. And I'm glad it'll be you who gets the final painting. It feels right, somehow.

Court reconvened at two o'clock. Dan and Adam had stood in Judge Lawless's chambers and recounted their interview with Abi. He'd showed no emotion and made no comment. He'd

331

called the prosecution and defence barristers in and they had agreed what would happen. They had no real choice.

'All stand,' called the usher, as Lawless stalked in to the court. He looked even grimmer than usual now, as if his own personal storm clouds were following him.

In the dock, Lewis Kiddey stood, visibly shaking. His eyes were fixed on the judge as he settled himself in his chair. He'd have been told what was going to unfold now, Dan knew that, but he wondered whether Kid could comprehend it. After six months in prison, awaiting trial for a crime he didn't commit, it must be hard to believe he was about to be freed, completely exonerated. He looked pale as Judge Lawless addressed him.

'Lewis Kiddey, this morning new evidence came to light which has a profound effect on the case against you. I cannot go into details as there may yet be another trial based on that evidence.' Abi, thought Dan, looking around at her in the public gallery. She sat, her eyes closed, seemed to be swaying a little from side to side.

'But it will not be a trial of you, Mr Kiddey,' continued the Judge. 'You are an innocent man and this case against you is now at an end. I am formally entering a verdict of not guilty and you will leave the court a free man, with no stain whatsoever upon your character. You may go.'

Gasps ran around the court, seemed to chase each other across the wooden panels. The journalists scribbled furiously. All eyes turned to Kid.

He sagged forwards, pressed his palms against the plate glass of the dock to steady himself. He looked disbelievingly around the court at the silent faces, all staring at him. Beside him, a security guard broke the silence as he ground a key into the heavy metal lock of the dock's glass door. He swung it open and stood aside.

Kid gaped for a moment at the open door, the symbol of his innocence. He took one faltering step, then another, haltingly walked out into the courtroom. He drew in a deep breath, as though savouring the air of freedom. He was just a couple of feet away, and Dan edged over and offered his hand. Kid shook it vaguely, uncertainly.

'Mr Kiddey,' said Dan quickly, pressing his card into the man's limp and trembling grip. 'My congratulations.' Kid's legal team, robed barristers, suited solicitors, were bearing down on him. He knew he had only seconds before the man was taken away. 'Here's my number. Please give me a call later on.'

Kiddey looked uncertain, his mouth hanging open. This was no time to be unusually modest, not if you want the scoop of your career, Dan thought. 'It was me who solved the riddle and got you freed today, Lewis,' he said. 'I did it. I saved you. I think when your lawyers have explained what's happened, you'll want a word. Please, call me as soon as you can. My number's on the card.'

'What?' shrieked Lizzie when Dan got back to the office and explained what had happened. 'I don't believe it. Bloody what?!'

He could see she didn't know how to react, a three-inch heel piercing the carpet, but her eyebrow in a peak too, quite a clash of emotions for her. An amazing story, yes, but the chance of another couple of sweet days of the trial gone too. And he'd only got to the collapse of the court case so far. Dan hadn't yet told her about solving the Death Pictures riddle, nor that call from Kid, so gushingly full of thanks, sobbing with relief. Yes, of course he would be interviewed live on *Wessex Tonight*, he'd be delighted. Of course as an exclusive, anything for the man who saved him.

No one had ever called Dan their saviour before and he wasn't sure what to say. It didn't feel quite right.

'I want most of the programme on it,' Lizzie gasped breathlessly when he'd finished recounting the story. 'No, make that all the programme! I want you to cut a report about everything that happened today. I want all the background to the Death Pictures riddle. I want you live in the studio to explain how you solved the mystery. I want Kid there with you. I want emotion. I want to see him break down in tears and thank you. I want us to call the TV awards panel and make sure they're watching. This will be our finest hour. Oh my

God, I can see the ratings now...'

It was a frantic afternoon, pulling together all she wanted, but Dan had enjoyed it immensely. He was flying in fact, all thoughts of the swamp banished, for now at least. When Lizzie left the newsroom for a meeting, he even had time to put in a call to the Nowhere Inn, a delightful fourteenth century place in the hilly countryside near Exeter. It was renowned for its food and drink and welcomed dogs too. Dan booked the best room for him and Claire for Saturday night. He thought they deserved it.

'What time would you like a table for, sir?' they'd asked.

'What time does the bar open?'

'Six, sir.'

'Six then please.'

There was one delicate call to make, to Adam. He'd expected to find the detective angry or at least sullen, but he was surprised.

'Hi, Dan, or should I say, Inspector Dan? You're getting pretty good at cracking these mysteries, aren't you? That's two out of two now with the Bray case. Not a bad success rate.'

'Thanks, mate, but all I was doing was trying to line my pockets and get myself a nice picture for my wall.'

'Balls. It was the challenge that got you. You couldn't bear to think of someone being able to outwit you.'

How well he knows me, Dan thought. Time to tell him about Claire, while he's in a good mood? No, don't spoil it. Another day.

'You're remarkably chirpy given what we've been through this morning,' Dan said.

'There's nothing to bother me there. I did my job and came to the best conclusion I could with the evidence I had. I shouldn't say this, but it was a brilliant piece of deception by McCluskey. It took everyone in. The other detectives who worked the case with me agree, as even do the High Honchos. They're delighted there'll be no media criticism of the force. You hacks are all too bound up in the puzzle finally being solved. We did everything we could. It was only when you cracked the riddle that we saw what really went on.'

Just one more thing to ask, Dan thought, and that leads into it nicely.

'I'm on the programme tonight to talk about how I solved the riddle and what will happen next. So I need a little bit of info if you wouldn't mind?'

'As ever. Of course. The usual rules apply. It didn't come from me.'

'Of course. What did you find when you went with Abi to the bank?'

'Exactly what she said we would. There was the answer to the riddle and a letter from Joseph outlining the plan in detail. It absolves Abi from blame entirely.'

Dan noted that down. 'But that's not the end, is it? She's still liable to be charged.'

The phone hummed with a sigh.

'That's the only outstanding matter now, and it's a tough one,' replied Adam. 'I've released her on police bail. She's not going to go anywhere. For what it's worth, I think she was acting entirely under Joseph's influence. He was clearly a dominating character and she was following his directions. We've had some discussions here with the Crown Prosecution Service already, and the view we're coming to is that she's unlikely to be charged. Very unlikely in fact. We can't see how it'll serve any public purpose. She'll probably be let off with a caution.'

A fitting ending, Dan thought. He'd believed Abi too. She was obviously totally devoted to Joseph. When would he meet a woman like that? The only one he'd ever loved hadn't exactly managed that, had she? She'd walked out on him. Thomasin...

Enough of that. There was Claire and the weekend to look forward to. No need to spoil it, wallowing in the pain of the past. No need to be defeated before you start. He'd done that with enough relationships.

'Thanks, Adam. We must meet up for a beer again soon, it's been far too long.' But Dan understood why. His friend was back with his family now, happy again.

'I'd like that. Come round and have supper with me and

Annie and Tom. You can bore Annie with the story of how you cracked the riddle.'

She won't be the first, Dan thought, or the last. Many, many people are going to be hearing about it, very many indeed. It would become his favourite anecdote. He doubted whether he would ever tire of telling it.

'OK, mate, I'd like that. Oh, just while you're on the phone, I know it's not your case, but is there any update on the Godley murder? McCluskey's dominating the news at the moment, but I'll have to keep an eye on Godley too.'

Dan thought he heard Adam swallow, but it could have been the mobile phone line.

'No, not really,' the detective replied. 'They're still investigating. The trouble is, there are no prints on the knife that was used to kill him, and there were half a dozen other inmates in the washroom when he was stabbed. They've all smeared his blood on them. Clever that. It means we can't work out who actually did it, and we can't charge all of them with murder. That would get thrown straight out of court.'

Another pause, and Adam's voice changed, from businesslike to... what? Relieved was the best way Dan could put it.

'The only real lead we have is that one of the inmates has a sister who was best friends with one of the rape victims. He's a bit of a hard man too. So we think it probably is him, but proving it is going to be very difficult, if not impossible.'

In the meeting after that night's programme, Lizzie was more effervescent than Dan had ever seen her.

'We've led the way on this story from the start, but tonight... tonight!!'

Was she going to break down in tears, he wondered? It was like watching one of those nauseating acceptance speeches at the Oscars. The adrenaline of being on air was ebbing, and he could feel the growing weight of the tiredness it had been holding at bay. He wanted to go home, go for a jog with Rutherford, then hit the sofa with a beer, to lie there and clear his mind. For the first time in ages not to think about a thing, not about the Death Pictures, not anything.

Lizzie was still talking, the words tumbling in a waterfall of excitement. 'It was wonderful, amazing, stupendous, to have the exclusive on solving the riddle, to have it done by one of our staff, to have Kiddey on live exclusively... well, words fail me.'

There was a silence as journalists, cameramen, picture editors, engineers, directors, all stared at her. Dan could read their thoughts. That was almost as big a story as the one they'd just broadcast.

'I don't know how we'll ever top this,' she continued. Being lost for words didn't last long then, Dan mused. 'Magnificent work one and all. Just magnificent. The drinks are on me tonight.'

He had a pint in the small but cheerful work bar, told the story of cracking the riddle again to a group of radio colleagues, then decided to go home. Rutherford would need a toilet break and he was feeling leaden with tiredness.

There'd been another development that Dan hadn't anticipated, and was finding oddly uncomfortable. A few minutes after he'd appeared on *Wessex Tonight* to explain how he'd cracked McCluskey's riddle, the newsroom phones had gone mad. There were scores of journalists from across the country – and quite a few international ones too – wanting interviews and pictures.

Dan found he wasn't enjoying the paradigm shift from reporter to reported. It felt like a switch from hunter to prey. A growing urge was encouraging him to escape the media attention and hide away at home. It had been an extraordinary few days and he'd had enough. It was time for some calm.

Fred on reception stopped Dan as he walked towards the automatic doors.

'That chap, he left something for you.'

'What chap?'

'You know, the artist fellow. The one who was on air with you tonight.'

Kid? What had he left?

Fred pointed to a bubble wrapped package, flat and about

four feet by two, the colours and details of a painting just visible within. There was a note attached. Dan picked it off and read it.

'The spell in jail made me a much finer artist and person. A major London exhibition is already being arranged of the works I painted while I was inside. This is the best of them. I'll need to borrow it back for the show, but it's yours. With my most heartfelt thanks always, Kid.'

Blimey, two new pictures in a day Dan thought, picking it up. And both worth tens, perhaps hundreds of thousands of pounds. I could sell them and retire. It would certainly be a way to escape the media attention. Perhaps join El on his holiday and extend it, stay a few months even. But then what would I do? I'd be bored within days.

He'd checked insurance premiums for fine art on the internet that afternoon and got a shock. There was no way he could afford to keep the paintings in his flat, not without turning the place into a fortress. And Rutherford would only bang into them and cover them with fur anyway. It wasn't how such works should be treated.

He knew what he was going to do. He was happy enough living as he did, didn't need money or great art. Solving the puzzle was what mattered to him, not the prize. The memory of that interview with Rachel was still vivid in his mind. Tomorrow, he'd find the numbers of a couple of charities set up to help the victims of rape and see if they could use a painting. A print of each would do him. It would be more fitting.

About the author…

Simon Hall

Simon Hall has been the BBC's Crime Correspondent in the south-west of England for three years. He also regularly broadcasts on BBC Radio Devon and BBC Radio Cornwall.

For more information please visit Simon Hall's website

www.thetvdetective.com

Coming soon from Simon Hall

Evil Coombe

Evil Coombe – a sinister Dartmoor valley hiding a dark secret.

A masked man breaks into women's homes, threatens them with a gun, but never speaks and steals nothing of value, only documents bearing their names. He leaves behind a series of notes addressed to Dan, boasting of plans for a great crime which will shock the country. Each note contains a riddle, the answer to preventing it.

A police marksman kills two men in frighteningly similar shootings. Detectives are suspicious, but can't be sure whether a crime's been committed. Their only clue is a cryptic password they find hidden at the man's home and a possible motive festering in his past.

Dan and Adam face baffling questions. Is the marksman a murderer, or just doing his job? Why does the faceless attacker steal only documents with women's names on? What is the great crime he's planning? And how to solve the riddles and stop it?

A young girl is abducted, and they realise they're hunting a psychopath, utterly bent on taking revenge on society, a once-brilliant man made demented by memories of war and the death of his best friend. They begin to break the codes, but he's always one step ahead... until the desperate search converges on Dartmoor...

More great crime books from Accent Press

Praise for Katherine John…

Katherine John is a best-selling author for Orion writing as Catrin Collier. She lives with her family in Swansea, Wales.

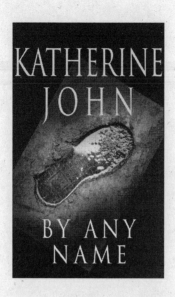

KATHERINE JOHN

BY ANY NAME

A bloodstained man runs half-naked down a motorway at night dodging high-speed traffic – and worse. Cornered by police, admitted to a psychiatric ward suffering from trauma-induced amnesia, all he can recall is a detailed knowledge of sophisticated weaponry and military techniques that indicates a background in terrorism.

Terrorist – murderer – kidnapper – thief; whatever he is, he remembers a town in Wales and it is to Brecon he drags Dr Elizabeth Santer with the security forces in all-out pursuit. There, a violent and bloody confrontation exposes a horrifying story of treachery and political cover-up.

Is Elizabeth in the hands of a homicidal terrorist or an innocent pawn? Her life depends on finding the right answer.